ABO

Harper Ford is an author, much of the time. She started out as a writer of historical novels, then found out she was funny during lockdown so decided to write contemporary romcoms too.

Hot Not Bothered is her second women's fiction novel.

www.harperford.co.uk

ALSO BY HARPER FORD:

Divorced Not Dead

Praise for *Hot Not Bothered*

'A gloriously uplifting celebration of middle age
and all it has to offer – bad as well as good. I loved it.'
Katie Fforde

'Bloody brilliant! A story that has heart, sass,
wit and wisdom. All the Bridget Jones romance drama
with added hot flushes and feminine rage. I devoured it.
Harper Ford is the voice of everywoman (over 45).
Laugh out loud, fist-pumping fabulousness.'
Helen Fields

'A hilarious take on the hormonal pressure cooker
of midlife . . . I loved it! So funny and relatable!'
Fiona Gibson

'A hilarious joy of a book that leaves you
feeling as if you've had a warm hug from a friend.'
Kate Galley

'Very relatable, very funny and an important
reminder of the power we have as women
when we come together.'
Jo Middleton

'Blisteringly honest and laugh-out-loud funny!'
Aliya Ali-Afzal

'Like having the biggest rant with your best friend.
Hilarious, relatable and compelling.'
Helga Jensen

'An absolute gem . . . A delightful blend of humour and heart. Five stars, without a doubt!'
Rosie Hannigan

'Deserves to be on the best books of 2024 lists! A funny, relatable, brilliant read. You'll devour it in one sitting!'
Annabel French

'Hilarious, hopeful and relatable!'
Rosie Wilby

'Heidi is a superb character who it was impossible not to love. The book is a joy from first page to last!'
Catherine Balavage

More praise for Harper Ford:

'A blast!'
Daily Mail

'A no-holds-barred, honest romcom.'
Platinum

'Hugely relatable!'
Heat

'An unfiltered, hilarious book . . . highly recommend!'
Best

'Honest, unfiltered, hilarious!'
Louise Pentland

HARPER FORD

hot
(not bothered)

avon.

Published by AVON
A division of HarperCollins*Publishers* Ltd
1 London Bridge Street
London SE1 9GF

www.harpercollins.co.uk

HarperCollins *Publishers*
Macken House, 39/40 Mayor Street Upper,
Dublin 1, D01 C9W8

A Paperback Original 2024

First published in Great Britain by HarperCollins*Publishers* 2024

A catalogue copy of this book is available from the British Library.

ISBN: 978-0-00-865133-6

Typeset in Sabon
by Palimpsest Book Production Limited, Falkirk, Stirlingshire

Printed and Bound in the UK using
100% Renewable Electricity at CPI Group (UK) Ltd

This book contains FSC™ certified paper and other controlled sources
to ensure responsible forest management.

For more information visit: www.harpercollins.co.uk/green

This book is dedicated to Kathy Kendall – sociology professor, horror fan, creative writer, incredible teacher, avid reader, dog parent, card writer and wonderful friend – who I was lucky enough to meet in a classroom in Oxford decades ago and I'm so very glad I did.

Chapter 1

You know the phrase, *I don't give a fuck*? When you're well and truly at the end of your tether and have nothing left to give? Well, I'm there with bells on.

Listen, I don't swear much, usually. I am not – as my mother calls it – a potty mouth. Or at least, I never used to be. The odd 'bloody' and 'shit' and a 'wanker' or two. But in the past year or so, as my health has declined, my rage has inclined. That's to say, I feel like a bloody volcano about to erupt. I heard my daughter say to her boyfriend the other day, 'I really don't give a fuck.' And I thought, yes, that's me. I have no fucks to give. My fucks are deceased. The supply of fucks I once owned are no more. My fuck bucket had a hole in it and it's totally depleted of fucks. If Mother Teresa came begging at my door for all the fucks I have to give, I'd have to send her away empty-handed. I'd say, zero fucks are available at Heidi's house. I'm Heidi Hobbes. And I'm fresh out of fucks.

1

My usage of the word 'fuck' has gone from about 5 per cent to 75 per cent, in my head anyway. I rant inside my head all the time, yet rarely does it reach my mouth. If someone as much as looks at me funny in Tesco car park, a diatribe of epic proportions detonates in my mind and buries them with an avalanche of invective designed to kill. But on the outside, mild-mannered Heidi simply gives an awkward smile. Inside, they're dead meat. But I'm not sure how much longer I can keep it all in. I've never known such rage. Where's it all coming from? Maybe I should take up kickboxing. Or axe-throwing. I need some way to channel this anger, because otherwise, I'm going to rival Old Faithful, the explosive geyser in Yellowstone National Park. That lucky bastard gets to shoot forth boiling water hundreds of feet into the air twenty times a day. I never used to feel like this. I never used to have this anger. I feel like I'm devolving into some kind of cavewoman. I'm not even sure who I am anymore. Who the hell is *this* Heidi Hobbes?

Well, the facts are that I'm aged fifty-two, a mother of two daughters, divorced and single, I work as an administrative manager at a college and I'm devoted to my home city of Oxford. When I'm dead, my life's ambition is that they'll write about me 'late of this parish' in the *Oxford Times*. Sometimes I feel that day will come sooner rather than later, because recently my health has fallen off a cliff. I feel crap most of the time and it's getting worse. I'm wondering if it might be the menopause, only because I keep getting spells where I feel really hot. They call them hot flushes, don't they? Or hot flashes? One of those. Maybe I am menopausal . . . I've got a Mirena coil in so

I don't have periods anyway, so I wouldn't know the menopause if it came up and bit me. I'm woefully ignorant about it. But anyway, whatever the hell is happening with my health these days, life goes on, and the kids still need dealing with; and my job still needs feeding like a ravenous beast; and the flat needs cleaning and tidying; the washing and ironing won't do themselves; dinners won't spontaneously combust and fly over to the kitchen table, like a scene from *Sword in the Stone* (and hasn't every mother who's watched that movie with their kids wished they had a magic wand that could do the dishes and pack up their whole house into a carpet bag?). Stuff needs doing. Life is bloody long and hard and will take every iota of strength and enthusiasm you have to keep going, to push through, to give a fuck. And I used to give a fuck about that. But today, the morning of Easter Sunday – when family and close friends are coming to my house to eat roasted lamb shoulder plus varied accoutrements – I have officially run out of fucks.

I'm in my kitchen and I'm surrounded by ingredients. Somehow I have to garner enough skill and gusto to transform them into a meal for eight people. Yes, eight. Now, normally, that would be the kind of challenge that would get my juices flowing. I love to cook. I really do. I'm not jaded from years of making tea for my family. It's actually one of my favourite parts of the day. Plus, usually, I'm a master of multitasking and can handle a meal for any number of folk any day of the week. But today, I'm feeling bamboozled. I switch on the dishwasher to clean all of yesterday's stuff I forgot to wash last night and then I turn to look at my kitchen island. I'm gazing at the cornucopia of foodstuffs on there and usually my mind arranges them in a logical sequence of jobs required to provide the feast. But today I'm looking at this white lumpy vegetable sat in the middle of the counter and I can't remember its name. *Brain*, my mind says. *It looks like a brain*. It does look like a brain. How ironic, since my own brain is on holiday right now. Or in a bloody coma. What the hell is this vegetable called? Do I really have to google what a BLANK is? How would I google it?

White lumpy vegetable that looks like a brain.

I type that into my phone. What comes up? Celery root. I look at it. No, it's not a celery root. What the hell is a celery root? Ah, there's a picture of the same thing. It's so familiar, I've cooked it a million times with a cheese sauce, I've roasted it with barbecue spices and served it with tahini dressing. It's delicious, it's a . . . I click on the picture. CAULIFLOWER. Oh, the relief! It's a cauliflower! The more I look at this word on the screen, the less it means.

Then I realise I've not had time to put on any make-up yet or brush my hair properly, so I turn on my phone camera and tap front-facing and my God, that was a dreadful idea. My face looms wrinkled and pale, the bags under my eyes are big enough for a fortnight in the Algarve. My usually neat shoulder-length brown hair now looks like I've been pulled through a hedge backwards. And I'm sweaty. Bloody hell, my face is shiny and not in a good way.

'You look like the wreck of the Hesperus,' I say aloud to myself.

Urgh, I can't bear to look. And I'm still wearing the hoodie with Debbie Harry on it that I threw on this morning, which I drag off over my head, messing my hair up even more. How did it suddenly get so bloody hot in here? I must go to the bathroom and have a cool shower and tidy myself up. I put my phone down and the cauliflower catches my eye again. How could I have forgotten something so familiar as a cauliflower? I go round all the other ingredients on the table and name them in my head, just to check I've not descended into complete dementia. I shudder. *Dementia* . . . the buttock-clenching fear of that word. My parents live all the way over in Norfolk and luckily both of them are still fully compos mentis. But dementia is the thing I fear the most for *myself*, because lately I can't remember a damn thing and it's terrifying. So I test myself on the vegetables:

- Aubergine
- King Edward potatoes
- Butternut squash
- Chantenay carrots
- Vine tomatoes
- Purple sprouting broccoli
- Petit pois

There! I *can* remember them all! Not so shabby. These are all the side dishes. But where is the main course? The meat. The centrepiece of any Easter Sunday meal. Where is the shoulder of lamb?

'What the hell are you doing, Mum?'

There's my nine-year-old, Ada, standing in the kitchen doorway staring at me with those long-lashed brown eyes, just like mine. Neither of us will ever need fake lashes, though I suspect Ada would rather die than wear anything so conformist. She's a rebel. In the eighties, she'd have worn an A for Alternative badge, like me and my mate Siouxsie did (obviously a pseudonym, real name Sharon). Ada has cropped hair at the sides and a big combed-over quiff on top and she wants to dye it blue, though school won't allow it. She's so cool. She's little, like me (but without the middle-aged spread). Small but mighty.

'I said, what – the – hell – are – you – doing?' she intones, as if I'm a hundred years old, in need of an ear trumpet.

'I'm cooking for eight people, that's what,' I snap, then regret it. Why am I so snappy these days?

'No, you're not. You've been staring at the food for ages, just staring at it like you've forgotten what a vegetable is. Are you losing it or what?'

She's not really asking me a question, just laughing at me. Mum being weird, as is the norm recently. She goes to the fridge to grab a couple of Cheestrings.

'We're eating soon,' I say automatically, as most mothers do when their kids come in for crappy snacks while they're toiling over a lovingly prepared, nutritious dinner.

'No, we're not,' she corrects me, correctly, and leaves the kitchen. She knows me so well, it's frightening. And she's uncannily almost always right about everything. She was named for Ada Lovelace, the mathematician who invented computers, or at least had a hand in it, so I was told by my ex-husband, a computer whizz. Somewhat ironic, since Ada is dreadful at anything vaguely techy. She's more of the intuitive type. *Arty-farty*, as my mum says and not meant kindly (though to be fair, she started calling me that when I became convinced in my teens that

I was going to be a hairdresser on a cruise liner, while playing violin gigs in my spare time). But she still calls me arty-farty, always in disparaging terms, and it's definitely meant as an insult. Which, come to think of it, is very unfair, since most of my job involves reams of data and highly technical stuff, which takes a lot of non-artsy braining to get right. So, yah boo sucks to you, Mum. I'm so glad she and Dad aren't here right now, which sounds mean, but honestly, they do my head in.

'Get a grip!' I tell myself.

I pick up a potato, grab a peeler and get to work. Today's side dishes are going to be:

1 Potatoes Dauphinoise
2 Pea and mint puree
3 Roasted carrots and squash
4 Steamed broccoli
5 Tunisian aubergine salad
6 An acre of roast potatoes to satisfy the kids.

I'm peeling and chopping and boiling and steaming and tossing and whizzing up and I'm in my happy place. I'm in the groove now. My brain has recovered from its previous inadequacy and I'm motoring.

People are starting to arrive. I can hear my ex in the hallway, bantering with our daughters. My other daughter Carly comes into the kitchen. I named her. She's twenty-two and obviously misnamed for my favourite singer-songwriter Carly Simon, as she's tone deaf and instead loves computers like her dad. She qualified last year to be an IT teacher, also like her dad. She works in a sixth-form college (which she chose instead of schools, because a) little kids annoy her b) she says summer terms at college finish earlier and she can go on holiday in school term-time. Smart girl). She's of small stature like me too, but she looks like him, the big, kind green eyes. She's almost all him, really. And like him, she's not musical in the slightest. Ada, however, streams music from every pore. She doesn't actually play an instrument, strangely; since she turned four years old, I've tried to encourage her to be a musician like me – or at least how I used to be, when I was a free-wheeling folk fiddle player once upon a time. I started Ada on a long line of lessons in piano, guitar, percussion, clarinet, trumpet: all the major food groups of the musical kingdom – but she hated them. She kept telling me that she loves to hear it but doesn't care about producing it. I finally listened to her and gave up. She exists with at least one AirPod in 24/7 and knows everything there is to know about pop music from 1900 to the present day. Carly, however, barely even listens to music. Instead, she's always plugged in to some podcast on science or economics or politics, again, just like her dad.

'Mum, are you okay?' says Carly, biting her lip. She's staring at me like Ada did, but she has a different demeanour: she looks worried. Her long, blonde-highlighted, dead-straight hair is pulled up in a chignon today, neat and precise. She comes over and puts her hand on my arm.

'Yes, I'm fine,' I snap. I really need to stop with the snapping.

'Can I help with anything?'

'Just deal with your father.'

'He doesn't need dealing with,' she says, softly. 'He could help, if you'll let him.' And she's right. Geoff is a good bloke, a truly good man. We were together from the same age Carly is now: twenty-two. We had a few years of freedom, wherein we worked but also travelled whenever we could (Prague and Salzburg city breaks, that kind of thing); bought a little flat, did it up; got married, then moved here. We had Carly when I'd just turned thirty. Then, after I forgot to take the pill a couple of days one month, I fell pregnant with Ada, aged forty-three. A mistake, which seemed awful at the time. I felt too old, too tired to do it all again. And I knew by then I was definitely not in love with Geoff anymore. In fact, I'd thought about us splitting up often, until I weed on that stick and it came up positive. But then this little miracle came out, who never stopped laughing, whose eyes lit up whenever I played her Fleetwood Mac or Joni Mitchell or Blur or The White Stripes or Vivaldi or anything really. She was such a joy, she still is. I can't regret her. But fifty-two seems too old to have a nine-year-old. When I was pregnant, the doctor called me a 'geriatric mother'. And I bloody well felt like it too. I feel too old for everything these days. Especially today.

'I'm all right, just let me concentrate,' I tell Carly. There's sweat running from my scalp down my neck onto my T-shirt. How the hell did I get so hot? I open the kitchen window. It's unseasonably cold out there, with frost on the ground. The icy air blasts me, incredibly refreshing. I just want to rip my clothes off and jump out of the window and roll around on the frosty grass verge in my underwear. This heat feels like it's burning from my chest into my brain and my head's going to explode. Reminds me of that terrifying 1980s movie *Scanners* with Michael Ironside. Oh, the fears we had back then about spontaneous human combustion! Why were we so obsessed with it? And quicksand. And rabies. And the Bermuda Triangle. None of them turned out to be half as much of a problem in adult life as we imagined as kids. If only my biggest concern right now was a rabid dog. Now *that* I could handle.

'Mum, I'm worried about you,' says Carly. Is she still here? Blimey, I was away with the fairies.

The doorbell ding-dongs and I tell her to answer it. I can hear the good-natured gruff voice of Toby from the basement flat, joking with Geoff, and the bell-like laugh of Toby's husband Danyal, who always brightens up a room. They met at work, five years ago, at the John Radcliffe Hospital. Toby is a nurse manager in his early forties with a tall grey quiff not unlike Ada's and Danyal is a paramedic in his late twenties with cornrows atop a buzz cut. They're absolutely gorgeous together, the Randall-Smiths. They got married last year and it was a blast. They want to adopt some kids, but no luck yet. They'll keep trying though. They're determined and have shedloads of love to give.

'You brought Pushkin!' I hear Ada yell from the hallway. Pushkin is their little ginger cat, who takes advantage of their crazy schedule of shift work to come up to our flat at all hours of the day and night and yowl incessantly outside our door. Ada is obsessed with Pushkin and the feeling's mutual. She wears him round her shoulders like a shawl and walks around the house like that, him looking princely and smug on his human throne, and her flinching from his periodical claw-digging to keep in place. Perhaps that's the basis of most relationships, flinching now and then from stabs of small pain to keep the equilibrium. That's definitely what marriage became for me, when it got to the point where every damn word Geoff said and every damn little thing he did irritated me to point of incandescent fury. And yet, that used to be all the stuff I loved about him once, many moons ago. Sad how a marriage can fade from a cheery photo to become the negative of itself, like a reverse Polaroid. I was so relieved when he moved out, I nearly cheered, except Carly was upset, of course, but she got over it. Ada was too young to remember it. We've all got on so much better since then, since we're not under each other's feet anymore. He's a good egg, is our Geoff.

Speaking of which, Geoff sticks his head in the kitchen and calls out to me.

'All right, Mrs?' He always calls me Mrs, even though we're divorced now. (Someone once sent me a letter addressed to Mrs Geoff Green, in that weird, prehistoric way they used to label women by removing their entire name and rendering them invisible.) He's smiling at me, in a hopeful manner – I know that look. He's checking that I'm not losing it. He does that a lot lately. His haircut is brutal; he's recently started shaving his head to avoid drawing attention to the balding centre bit and it actually really suits him, mostly because he has such a nice face. I've always liked his face, but was never stirred by it, or his body, really. We were more like friends or siblings than a couple. We mistook friendship for marriage, we

11

realised, years later. After we separated six years ago and I reverted to my maiden name, Geoff moved into the basement flat next door, something we agreed upon as Ada was only three and his proximity made co-parenting that much easier. The girls and I inhabit a three-bedroomed flat at 30 Walton Crescent, North Oxford, just along from leafy Woodstock Road and trendy Little Clarendon Street. We live in a large house that has been split into flats, comprising numbers 28 and 30 Walton Crescent. We live on the ground and first floor, with Carly's bedroom in the attic (though she's saving up with her boyfriend Matt for a deposit on their own flat). Toby and Danyal live in the basement flat below us. Then Geoff is in the corresponding basement of number 28. Above him, live our final guests of today, Alia and Rich Watson, who are coming *sans* children, thankfully. I know for a fact I could not cope with eleven rowdy people in my flat today. Luckily, they'll be dropping off their three kids at their Nanoo's house, before they come here for lunch and a well-earned break.

Then, as if my thoughts have summoned their presence, the doorbell rings and before I have a chance to let Geoff know if I'm all right – which I'm getting the distinct feeling I'm not – he retreats to open the door. I grab a damp dishcloth and wipe my face with it, mopping up sweat. I can hear him welcoming the Watsons. Rich and Geoff immediately start telling filthy jokes and guffawing, which I'd love to join in with, but something is niggling at me, something is not where it should be, something hasn't been done . . . But for the life of me, I've not got a clue what it is. *Work, brain, work, for God's sake!*

In comes Alia, her hands full with a huge clingfilm-topped glass bowl full of something green and fabulous, and a large foil-wrapped package. The scents of her glorious South Asian cuisine fill the kitchen and I'm so grateful to have another great cook to help me, as I'm honestly starting to think I'm losing my mind.

'All right, my darling?' she shouts in her glorious Essex accent (from where she moved to Oxford aged nineteen running away from her family, but that's a whole other – quite incredible – story for another day). Her black hair with cinnamon highlights and a curtain fringe tumbles over her shoulders and her eyeliner is absolutely on point. She's forty-three but looks at least ten years younger. 'I come bearing naan breads – homemade, of course, darling. None of that shop-bought crap I've seen in your freezer. Oh yeah, I know you get a Tesco Finest peshwari naan from time to time, you traitor, when I can cook you up a naan any day of the week. Now, since you're doing lamb, I've also whipped up my special salad, with red onion, cucumber, tomatoes, coriander, lime, salt and sweet chilli. Plus I've nestled a little pot of my green chilli and coriander chutney in there too.'

Alia puts the stuff down on the counter, then comes over to me, arms outstretched, ready to haul me in for a much-needed hug. And for a split second, I think I'll start sobbing when her arms go round me. Why do I want to cry?! This is one of my favourite days of the year. I love celebrations, or any excuse to cook for other people and socialise in my kitchen – and my family and good neighbours are all here and I should be on top form. I won't cry, I'm determined.

'Don't hug me, I'm too sweaty,' I say. 'Thanks for the wonderful food.'

But Alia knows me too well. We've lived beside each other since our kids were tiny.

'What's up, my love?' she says, scrutinising me.

'I don't know . . . There's . . . something . . . not quite . . .' I trail off.

'You can tell me, darling,' says Alia.

I suddenly get a rush of memory and look round at the big oven, terrified it's not on, because I really need it to have warmed up by now. But it is on, it's okay. Then, it comes to me.

'I haven't got the lamb out of the fridge. Damn!'

'I'll get it!' she says brightly and goes over there. Why on earth haven't I got the meat out yet? I should've done that before I started messing about with the side dishes.

'Where is it, love?' she says.

Where is it?! *In the bloody fridge*, I want to snap! *Right in front of you!* It's usually kids who ask such dumb questions and you realise you'd have saved everybody precious time by doing the damn thing yourself in the first place. I stomp over to the fridge and look in, ready to grab the huge hunk of meat I need to get in that oven sharpish, as it's 11am already and we'll all be eating at midnight at this rate.

But . . . it's not there.

'Where is it?' I mutter.

'That's what I said!' jokes Alia and laughs, but stops when she can see I'm not laughing, I'm not even vaguely amused at all. Where the hell is my lamb?!

'You must've got it out earlier, darling. Let's see.' Alia starts looking round the kitchen, as if it's playing hide and seek and might leap out at any second. But it's nowhere to be seen. I picked it up from Tesco yesterday, plus all the veg. I put it in the fridge. But all the veg are out. So where is the meat?

'Geoff?' I call, out of habit more than anything. After six years apart, his is still the first name that pops into my head when I need help.

He appears at the door.

'We can't find the lamb, Geoffrey,' Alia says and I glance up and see him raise his eyebrows, like he's dealing with an elderly relative who's lost her marbles.

'Hey!' I snap at him. 'What was that look for?'

'Where's this lamb then?' says Geoff, cheerily, side-stepping the issue, lifting up a cloth and opening a cupboard and looking behind the kettle.

'Don't be so stupid!' I shout at him. 'It's a huge lump of meat. It's not going to be hiding under a cereal bowl on the draining board.'

At that moment, both of my daughters come in. They've heard the tenor of my voice and have appeared to see what's up. Behind them, Toby, Danyal and Rich are gathering, looking over the tops of my short children's heads and peering into the kitchen, Danyal grinning, while Rich looks curious and Toby looks like he can smell trouble.

'Can we help?' calls Danyal.

'She's lost the lamb,' says Geoff and that's it. That's the final straw.

'I HAVE NOT LOST THE LAMB!' I yell at him. 'How can a person lose a shoulder of lamb? It's ridiculous!'

'Let's look for the lamb then, Mum,' says Carly, looking really worried now.

15

'We're going on a lamb hunt!' shouts Ada, sing-song, oblivious and enjoying this immensely.

Then everyone's in the kitchen, three women, four men and a feral child invading my space and looking in stupid places, like the broom closet and the shoe rack. Geoff has found the lamb's plastic wrap in the bin, so we know at least that it was in the house at some point, indeed, it was in this kitchen. Then, Alia says, 'I bet it's in the freezer, darling!' and goes over there and my memory kicks in again and I remember pulling open a big door and putting it in, but it wasn't the freezer. It was . . . somewhere else. A cold sweat comes over me and I turn and look.

The dishwasher is churning away and I grab the door and pull it down and steam billows into the room and there's that little splash you get when you interrupt its programme and it spits at you in retaliation. And there, nestled amidst the shining crockery and cutlery, is a perfectly washed and gloriously soapy shoulder of lamb, half cooked and half raw, the cleanest shoulder of any creature that has ever been. And it is utterly ruined.

Ada sees it first and points and laughs like a drain.

'HAHAHAHAHAHAAAAAAAA!'

Oh, that laugh I love so much grates at that moment, as harsh as a banshee. And Danyal is laughing too – they get on like a house on fire, those two – but Rich just looks horribly uncomfortable and Toby tries to be helpful, saying, 'You know, Heston Blumenthal cooked something in a dishwasher once apparently.'

My wrath is bubbling up in me now.

'Thank you, Toby,' I spit out, 'but it's a bit fucking late for that, considering the lamb has already been washed with detergent and is cleaner than a duck fart but totally and utterly inedible and I've got eight hungry people in my kitchen like chicks in a nest with gaping open mouths screaming FEED ME FEED ME.'

I can hear myself and I don't even know who this person is. Neither does anyone else, by the shocked, embarrassed looks on their faces.

Alia and Carly simultaneously come towards me, saying, 'It doesn't matter, darling' and 'We've got loads of food, Mum' and other reassuring things, then Geoff hands me a glass of grape juice as consolation – it's my favourite since I had to give up wine – but none of it helps and I'm boiling up like Old Faithful and then I explode.

'EVERYBODY OUT!' I scream. 'GET OUT! GET THE FUCK OUT OF MY KITCHEN!'

And I hurl the glass of grape juice on the kitchen floor and it smashes spectacularly, the dark liquid splattering the kitchen units like watery blood.

Happy fucking Easter, everyone!

Chapter 2

I work at a college in Oxford. You might be imagining the dreaming spires, Inspector Morse and all that. But no, I don't work for the world-famous University of Oxford. Instead, I work at the Miriam Margolyes University of Further & Higher Education, abbreviated to MMUFHE and known locally as MUFFY. And yes, the college swimming club is called Muff Divers. You might not know that Miriam Margolyes grew up in Oxford, hence the dubious honour of having this place named after her. I'm inspired by Miriam Margolyes often as I love her honesty and integrity and regularly ask myself, *What would Miriam do?* The organisation that owns the college runs a bunch of other colleges across the country and is called the enigmatically generic title of Metropolitan New Group Education, abbreviated to MNGE, otherwise known as MINGE. You couldn't make this shit up. Remember City University of Newcastle upon Tyne, that had its proposed name changed at the last minute because of its initials . . .?! That really happened. So yeah, I work for MUFFY as part of MINGE. Sometimes I feel like my whole life is a cosmic joke.

I won't bore you with the finer details of my job as resource and planning manager, but year round, I'm involved in helping the place run smoothly, ensuring the college delivers the right courses, that we're spending taxpayers' money correctly. I'm dealing with defensive pissed-off managers below and impatient, exacting directors above, while multitasking the administration of the current year's intake of students with next year's. There is no time of year when it calms down, there is no summer holiday, there is no let up. It. Never. Ends.

I'm talking about it to my work besties – Brenda and Kim – one lunchtime in the shiny refectory at work.

'I'm good at my job and I do like it. I like most of the people I work with. But . . . it was never my dream career, you know? I didn't sit at my window when I was seven and wish on a shooting star to be a resource and planning manager for MUFFY as part of MINGE. No, I did not.'

'Is anyone really happy in their jobs?' says Brenda.

'People who make those cakes that look like hamburgers and shoes and real things,' says Kim. 'I bet they love it. And florists. Everyone's always chuffed to see you if you give them flowers.'

'Except at funerals,' adds Brenda.

Kim continues, 'Well, yes. You couldn't turn up there with lilies grinning like an idiot.'

I'm so glad I have these two to keep me smiling. Brenda Bennett. She's the exams officer and she's always got my back. She's twelve years younger than me, just turned forty, but gets me like we're sisters. With only one brother (one I never really got on with) and no sisters, my female friends are like gold-dust to me and Brenda is one of my key supports. She lives with her girlfriend Kim Huynh, also in her early forties, who's a curriculum manager. Brenda, Kim and I tend to hang around together at work events and support each other during the day, but we don't see each other that much outside of work (mostly because we're always bloody working).

'Thing is,' I carry on, 'I've always been good at my job, even when I don't like it. But lately, I'm losing it. My brain used to be able to maintain this high level of technical accuracy for twelve-hour stretches from 7am to 7pm. But now, my brain stops braining around 2pm. I've no idea why. I could set a clock by it. I had Mick Pickley – mansplainer extraordinaire – turn up at my door last week, saying, *We're all waiting for you upstairs*. Then I was supposed to be handing out a bunch of materials and I not only forgot to bring them, I had no memory of producing them or where I might have put them if I had. I bullshitted my way out of it, but I could feel my face go bright red, like a bloody apprentice.'

What I don't admit is that all this forgetfulness is quickly getting worse and it frightens the shit out of me. Work was always the place where I was in control. Home and parenthood are crazy, but work I could always handle. But not anymore. What the hell is happening to me?

We're surrounded by students and staff chowing down on jacket potatoes, superfood salads and loaded fries. All that food makes me feel sick to my stomach. I'm picking at a plain chicken sandwich, while Brenda eats a burrito, tucking her blonde bob behind her ears to keep it out of the way. Kim has long shiny black hair I'm very envious of, tied back in a loose ponytail today. She's eating a roast dinner, served in a polystyrene tray. If I had a full roast at lunch, I'd be asleep by one-thirty, then probably on the loo by two. My bowels are my enemy these days.

'It's perimenopause, I bet you anything,' says Brenda. 'My older sis is going through it. She left her car keys in the fridge the other day. Then she cried for a half-hour because she dropped an apple on the floor.'

'I don't even know what *peri*menopause is,' I say.

'Neither do I really, but I've heard it's the bit before menopause, before your periods actually stop. I think that's what it is, anyway?' says Brenda, looking at Kim for confirmation, who hunches her shoulders and says, 'I haven't got a clue. I'm trying to pretend it'll never happen. I've got enough shit to deal with.'

'Why is it I'm so ignorant about this?' I say, my annoyance rising, not at Brenda and Kim, but at the state of women's education about their own bodies. 'All of us are pretty clueless about it, by the sounds of it. We all get the period talk, but none of the menopause talk.'

Kim says, 'By rights, there should be a menopause nurse at every GP surgery. But then, that would cost money.' And she shrugs her shoulders again and carves up another roast potato. I can't manage this chicken sandwich and I just want to hide in the toilet. A wave of nausea engulfs me. Maybe I should eat. Maybe I'm just hungry. I used to love eating, and cooking, and eating. And eating. And never really struggled with my weight. Now I'm gaining weight but at the same time, I'm sick of food. My body feels like a battleground and I'm losing.

'See your doctor,' says Brenda. 'Get a test, a blood test for your hormone levels. That's what my sister had. It'll tell you what's going on, I bet.'

I promise Brenda I will. But, you know, life is busy, isn't it? Who's got time to be sitting on the phone at 8.30am trying to get a same-day appointment, because my GP surgery doesn't let you make appointments in advance anymore? I keep putting it off, as you do. It's a couple of weeks after the disastrous Easter Sunday debacle, and I've made up with my friends and family, who all forgave me instantly, bless them. But they're worried, of course they are. Geoff keeps telling me to see a doctor. Carly keeps telling me to see a doctor. Ada keeps telling me that there are too many ostriches being born in the zoo she built in her favourite computer game of *Rollercoaster Tycoon*. And that's good – not the ostrich birthrate boom, but the fact that my kid should be asking me about things like that, and not worrying about my health. That's my job, not theirs. And I say as much to Carly.

'Mum,' she says, one evening in the kitchen after tea, while we're clearing up. '*Please* will you make this appointment with the GP?'

'Yes, yes. I've told you I will.'

'I know you've told us. But you've said that several times now and still not done it.'

'Carly,' I say and put down the pressure cooker lid from my Ninja, eyeing the filthy element that's covered in cooking grease. I still haven't cleaned it properly since I bought it a few weeks ago. I told myself I'd clean the Ninja after every single time I used it. But have I? Have I bollocks. 'I have a Ninja to clean . . . at some point. And a gazillion things to do for work. And the flat to clean. And you guys to take care of.'

'I know how busy you are. But I don't need looking after. I'm a grown woman. And I help with Ada and the flat. And I can do more, whatever you need. Just tell me what else needs doing and I'll do it.'

Carly comes over and tries to put her arms around me, but I just feel stiff and awkward. I let her hug me and I do appreciate it. I just feel so unlovable these days.

'That's great, love. And thank you. I mean that. But honestly, nobody ever does stuff around the house the way I like it, so it's just easier to do it myself. It'll take just as long to explain the best way to clean this or iron that or fold the other, so I may as well do it myself.'

'That's because you're a control freak.'

'I am not! I resent that! It's just that . . . my way is the best way. The only way.'

'So you're a fascist.'

'Nice. That's really nice from my first-born.'

Carly throws down the tea towel she's been holding and I know she means business now. Look, it might seem like I'm being mean to my daughter when she's just trying to help. I know that, believe me, I do. But I can't help the way I feel. It's irrational, I'm aware of that. But I very rarely talk to either of my kids about my problems. I'm hardline about it i.e. it's not their problem and a parent shouldn't load their stuff onto their kids. It's how I've always been with my kids and even to a certain extent with my ex and my friends. I don't know why. Maybe it's because I felt I could never share my problems with my parents, so I became insanely self-sufficient. Whatever the reason, I always feel intensely uncomfortable about going on about my problems with most people, especially my kids. But anyway, Carly has thrown down the towel, or thrown in the towel? I'm not sure which yet.

'Just call the bloody doctor. Do it on a Friday when you don't have as many meetings. That's what you always tell me. Things get done on Fridays because they're quieter. Do it then. And if you don't, I will ring your GP surgery one Friday and do it for you.'

'Don't you dare! I'm not elderly and infirm! Not yet.'

'I will. And there's nothing you can do to stop me.'

She gives me a smug smile and closes up the dishwasher. So, she means business. Carly has spoken. I'll be damned if I let my kid tell me what to do. I stomp off to my room in a huff, all the time knowing she's absolutely right, that I'm being an idiot and that I'm lucky to have such a thoughtful daughter. Just before I'm about to slam my bedroom door ridiculously in protest, I call out to the kitchen, 'Carly?'

'Yes?' she replies, with a world-weary tone I bet she usually reserves for the more trying kids in her classroom.

'Thanks, love,' I call out sheepishly, if one can shout in a sheepish manner.

'You're welcome,' she says in the same tired tone. I'm a great mum, I know that, but I am also a pain in the arse. Fiercely independent to a fascist degree (apparently).

So, not long after Carly's intervention, one Friday morning, I ring the doctor. I'm number seventeen in the queue and they are currently receiving a large number of calls and my call is in a queue and will be answered as soon as possible. You know the spiel. And I'm on the phone for twenty-five minutes, trying to type emails at the same time as listening to phone muzak, but I persevere and get my appointment for that morning at eleven. I cancel a meeting I was supposed to have with a manager and apologise profusely, then I rush down there and see a GP I've never met before, one of the many locums who frequent my surgery. I tell him my symptoms and he peers at me, does my blood pressure, temperature, then shakes his head.

'Probably is perimenopause,' he says gruffly. 'Make an appointment with the nurse for a blood test,' and hands me a form. I have been dismissed. I see the woman at reception and the soonest appointment to see a nurse for a blood test is three weeks away. So I wait. Meantime, my symptoms have progressed. Along with the forgetfulness and hot flushes and nausea, I've also developed a constant acidy heartburn, which has me swigging Gaviscon like I used to neck White Lightning in the 1990s. And, mortifyingly, I have wind. Not just the odd little fart to hold in. But full-on bloating, and a queue of massive cheek flappers clamouring behind my sphincter, eager for freedom. The other day, I was late to another meeting and rushed in, dropped my phone on the floor, bent down to pick it up and let out a thunderclap. I instantly coughed like mad, trying to cover up the sound, as if nobody had noticed, but everyone had; they were sitting there wide-eyed, with my line manager Mick Pickley barely suppressing his laughter and the principal looking like she was going to vomit. I told Brenda and Kim about it after, my eyes filling with tears, and although they did their best to comfort me, they couldn't help but piss themselves laughing. I mean, if it's happening to someone else, it is funny! Farts are funny! But they soon realised I didn't find it amusing in the slightest. Brenda gave me a hug and Kim held my hand as I sobbed about it. I know they meant well. But I felt like a freak. It's just not ladylike, is it? Farting in public. It's daft when you think about it, the way we're so disgusted by natural bodily processes, especially women's bodies. It shouldn't be that way. But my God, it felt like the worst moment of my life.

Something has *got* to change. So, finally, I have the blood test and then I'm waiting for the results. Checking the NHS app every day and still nothing. I'm sitting in the car after work on a rainy Monday in May and I ring the surgery and ask the receptionist for the results and she finds them, at last. She says the blood test confirms I'm in perimenopause. *So, it's happening*, I think. *The beginning of the end*. And the receptionist adds that there's NO FURTHER ACTION. No further action? Surely, this milestone in a woman's life demands some action, some kind of recognition. Do I get a sash? Should I get a bottle of champagne? Urgh, I remember I'm off alcohol, not by choice, I hasten to add. The damn stuff gives me intense diarrhoea, as does coffee. Another symptom. I have developed a sensitivity to two of my favourite things in life. Thank heavens I can still eat chocolate and cake, or I'd hurl myself into the Oxford Canal. Canals make me think of Norfolk narrow boats and . . . oh, shit. I suddenly remember I've got the monthly video call with my parents and kids tonight. I'm sure we all hate it equally, but we force ourselves through it, God knows why. I drive home, thinking about the test results. So, I'm in perimenopause. Since hearing that word from Brenda, I'd done a little bit of googling and found out it is indeed the bit before the menopause official. It says it can last for seven to ten years. A decade of all this crap? Kill me now. I also read that the strict definition of menopause is a year without periods, apparently. Though other sources say that can last seven to ten years as well, so I'm more confused than ever. Again I wonder, why the hell is this stuff not taught to us? Why are we having to rely on Dr Google to educate ourselves about something that will happen to the vast majority of women i.e. just under half of the world's population?!

I'm back home, dinner is done, the kitchen is done, it's approaching 8.30pm and it's time for the monthly parental video call, known colloquially in our house as The Curse (i.e. about as welcome as your period). My mum and dad moved from Oxford to Norfolk ten years ago when they retired, thus their recent idea to keep in touch via Zoom. I hate using Zoom at the best of times but to do it with The Olds is torture. Look, they're nice enough people in comparison to some, I mean, they haven't murdered anyone's hamster lately. But they are hard work, and it's not just me who feels that way. Carly and Ada find it trying too, but Ada is young enough to make the effort and Carly is old enough to understand it needs doing, though she and I always eye roll when the first Monday of the month comes around. Why it has to be a Monday is another bugbear of mine, but my parents say they're too busy every other damn night of the week with their clubs and the parish council meetings and other aspects of their post-work-life activities. I'm not being a bitch about all that; I'm honestly glad for them they have such busy lives. But I tell you what, the way my life is now, when I retire I am doing fuck all. Binge-watching Netflix until I finish it. That's it.

So, Mum and Dad on Zoom. There they are, Dad with a full head of thick white hair, of which he's very proud, and he has the large brown eyes that Ada and I inherited. Mum has cheekbones to die for, with a severely short grey cut, a touch of Jamie Lee Curtis about her. Everything about them seems smooth and efficient, unlike the chaos of my life. We hear about their many hobbies and gossip about their friends and the girls tell them about school (same for both, one as pupil, one as teacher). Then the kids retire gracefully (or basically trot gleefully from the room) while I'm left with the parents to do the bit where they rip my life to shreds. I usually try to get out of that part, but one or the other always does this thing where they tell the girls to go because they 'want a word with Mummy'. Often, I'll say I have a pile of work to do, or an online meeting, or whatever, but tonight they insist.

'I rang Geoff the other day,' says Mum, 'and we're all worried about you. What's happening with your health?'

'Why are you ringing Geoff?' I say, annoyed. 'He is my ex, you know. If you want to know anything, talk to me.'

'We would, but you never tell us anything!' says Mum.

'We do a video call every month!' I say, already exasperated. What else do they want? Daily minutes?

'Geoff's a good man,' says Dad with a nostalgic air, randomly swerving off the subject, as is their wont.

'Such a good man,' says Mum. 'You know what we think about that.'

'Yes, I don't need to hear it again, thank you,' I say, trying to stay polite for as long as I can. They regularly tell me that splitting with Geoff was the worst mistake I ever made. They want us to get back together. They think I'm a fool for letting him go. I think they're interfering busybodies.

'And what about Ada's hair?' says Mum, suddenly. See what I mean about the subject-changing madness?

'What about it?'

'It's weird,' says Dad. 'Not like Carly's. Hers is lovely. She always looks so professional.'

My parents have often said that Ada and I are weird and – that epithet again – arty-farty. Dad in particular thinks Carly and Geoff are the bee's knees and only really wants to hear about them – he's an ex-civil engineer and approves of their scientific bent, even if it's 'only computers'. Neither of them seem to appreciate Ada's sense of joy and enquiry into the wide world. They only recognise that she's unconventional and they don't like it.

Mum adds, 'I suppose Ada being rebellious is just one of her odd *phases*.'

'I hope not,' I say. 'I hope she stays that way forever.'

'God forbid!' says Dad. 'None of your brother's children look that way. His little girls dress and act like little girls. None of this arty-farty stuff with the hair . . . Your brother is doing so well, have you spoken to him lately? He's in India just now, in charge of a stadium build out there. Just marvellous! And Larissa is doing a brilliant job with the children, all five of them.'

Oh God, here we go. The golden child, my younger brother, Lance. He's a civil engineer, just like Dad. He married Larissa – a yummy mummy who worships Mrs Hinch and runs her own business selling shampoo bars – in their twenties and subsequently had five perfect children. I never hear the end of Lance and Larissa's stellar accomplishments.

Mum says, 'Little Oscar has just started at my old place St Matthew's, did you know? He looks so adorable in the uniform, that beautiful little straw boater, really takes me back. Just marvellous. I could've been his headmistress now, if they hadn't dumped me.'

Mum was the headteacher of a private prep school just outside Oxford for decades and never wanted to retire. She claims she was forced out like Thatcher and described in great detail how she cried in the car like the PM did, on the way home from her leaving party.

'I could be doing that job still,' adds Mum, misty-eyed. 'If it wasn't for my gout.'

This is new. I ask, 'Oh, you have gout? That's rotten. How is it?'

Mum carries on, 'But they have a man running it these days, some upstart in his forties, from Romford, of all places, and used to be a *PE teacher*, for heaven's sake. Not an academic subject like mine. Not like geography. Oh, how I wish one of my children had become a geography teacher. I mean, Lance was always going to be a gifted engineer. He always took after your father. But if only you'd followed in my footsteps, maybe you'd be leading St Matthew's as we speak and you'd be Oscar's head. How super that would be!'

Dad says, 'Well, at least she's not a violin teacher! Imagine that! No money in it. Like we told you at the time.'

Mum always wanted me to be a geography teacher like her, but they were both pleased at least that I didn't become a travelling musician, like I was threatening to when I took Music at Exeter University, all those years ago.

'I have a perfectly good job now,' I sigh, inordinately tired. I need this Zoom from hell to end. I can feel a hot flush starting in my chest. It's tingling there and soon it'll rush to my head.

Dad adds, 'Well, you weren't really a good enough musician for it, were you? Not like Nicola Benedetti. Now there's a violinist.'

'I prefer folk and pop to classical,' I say, pointlessly.

'Yes, but that's not proper music, is it?' says Mum.

I've had enough of this. What would Miriam do? She'd tell the pair of them to fuck off. But I'm not Miriam, more's the pity. So I feel a sense of duty to keep up the charade that all this is necessary. Plus I'm feeling a bit needy, since I've heard I'm officially beginning my menopause journey. Of all people, shouldn't I be able to talk to my own mother about it? Maybe she'll have some maternal wisdom to impart. 'Look, I must go in a minute, but you did ask after my health, so I'll just let you know that I have seen a doctor and I'm in perimenopause.'

'What on earth is *peri*menopause?' says Mum. 'I know what menopause is but not heard of this *peri* version. Sounds like something to do with fermented pears. Or itinerant teachers.'

Dad looks alarmed and says, 'That's my cue to bow out,' and leaves the chat.

I explain to Mum, 'It's pre-menopause, the stage leading up to it. But to be honest, I don't know much more about it. I need to research it.'

'Why on earth would you need to research it? It's like researching menses. No need! They just happen. It's a natural part of ageing. And thank God menses end, which is cause for celebration, surely.'

'Well yes, absolutely. The end of the curse is certainly a great thing for many women.'

And the irony that we call this monthly phone call The Curse is not lost on me. And usually I wish it would come to an end as quickly as possible, yet . . . tonight, I'm wondering if Mum might actually be able to help me. After all, if you're lucky enough to have your mum still around when you hit menopause, shouldn't she be the first person you'd talk to?

'So,' I go on, 'how was it for you?'

'How was what?'

'The menopause.'

'Oh, I barely remember it.'

'Really?' I'm feeling hopeful. Maybe it won't be so bad for me, if it wasn't for Mum.

'I never had any problems with the change, I breezed through it. There's an awful lot of fuss made about it nowadays, as if women deserve special treatment for just being women.'

'Well, I'm not saying that. But there does seem to be a lack of information around about it.'

'What information would you need? You suffer and you move on.'

Oh dear, I don't like the sound of that, for her or anyone. 'Did you suffer then, Mum?'

'Of course I did.'

'I thought you breezed through it.'

'That's because I'm made of sterner stuff. Everyone suffers, dear. That's life. I thought you'd know that by now, at your advanced age. You really ought to stop dying your hair, you know. It ages you. Grow old gracefully.'

'Thanks,' I say with a sigh. But I want to pursue this. It's so rare that Mum opens up to me, I want to know more. 'But, what symptoms did you have, when you were going through it?'

'Oh Christ,' she snaps. 'I don't want to talk about all that personal stuff.'

'Did you get HRT though?'

'Oh, all this HRT rubbish. Why does everyone these days think they need external assistance to get through the slightest inconvenience in their lives? Plus, it causes breast cancer, you know.'

'Mum, I think that's all been debunked now. HRT helps loads of women, apparently. Didn't your doctor try to help at all?'

'Help? I never had any help, with anything! These days everyone bleats about help! It's pathetic. Nanny state and childish population. Help yourself and don't bother others. Put up and shut up, that's my mantra. Anyway, must go. You haven't even asked how I am, as usual. I've got gout, but you wouldn't be interested in that, as you're the one with all the problems, aren't you?'

'I *did* ask about your gout just now but you didn't answer!'

'No, no, it's all right, I have your father, thankfully. What with your brother's success meaning he's too busy to call at all and your indifference to my suffering, I'm lucky to have your father, as annoying as he is. Bye bye for now. Good luck with the *PERI*menopause or whatever it's called.'

And she clicks out of the Zoom and there I am, alone, staring at a white computer screen telling me my meeting has ended. My hot flush floods my head with heat and I start sweating like a cornered thief. Stress can bring these on. And my parents are the epitome of stress.

Chapter 3

Thank God that's over. It was a particularly irksome parent duty call tonight. I remind myself never to reach out to Mum or Dad when I need help. They're just not capable of it. It's like they missed a gene, the one for empathy. Thank heavens I didn't miss that gene. And that Geoff is such a good bloke, that our kids didn't inherit my parents' smug coldness either. But whatever my parents have to say about Geoff, and even knowing myself that he's probably the nicest bloke I ever met, I am *not* getting back with him.

I do generally feel extremely single these days and – yes, I'll admit it – I'm lonely. I value my independence so much though and I'm so glad I don't have to live with a man anymore. I've loved the freedom in my home of the last six years. I don't have much of a sex drive but I do miss intimacy – that is, the cuddling and the closeness. But I can't be bothered to meet someone and do all the groundwork necessary to build up to being comfortable enough to be intimate. And wouldn't they want sex anyway? I couldn't go into any relationship not wanting sex, any man would refuse that, wouldn't they? I've heard about asexuality, but I don't feel that's me either. I think I am still a sexual being, somewhere deep down. It's not gone, it's merely dormant. Maybe I would be up for it with someone I found really attractive. I mean, I do still fancy movie stars, especially those of the distant past like Cary Grant and Danny Kaye – apparently those two had a torrid affair, which is the sexiest thing I can imagine actually – what does that say about my sexuality?! I've no idea. I had a few flings in my late teens and early twenties, but since meeting Geoff, I've had no sex with anyone else, or since splitting up. I have no idea what I want in bed, but for now, I want nothing to do with it. I feel ancient and ugly and farty and unlovable but also, I don't want anyone bothering me with their pesky physical needs. I've got enough crap to cope with. I'm in perimenopause. And I'm only just starting. What if all this . . . just . . . gets worse? And worse? Terror grips me. Stuff what Mum says, I *do* need to research this. I need to know what I've got in store for me. I need to know what's coming – as I've no idea what it all involves, hot flushes and forgetting stuff and what else? Am I immediately going to start sprouting long black hairs from my chin? Am I going to go completely insane??

Right, time to do some more googling. One site says that going into perimenopause and then menopause is a kind of reverse puberty. Ah, I like that explanation. When you're a teen, your body floods with all these crazy hormones, driving you mad. Then in your forties onwards, the same hormones decide to bugger off, also driving you mad. What fun women's bodies are. So, what have I got in store then, as my hormones fling themselves into the sea like a bunch of lemmings? I click on a list of the most common symptoms and I have a few at the beginning of the list:

- Hot flushes – I've had some of those, particularly when I'm stressed out (see Easter Sunday). Oh and apparently it's flushes in the UK and flashes in America. Flashes sounds more theatrical and exciting, while flushes more ladylike and nineteenth century. Typical. I want to be dramatic, not like a corseted Victorian fainting at every turn.

- Mind fog – I didn't know that's what it's called, but yeah. Big time. I actually forgot my own middle name the other day. (Veronica, if you really want to know. Maybe my mind blanked it out because it's so awful.)

- Digestive changes – you can say that again, Windy Heidi (as surely my secret work nickname must be by now).

- Weight gain – oh boy, have I ever. I now have the deportment of a corgi. I've abandoned jeans forever in favour of jeggings.

- Decreased sex drive – well, absolutely. Although I've had that more or less since Ada was born, so I'm not sure if that's just my life now.

37

Then there's all these other symptoms on the list, including:

- Dry vagina
- Stress incontinence
- Osteoporosis (something to look forward to)
- Depression
- Anxiety
- Recurrent UTIs (as if I don't wee enough already . . .)
- Migraines
- Burning mouth (why?!)
- Tingling in hands and feet
- Mood swings (no shit, Sherlock)
- Breast soreness
- Fatigue
- Allergies
- Dizziness
- Restless legs (random?!)
- Brittle nails
- Dry skin
- Night sweats
- Bloating
- Irregular heartbeat (terrifying)
- Dental problems
- Body odours (GREAT)
- Hair loss
- Electric shocks (WHAT ON EARTH?!)

Okay, OKAY. That's quite enough of that! Reading that list has brought me out in hives, figuratively anyway. It's the most terrifying list of curses heaped upon womankind I've ever seen. Is this normal for everyone? Is this what will happen to me?? Is this the life I have to look forward to, for the next nine or ten YEARS??? Blimey, if men experienced all of this stuff in their midlife we would never hear the end of it. In fact, they'd probably all get ten years off work and a cold beer in order to recover.

Oh God, I can't take it. I need help. I don't want to google anymore. It's too scary. I need to hear from real women who are going through this. But there's a problem with this:

a) my best friends Brenda and Kim from work plus Alia from next door are all in their early forties and not in perimenopause yet

b) I don't like anyone else.

For real. I'm just not a people person. Apart from Brenda and Kim, I don't mix with others at work really. On the rare occasion I join in a works do, I tend to hang about in the corner with my two besties, before I sneak out early to go home, where it's safe, and I don't have to make cringey small talk. I don't like going out much at all, to be honest, as the world is far too . . . peopley. So, how can I hear from these real women? I know . . . the answer to every niche interest on earth: Facebook Groups.

The modern solution to every variation on life you can imagine (and many you can't). The other day, I was invited to join a group that worships sweetcorn. So yeah, there's all sorts. I search on Facebook for menopause groups. Wow . . . there are so, so, so many. I can't possibly join all those. There are groups for diet and menopause, exercise and menopause, anti-HRT and menopause, men and menopause, natural therapies and menopause, sex and menopause, mental health and menopause, farming and menopause – what?

Yes, I read that right. There's a bunch of menopause groups just for the seven or so relevant women in your local village or hamlet, or group names with pleasing alliteration, like Menopause Mentality or Menopause Mania or Menopause Manchester (they won the menopause name-matching lottery, although the Mendips would be even better, if they had bothered to set up a group). Then there's a whole other list about Perimenopause, with the added challenge of finding words beginning with P to fashion a catchy group name (from Power to Practitioner to Positivity. Someone needs to invent a group called Petrified of Perimenopause or . . . Pissed Off with Perimenopause. I'd join that). I choose the most generic-sounding one, Perimenopause UK. It's vague enough to avoid the niche weirdness of alternative therapies (I like to think I'm open-minded, but when it comes to my health, I want medicine, I want legal drugs. I don't want essential oils and invisible massages) and it's specific enough to avoid American groups where the US healthcare system would add another layer of confusion to my already menopause-addled brain. I have to answer a couple of admin questions and then I'm in, no wait time to be approved. That's nice. I can start looking through all the posts to cheer myself . . . up . . . hang on a minute. I'm reading post after post after post about how awful perimenopause is.

Urine infection 14 months, no let-up, don't know what to do

Hot flush today 7 hours long. Any advice?

Itchy skin so bad please forgive pic but need to show you my legs look like cat scratching posts what can I use please?

Dr said my vagina has 'atrophied' permanently and I don't understand. Anyone been told this?

4th hospital visit of the month with random allergic reactions. Is this menopause or something else? Please help.

Bloody Nora. This is horrible. I thought I'd find comfort in a group of like-minded women all going through the same thing. But what I've found is a litany of despair. Everyone is desperate, everyone is sad, everyone is crying out for help. So I look at the comments. Surely there is some help out there. A problem shared and all that. If Mum can't help, maybe these random Facebook women can.

For the hot flush post, some of the comments read:

Nothing works just have to grin and bear Im afraid sorry

Go outside

Cold baths

Excuse to eat ice cream

Hot baths

The best remedy for menopause symptoms are to be found with Dr J. J. J. James of Tottenham, all natural remedy pills vitamins and minerals tablets for you. Click here.

Oh bloody hell, here we go. The scammers have arrived. There's loads of them, the more I look, some with ADMIN replies to alert the group. But even some of the non-scammer answers sound scammy.

Lemon verbena tea & manuka honey. Works wonders for all menopause ailments.

It sounds counter-intuitive, but you need to reset the balance of your system and introduce heat inside to drive the heat out. Yoni steaming will banish all hot flushes. I swear by it.

Kopi luwak coffee. It's the only thing that works for me. Well worth the expense. To which someone replies, *That's the monkey shit coffee, isn't it?* And someone else adds, *Civets actually.* Then, *What the hells a civet?*

Are these people for real?! What the hell has civet shit or pricey honey got to do with hot flushes? I want to help all these women; I want to give advice, or google stuff for them, or recommend books, or tell them I'm sending hugs and to keep smiling. But you know what? I'm too damn tired. I can't take on all these poor women's problems as well as my own. And their miseries are freaking me out. What if I get a seven-hour hot flush? What if my vagina ATROPHIES?

I slam shut my laptop lid. That way madness lies. I can't bear it, not right now, not on a rainy Monday night, washed out from work and kids and house stuff and parents. It's all too much. Maybe I'll have the strength to join more menopause groups and find a more positive one, one that doesn't scare the bejesus out of me.

I'm staring at the closed laptop lid when Ada comes in.

'Can I play The Game?'

She means *Rollercoaster Tycoon* AKA The Game. She has her own laptop and a Nintendo Switch hooked up to the telly, but with all that technology, she still loves the decade-old game I have on my computer that we played when she was really little. She likes building the coasters, setting up zoos and creating water parks. She'd rather play that than just about anything. I get it. I could murder a game of *Pong* about now. That's how melted my brain is. Even *Space Invaders* would be too stressful.

'Sure,' I say and open up the lid. I see I have a tab open with the minutes for tomorrow's Very Important Meeting that I can't remember the name of right now, and realise I was working on that just before The Curse occurred. I quickly tap into it and add two more things to the minutes that I've just remembered, one about finance and the other about timetabling. Then I need to name the document and save it.

'C'mon, Mum,' says Ada, tugging at my sleeve like a toddler.

'Okay, okay,' I say and . . . what was I doing? Ada has jumped in and navigated to the Home page, already clicked on the game and it's loading.

Oh well. I go downstairs to make a cuppa and look for a romcom on Prime. I can't be doing with anything taxing – tonight is not the night for *University Challenge* or *Only Connect*. I need something schmaltzy and meaningless to wash over me for a while. I sit there for twenty minutes, not taking a moment of this movie into my head. It's just televisual wallpaper. Then I suddenly remember I was in the middle of the minutes for tomorrow's meeting and I go back upstairs. I tell Ada to pause a minute and I go to find the document and it's gone.

'Where was that document? Have you closed anything?'

Ada lifts her hands up, palms out, to show her lack of criminality. 'I haven't touched a thing, Mum.'

'But where is it then?' I say, looking through the tabs: Zoom, Facebook, Word. But no meeting minutes. I look in Recently Saved Files, I look in My Documents. But it's nowhere to be seen. I don't know where else to look. I don't think I even named it. I can't remember the last two things I added to the list. I can't remember any of it. I'm a useless, mind-fogged, perimenopausal mess. I can feel my blood pressure shoot up and my patience suddenly evaporates.

'Look what you've done!' I snap at Ada. 'All that work, lost forever!'

'It wasn't me!' she cries, pushing herself away from my desk with a kick, my office chair spinning as she turns and jumps out of it, stomping out of the room.

She's right. It's not her fault. Blimey, I'm a terrible mother. I'm a terrible person. Who the hell is this old battleaxe? I go to Ada's room, to where she's retreated. I say sorry through the closed door and hear her grunt back, *Okay*.

I go and sit in the kitchen, as it's coolest in there. I stare out of the window I'd forgotten to close the curtains of and it's all dark out there. I stare into the blackness. Jeez Louise, that's depressing, but somehow compelling. The call of the void, they call it. I look away from that. I watch the washing machine starting its spin cycle instead, my mind zoning out at its white noise. What's happening to me? What happened to the Heidi I used to be? When I was a kid, younger than Ada, I watched this show on TV that I firmly believed was named after me and made only for me: *Heidi*. Blimey, I can instantly hear the music in my head right now. Dah da-da dah da-da dah dah . . . And little curly-haired Heidi with the perfect smile, frolicking in the Swiss Alps with her grandpa and Peter the goatherd. It was originally in German, I think, but it had this English dubbing with a weird accent, so she'd say, GREND-FARTHER like she was from downtown Johannesburg. Gosh, I bloody loved it. I watched it religiously. I wanted to step into the telly. A few years ago, I visited Zermatt with Geoff and the girls and from the cable car saw these wooden huts in the mountains and thought, *Why can't I just live there and make strudel and raise goats? Why can't life be that simple?* I feel that right now more than ever. I'm on one of those carousels I rode at the Witney Feast when I was a child, the Galloping Horses. I'm on it and we're going round and round so fast, and the luridly painted ponies are leering at me, and my head is spinning and I want to scream, STOP! LET ME OFF! But it's not a fairground ride, it's my life. And I'm barely hanging on by my fingertips.

I want to go back to the carefree days of Heidi in the mountains. Then schooldays and summer holidays. Then university and playing up a storm on my violin for various folk bands in the pubs. They hated that, the music department at Exeter. So old-fashioned and traditional. The professor only approved of classical music (like my parents) and poo-pooed folk or pop, even Gilbert and Sullivan being frowned upon. I used to play that fiddle up a storm. I was bloody good at it too, whatever Dad says. I know I was. But I put it away when I left uni and couldn't get a job. I didn't want to teach, again, whatever Dad says. It was never on the cards for me. I just wanted to perform. But that doesn't pay the bills, so I learnt to type and got a secretarial job at Oxford University Press. It was only ever meant to be temporary, while I worked up enough of a network to start performing all over the UK. I took songs everyone knew and I adapted them for the violin, feverishly writing my own variations, all by ear, by memory. I stored hundreds of tunes in my head back then. My fingers moved at a thousand miles per hour. My body swayed and absorbed the unspooling line of sound from my violin. Not an achy joint or a forgotten word in sight. Just me and the music. But my musical career never took off, and the temp job became permanent. And I got swallowed up by the world of administration. Then came Geoff, and our life together, and the kids. And I put my violin away in its case. It's stayed there ever since. It's in the attic now.

The washing machine clicks off and it's done. It plays a little tune when it's finished, to alert you politely to the termination of its operation. Bizarrely, my washing machine plays a twinkly rendition of Schubert's 'Trout Quintet', note perfect. That's about the height of the musical interaction I have these days. You couldn't get more middle class and middle-aged than that if you tried.

What happened to the freewheeling, fiddle-plucking, fearless and feisty Heidi I used to be? Is she dead and buried? Or simply waiting, like my violin, stowed away in the attic, gathering dust? Could she be rediscovered, reborn, revitalised? I feel suddenly galvanised by the thought, until it dawns on me that anything involving discovery, birth or vitality sounds utterly exhausting. And I have no energy left for any of it. As I said, I have no fucks to give. I let out a long, protracted sigh.

The washing needs putting in the dryer. Back to reality.

Chapter 4

I've ordered a couple of books from Amazon about menopause. I've only gone for the celebrity ones as I don't trust some of the other self-published ones by self-appointed women's health counsellor Dr Fenella Smith-Smythe, or whatever the hell weird name they all seem to be called. And you just know they're not a medical doctor, but instead have a PhD in Alternative Bullshit. Don't get me wrong, it might work for some people and that's great for them. Even if it's just the placebo effect and it helps, then that's a good thing, right? Plus, what do I know? There are more things in heaven and earth, Horatio and all that. But I do tend to have an innate mistrust of anything self-helpy. At least the celebrity ones have an actual medical doctor writing alongside them, so Davina McCall and Mariella Frostrup it is. I read chunks of them in bed and it's fascinating stuff. I'm learning about the history of how menopause has been viewed over the centuries (clue: it's never good), as well as how little training seems to be given to GPs on it and how different the experience is for each woman. But it's worrying too, like the Facebook posts – all these women having the worst time of their lives. So I don't read the books too often, just dipping in when I have enough mental energy. I'm still googling as well, to supplement my book knowledge. There is lots to learn but also some of it is unhelpful, confusing and contradictory advice, multiple doctors giving different guidance – like some saying yes, some saying no to HRT, the difference between male and female doctors on this subject (and gynaecology in general), confusion about symptoms and treatment and anodyne comments on medical websites, where they advise women to get more sleep and reduce stress and other such generalisations, which is about as much use as telling the *Titanic* to avoid icebergs.

I go back on Facebook and join more groups, including some midlife ones. Every symptom and approach under the sun is to be found here. Plus it's still miserable reading about everyone else's problems, although it can be heartening – sounds bitchy, I know, but some days it's a relief to see that others are worse off than me. So far, anyway. The constant posts in the groups are by turns scary, full of frantic positivity, oodles of drama and some inspiration, but mostly depressing or scaremongering and there seems to be reams of misinformation – people answering in the comments that they swear by this or that dodgy-sounding therapist or supplement or vitamin or various other very expensive things from Holland and Barrett, which to my mind all seem to sound more and more like snake oil. I feel like Dorothy listening to Professor Marvel in *The Wizard of Oz*. I can't afford to spend hundreds on vague pills and potions, just in case one ingredient of one of them may or may not work on one or less symptoms, with the added risk that they'll all start contraindicating each other and make you more sick. The more I read, the more it doesn't feel like a community, rather a ragtag group of people who have one thing in common which in turn divides them, because nobody's experiences are quite the same. I turn off all notifications! And some of the more frantically positive groups piss me off so much, I'm back in volcano territory. No, Juniper or whatever your name is, I do not feel energised and enlightened by this new phase in my womanhood, I feel like shit. Most of the groups, I visit less and less, until I absent myself altogether. I don't write flouncy *I'm outta here* posts announcing my departure. I'm not an airport. I simply, and quietly, click on Leave Group. And always breathe a sigh of relief. Wherever help is to be found, it's not on Facebook. I'm at a loss as to what to do next. I'm feeling very alone, to tell the sad truth.

And then this happens . . . I'm at my desk at home and I've just exited another depressing Facebook group, when I start going through all the day's work emails I haven't had a chance to read yet. I come across one to all staff, from the CEO of MUFFY, and one of the head honchos of MINGE. Its subject is *SUPPORTING OUR STAFF WITH MENOPAUSE*. Aye aye, what's all this? What does our male CEO – an ex-Aldi manager in his late fifties called Steven Quaife – have to say about menopause then?

To All Staff To Whom This Applies is the awkward opening gambit in massive font. They don't want to start with anything about women or womyn or womxn or people with wombs or anything of that ilk, as it terrifies these guys that they'll use the wrong epithet. So, they keep it as vague as possible.

Here at MMUFHE, we pride ourselves on our policies developed to support each and every one of our staff, whether they be in executive or senior management, teaching, administration, HR, finance, marketing, commercial, resources, estates or any other department of the college. Those going through the later-in-life stage known as perimenopause and menopause are at an age where they bring extensive wisdom to the educational table and are valued, mature members of our community. We esteem and cherish these elongated life experiences of said elder workforce and wish to extend the hand of help, sustenance and facilitation to them.

Someone swallowed a bloody thesaurus. Cut to the chase, Quaife.

We have canvassed opinion and after a panel discussion, we have drawn conclusions. We have really listened to your needs and we are here to support you all. With this in mind, the senior and executive management teams have banded together in an unprecedented step to confabulate at great length of how best we are able to support our staff coping with this unfortunate disorder. We have boldly taken the appropriate steps to now be able to offer a new initiative to underpin and boost the vital roles these *staff provide. For all those currently going through perimenopause or menopause*, we are delighted to announce that we can now offer a desktop fan of modern, innovative design** to keep cool those afflicted staff members, even on the hottest day of the year, free to all users.*** No longer will our workers need to endure the heated moments of discomfort that have previously tormented and plagued them at work, all while attempting their very best to continue with their essential and treasured vocational roles while suffering under the cosh of their gendered inheritance. Please contact HR in order to avail yourself of your new best friend that will live cheerfully on your desk, assisting you at all times to overcome this temporary, short-term infirmity and instead enable you to look forward to a new, triumphant phase in your working life.*

Very best regards,

Steven Quaife, BSc (Hons), FAW-trained, ECB Foundation Coach, CEO of MMUFHE as part of MNGE.

*All those applying for the desktop fan must bring both a medical certificate from their GP or private gynaecologist and hormone replacement therapy prescription as evidence of perimenopause or menopause, presented to HR before order of desktop fan is actioned, as orders will not be merely rubber-stamped via oral testimony. Orders will be rejected without both items of written evidence.

**Plugs into USB port plus solar-panelled, thus meeting our green energy pathway commitments laid down in this year's Action Plan, Section 73, Subsection 4g.

***75% of the cost of each desktop fan must be met by individual members of staff and payment will be taken from monthly wages in one lump sum and instalments will not be considered or approved as viable. No other fans are available or should be used by staff, due to health and safety regulations. (Cost of each fan is £399.99 RRP.)

Oh.

My.

Fucking.

God.

THAT'S IT! The final straw has lightly wafted down upon my pain-riddled lower back. I have reached the last vestiges of the frayed straggly threads that constitute the end of my tether. I have waded across the raging river and – up to my tits in the rampant torrent – there's no turning back now. I've had ENOUGH! This email from Steven Quaife – AKA Stevie Queef, as everyone at MUFFY calls him behind his back – has finally tipped me over the edge. The question is . . . what would Miriam do?

I hit Reply All and a fresh, pristine screen pops up for me to type my reply.

> *Dear Stevie Queef,*
> *I've never read such a pretentious pile of drivel as this email to which you've just subjected every member*

of your long-suffering staff. Reading that has had such a profound effect upon my ever-increasing rage, that you're bloody lucky you're not in the room with me right now, as I've finally lost my shit. I think I'm going to hit someone. I think I might actually punch someone's lights out and that someone might be you, Steven Quaife, BSc (Hons), erstwhile of Aldi, whose qualifications are so pathetic you've actually included your First Aid at Work certificate in your bloody email signature, as well as your entry-level England and Wales Cricket Board coaching credentials. This is the man who rules us all. So, after careful consideration by you, alongside the entire SMT and EMT at the Miriam Margolyes University of Further & Higher Education, you lot of pointless arsewipes have come up with . . . THIS. This is your ingenious solution to coping with the devastating complexities of menopause at work. Free desktop fans?! And they're not even free! You bastards only pay for a quarter of the cost! And the rest is taken from our hard-earned wages as a lump sum! Plus we have to pay our GPs for a medical cert to prove we're menopausal! Plus there are plenty of menopausal women who are not even on HRT or can't be or want to be but their GPs won't let them. And we're not permitted to use any other fan but the 400 quid one you undoubtedly got some dodgy deal on a job lot for from your backhander business mates, the same shady wankers I bet who installed the tacky-as-fuck water feature in the lobby last year that cost the college FIFTY THOUSAND POUNDS! And I don't even have a fucking printer in my office!! I have to go to the next floor down to print out a document! And now this fan bullshit. Why is a fan £400 anyway?! For that, I'd expect it to give me a cuppa and a head massage. Plus with these fans on our desks, it's just another way of singling out women with menopause as the office freaks, isn't it? Unclean, unclean! Why not paint a big red X on our desks while you're at it? And what about the women who don't have desks, who work elsewhere in the college? How is a desk fan going to help them?? And the fan isn't even the worst thing – after all your professed research, you've come back with hot flushes as the only symptom of menopause and fans as the only solution, instead of what we need, which is to connect with other women and be given a space to talk about menopause as opposed to hiding behind fans. Actually SPEAK to each other. Oh and don't get me started on the management-speak bullshit of your email. The pomposity of the verbiage is un-fucking-believable! The absolute total audacity of the whole fake helpful bullshit you're touting at us, dressed up in posh language so us dullard drones won't notice the whole thing is a nod at workplace support at best, a scam at worst! You total and utter bunch of bastards. If I had the nerve, I'd resign. But there's no point, because I'm convinced every other workplace in the whole damn country will be the same as this one, pretending that women and men are equal, despite the gender pay gap, useless childcare support and wilful ignorance about women's health. FYI hot flushes are only one of dozens of possible symptoms that a woman experiences throughout menopause and all the fans in the world are not going to help me when I'm drowning in nausea and forgetting my own fucking name. I'm so sick and tired of this idea that women's bodies are non-standard, that women's issues are extra, are alternative, are for special consideration. We've come no further than Adam's rib, for fuck's sake! White, middle-class, heterosexual men are the norm and everything else is seen as abnormal. And I for one am sick to bloody death of it. I call for revolution. Sisters, unite against these twats of the first order and rebel! We won't take this shit anymore! Fire me, if you dare! I will arise from the ashes and eat men like air! And that's a butchered quote from feminist poet Sylvia Plath, not that you'd ever know, you cricket-coaching cretin with verbal diarrhoea. Fuck off back to Aldi.

   Yours sincerely,
   Heidi Hobbes (grade 8 violin)

Of course, I don't send it. I sit there and read it back, chortling all the way. If only I had the balls big enough – or rather, the ovaries – to actually tell my useless bosses what I really think of them. Another big sigh from me . . . and I scroll back to the top to start deleting the whole damn, beautiful thing. For a moment I pause, thinking about saving it to Drafts and showing it to Brenda tomorrow and we can have a little giggle about it.

'Mum, the game,' says Ada, suddenly in my doorway.

'Bloody hell, you gave me a fright,' I say, swivelling round at her voice. 'How long have you been standing there?'

'I said twice – can I play the game? – and you totally ignored me. You were just typing really fast and angrily while your face was going red.'

I get up and go to give her a hug, which she tolerates. I need it much more than she does. 'Sorry, pet. I was miles away. Just living for a moment in a better world inside my head where we can say what we really think to anyone and never have to pay the consequences.'

Ada lifts her chin and says, 'That's how I'm going to be when I'm an adult. I'm just going to say whatever I think and people will just have to deal with it. People worry too much about what people think of them. I just don't care what anyone thinks of me. Never have and I never, ever, ever will.'

'I hope that's true,' I say, smiling down at her sweet, earnest face. 'Life's a lot easier that way, kid.'

Ada shrugs and goes over to my laptop to play The Game.

I go down to fill the dishwasher with the remnants of tonight's dinner to find that Carly's already done it, before she headed out for a night at Matt's. Ah, she's a good lass. I'm relieved I don't have to do it, as I'm absolutely knackered. I collapse on the sofa and start doomscrolling on Facebook. I scroll swiftly past any of the menopause or midlife group posts, as I really can't be bothered to think about all that tonight. I need a break from my biological destiny for an evening, thanks very much. So I share a couple of videos of ducklings following a golden retriever, and a cat who lost a leg and survived cancer and lived a long happy three-legged life with his new owner. Feel-good stuff. I need this nonsense, to avoid the call of the void. I'm scrolling on looking for more happy vibes and see a couple of lads called Funkanometry doing a fab dance in a square in Canada, set to 'Stayin' Alive' by the Bee Gees. Ohhhh, I bloody love that song. I used to play that record over and over and over again when I was a kid. I google it – yeah, it came out when I was six. That's so great to see these Gen Z boys discovering such a classic! That's cheered me up a treat.

I reach over and grab my earphones from the coffee table and put them in, find the song on my playlist titled *Old School Shit* and start listening. Oh, God, the years drain away and there I am, dancing round my room in my ra-ra skirt in 1981 aged ten listening to this classic from 1977, thinking my moves are the best moves that ever moved, and that the Bee Gees are the greatest band in the world, apart from Blondie obviously. If I had the energy, I'd get up and dance right now, but I'm too bloody knackered. Stretched out on the sofa, I tap my feet and twitch my hips and nod along to the beat, and I close my eyes. Life was uncomplicated back then in the seventies and eighties – I mean, I know middle-aged folk like myself say stuff like that all the time, but it really was. No mobile phones, no internet, no Instagram, no Spotify or Netflix. Just three television channels and there was the Top 40 on the radio on Sundays and you'd set up your tape recorder to record the songs you wanted and had to have the reflexes of a house fly to press pause at precisely the right moment so you didn't get the DJ's voice ruining your mix tape. There was *Dial a Disc* on the phone where you called up and listened to your favourite song thirty times until your dad gets the phone bill and clouts you round the ear. You'd take holiday camera films to Boots Chemist and get the photos back two weeks later and, my God, the excitement of going to pick them up! You had to wait for everything, nothing was instant (except Mellow Birds coffee with a heaped teaspoon of Nestlé's Coffee Mate). You weren't assaulted twenty-four-seven with thousands of images of people who look better than you ever will inside a tiny computer that rests in your hand. If you weren't in the same house as someone, people couldn't get hold of you unless someone answered the one telephone tethered to the wall, on the table in the hallway. You could go out and disappear into the day and never be bothered by a soul. No constant notifications in your pocket reminding you of your endless responsibilities to other humans. Even the nineties were still pretty innocent, as the internet, email and messaging didn't become mainstream until well into the decade, and the height of technology was typing up my uni essays on my Amstrad Word Processor (before I'd ever heard of Sir Alan Sugar and *You're fired*), with its blinking green cursor on a plain black screen. Happy days! I wish I could be back there right now, in that ra-ra skirt, no responsibilities, no job, no mortgage, no kids, no menopause.

The song comes to an end and Simon and Garfunkel's 'Bleecker Street' comes up next. Oh crikey, the beauty of those guys' voices, the sad reflective yearning of their songs. It makes my soul ache. Now I'm back in my heartache-ridden teens, wallowing in self-pity as I listened to sad songs then rewound the really scrunchy saddest bits because they didn't hurt me enough the first time. Would I really want to be a teen again? Maybe not. Actually, definitely not, when I think back to the bad perms and my heart repeatedly broken by a string of useless, heartless boys. No, if I could go back to my youth, à la some magical body-swap time-travel movie – I'd go back to the early nineties, turning nineteen in the first year of the decade. Everything was before me then, everything was possible . . .

God, I feel depressed again now. Plus I've got a bad tummy tonight. It's churning around and thank heavens I'm on my own in here so I can fart at will, because they're coming out at a rate of knots tonight. I light a candle in case I stink out the whole house. Urgh, middle-aged bodies are excruciatingly embarrassing. The gloom of my present predicament fills my mind again and I go back to my phone for comfort. Whatever I may miss about my simpler childhood, I am addicted to the distraction techniques of my phone and I go on Instagram and watch some biscuit-decorating videos for a long while, then go on doomscrolling, the sounds of my youth still playing in my ears: Steeleye Span, Pearl Jam, Portishead. They're too nostalgic, so I turn off the music. I can't cope with all that wallowing tonight. Then, a Facebook notification pops up at the top of the screen. I've been invited to an event. What? Nobody ever invites me to anything, because anybody who knows me knows that I always say no. I don't even agree to Friday night drinks down the pub with my colleagues, because, well, *people*. But also, I can't drink alcohol, so what's the point? I click on the notification and up pops a green circular logo and it's the University of Exeter. What's this? Some kind of dreadful alumni thing asking for cash? You're literally bankrupting teenagers with your fees these days, University of Exeter, so no, I can't afford to send you a donation, since I'm still helping my twenty-two-year-old save up for a house deposit because she's already in so much debt, another shit thing about these days. But no, the title shows me that it's not about that. It reads *CLASS OF '94 REUNION!!!*

Hang on, that's me! I graduated in 1994. What's this all about then? I click on the post . . .

Chapter 5

I tap on Meet Your Host and a picture pops up. Oh my God, it's that girl that used to play the flute and the bloody harp and had rich parents and was utterly insufferable. Christ, she hasn't aged a day. She has the exact same long, dead-straight, sandy-coloured hair hanging down each side of her face like beige curtains, which just about sums up her personality. I read on:

Hi! It's Serena Lightfoot here! Remember me?! Of course you do! And I'm sure you will never forget our beloved time at Exeter Uni either. So, here I am to take you right back to those halcyon days of thirty years ago by gathering us all together at Reed Hall, Exeter on Saturday 5th October for a reunion dance! There will be a bar and buffet, along with a 1990s-themed disco and a sumptuous celebration cake courtesy of my highly successful bakery business CUTEY CAKEY. I've invited everyone I personally remember, but if you're still in touch with any of our Class of '94 compadres from that wonderful time, then please do send their details to me and – once I've done the due diligence of proper checks and providing they are bona fide graduates of '94 – I'll invite them too. Let us know you're coming by clicking on the Going button, or if you're not sure yet, why not click on Interested, just so we know you've seen this post? Come along and relive our glory days on – remember, remember – the 5th of October! What have you got to lose?! Comment below to start the conversation and get us all chatting again. See you there, darlings!!!

Blimey. Serena Lightfoot. I haven't thought about her for nigh on thirty years. So now she runs a bakery business called . . . Cutey Cakey?! Oh my God, this is priceless. A couple of people are commenting already. I don't recognise the names. Ooh, there's another one, some girl I vaguely remember called Sally who was really into medieval music and played the recorder (yes, they let adults play recorders and they have really big ones too with keys on and everything – actually, joking aside, tenor and bass recorders are rather gorgeous). Who else? Nobody yet. How weird that this should pop up tonight, when I was reliving my youth in my tired old mind. But then, I've been doing that so much lately, it occurs to me that maybe I'm not the only one. Maybe it's a zeitgeisty thing and Serena Lightfoot has been sitting there thinking about her glory days too but, unlike me, doesn't have a people phobia and decided to do something about it.

So, am I going to go to Reed Hall in Exeter on Saturday 5th October to boogie on down with the old 'compadres' from my alma mater?

My overwhelming reaction is my brain yelling NOOOOOOOO like Munch's *The Scream*. Won't it be the most appalling cringefest? However, another thought occurs to me: that the timing is incredibly fortuitous, because I always take a few days off in the first week of October, after the madness of September enrolment and new arrivals, and to recharge before the next round of planning begins. So this party would come at precisely the right time for me. Seems strangely serendipitous . . . Comments on the post start popping up thick and fast. Wow, Serena must have kept in touch with everybody she ever met at uni. I literally don't know anyone from those days anymore, not a single person. I'm trying to imagine walking into Reed Hall all these years later, with my menopause belly and my dry hair and corgi legs and . . . I shudder. I can't bear the thought of it. The humiliation. Most of them won't remember me anyway – I was never exactly the life and soul of the party – and even if they do, they'll all be thinking, *Wow, she really let herself go. That Heidi Hobbes used to have gloriously long wavy brown hair down to her bum and a trim little figure with perky tits and bloody hell, look at her now. What a mess.* I can't bear the thought of it. But then another notification pops up.

Nathan Wheeler tagged you in a post in **CLASS OF '94 REUNION!!!**

Nathan who? Nathan . . . Oh my days, it's Nate! The guy I shared a house with in my final year, along with another lad called Luke (Luke something . . . his surname escapes me). Nate Wheeler . . . A surge of feeling sweeps over me like a tidal wave, making every inch of my body tingle and hum. It's so instant and intense, it completely blindsides me. I close my eyes and breathe in deeply to calm myself. Am I having a hot flush? No, it's something else. What is it? It's something I've not felt in so long, that I'd almost forgotten it. It is desire. Eagerly, I click on his notification and read his comment.

Hey Hobbes . . .

Oh, hey, Wheeler. Hey, Nate Wheeler. Hey, superstar pianist, love of my final uni year and subject of many a sexual fantasy for many a year. Despite a couple of boyfriends before uni, Nate was my first proper full-on crush. You could say, my sexual awakening. And here he is again, after all these years and he's having the very same effect he had on me three decades ago. I realise in all the excitement I haven't clicked on his profile pic yet. Will he have aged badly like me?? Here we go . . .

Well . . . the answer is decidedly no. He has aged spectacularly. It's not fair! Why do some men look better and better the older they get? Silver fox, that's what they call them. Nate's actually still got a full head of blonde hair, thick and brushed back and streaked with grey I can see, as I enlarge his head in his full body shot. It's a picture of him on stage playing keyboard with some band. He's wearing jeans and a tight T-shirt with raggedy hems – just the same look he used to sport back in the day – and it shows off a very decent body for a man his age, with bulging arms and those beautiful hands just out of shot. How I used to love to watch him play piano with those hands. He must still be performing then. Crikey, I must answer his comment! I'm not playing hard to get. I'm just busy drinking in this image of this still-beautiful man. What a looker! What the hell am I going to say to him?!

But then, another notification pops up immediately. It's a Friend Request from Nathan Wheeler.

I've never clicked on anything so fast in my life. And moments later, DING. There's a DM incoming. I go straight to Messenger and there sits his first private message:

I'll go if you go . . .

Jesus, that's the sexiest five words I've heard in a long time. Be cool, Hobbes, be cool.

Hey Nate! How's life?

Pretty good. How's about you?

Bloody awful, to be honest. Too much work, too much responsibility, too much adulting.

Ah yeah adulting. Overrated concept. We wanted to be adults so bad when we were kids. Now look at us.

Exactly!!!

I delete two of the exclamation marks before I press send. Three of them seems excessively keen. God, what a rush this is. Messaging with Nate Wheeler.

What are you doing now? he asks.

I think, Lying on the sofa watching a romcom, contemplating never standing up again. But I write instead:

Just back from the gym. Hot yoga tonight.

I cringe the moment I've sent it. Who am I kidding?! But I can't admit to glorious Nate Wheeler the awful truth that I'm fat and exhausted and washed up.

Nice. But I meant, what job are you doing?

Oh right! I'm an administrator at a college. Don't get too excited. It's not half as glamorous as it sounds. What about you?

We've all gotta earn a living. I'm still playing keyboards in the industry. Still keeping the music alive.

His actual job is a musician? Wow, that is impressive. How on earth does he make a living though?

That's great! Do you teach as well?

Fuck no. Kill me now, rather than do that.

67

Right?! Agreed!

*No, I'm a session musician, accompanist, soloist. Plus I
run a small recording studio in my back yard.*

Gosh, even more impressive. He kept on with his music.
He's still playing and collaborating and recording all these
decades later. I feel a pang of envy in my gut. Or is it that
chocolate I snaffled earlier coming back to say hello?

Do you still play? You were a cracking violinist, Hobbes.

Oh, stop. I was average at best.

I'm lying. I know I was better than that. And it gives me
a thrill to hear him say it too.

*No you weren't. Stop bullshitting. You were talented AF.
Do you still play then?*

*I try to keep my hand in, yeah. I do a gig now and
again.*

I lie again. I can't bear to admit that I haven't touched
my beautiful violin in years. Why haven't I? It feels more
and more like a crime that I haven't, especially now I'm lying
about it.

Glad to hear that. Would love to hear you play again, Hobbes.

My stomach twists with nerves. He'd love to hear me

play? I'd love to hear me play, it's been so long. But what if I've lost it completely, all that talent and facility I used to have? Maybe it's atrophied, like that poor woman's vagina.

Well thank you. You too. So you still play gigs?

Yeah I toured with Coldplay year before last and now focusing more on folk this year, mentoring some UK bands. Plus I was a session musician with Daryl Hall last year.

OH MY GOD!! I tap out and send before I have time to think how fan-girly that is. It is damned impressive though.

He replies with a blushing face emoji.

What's Daryl Hall like? Sara Smile is my favourite song of all time!

He's such a lovely guy. And that voice. It's the perfect instrument. He hasn't lost it. Sweet and pure as ever it was.

I must admit, I'm a little bit starstruck, Nate!

Don't be. It's just me. And it's just my job. Have you heard from Luke recently?

Our other housemate, Luke. I still can't recall his surname – as I've forgotten so many things – but Luke shared a house with me and Nate from '93 to '94, after which we all left Exeter and went our separate ways. Luke and I stayed in touch for a while, the odd letter or phone call. But time moved on and marriage and pregnancy came and our friendship faded away, as often happens in life. But I do remember that Luke was such a nice chap. We all had a hoot together. I mean, I was lusting after Nate who we barely saw, as he was so popular and in demand. Thus Luke and I hung out quite a bit, in between gigging and writing our dissertations. He was a good friend then.

No, I've not kept up with Luke in years. Have you?

Not for years. Great guitarist. Not sure if he's coming to the reunion too.

I never said I was coming!

Why not? You've gotta come, Hobbes. Like I said, I aint going if you aint.

I never go anywhere! I've got two kids and a full-time job and no time to myself.

You go to hot yoga.

Even that was a lie!

I'll think about it . . . I type, hesitantly. Something tells me I want to play a little bit hard to get with the gorgeous Nate Wheeler. I've been altogether too keen so far in this conversation, I feel.

70

You do that . . .

There's that little frisson again. If I were typing my thoughts on a phone right now, I'd add that emoji with hearts for eyes, just for myself. I wouldn't let him know how thrilling it is just to think about him again after thirty years, let alone message with him. A wave of excitement and fear makes me tingle all the way up my spine and into my ears. I suddenly realise that this desire – this out and out LUST – has been lying dormant inside me all this time and now it's been turned on like a light switch. It really is that instant. And I thought those days were over. I thought it was dead. But all it needed was a spark. All it needed was Nate Wheeler.

I'm off now, Hobbes. Places to be and people to see. Let's catch up again soon.

Sure. Take care. And thanks for reaching out!

My pleasure. A bientot.

And then, as swiftly as he reappeared in my life, he's gone. Well, well, well . . . Nate Wheeler! I can't quite believe it. I think back to the summer of '93, when he turned up on my doorstep during a heatwave. I'd been living with two girlfriends studying languages in my second year and they both left to go on their year abroad and I had to find two people to occupy their rooms, so I wasn't left paying rent on a three-bedroomed house I couldn't afford. So I put a note up on a few noticeboards. Nate and Luke were the first to get in touch. Well, Luke was. I knew Nate a bit, as we were taking music together. But I didn't know Luke. He was studying engineering, yet was also a musician in his spare time. He and Nate became friends via the local music scene and moved in very different circles to me. I was with the decidedly folky folk, while Nate hung out with rock gods and their groupies and Luke was more of a classical guitar type, though I later found out he played in a band too, writing their own stuff, introspective and sweet, kind of Nick Drake-ish. Luke rang my house phone and we arranged for him and an unnamed mate to come round to view the house.

I'd been watching Nate Wheeler from afar for two years and never even spoken a word to him outside class, in all that time. So when he appeared behind Luke that day, I was a tongue-tied fool. Nate was charming though, so utterly relaxed in his own body, he was nearly horizontal. He actually said they'd take the house before he'd even seen the bedrooms, winking at me as he did so. Luke said yes too and they moved in a few days later, sweating through the late August afternoon, carting in amps and leads and pedals and instrument cases, which filled the front room. I'd only ever lived with girls at uni, so the sudden arrival of all that male odour and paraphernalia was quite a shock to the system. Nate was a slob and left everything in a mess, but thankfully Luke was considerate and tidy by nature, so between us we kept the house in order, regularly berating Nate for his slovenly ways, who always took it good-naturedly. Neither of us could be mad at Nate for long. And really, he was hardly ever at home, always out partying, gallivanting, experimenting with various substances and returning at dawn smelling of booze and weed, the eternal rebel. Mostly, at home, it was me and Luke, holed up in our bedrooms tapping or scribbling away at our final-year assignments. Suddenly, the flavour of those long-lost days wafts across me like a scent on the breeze and I'm there, in my little attic room, one wall stained with damp from the leaking chimney stack – which my Devonian landlord called a chimley – in that tall, thin house on a long tree-lined terrace in Exeter. I haven't thought about that place in, what, twenty years? Thirty? Now, it seems like yesterday, those full days and late nights of reading and taking notes and typing up, meeting Luke in the kitchen for breaks from our dissertations, making a quick cuppa and back to it. How companiable he was, what an easy-going housemate.

Then, as the memories flood back, I recall now how much I was in love with that impossibly glamorous pianist and was certain that he did not reciprocate. Nate was forever friendly with me, gracing my cheek with a peck when I did the washing up that was actually his turn or giving me a grateful hug when I made him fried-egg sandwiches as a hangover cure. Nate was always nice to me, and genuinely seemed to enjoy hanging out with me. But he never made a move. And I never had the nerve to tell him how I really felt. That I saved for Luke, who listened seriously and never tried to give me advice. He'd invariably have his guitar on his knee in the living room, picking away at it while I wittered on about Nate. He was a good listener. Then I remember that after Christmas of that final year, Luke inherited a car from an older brother, a beat-up royal blue Citroën 2CV, an eccentric little car that had a friendly face and a roll-back canvas sun-roof.

For those last few months of final year, when we took a break from working, we'd potter off in the 2CV onto the moors of Devon and visit country pubs, play chess or read in front of roaring fires in the cooler days or sit on pub garden benches in the warmer ones, chatting about life and music, mostly music, smoking roll-ups and nursing one pint of bitter as long as we could and sometimes ordering chicken in a basket if we were feeling particularly flush with cash that week. Everything was so simple then: essays and beer and chips and ciggies. And music, always music. My God, how I miss those days.

Why did we lose touch, Luke and I? And Nate. I really can't recall. There was something about Exeter at that time, a kind of halcyon remove from the real world. Once we all left it, the bubble burst. The dream was over and we went off into our real lives, our adulty ones. I didn't have social media or email or even texting in 1994, so had to write letters or make phone calls and blokes just didn't do that as much as girls did. And so the years passed and those faded into almost sepia memories. I'm as far away from that Heidi Hobbes as I am from death, or maybe even more so, if I kick the bucket before I'm eighty-two. I haven't seen Nate or Luke in thirty years. It was another era, part of history now, which makes me feel a thousand years old.

I pick up my phone again and go back onto the reunion invitation post. I scan through the names and look for Luke, but he's not there. What was his last name? Something like Berry or Berwin or . . . Beresford! That's it. I do a Facebook search for Luke Beresford. I scrutinise the tiny thumbnails to see if it looks like him, like the

Luke I remember, who used to have thick, chunky, shoulder-length dark brown hair tucked behind his ears and round wire-rimmed spectacles all those years ago. But I can't find anyone who looks remotely like him. I need to ask Nate if he has any contact details for Luke. But I don't want to message Nate again so soon. Far too keen. I don't even know why I think that, I mean, I'm not twenty anymore! Who cares if he thinks I'm over-keen? *I do*, I realise, with a shock. I care very much and there's no way I'm going to text first. Stupid, really, but that's how I feel about Nate Wheeler, as if he's a project that will need careful planning and scheming to achieve; the thought of him is all a nebulous mixture of lust and nostalgia, excitement and hope, though God knows why. He's just a bloke, after all. But what a nice surprise of a weekday evening. I grin, really grin, for the first time in ages. Hearing from Nate Wheeler has had a tremendous effect on me: instead of wallowing in memories of a time long lost, suddenly the past has jumped up and texted me. The Heidi Hobbes I once was is there again, buried deep in me, my freewheeling younger self. Perhaps she never really went away.

I go back to the Facebook reunion post and tap Interested. I feel invigorated! Just from seeing that Interested status pop up! I hop up from the sofa, suddenly full of verve, unsure of what to do with this uncustomary burst of energy. Not hot yoga, that's for sure. I decide to gift it to my daughter, who usually gets the miserable, worn-out version of me. So I trot upstairs to see Ada and give her a kiss. She's playing The Game on my computer again, but turns and her eyes light up when I come in, which gives me a little pang of guilt and love, that she's so pleased to see her silly old mum.

'Can I build an ostrich enclosure and put too many birds in, so they breed wildly and overrun the zoo?' I say.

'YES!' shouts Ada gleefully and I drag a chair in from her room and we play *Rollercoaster Tycoon* till way past her bedtime and mine. I'm so tired by the time we're done, I crawl onto my bed without even brushing my teeth, as Ada shuts down the computer for me. And, happier than I've felt in quite a while, I conk out like a light.

Chapter 6

The next thing I know, it's morning and my alarm is going off. Best night's sleep I've had in ages. Now it's time for work again. The toad work, as the poet Larkin called it. How bloody right he was. Shower, hairdryer, clothes and cereal for two; saying bye to Ada before her dad does the school run; then traffic jams, car park and stairs. I'm a bit late today and should've been at my desk earlier, but I can't face it just now. I'm so utterly, inordinately exhausted. When did life become so unbearably tiring? I go to the ladies' and into a cubicle. I don't need a wee. I just need a moment of quiet before I face the intensely peopley place that is the open-plan, desk-cluttered MUFFY administration office. I put the toilet lid down and sit on it, looking at my phone. I can't bear to look at work emails; that can wait until I get to my desk. I check to see if Nate has messaged again: not yet.

I google Nate Wheeler. His website comes up, with various pics of him performing. So he wasn't bullshitting – there are crowd shots of Coldplay and Daryl Hall performing with other close-up pics of just Nate playing keyboards on stages. On another page there are pics of Snow Patrol and Suede gigs. And there's another pic of Nate with his arm around Brett Anderson of Suede! My housemate Nate, hanging out with Brett Anderson! Suede! My God, one of my favourites of all time. The coolest of the cool! All I want to do right now is plug my *Old School Shit* playlist into my ears and dance to 'Beautiful Ones' by Suede and all the other Britpop classics of my uni days. Instead, I'm stuck on the loo in an admin building with exactly three minutes left before I ought to be back at my desk. I look around Nate's website a bit more. He does have a recording studio at home. It's in the Orkney Islands, bizarrely. He's got a lovely-looking house and studio up there, by the pics. I'm in the wrong job, I really am. It looks huge, the house. With his own private studio. There's one in the eye for my parents, who said being a musician would never amount to anything. I envy Nate Wheeler. But even more than the money, I envy the fact that he never sold out his dreams and got a normal job, like I did. I had plans, so many plans, to travel the world and perform and compose and . . . other hazy possibilities that I hadn't formulated fully but would surely unfurl in the bright, shiny future I expected would come to me back then. But, as ever, nothing works out the way you expect, and I met Geoff and I fell pregnant . . . and here I am. A cold sweat prickles my face. I feel a bit ill. Is it menopause symptoms? Or is it the realisation that I had a life mapped out but getting pregnant was the turning point that ruined it all? I don't regret my children, either of them – how could I? I adore them, I'd die for them without a second thought.

But it occurs to me that, if I hadn't had Carly, I might be like Nate now, an accomplished musician, fulfilled, contented, simultaneously at peace yet also energised by my fabulous life. Maybe I'm in the wrong life now. At some point thirty or so years ago, there was a fork in the road and I chose to go down one and not the other, never to return. There's that idea of the *unlived life*, curving away into an alternate future like a railway track. What if I made the wrong decision back then? What if my life is on the wrong track? And is there any way on earth to get it back on the right one? Brett Anderson is singing LAH LAH LA LA LAH LA LA in my mind's ear and all I want to do is escape this bloody toilet and – I admit it – this damned crappy life I've made for myself. But I know I don't have the energy or courage to do anything about my life. I can't throw a hand grenade into the middle of my fifty-something existence. I can't even face the idea of going to a uni reunion.

I look back at the Facebook post and see my Interested tick there and feel a bit panicky. Could I really do it, travel down to Exeter and meet all those folk from the past, with all my anxiety and ailments and general misanthropy?

'Maybe I could . . .' I say aloud.

Then, two women come into the ladies' chatting away and I shut up. I don't want everyone to be talking even more about me, after the farting and the forgetfulness and now talking to myself in the loos. But . . . I hear my name . . . and these two *are* talking about me. Why the hell are they talking about *me*?

'So brave. I mean, it's the stuff we think but we'd never say it,' says one woman. It sounds like Mary, one of the senior accounts staff.

'I know, right?!' says the other woman. That's one of the young finance bods, Famke, I think it is. 'Calling him Stevie Queef, to his face!! Well, on an email anyway. But to everyone! To All Staff! Heidi's a legend, I tell you. This'll go down in MUFFY history, even if she gets sacked.'

'Especially if she gets sacked! A martyr for the cause!'

I'm off that toilet quicker than shit off a shovel. I open the cubicle door and both women look round and clock me.

'What's this all about?' I say, breathlessly, my heart starting to thump now.

'Oh my God, you gave me a shock,' says Mary. 'It's like we summoned you!'

'What are you talking about, Mary? What's all this about me getting sacked?'

Famke looks embarrassed to have been caught out gossiping, but Mary's been at MUFFY even longer than I have. An old hand with the figurative hide of a rhino, she doesn't give a flying fart what anyone thinks of her.

'That email you sent to all and sundry about the fans. It was bloody marvellous, love.'

'But I didn't send it! I saved it to Drafts!'

'Erm, no. You didn't,' says Mary, emphatically. 'It went to every single staff member with an email at MUFFY. And *everyone* is talking about it.'

Famke gasps. 'You mean, you sent it . . . by accident?!'

My mind races back to last night, when I finished typing my monumental rant, then Ada came in and . . . Oh God, I didn't save it to Drafts. Or maybe I did, but it was still on there, unsent, then Ada went on The Game and maybe she clicked something by mistake or . . .

'Oh FUCK . . .' I whisper hoarsely and Famke giggles.

'This is even better gossip!' says Mary archly. Then even the thick-skinned Mary can see how upset I am. My eyes have filled with tears and they're rolling down my cheeks onto my hand which is clamped over my mouth. I turn sharply to look in the mirror, using the tips of my index fingers to wipe away the black stains from my supposedly waterproof mascara. My stomach instantly starts churning and I can tell it's going straight into fight or flight mode. Oh God, not now, please not now. There I was, on the loo, wishing away my current life and it's as if some messed-up fairy godmother has heard me and granted my wish. I'm going to lose my bloody job! But what will happen about the mortgage, the bills, Carly's house deposit, Ada's future?!

Mary puts her arm around my shoulders, while Famke slinks off out of there, leaving the drama to the middle-aged women. 'Come on, love. You've been here forever. You're practically an institution. They won't sack you for this. You're just going to have to eat a helluva lot of humble pie, that's all.'

'Oh Christ, what the hell am I going to do?'

'Who's your line manager again? Pickley?'

'Yes, the marvellous mansplainer.'

'Shit. Oh well, it is what it is. Go and see him now. Tell him it was all a terrible mistake, a joke gone wrong. Blame menopause, say you had a mini mental breakdown due to hot flushes.'

'I'm not blaming menopause! That makes it sound like any of us going through it aren't capable of our jobs. That men were right about us, that we're deficient, unreliable. That there shouldn't be women fighter pilots because they

81

might be on their periods and start killing their own indiscriminately. That women's hormones are liabilities!'

Mary grabs my shoulders roughly then. 'Hey!' she yells and I freeze. 'Snap out of it, woman. You're rambling like a lunatic. This isn't you. This is menopause talking. I know because I went through it a few years back. But I'm fine now and so will you be. Get a bloody grip. Clean up your face and get out there and apologise to Pickley, tell him you'll apologise to Stevie Queef and get it sorted. All right?'

Mary has shocked me into pulling myself together. She's right. I can do this. I have to do this. She stays with me until my face looks slightly more like an administrator and less like a clown caught in the rain. I'll thank her later, buy her a nice bottle of red. Then my bowels tell me in no uncertain terms that I need to be alone, totally alone, in this ladies' room.

'Mary, I need the toilet urgently and I don't mean a wee. Could you . . .?'

'Bugger off? Sure. Good luck. Get straight over to Pickley's office when you're done.'

'I will.'

Oh Christ, thank God she's gone. I rush to the loo and . . . well, it ain't pretty. I'm in there quite a while. My stomach is cramping, I'm sweating and feel faint. I hate my body, HATE it. Just when I need it, it lets me down. Finally, after plenty of wet wipes and deep breathing and thrice the recommended dose of Imodium, I'm ready to face the world. Or at least, my boss. I walk over there, still feeling rotten, and I knock on Pickley's door and walk in. I have to run the gauntlet of his assistant, Natalie, first.

She's about half my age and raises her eyebrows at me in a way that infuriates me so much I want to slap that look off her carefully made-up face. There's that rage again. One minute I'm in floods of tears, the next I'm thinking KILL KILL.

'Is he in?' I say, trying to muster as much dignity as I can.

'Yes. He's expecting you. Or at least, he was about to go out and hunt you down.'

Oh shut your stupid face, Natalie, I want to say. But I've done enough career-crushing for today. I knock on his door and walk straight in. I have to grasp this situation by the horns. My rage has fuelled my energy now. Operation: Save My Job.

Pickley looks up from his desk and frowns.

'Ah,' is all he says, then he raises his eyebrows too, the same way his simpering PA did. I want to smash his chops as well. But I contain myself.

'I've come to apologise about the email. And explain,' I say. 'It's all a terrible mistake.'

'Take a seat, Heidi,' he says blandly. That rings alarm bells. He never calls me by my name. I honestly wondered sometimes if he even knew what my name was, despite managing me for the last three years since he was appointed Head of MIS (I use the term 'managing' very loosely). He was most definitely promoted beyond his capabilities. He's in his late forties, he has greying hair that he's tried to style with wax to look a little bit Elvis-ish, just a hint of a quiff, not enough to look inappropriate for a senior manager but enough to give him what he thinks is a dash of cool. I just think he looks like a bit of a twat.

'Let me start, please, Mick. This is all a misunderstanding. I wrote that email as a joke, then my daughter went on my computer and must've pressed send by accident.' I feel rotten throwing Ada under the bus on this, when it's just as likely I did it myself. But hey, she doesn't work here and I do – not to mention, she's nine and carefree and I'm fifty-two with a mortgage to pay.

'How it happened is not the issue,' says Pickley, placing his elbows on his desk and his fingers together in an irritating arch. 'The fact that it *has* happened is the issue. This is very serious.'

'I know it is. But it was an error on my part, just an error.'

'An error of judgement, certainly,' he says. 'And might I remind you that your role at this institution is a senior one, which carries substantial responsibilities in terms of accuracy and . . . and deportment?'

Deportment? What is this, *The Prime of Miss Jean Brodie*?

'I know that, but—'

'As I say, you are in a senior role here. And though the SMT and EMT would always welcome your views on any given subject on the agenda, we'd particularly find it useful to liaise with you on matters pertaining to the subject at hand. Your senior position and your station in life means you'd bring a powerful perspective to such a discussion. And, as the saying goes, with great power comes great responsibility.'

Oh pipe down, Pickley! He thinks he's Uncle Ben from *Spiderman* now.

'Yet the manner in which you chose to express those views was unfortunate, to say the least, and unprofessional to say it kindly, while others might say it was downright incompetent. What kind of message does it send to younger members of staff when old women . . . or erm . . .'

He stutters. Old women?! I can't be more than three or four years older than him, the wanker!

'Let's say, a more senior female professional such as yourself is setting such a bad example. There are ways and means of expressing an opinion and this is not one that we would ever accept here. Not to mention the insults directed at specific members of staff. And overall the negative message of ingratitude that pervades the whole email, mocking the kind offer given to all female members of staff of a certain age, or of any women suffering with the . . . with the . . . rigours of the . . . *men-o-pause.*'

He says the last word like it's filth. He mouths it like it might infect him. Christ, I tell you, the fact that I haven't murdered anyone at work yet is testament to my powers of restraint, if nothing else. I feel that rage bubbling up in me again and – despite the fact I came in here to eat humble pie and try to save my job – bloody hell, she's gonna blow!

'Now listen to me. LISTEN TO ME. I meant every bloody word of that email and I'd send the whole damn thing again a hundred times if it'd make someone round here actually listen to what women like me actually need,' I say, but it isn't me who says it. I'm as surprised as he is. It's like my rage has taken its own persona and inhabited my body, like Lily Tomlin leaping inside Steve Martin in *All Of Me.* But, for once, I'm glad my rage is there. Even sitting there knowing my job is on the line, I can't bear this silence any longer. I have to speak, I have to be heard. 'Forcing staff to buy overpriced fans is a bloody ridiculous way to pretend to help them. If you can afford a water feature, you can afford training that goes beyond a cursory glance at this issue that affects so many valued members of staff here and at every workplace. Look, I'm sorry if I offended anyone. I'm sorry it makes me look unprofessional. But I'm not sorry I sent it. I stand by it. Every word in there about the menopause and about the way women going through it are treated so shabbily by this institution was true. I may regret the way I did it, but I don't regret the message. And if you sack me for this, I won't go quietly. I'll go for wrongful dismissal and I'll go to the *Oxford Times* and I'll make such a stink about it, I'll deluge MUFFY and MINGE with so much legal and media bullshit, that you won't know whether to scratch your wristwatch or wind your arse.'

And there, channelling Dolly Parton in *Steel Magnolias*, I'm done. I'll probably be sacked now. But maybe, just maybe, I'll have unnerved him enough to make him think twice. I had no idea any of that stuff was going to pour from my mouth. It was my rage talking. I need to give her a name. I think I'll call her . . . Blondie, that post-punk powerhouse. Yeah, Blondie has spoken. Deal with THAT, Mick Pickley.

He's shocked, I can tell. He doesn't know quite what to say. He raises his eyebrows again, and laces his fingers together and clears his throat.

'I'll need to liaise with Steve about this. You'd better get back to your desk and get on. We'll be in touch. You're still employed here, Heidi. For now.'

I don't reply. I stand up and walk out. I'm done with any idea of begging. Blondie wouldn't beg, Miriam Margolyes wouldn't beg. Yes, I screwed up. But I know I'm right. Wow, this new me is rather wonderful. I've never been bolshie, never made trouble, never spoken out. I couldn't even tell Nate Wheeler I liked him for a full year when I was twenty-one and beautiful. But now, at fifty-two, it's like I just don't give a damn anymore. I suddenly realise that having no fucks to give can work both ways: yes, you can feel worn out and tired of everything. But you can also have zero fucks left to care what people think about you. And I realise that's where I am now. And it feels pretty damn good.

I go back to my office, suddenly worried about all the gossip that will be circulating. But when I walk in, I glance up and people are smiling at me. It's mostly women in the admin office, to be fair, but every person in there is smiling and some are nodding and others give the thumbs up. I see Brenda and she starts clapping loudly and there's a ripple of laughter while a few others join in. I grin, abashed, then sit down. The hubbub dies down to a few whisperings all around the office. Brenda comes over and gives me a hug around the shoulders.

'I take it sending that magnificent rant was an accident, right?'

'Oh God, yes.'

Brenda adds, 'I didn't even see it till I got to work. You know I turn off all my phone notifications at night. I can't be bothered with them. If I'd known, I would've told you last night, love.'

'I know. It's okay. I do that too. And I've no idea how it actually got sent. It might've been Ada, but just as likely was me being absent-minded, as usual.'

'What did Mick say?'

I tell her that apparently Pickley is right now considering my future with Stevie Queef. She tells me they wouldn't dare sack me about this.

'Menopause is such a hot topic!' says Brenda. 'The negative press would ruin them.'

I get on with my day. I try to focus, but it's a losing battle. To distract myself, I look on my phone for messages from Nate but there aren't any, so I send one to him. Who cares, really, who messages first? We're not fifteen. (And anyway, he messaged me first last night, so it's my turn basically.)

I may have just got myself sacked from my job that I hate.

He answers immediately, I'm amazed to see.

Brilliant. Why? And how? I'm agog.

I don't want to admit it's about menopause, as I feel like it makes me sound a million years old and I want to sound all young and slim. (I know, it's stupid. But it's how I feel.) So I tell him the story with judicious edits about the subject of the email or my subsequent reply.

He replies, *I think you may well be my hero.*

Gosh, here comes that wave of desire again! What a twenty-four hours it's turning out to be. First, Nate Wheeler pops back into my life, then I stand up to my bosses with such fervour, it might get me thrown out on my ear. Just shows, you can never predict life. You're bumbling along ploughing the same old furrow then a landmine explodes and nothing is ever the same again.

My desk phone rings and I put down my mobile. It's Natalie, telling me to come to Mick's office 'as soon as is convenient'. Urgh, my stomach lurches. This is it. Now I will find out my fate. But I hold my head high as I walk over there. I don't knock on the door, I don't wait for Natalie to buzz her boss and give me permission to enter, I just keep walking right into his office. And come face to face with, not only Mansplainer Mick seated smugly behind his huge desk, but also, lounging in an executive armchair with his executive pinstripe-clad legs stretched out in front of him, is the one and only CEO of MUFFY, Steven Quaife.

It's time to face the music . . .

Chapter 7

Mick leads the assault. He basically makes the same speech he gave me before, but Quaife doesn't know he's said it all before and I do, so Mick is trying to sound forthright for his boss while also knowing I know he's repeating himself, so he's a bit stuttery and red-faced. Quaife hasn't moved a muscle since I entered the room. He's watching proceedings with a hint of a smile. He doesn't have a face like thunder, as I expected he would. I mean, I did tell him to fuck off back to Aldi. And I dissed his qualifications mercilessly. Does he, perchance, look slightly amused? I'll need to take advantage of that, yet tread carefully. This conversation could go either way. Once Mick has finished his initial drubbing, I jump in and address myself exclusively to Quaife.

'I do apologise, Steven. This kind of action is not typical of me, I hope you know that. I've served the college for many years and nothing like this has ever happened. I'm afraid my rage got the better of me and I typed it out. I certainly did not intend to send it. My daughter sent it on by accident. However, as much—'

Quaife interrupts. 'Well, girls and tech is never the best mixture.'

Yeah, he actually said that. His face is so pleased with himself, he'd give the Cheshire Cat a run for his money. Whatever hackles are, he's got mine right up.

'She's extremely bright when it comes to tech actually,' I exaggerate. I mean, Ada is extremely bright. But she's a bit cack-handed with tech. However, he doesn't need to know that. It's the sexism of his comment that bugs me. 'But she's nine and she makes mistakes, as do we all.' I have more to say, but I sense it'd be prudent to let the man say his piece and give me a dressing-down, as is required, after the way I humiliated him in front of his entire staff. Quaife is not pleased with my last comment and his face has morphed from amused to annoyed. Oh God, here comes the fear again. Surely, I am going to be sacked. This is it.

'Your action was unfortunate, accident or not. Your thoughts on myself were unwelcome. They were of a personal nature that says more about you and your prejudices than it does about your target.'

Sheesh . . . I mean, I guess he means the Aldi bit.

'I shop at Aldi,' I say, uselessly, which serves to annoy him further.

Undeterred, he goes on: 'Email communication is the norm these days, of course, yet we all know the capacity it has for error, some of which can be extremely serious legally; from Hillary Clinton to Suella Braverman, many of the great and the good have fallen foul of email mishaps.'

Did he choose two women on purpose?! Either way, I

can't tell yet which way he's gonna go with my case – for or against?

'And they've had to pay the price.'

Here we go . . .

'However, in your case, this is complicated by the content of your . . . complaint. Its subject matter. The – shall we say – delicate nature of the issue of menopause.'

Ooh, this could turn the tide in my favour. And at least Quaife says the word plainly, without Mick's obvious distaste for it.

'It might interest you to know that I read your email out to my wife last night.'

I raise my eyebrows unconsciously. Is that a hint of a smile about his lips again?

'And she laughed.'

My eyebrows edge higher.

'Then she applauded.'

I actually snort. I'm so keyed up, it just comes out. I fight to reset my face to the required seriousness. Mick looks disgusted with me. Quaife goes on.

'She agreed with almost every word you said . . . almost. She'd rather I stayed here on a CEO's wage . . . than fuck off back to Aldi.'

I stifle a grin, but I think he's actually amused. I think it might – just might – be okay . . .

'But she agreed with every word you said about menopause. And about our stance on the issue. Now, happy wife, happy life, they used to say. I don't subscribe to such outdated sexism.'

You sure about that, Stevie, with your crass girls and tech remark? Thing is, even some folk who like to think they're woke, they don't notice when they're being sexist or whatever. It's these micro-aggressions that add up day after day and get you down. But at least he's making an effort now. And really, I am totally in the wrong about what I did, and he's giving me the benefit of the doubt. Or at least, his superstar wife is! I need to meet that woman and shake her by the hand! Anyway, Quaife continues.

'However, her point was taken, that despite the insults, the underlying argument you present is a fair one. We do need to do better to support our colleagues in this complex issue. And that is where you come in, Heidi.'

He pauses there, for dramatic effect. Again, without thinking, I blurt out, 'What now?' *Christ, woman, get a grip. You're an articulate senior administrator, not a grumpy teen.* 'I mean, I'd be happy to discuss this further with EMT and SMT. Granted, the email was an unfortunate vehicle for my argument, but I stand by what I said. Menopause needs more than an over-priced fan.'

'So, you've apologised to the two of us, yet I would require you to send another email in apology to All Staff. Do you accept that?'

'Of course. No problem.'

'Then, there remains the issue at hand, that is, how we can support our staff going through menopause. I want you to lead this issue, Heidi. You'll set up a menopause support group, create it, promote it, run it, however you see fit, perhaps fortnightly meetings, for the foreseeable future. Reach out to all affected staff to show them that they are listened to, they will be heard. If you carry out these two tasks – the apology and running a support group – then this error of judgement will be deemed, by myself,

EMT and SMT to have had a line drawn under it and to use it a jumping-off point for a new era in our college's support and understanding of a crucial time in a woman's life. Are we agreed?'

I have to say yes, of course we are. I'm boxed into a corner, but also I want to keep my job. And I did fuck up, rather spectacularly.

'Absolutely. That would be my pleasure,' I say with a fake smile. But inside, my misanthropic alter ego is cowering in the corner. Me? Being peopley?? Actively seeking to create a group that I am forced to not only run but turn up to every damn fortnight and talk to strangers about my private doings??? Oh God, it's my idea of hell. But needs must. It's that or the chop, it seems. And despite Brenda's assurances that I could take them to tribunal or whatever if they sacked me, I did personally insult the CEO in front of every member of staff, figuratively speaking. And I guess I've got off lucky. So, menopause support group here we come. It'll be like Facebook, but a hundred times worse, as I'll have to meet these people face to face. And pretend to enjoy it. Urgh.

Back at my desk, Brenda's out at a training session the rest of the day, so I don't talk about it with anyone. I have to settle down and focus on writing this apology email. I can eat humble pie if I have to.

> *To All Staff*
> *An email was sent from my computer yesterday evening that I wrote, yet it was never intended for public consumption. I wrote this email as a form of stress relief for myself and regretfully those feelings*

were made public due to human error. I would like to apologise to all staff, and specifically to our CEO Steven Quaife, for the style and tone of the email, particularly the insults found therein. These were made in a moment of rage and were entirely inappropriate and unprofessional. I have discussed the matter with both my line manager, Mick Pickley, and with Steven Quaife. The matter has now been resolved and I want to thank both for their understanding and clemency. To repeat, I apologise to all staff for this oversight in my professional conduct and want to assure you all that nothing like this will ever happen again on my watch.

Best regards,
Heidi Hobbes

Will that do? Does it have the right tone? Brenda's not here for me to ask. I think it's okay. I really want to say something about how I meant every word about the menopause stuff though, but it doesn't seem prudent. I got away with it and I don't want to rock the boat. And I won't mention anything about the menopause group as yet. I'll save that for another email. I take a moment to reflect on how close I came to facing a formal disciplinary, for the job that pays the bills and takes care of my daughters. It's a wake-up call, that's for sure. I have to organise myself better, to make up for these memory lapses and lack of concentration. But what's the answer? Even more Post-it notes than the hundreds a week I already use? I think of that bit in *Bruce Almighty* when Jim Carrey and his room is smothered in a million Post-it notes and that's how my life feels right now. Something has to change, so I can get a hold of things. And now, on top of all that, I have to set up and run this damn group – as if I don't have enough shit to deal with! Christ, it never rains but it chucks it down.

Okay, so, it's time to craft this menopause group email. I'm feeling a bit queasy, after my run-in with the executives. I need to focus. I leave my desk and go down to the refectory and buy a mint tea. It's nothing like as nice as coffee used to be, but it's refreshing and helps with my tummy a bit. I sit down in a quiet corner and look at Nate's website again, then go through his social media, namely a Facebook page and Instagram. His private Facebook has virtually nothing on it except other people tagging him in posts. On his public stuff, he doesn't post that often, yet there's plenty of interesting stuff to scroll through. Mostly pics of his recording equipment and instruments, other musicians, audiences, hotel rooms, city streets, architecture, parks, skies, food, a friend's dog, another friend's baby. Hardly any of him. Virtually no selfies. That's good to see; makes me feel he's not vain, though he has every right to be, considering how handsome he is. I know looking at someone's socials represents only the thinnest slice of who they really are, but from these images I like the guy he seems to be. I like his life. I like the way he focuses on the music and on his surroundings, not on himself. If I knew nothing about him, I'd still like him. Then I remember that I do know him, or I did, and his latest reply is sitting in my inbox right now. I go on to Messenger and there's that message from Nate about me being his hero. This cheers me up a treat. I reply:

Update: I've survived to live another day.

Again, he replies straight away. Does this guy never work? Whatever the reason, I like that he's so available.

What happened??

I had a grilling from my line manager and the big boss and I'm off the hook. I just have to set up a kind of staff support group. Not my cup of tea in the slightest, but it's better than the world of shit I might've ended up in.

Again I manage to keep out of it the exact reason for the support group and luckily he doesn't ask.

You don't like support groups?

I don't like people.

I hear ya. Sounds like the lesser of two weevils though. I hate bosses more than I hate anyone.

You're not wrong! It's one of the worst things about my job, apart from all the other worst things.

I must admit, being a freelancer has its bonuses.

Sounds like heaven to me right now. If only it paid the bills as well as permanent jobs.

Why didn't you stay in the music business, Hobbes? You were brilliant.

Life . . . happened. Bills needed paying. I had a kid, then another one. Being an artist doesn't pay for that, not for most artists. It's incredibly impressive that you're still in the industry.

Doesn't your husband help out?

Was that a genuine query or a convenient segue to find out if I'm single or not?

I'm divorced. He's a great co-parent. Nice guy. Earns a reasonable wage. But neither of us earn enough for me to give up the day job. How about you?

How about me?

You have kids, married?

Urgh, that sounds too direct. Too late. I've sent it now.

No to both. Never worked out for me. And yeah, I know it makes me sound like a sad fuck.

It really doesn't.

I mean that. Actually, right now, it sounds like heaven. Total freedom, no responsibilities, nothing to tie you down.

Nate replies, *You're kind. I know I've wasted opportunities for good relationships with good people. But somehow, the music always won. The music was always there, when other stuff went to shit. Even if I forgot it for a moment, it was there, waiting patiently.*

Oh God, it's like he's reading my mind. Right now, my violin is still sitting in my attic. It doesn't begrudge the years it's been left there. It's like he just said. It's waiting patiently.

God, I know exactly what you mean.

You do? How so?

I really want to tell him everything, suddenly. I've tried to be cool with the lies about hot yoga and yes, of course I still play fiddle. But now I just want to confess all, that I abandoned music years ago and now I regret it dreadfully. I want to tell Nate because I know he'll understand; he knew that part of me when I was young and filled with dreams and music. He's the only person I know right now who truly gets it.

'Heidi, do you have a minute?'

What? I look up from the world of my phone and Mick's PA Natalie is staring down at me. I see behind her that the refectory has filled up with people, all talking loudly, and I hadn't noticed any of them arrive. Oh shit, what the hell is the time? Christ, it's half eleven! I've been down here for over two hours! How on earth did I lose that much time??

'Why?' I snap.

She grimaces – blimey, she hates me – then says, 'Mick's just wondering when you're going to send round the promotional materials about the menopause group.'

'What promotional materials?'

'Well, the email, at least. He wants it sent. So everybody can . . . see.'

'See what?'

'That you've been . . . you know. Dealt with. Appropriately.'

'Chastised, you mean.'

I can see from her face she doesn't know that word. Ha! Good.

'If you could send it ASAP?' she simpers, then turns on her lofty heel and departs.

I must get upstairs. I ought to buy a sandwich, but I'm still off food. I don't want any more tummy issues today. My mint tea is stone cold, untouched. Oh well, I quite like it that way. I go back upstairs to my desk and start writing the email. Promotional materials? I don't want to promote it! I'm going to send this email and hope nobody replies and then I can draw a line under this whole mess and move on. My unintended two-hour sojourn downstairs has put me massively behind on today's burgeoning in-tray. At least I didn't miss a meeting. I rattle out an email to all staff telling them about a menopause support group, time and place TBA. I make it sound supremely uninteresting and uninviting. There, done. I go to my email inbox and find I have 112 unread emails. Oh, Christ. I have so much to do, I decide I'm not going to do any of it. I pull up Facebook on my desktop rather than phone, so it'll look like I'm working. I go back to Nate's unanswered message.

You do? How so?

I want to confess that I've abandoned music altogether. But I feel too embarrassed that I already lied about it. I've just re-met this glorious bloke and I don't want to mess it up before it's even re-begun. I think back to those heady days of our final year at Exeter, the gigs, the concerts, the practice sessions, the essays on musical history. I marvel again at how I let all of that fade away once I left uni. How easily I gave up our obsession, how in that house we were enthralled by our muse, defined by our music, the pair of us, me and Nate. And Luke too, of course. He was an engineer, but he almost breathed music. He was welded to his guitar. He carried it from room to room. He was damned talented too. He could pick up any stringed instrument and play, more or less. Anything guitar-related anyway: banjo, lute, mandolin. He could play any tune on them too, any old thing you wanted. How good it was to be in a house where music wove the fabric of everyday life. Did Luke leave it behind like I did, as he moved into his working life, to become the engineer he had trained to be? Did he abandon it, as I did?

I go back to Nate's last message. I reply:

That's a long story. In the meantime, have you heard from Luke yet about this reunion? I tried looking for him on Facebook – Luke Beresford, right? – but couldn't find him.

He doesn't answer straight away. I answer a few work emails, then his reply pops up.

Luke changed his last name after we left uni. His dad had an affair and his parents split up, then he changed it to his mum's surname. I remember him doing that, but I cannot for the life of me remember what it was.

If it comes back to you, let me know, will you? I'd love to have a chat with Luke again.

I'll see if I've got it in an old address book somewhere.

Thanks Nate. Gotta work now. Catch you later.

Definitely.

That last word gives me a buzz. In fact, it sets me up for an afternoon of work. I know I need to get the tricky stuff done before 2pm, when my brain shuts up shop. So I plough through the most complex work stuff in the next couple of hours, then go onto more admin-style tasks that don't require much thought. But even this easy stuff is beyond me today. It's been a hell of a day and I just know my brain isn't going to play ball, so I slope off early. I get home and sleep on the sofa for an hour before Ada gets home, then Carly a half-hour later, but both of them are off out tonight. Carly is going to the cinema with an old girlfriend and Ada is out at Brownies which her dad always takes her to, then to McDonald's after and a sleepover at his. They do that on the same day every week. So by 6pm, I'm alone in the house. What shall I do with myself? I know exactly what. I go upstairs to Carly's floor and open up the attic and pull down the steps. Up I go. It's dusty and spidery and I shudder. I have to move a few boxes until I find it. Or should I say, her. I always thought of my violin as female.

'There you are,' I say aloud. I carry her case down the steps, push them back up and close the attic hatch. I take her to the living room. I don't even have a music stand these days, not that I have any violin music left. All long gone. What sort of state will she be in? I open up the case and wouldn't have been surprised if a cloud of moths fluttered out. But she looks surprisingly good, encased in her velvet bed for all these years. Will I have forgotten everything? How to tune her, how to bow, how to pluck? I sound out each of the four strings. The tuning is all over the place. I don't have a piano or tuning fork to get the right G, but I guess where it might be. (I don't have perfect pitch, though Luke does, or did. He was my tuning fork back in 1994.) Then I remember that times have moved on and I can find an online tuner on my phone, so I do. There we are, that's better. I bow all four strings, G, D, A and E. It's so pleasing that they're all a fifth apart. I sound a bit scratchy, so I bow more firmly and there, it sounds much better now. I play a scale of G major, two octaves. Wow, it's amazing how quickly it returns. I try it again, faster this time. It really is like riding a bike.

I tire of scales quickly – I never did like them – and try to think what pieces I used to play. There's one on the edge of my mind that was my absolute favourite, one of the tunes I adapted myself for violin from a song. But what was it? With my useless memory, what hope will I have? But immediately, it leaps to the front of my mind. 'Wichita Lineman' by Jimmy Webb, made famous by Glen Campbell, adapted a hundred times or more by countless other artists. It's a classic, it's a beauty, it's the best song ever written, some say. So, when it comes to music, my menopause mind is bypassed and goes straight there. I'm thinking about where I first heard it and I cannot for the life of me remember. It just seems to always have been in my head, wafting through the house when I was a baby perhaps, just like that Paul Simon song, 'Late in the Evening'. This song, 'Wichita Lineman', is such an odd one, such a curious story it tells. There's a man, a telephone line engineer, driving around some Midwest state, the long, lonely roads and unmatched distances of America. He's thinking about his job, how he'd like a break, but if the weather turns snowy it'll make his job a hundred times worse. But all the while, he's thinking about someone, who feels so present to him that this person's voice is vibrating down the lines to him from wherever they are, but he can't go there, as he has to stay and work, to stay on the line for who knows how long. There's been argument about where the song came from, being set in Wichita, Kansas, but they say Webb was inspired to write it after seeing a lineman up a pole on a remote road in Oklahoma. Many, many people over the years have eulogised about 'Wichita Lineman', have talked endlessly about what it all means, if it's a metaphor for a deeper truth. I'm not sure there is more in it than itself. I'm not sure there needs to be. Like Van Gogh's *Sunflowers* or Monet's *Water Lilies*. They are just themselves. I heard that Webb said the song was unfinished. And it feels that way, too short, too perfect though. It doesn't need another note or word to complete it.

I close my eyes and my muscle memory finds the starting note. And I play. The melody unspools, filling the years between the nineties and now. I am transported. I keep my eyes closed, my fingers finding every note, every bow, every phrase. The melody sings out and my bow double-stops, playing two strings at once, to add in harmonies. I am twenty years old. That wave of desire and longing sweeps over me again, but it's not for Nate Wheeler. This time, it's for my first love: my violin. I play the same tune over and over again, perfecting it each time, adding new grace notes and rhythms, allowing my fingers to improvise around its simplicity.

When I open my eyes, they are clouded by tears. I'm crying at full pelt now, sobbing, in fact. I can't even begin to explain to myself where this avalanche of emotion is coming from, so I just give in to it. After a while, the sobs start to dry up and I'm snivelling and starting to recognise where I am again. I'm back in my house, aged fifty-two. I've been playing for a half-hour and my back is aching, my shoulder is aching, my wrists are aching. That didn't happen thirty years ago. Plus my eyes feel like I've been punched up. I know when I'm beaten. Reluctantly, I put my fiddle away and close her up. I feel physically exhausted – today has been a trial, and that outburst of sobbing didn't help – but my mind is buzzing with the thrill of music. I go to bed and check on my phone for replies from Nate. Nothing as yet. I hope he finds Luke's name. It'd be great to talk to him again. He loved 'Wichita Lineman' too, I seem to remember. I have a quick look at my work emails, only because I want to see the one I sent myself before I left this afternoon, with a list of everything I needed to do tomorrow at work, as a reminder. I'm basically my own PA (because MUFFY is too mean to give me a real one). Lo and behold, above my own email are four new ones from four people I've never heard of before: Cheryl Hughes, Niki Michaelides, Rhona Morgan and Joy Beyioku. And all four are replies to the menopause support group email. And all four are saying yes, they would love to attend. Bloody hell. How dare they be so damn keen. So it begins . . .

Chapter 8

In early June – a breezy, warm day that messes my dry hair up a treat – the day of the first menopause support group meeting arrives. I timetabled it at lunchtime, hoping that means that nobody will want to come, as they wouldn't want to give up their precious lunch hour. But the tactic didn't work and here I am, going upstairs to an empty room on the top floor in the far corner of the admin building, again hoping nobody will find it so nobody will show up. I've been in there before for a dreary training session and it is a depressingly poky room with mud-coloured carpet tiles and a blackboard left over from the olden days. Again, I'm foxed as when I arrive, ten minutes early, I peek through the little criss-crossed viewing window in the door and see there's already three people there, chairs out in a circle. I wonder where the fourth person is. They've beaten me to it and they're already chatting away. Maybe they don't even need me! I could just slink away and let them get on with it. But I can't do that, I know. Pickley and Queef will have my guts for garters. Can't fault how keen these three menopausal women are. I'm just pissed off all my tactics didn't work. I know it sounds a bit mean, me offering help to those in need and actively planning that nobody will say yes. I know it's not my finest hour. But honestly, I have enough to deal with. And this is just another damn thing on my list. Plus it's a thousand miles outside my comfort zone. Urgh. Time to put on a nice face and slog my way through this hell. I smile brightly as I come in, suddenly self-conscious as I walk to grab a chair, hating the navy slacks I have on that I've had to unbutton at the waist as they're too small for me these days, horribly aware of the fact that my pale blue blouse I used to love is now gaping at the tits because that's too small too. I still haven't admitted to myself that I need to buy a whole new wardrobe. I keep expecting the weight to fall off and I'll emerge as my once slimmer self, like an elegant butterfly from a dumpy caterpillar.

The three women stop talking immediately and look expectant. I sit down and introduce myself as the one who started the group and everyone nods. I can turn on the charm when I need to, in meetings and social situations if I absolutely must. Probably nobody even notices how intensely uncomfortable I am doing it, or how utterly drained I always feel afterwards. But I am quite good at it, nonetheless.

'And you all also probably know me from the infamous email I sent out ranting about desk fans.'

I decided on the spur of the moment to grasp the nettle and address the elephant in the room, and other clichés.

Two of the women smirk knowledgeably, but the third looks nonplussed.

'I don't get emails,' she says. 'I only found out about this and emailed you because my friend told me about it.'

'Oh, it was really good,' says another shyly.

'WhatsApp it to me?' the other whispers loudly and her friend nods. Or at least, I assume they're friends, since they have each other on WhatsApp.

To act professionally, I feel I should add, 'Well, it was all a horrible mistake. It was never meant to be seen by human eyes. But anyway, what's done is done and here we are.' I sigh after that, involuntarily. Then I worry I sound negative about this group, that I've let it slip that the email debacle has led directly to setting it up.

'However, I am delighted you're all here and want to thank you for coming. We're here to talk about menopause and be a support to each other.'

I suddenly realise that I haven't planned out anything for this meeting. I mean, I had a billion other things on my to-do list, but also I just assumed you get a bunch of women in a room and they'll talk about anything, won't they? But now I feel the pressure, that they're looking to me for some sort of leadership. I've never been a natural leader. I like sitting on the fringes of things, observing, taking notes, getting the donkey work done. I never wanted to be in the spotlight, even as a musician. I much preferred playing with others. I was never a natural soloist. Yet here I am and these three women's expectant faces want me to provide them with something. God knows what, but I need to deliver.

'I think it'd be helpful to introduce ourselves first, so at least we know names. So, you know who I am, but I'll just reiterate. I'm Heidi and I'm a resource and planning manager. Just to add, I'm fifty-two and recently had it confirmed I'm perimenopausal.'

I pause. I lost count of the number of times I said 'just'. I know there's so much more I could say, perhaps even should say. But I can't bear to. I don't want to tell all my private doings to these strangers. Just because they're women doesn't mean they'll understand me, or not judge me. So I don't say any more. I simply turn to the woman on my left and say, 'Would you like to go next?'

Christ, I HATE it when you're in a group and someone says *let's introduce ourselves, shall we?* And sitting in the circle waiting for your turn, like lining up for the guillotine. And now here I am inflicting it on others! But I realise that the reason group leaders suggest this monstrosity is not only to get to know people's names, but also to take the damn focus off themselves for a minute.

The woman on my left begins. She's the one who said my email was good. She's petite, even shorter than me, I think, and very slight, with long, straight blonde-brown hair wound up in a tight bun at her neck, dressed in a crisp white blouse and calf-length, flowery, summer skirt. 'Hello, my name is Cheryl. I'm a receptionist in the HE building . . . Cheryl Hughes. Sorry, I forgot to say that . . . I've got menopause . . . or I mean . . . I'm in menopause, or however you say it. Oh, and I'm fifty.'

And that's all she's going to say about that. A silence looms.

'Thanks, Cheryl,' I say, suddenly realising I'm going to have to remember everyone's names with my shit memory.

But at least there's only three of them. Number one, Cheryl the softly spoken receptionist.

We all turn our gaze to the next woman. She looks a bit like me, with a short, stout body dressed in comfy, grey loose-fitting trousers and brown top. Her hair is cut very short, very close to her head, grey with dark streaks of her natural brown. God, I'm terrible at this group leader malarkey. I'm supposed to be welcoming. 'And you are?' I say, then realise that's worse than silence, isn't it? I mean, I hate the sound of my own voice saying that. It sounds so passive-aggressive. Plus I really need my internal monologue to stop over-analysing everything. *Focus, Hobbes!*

'Hi, I'm Rhona, Rhona Morgan. I'm a cleaner in the HE block and I'm forty-eight. Cheryl told me about this menopause support group. So, here we are. I'm in perimenopause. I'd say my biggest struggle is the physical one, as my job means I need a lot of physical get-up-and-go, you know. I'm very anti-HRT. I like more alternative therapies, you know, natural therapies. I don't trust doctors, not any of them, never have and nobody can persuade me to change my mind on that one. Anyway, I'm married, no kids. No particular reason why, we just chose not to. Some people do that, you know. It's not always a tragedy. We just didn't want to have kids. My husband is very nice. He's supportive. He's a godsend. I don't know where I'd be without him. We got married young. Nice registry office in Swansea, before we moved here for his work. I don't believe in God actually. Neither does he. I went churchy for a while when I was a girl, because of Brownies, I think. But I'm not bothered about church anymore. Too much standing up and sitting down and standing up again, you know.'

111

All right, chatterbox, wanna tell us your bra size and your O Level results while you're at it? God, my inner voice can be such a bitch sometimes. *Remember, Hobbes, it'll be much easier if these women want to talk, because then you won't have to.* Number two, Rhona the anti-HRT cleaner.

'That's great, Rhona. Thanks so much.'

Last up is a tall, imposing woman, exquisitely dressed in a maroon power suit, with a short salt-and-pepper afro styled in a pixie cut. And before I have to do the embarrassing *And you?* bit again, she speaks first and says, 'Right, so I'm Joy Beyioku and I'm a sociology lecturer in HE and I'm fifty-eight, thus going through a very late menopause. I'm rather anti-alternative therapies and very pro-HRT. I'm afraid I won't be recommending essential oils and dried bark tea anytime soon. I do feel a lot of this alternative approach can be quite dangerous.'

I can't help it. Knowing I shouldn't, I glance back at Rhona, our pro-alternative therapies group member. She is frowning very obviously. She takes a deep breath in, raising her hand. And at that moment – when it seems that our number three, Joy the straight-talking lecturer, has quite deliberately triggered our number two, Rhona, to start a stand-up row before we've even finished introducing ourselves, which doesn't bode well for our fledgling support group – the door opens and another woman appears.

'Oh God, I'm so sorry,' she says. She looks too young for this group. She must be looking for another meeting.

'This is menopause support,' I say. 'You're probably looking for something else.'

'No, that's it. I got lost. I'm such an idiot.'

It really bothers me when people say that about themselves, especially women. There's too many out there who put themselves down routinely and it just plays into the hands of the bullies out there too.

'Not at all. It's a bloody rabbit warren round these parts. Come in and take a seat.'

She smiles and shuts the door behind her. Joy stands up and fetches her a chair from beside the wall and places it in between her and Rhona, a nice gesture which means our new lady won't feel out on a limb. Joy doesn't look too annoyed she got interrupted, but I look at Rhona and she looks like she really has had her nose put out of joint. Cheryl looks awkward as hell. I'm quite glad this new woman came in at that moment and diffused the situation.

'We're just going round and doing the dreaded introducing ourselves a bit. I'm Heidi and this is Cheryl, Rhona and Joy.'

Everyone says 'Hi' to the newbie.

She replies, 'Hi and thanks. Really sorry about being late. Erm . . . so yeah, I'm Niki Michaelides.'

It goes quiet, so I add, 'Maybe a couple more details, if you don't mind, Niki? Like your age and where you work?'

It seems fair, since we've all said at least our age and job. And, truth be told, I only really say it because I want to know how old she is. She looks twenty years younger than me, so either she's got the greatest skincare routine in history or she's in early menopause, I'd wager.

'Oh, yeah, sorry. Well, I'm a success coach for plumbing and electrical students based in the FE building. Basically

113

that means I'm a kind of personal tutor for lots of lovely but foul-mouthed and smelly boys. And I'm thirty-six.'

She doesn't say any more, our number four, Niki the youngling tutor. She's stunning, there's no other word for it. Big smile and liquid dark eyes, thick and wavy black hair, curvy with a big bust and tiny waist, dressed in a close-fitting pale green suit and dark green jersey top, tucked in. God knows how the plumbing and electrical boys manage to utter a word to a tutor that gorgeous!

It's my turn now. What the bloody hell am I going to say? Why didn't I prepare anything? Everyone's staring at me expectantly. I should've brought handouts so everyone could stare at them instead. Get it together, woman, and say something, anything.

'So, welcome to our menopause support group.'

That's a good start, but I'm looking at these four women and my icy resolve that I never wanted to do this damn thing in the first place is starting to melt. They're all in this menopause shitshow and I'm guessing they're struggling with it so much that they've made the decision to give up their lunchtime to come for help in person, and not just join a Facebook group or read a book. They deserve more than a cursory attempt to keep my job. So, I decide I'm going to make the best of this. And that starts with putting myself out there and trying to be as honest as I can.

'I really appreciate you all coming here today, especially at lunchtime. I want to start by saying I'm no expert on menopause. I've no training to be here doing this. I'm having a really hard time with perimenopause myself. And I'm really bloody angry about the way menopause and women's biology in general is treated in the workplace.

And in the wider world as well. I mean, why don't I know more about menopause? Why am I so ignorant about my own body? I can't be the only one. And why is there so much conflicting information out there about how to deal with menopause? It's a minefield. I've only just started and I'm massively confused already. So, please don't look to me for much clarification on how to cope. I wish I could do that, for myself and for you, or any women suffering with this. But I hope that merely by meeting and talking, we might be able to get somewhere together. I just wanted to say that up front and I hope it's not too disappointing to hear I'm no expert.'

'Personally, I'm tired of so-called experts,' says Joy, our lecturer and HRT fan. A couple of the others nod along with this. 'I teach sociology and a significant part of my practice is teaching medical students. They're all supposed to have some sociology training, so they can start to see their patients as people with lives and not just bodies that need fixing.'

'What a great idea,' I say. 'I didn't know that happened.'

'Well, yes, it's a great idea in theory. But you wouldn't believe the resistance I meet. So many see it as a waste of time. I've had all sorts of reactions, from annoyance to absence to anger and even the height of rudeness. I met a doctor once who told me in a downright disdainful manner that '*I skipped all my sociology lectures and went to a strip club instead.*' And he wasn't joking, deadly serious.'

'Bloody hell!' I say. 'What an arsehole!'

Everybody laughs. I didn't mean to swear, but I think it's warranted for that arsehole of a doctor. And I think it might've relaxed everyone a bit.

Our youngest member, Niki the tutor, joins in. 'You know, I'm not surprised to hear that. Because I'm a bit weird because I'm having such an early menopause, I've talked to so many doctors now. And I'm sick of them. Some are nice and helpful. But some are just horrible.'

'Especially the men,' says our alternative therapy fan, Rhona, the cleaner. 'The things my male doctor said to me. It's disgusting. The way they patronise us women! Makes me sick. He told me I was imagining it all. He wouldn't even let me have a blood test. That's why I've started treating myself, with home remedies and other stuff. How can men understand? You know, what we're going through? It's like having a man as a midwife. It's bloody ridiculous!'

We haven't heard yet from perhaps our shyest member, Cheryl the receptionist. You'd think she'd be fine with talking since she has to talk to people all day in her job. But actually, there's a big difference between saying *Hello, how can I help you?* and telling strangers what's going on in your lady parts. So, I turn to her and ask, 'What do you think about that, Cheryl?'

She looks a bit mortified, but I am starting to feel like there are some alpha members of this group who will speak easily and might end up dominating the conversation. Which is fine in some ways, but also I'd like to give everyone the chance to be heard, without making them feel too uncomfortable or picked on. Let's see how quiet Cheryl responds to this tactic. And you know what, she really surprises me.

'I think that's bollocks.'

Rhona, who could be offended by this and is so wound up I worry she might fly off the handle, instead laughs and that lets us all laugh too. My assumption that Cheryl and

Rhona are friends is confirmed further, as she seems quite used to this kind of response from Cheryl.

'Please, tell us why!' I ask Cheryl.

'I just mean, I don't think it's about if you're a man or a woman,' Cheryl continues. 'The nicest doctor I've ever had is a man. A Scotsman with a lovely, lilting Highland voice and a huge beard, looks like a bear of a man. And he put me straight on HRT, no bother. And he always listens. And I've had horrible women. I had two women doctors fit my Mirena coil and both times I was in agony with tears streaming down my face and they were both cold as ice and said, *It shouldn't hurt you that much* and I was like, *Well, it bloody does*.'

'Me too!' I cry. 'The Mirena coil bit! It hurts like hell! Why on earth do they say it won't hurt? I've dreaded it both times I've had it put in!'

'And me!' chimes in Niki.

Joy adds, 'I've not had a coil but I've certainly had some unhelpful women midwives. I had a miscarriage and asked my GP for an early scan with my next pregnancy as I was so paranoid. He said yes fine, then when I went for my booking-in appointment, the midwife said there's no way I'd be getting an early scan. '*Lots of ladies have miscarriages, you know*,' she said in such a brutal, offhand way like it was nothing.'

'Sorry to hear that,' says Niki, looking at Joy with such compassion and understanding in her eyes, which I now see are shining with tears. Oh God, maybe Niki has had miscarriages too. Poor woman.

'I suppose I stand corrected then!' says Rhona good-naturedly, but she folds her arms and looks peeved.

'It's not about being right or wrong,' I say, as I don't want Rhona to feel shot down in flames in our very first session. 'We're here to share our experiences and hopefully help each other. I don't know about you, but it's really refreshing for me to hear such different experiences. It's easy to assume a lot about . . . well, about everyone and everything really. About menopause. And about the medical profession. It's actually really heartening to hear good stories about male doctors. And to know that perhaps the key thing is to find a doctor who is understanding and helpful, whatever gender or background they have.'

'Definitely,' says Joy. 'It's empathy they need. If they don't have empathy, they have no business being in the medical profession, in my view, especially GPs. And you should shop around until you find the right one.'

'I can't afford to go private!' cries Rhona. 'Not on a cleaner's wage. Not all of us are rolling in money, you know.'

'People spend a fortune on these alternative remedies though,' Joy counteracts, calmly.

'We're not all lunatics, you know! Just because I don't trust doctors doesn't make me an idiot! And while we're about it, I'm not spending a fortune on remedies, *actually*, as most of them I make myself at home. You don't have to buy those pricey turmeric and black pepper capsules for joint pain. You can take a teaspoon daily of the real thing, which costs a lot less.'

Rhona is seething. She looks like she's going off the deep end. Joy, however, is cool as a cucumber, no ruffled feathers whatsoever.

'Okay, fair point,' Joy replies. 'But what I meant wasn't about going private but trying different GPs at your usual practice. Unless you have a tiny one with only one doctor. That's all I meant. Sorry if it came across as privilege. It really wasn't.'

I can see there might be a big problem between Joy and Rhona. I don't want there to be bad feeling in this room, and so early on. I'm going to jump in to intervene, but then Rhona says something I didn't expect.

'Look, sorry. I'm sorry . . . I mean it. I really am sorry, Joy.' Rhona gives out a great sigh, not a put-on one, but a real one. She wipes her eyes and sighs again. Everyone waits. 'I just get this . . . rage. This awful rage. Everyone annoys me. Everyone makes me so mad. I'm sure you're a lovely person, Joy. And I have no business foisting my opinion on you. I just . . . Nothing works, you see. Nothing has worked. And I've always had faith in this stuff, you know? But recently, I just lose my temper all the time. Sometimes I just can't control . . . well, this terrible rage that comes out of me.'

So, I didn't need to step in after all. This honesty bomb from Rhona has put us all at ease.

'Thank you, Rhona, but honestly, there's no need to apologise,' says Joy. 'I'm an academic and I've put all my faith in science. But even so, I've found that doctors have let me down at every turn. Yes, I've gone private, but even that's been a mixture of helpful doctors and downright quackery. And there just isn't anyone to talk about it with. I have three sons, so they don't understand. And anyway, Rhona, I shouldn't be foisting my own opinions on you. You must do whatever you feel is right, of course.'

'Thanks, love,' says Rhona simply and they smile at each other. Wow, this is rather lovely. I didn't need to step in at all. Everyone here is just trying to get through it all in their own way.

I say, 'Well, just look at that email I sent everyone! I didn't mean it to become public, obviously. But I simply had to write it down. I had to get it out of my head or my brain would explode! And I know I've snapped at everyone in my house and beyond hundreds of times in the last few months. And rage is the right word for it, Rhona. I've never known such rage! I've actually given my rage monster a name!'

'What is it?!' says Rhona, laughing. 'I haven't got a name for mine yet, but maybe I should!'

'I've christened her Blondie! My all-time girl crush and rock queen.'

Everyone laughs at that, plus Niki says, 'I think we should all agree to name our rage now.'

'That's homework for next week then!' I say.

Well, well, well. This is going really well. We've still got some time left, so I decide to pull the disparate strands of our conversation together and try to formalise it a bit.

'Thanks everyone for your contributions so far. I think what might be helpful is to finish this session with a few words from each of us about what our experience of menopause has been so far. Just a quick summary of your main experience of it so far would be useful, I think, so we can hear what we're dealing with. Then, in the coming weeks, we can start to break these down into more detail on our actual symptoms and hopefully help each other to find some answers or at least some coping strategies. How does that sound?'

Everyone nods and agrees and off we go. As the other women speak, I make a mental summary of their summaries:

Cheryl Hughes, fifty, receptionist in the HE block. She says she feels ignorant about menopause and wants to educate herself. She's really struggling with various symptoms, about which she's very embarrassed and doesn't give much detail. She's on HRT and it's helping a bit but not fully. She's got one daughter in her twenties, now left home. Plus she mentions her husband and doesn't say much about him, but she looks a bit uncomfortable when she says it's just the two of them at home now. I'm not sure why, but I don't like the sound of him already.

Rhona Morgan, forty-eight, cleaner in the HE block. She says Cheryl told her about the menopause group and so they came together. She's in perimenopause and struggling physically, as her job requires a lot of physical energy. Her husband tries to help rather cluelessly, but he wants her to seek more medical intervention than the alternative approaches she favours. It's clear she knows some of her therapies are not working but she doesn't want to give up on them.

Joy Beyioku, fifty-eight, sociology lecturer in HE. She's going through relatively late menopause and is pro-HRT and seeing a private gynaecologist. She is long-term divorced, single currently and her three sons are in their twenties and thirties. She more or less raised them alone. Her sons live all over the world, in Canada, Nigeria and Northern Ireland, and she's clearly massively proud of them. Her parents have long since died. The overwhelming impression I get is that she's lonely, but pretending not to be.

Niki Michaelides, thirty-six, success coach for plumbing and electrical students in the FE block. She's in early menopause, something she never expected to happen. She also has a range of other health issues, which menopause has exacerbated. She isn't on HRT as she's on so many other meds, she feels like she's rattling already. No partner or kids, or at least, she doesn't mention any. Her voice throughout is unerringly bright, but I feel like there's a sadness behind those eyes and I don't know why.

So that's my completely unqualified psychological examination of our group. And that's the end of our first meeting. And crikey, it actually went a billion times better than I thought it would. And though we've talked non-stop for an hour, it's clear we've barely scratched the surface. There's going to be so much more to discuss in our next meeting in two weeks' time. It's actually really energised me, not drained me, as I thought it would. I'm amazed how much better I feel. And what a fascinating bunch of women. I surprise myself by realising that I'm really, really looking forward to the next session.

Who knew that three such momentous things would happen in my life in such a short space of time? I'm back in touch with the lust of my life, Nate Wheeler; I nearly lose my job due to menopausal rage but end up saving it because menopause is the topic du jour; I meet a group of women in a setting I'd usually rather die than be in and it turns out to be a wholly positive experience. On the way back to my desk after the meeting, I'm feeling pretty damn pleased with myself. I go to the refectory to grab a sandwich and a mint tea before it closes, sit down to eat and drink, and go on Messenger. I might message Nate in a minute to tell him how well the group went. We've been chatting a bit since that first day, not every day, but now and again. And it's still just as exciting. I get a little frisson every time his Messenger bubble pops up on my phone screen.

Then I see on Messenger that there's that little red blob telling you there's a new message waiting from someone, but when I go to my conversations list, there isn't one there. It could be a message request, I suppose. It's usually weirdos and scammers behind those requests, but something tells me to check it out anyway. And I'm so glad I did. Because it's from someone called Luke Jones. And instantly, at the first brief glance at the tiny thumbnail, I know it's my old housemate Luke Beresford. I don't even need to look at it properly. I haven't seen that face in thirty years but I realise in that moment it's as familiar to me as family. Isn't it weird how your memory works like that? Some image bobs up into your life again after literally decades and your brain instantly recognises it as a core memory. And yet at the same time, you can't remember where your car keys are when you're holding them in your hand. I click on Luke's message and see what my long-lost friend has to say to me after thirty-odd years . . .

Chapter 9

Is this the Heidi Hobbes that used to play a wicked Wichita Lineman on her fiddle?

Wow! I can't believe he remembered that! I couldn't even remember his full name at first. Now I feel bad!

It is indeed! I reply. **In fact, I played it just the other day after not touching my violin for years and it absolutely made me sob.**

It's a beautiful song. And the Glen Campbell version floors me every time. Did you know Prince said his favourite guitarist was Glen Campbell?

I did not know that! It occurs to me you always had these fascinating facts about musicians up your sleeve.

It's true, Luke really did. I recall now I learnt so much from him that year, about the music world. He saw pop stars as real people, not royalty. Real musicians with influences. I used to enjoy talking about music with him. A memory pops into my head of him telling me that every musician stands on the shoulders of the teacher who taught them, and the teacher who taught their teacher, all the way back beyond distant memory to the first humans who made sounds that moved us. What a great image.

How the devil are you, Luke?!

All's well here. The thought of any sort of reunion would normally make me shudder, but I'm considering it.

Me too, on both counts! I'm not a very peopley person, but there's something about those Exeter days that has been haunting me recently! So I'm tempted!!

Strangely enough, me too. It's been in my mind a lot. Maybe because it's 30 years this year since we graduated (which seems impossibly ridiculous. I mean, the 90s were only a decade ago, weren't they?)

And I was twenty-two a decade ago, surely!

Then I have a closer look at his profile pic. And the truth is, he is the one who seems to have been preserved in aspic. There's a few wrinkles, and his hair is a little shorter, but he looks exactly the bloody same.

You, on the other hand, haven't aged a day.

My knees would disagree with you there. And my carpal tunnel. Too much guitar playing.

Oh, do you still play? I remember you plucking away on any stringed instrument you could get your hands on, then carry it from room to room, like it was surgically attached to your body.

I do still play, yeah. I have a day job but still play guitar for fun. I do gigs with a mate of mine. I live all over with my job. I'm in Boston, USA right now and for the next few months.

What job do you do?

I'm a systems engineer, in the energy industry. I'm based at Shell TechWorks right now. Doesn't leave much time for guitaring, but I sneak it in when I can. How about you?

I'm an administrator at a college. I'm . . . not enjoying it much these days.

I bet you're good at it, as you were always the most organised in the house. And the one with the best eye for detail. You used to tell me my low E string was always slightly out of tune, do you remember?

I do NOT remember that! You're the one with perfect pitch!

126

That's just a quirk of nature. You had a better ear for music than any of us.

It's so odd to think of myself as being defined by music back then. Nowadays, I feel like I'm defined by only those things I don't care anything about, like how I meet deadlines efficiently, or how well my lasagne turns out.

Luke adds, *I'm genuinely sorry to hear you haven't touched your violin for years.*

You know what, I am too. I can't believe I allowed that to happen, in some ways. In other ways, I know it's normal, as life gets busier and more complicated. Once you have to start proper adulting, music tends to take a back seat.

It does, so you have to make room for it. I hope you playing Lineman means you're back into it again?

Not quite. Weirdly, I feel guilty every time I see my violin case, leant up against the wall in my living room. I realise I've been avoiding taking it out again and feeling the same way I did. It was pretty overwhelming. I really did sob. I'm not sure what I was crying for. Something I'd lost, I think. Also, fair warning, I'm a menopausal nutcase these days, so I could just as easily be crying at a Jimmy Webb song as a slightly overboiled egg. Some days I feel like I'm totally losing my mind.

Blimey, where did that truth avalanche come from?! He'll probably run a mile. I'm sure when he messaged his old housemate he didn't have histrionics in mind. But then, you know what? Stuff that. I don't have anything to lose. I just want to be myself. I always was that way with Luke back then.

My ex-wife had early menopause and really struggled. It's a bloody awful thing to deal with. I'm not surprised you sobbed. Music is so often the key to unlocking emotions and memories. For me, it's even more powerful than scent in bringing back moments from my past. I can hear a snatch of a song and I'm transported to my youth and there's this terrible yearning.

Yes! It is exactly that, a terrible yearning.

I know just what you mean. What do you think we're yearning for?

Something that's lost, as you say. Freedom. Optimism. Innocence.

Never such innocence again, as Philip Larkin said. He was talking about the First World War, so at least we didn't have to deal with that shitshow!

Well yes, my grandad fought in that war, so I know if he were still here, he'd be scowling at us for our pathetic self-indulgence when we moan about not having the right kind of oat milk in our lattes. Doesn't make it any less

128

powerful though, that loss of innocence we all have to go through. Larkin also said, They fuck you up, your mum and dad. And he was right about that too.

Oh crikey, wasn't he just! I try to think back to what I knew about Luke's parents, and it's virtually nothing. But then I recall what Nate said recently about Luke's dad having an affair and Luke changing his name to his mother's maiden name. That's quite the response from a twenty-one-year-old chap, discarding his father's name. It must have been a very big deal in his life. Interesting . . . and I can certainly relate to a difficult relationship with parents.

Amen to that, I reply. Then my desk phone rings and I remember I'm at work and I'm supposed to be doing a thousand other things instead of taking a trip down Memory Lane with Luke Beresford (now Jones).

I've got to go and do tedious worky things now, though I'd much rather chat about music!

Same and same. I'm glad that strange woman on Facebook organised this reunion. I vaguely remember her playing the harp at a party once and nobody was listening, so she got up and locked it away in her car so nobody would spill beer on it, but thought it might get nicked so she threw a blanket over it and it sat there on the back seat looking like a kidnap victim. I never liked her but I like harps. I liked Harpo Marx playing one, anyway.

129

I haven't thought about Harpo Marx in years! God, he was brilliant! And his brother – Chico, is it? – playing the piano, with all those tricksy comedy things he did with his hands. I need to go watch a Marx Brothers film now!

They were the dog's bollocks. Bloody loved them. And Harold Lloyd.

I've got a hoodie with Harold Lloyd on it!

You fucking haven't.

I fucking have.

That's nuts. I've got him as a screensaver on my laptop, hanging off that clock in New York. He was my hero when I was a lad. I wanted to do his job. Be funny, act up a storm, but never have to speak to a soul.

You talked plenty to me when we shared a house.

That's because I was comfy there. In the real world, I don't like people very much. They set me on edge a bit. I was walking under a big umbrella in the rain the other day and it was see-through, and I was looking through it to see where I was going, and it occurred to me that I'd be quite happy to go through life like that, behind a plastic screen with blue raindrops painted on it, so I never had to deal with other people talking and looking and just existing.

Hear hear to that!

Oh Christ, my desk phone rings itself off. Whoever was trying to get hold of me with their neediness has gone away empty-handed, all because I'm messaging on my phone with someone I've not spoken to in three decades. I must focus! It's coming up to 2pm, that's why my brain is losing it. But I must get back to work.

You need to work, replies Luke, reading my mind. *And so do I.*

The toad work.

The toad work.

We both typed that at exactly the same time! Of course, he's a Larkin fan.

JINX!!! I reply.

You got me. Back to work we go. More later?

More later.

Later x

Later x

Work is crazy the rest of the day, but I get through it with a kind of warmth in my belly, and it hasn't come from drinking the canteen mint tea. It's from Luke Beresford-now-Jones. It's from finding an old friend again.

And falling into talking like falling off a log. It's really nice to have a man as a friend. I don't have many, mostly women, and not that many of them. I'm a one or two besties and many acquaintances type person. I could quiz Luke about the best way to impress Nate, maybe. I mean, he knew him well back then.

I realise as I'm driving home that we didn't mention Nate once. I must tell Nate I found our old housemate. I'm sure he'll be delighted. I'm actually quite surprised they've lost touch. But that's the way life goes, I guess. Things fall apart, as T. S. Eliot wrote. I wonder if Luke likes Eliot much? I don't particularly, I just love little snippets, like how he said his life was measured out in coffee spoons. I much prefer Larkin, mostly because he says fuck and he loves jazz. And he knows about sadness. And yearning.

That evening, I get my violin out once more and play a few tunes while Ada and Carly are out again, this time at a roller disco, of all places. I'm not brave enough to let anyone else hear it yet (except perhaps Alia, Rich and co through the walls and Toby and Danyal through the floor, though they haven't complained so far). I'm finding my fingers with my violin again. I'm reacquainting myself with her. I'm working on getting her to forgive me, for abandoning her for so long. We're getting to know each other again. Like with my old housemates. I put my violin away and message Nate and tell him about Luke. He doesn't say a lot, except *Jones yeah that's it*. So I leave it and message with Nate about Orkney instead. He sends me lots of photos of the wild landscape there and it looks glorious. The peace! The space! I'm cramped up in this Oxford townhouse with all these people living on top of each other and wild Orkney looks like heaven to me right now.

You're welcome to come visit anytime, Hobbes, writes Nate.

Thanks! Sounds like a nightmare to get up there though! How on earth do you manage to get to your gigs and so forth, living so far off the beaten track?!

I don't do gigs when I'm here. I actually split my year between Orkney and the rest of the world. I come up here in June and stay till the end of September. It's my reverse hibernation, where I come to bask in the northern sun and retreat from the world for four months. After that, I go back to Chelsea and my travelling life.

What's in Chelsea?

My London flat. It's small but perfectly formed (a bit like you . . .)

I am petite height-wise but little does he know I'm not petite in width, less Kylie Minogue and more Danny DeVito. I haven't sent him any current body shots yet. I intend to never do so, if I can get away with it.

I really am in the wrong job. And the wrong house. I feel like I live with the Pontipines some days. You wouldn't know them, It was some weirdy weird kids programme my youngest used to watch, like a bad acid trip.

Haha I do know them cos my niece was obsessed with In the Night Garden. *And you're absolutely right about the acid trip. What were they thinking?*

Right?! Scared the shit out of me.

Haha but look, about Chelsea and Orkney. I don't want to sound like a rich prick.

That's ok. You're allowed to be rich and not a prick. Maybe.

It's only that I need a London base for work. But I need to escape too. I need my own space as an artist. Now I sound like an artist prick.

Yeah you kinda do actually ;)

I can't get away with anything with you, Hobbes.

No, you can't.

I kinda like that though. Keeps me on my toes.

Good.

There's a pause, and that frisson again. Blimey, I'm so attracted to this man. Texting with him is like champagne and oysters. Actually, better than that. Oysters never appealed to me. Or prawns. Bugs of the sea. This is pure

134

adrenaline and serotonin and endorphins all wrapped up in a blonde rock god, who wants to talk to little old me, with my corgi legs. And that's another reason not to travel up to Orkney and see him (apart from all the other thousand reasons, like work and kids and my anxiety about leaving my house, which is a new menopause symptom that's been creeping up on me recently). I don't want him to see me fat. If I'm going to this reunion, then I'm going to have to lose a ton of weight before October. If he sees me this way, he'll be off like a shot, I'm sure of that. The longer I can prolong this bodiless messaging, the better. I can pretend I'm as beautiful as he makes me feel. Oh Christ, that's a bloody sad thing to say, isn't it? What kind of feminist am I that I need a man's validation like that? But however I try to reason it, with my feminist head on, my Heidi heart isn't in it and deep down I feel bloated and uncomfortable in my old clothes and no amount of feminism is going to make me feel better about that right now.

Ada and Carly come back and regale me with tales of how many people fell over at the roller disco and which were the best tunes to skate to: 'Sweet Escape' by Gwen Stefani, apparently, had just the right speed and rhythm. Ada goes to wash her hair and I chat with Carly for a while on the sofa.

'I see you've got your violin out of the attic,' says Carly.

'Yeah, just trying out a few old tunes.'

'But only when we're out?' she says, eyebrows raised and a little smile.

'It's just been years, love. I didn't want to make a racket in front of you lot.'

'I bet it's not a racket, I bet it sounds amazing. I'd love to hear you play, Mum.'

'Oh stop. It doesn't sound like anything yet. Maybe when I'm a bit more used to it. I need a few more evening sessions when you two are out. Thanks for taking her to the disco, by the way. You're a super sister, you really are.'

'Oh, stop yourself. I'm a big sister and that's my job. Anyway, it's a laugh. Hanging out with Ada is always a laugh.'

I reach over and stroke her hair. It's so soft and bright, her green eyes looking stunning in this light. I really do make beautiful children, if I say so myself. 'My gorgeous girl,' I say. She kisses my hand. She's such a good kid. 'You know, maybe it wasn't such a bad idea to have you young and another kid so old. Built-in childcare!'

'Oh right, I see!' says Carly, fake mad. 'That's all I'm useful for, eh? Like those siblings that are born to be organ donors for the other kid. That's my lot in life, to be Ada's babysitter!'

'Yeah, pretty much. Till you have some of your own.'

Carly grimaces.

'What's that look for?'

'I don't know really. I just can't imagine wanting kids, not right now. Maybe ever, I don't know. I like being a grown-up too much. I want a place of our own for me and Matt. I want to go out with my mates all the time, like I do now. I want to go on holidays in the sun and just relax and not have to deal with screaming kids.'

'Maybe you won't have kids then,' I say.

'You look disappointed,' says Carly, biting her lip in that way she has when she's worried about me.

'Do I? I'm not actually. I mean, I'd love your kids to distraction, Ada's too. But also, I wouldn't want my desire for them to be the reason either of you choose to have kids. If you don't want them, that's fine by me. I'd much rather you have your freedom.'

'That's what I worry about,' says Carly, looking down at her clasped hands. 'That we took away your freedom, Mum.'

'Oh God, not at all! Don't ever think that!'

'No, I mean, let me finish. Seeing your violin out again. And realising you were the same age I am now when you had me. I did take away your freedom, and maybe your music career.'

'Hey,' I say. I take her hands and hold them in mine. 'That's not true at all. And I was a grown-up, just like you are now. I made my choices and I was happy to. Absolutely no regrets, none whatsoever. I've loved our lives together, and I love our life now.'

'Okay, but I'm not sure that last bit is true, is it, Mum? You seem so unhappy these days. I'm so worried about you.'

It makes your heart ache when your kids turn from being wholly self-involved to worrying about you. It feels against the natural order of things, but also it's rather wonderful. 'That's just the menopause stuff. It's hard. But it'll pass, one day. Things will be better.'

Carly doesn't look convinced. 'All right. But I'm glad you're playing your violin again. Why not get in touch with some of your old musical friends? You could start up a group or something. Get you out of the house.'

'I spend quite enough time out of the house, thanks!'

'Mum,' she says, very seriously. 'You NEVER go out. Not for fun. Maybe starting up a band or joining a musical group or something would be good for you.'

'Oh, stop trying to mother me. And anyway, I am in touch with some of my musical friends, I'll have you know. I've been messaging with a couple of my old housemates from uni days. They got in touch through Facebook.'

'Ooh, have you? The sexy one?'

That surprises me! Can she read my mind? 'How do you know that?'

'Ooh, it is the sexy one! Is he married?'

I can feel my cheeks go hot.

'Ooh, you're blushing! He isn't then?'

'Stop saying "Ooooooh"! Look, it's nothing. We're just chatting. How do you know about the sexy one anyway?'

'You told me all about it, when I went off to uni. You told me not to fall in love with my housemates, because it's too hard to live with. You said just make friends with boys instead. And then I moved in with Matt and we fell in love and you said, "There, you did the exact thing I told you not to do, just as all daughters do."'

And she laughs at me. I have no memory of this conversation whatsoever.

'What's his name then?' says Carly, all excited. 'I want to look him up.'

'No way, I'm not having you stalking.'

But she begs me and I tell her it's Nate Wheeler, as long as she doesn't follow him or friend request him or whatever. She finds him.

'Wow, Mum, he's a total silver fox! He's hot as all hell!'

I blush again. She's looking at his profile pic on Facebook. I gaze at it too.

'Oh God, I know. He really is.'

'So, what's happening? Is he coming to see you? Take you out on a date? There's this new Italian on Little Clarendon Street. You should go there.'

'Slow down, Speedy Gonzales. He's up in the Orkney Islands and staying up there till September, apparently.'

Carly makes a face about this. 'What?' I say.

'Nothing. Just, if a person really wants to see someone, they'd come from the ends of the earth, that's all.'

Now I regret telling her. 'Look, we're just friends. That's all. I'm chatting with our other housemate too, Luke Beresford. I mean, Luke Jones. He changed his name. We're just friends, the three of us. That's all. Stop getting ahead of yourself.'

'Ooh, a love rival! A ménage à trois!'

'Oh SHUT UP!' I say crossly and stand up.

'Hah, I've hit the nail on the head there, haven't I! Touched a nerve!'

'Oh stop it, child,' I say and stamp out of the room and go to the kitchen. She's annoyed me. Carly does this, grabs onto something and won't let it go. Blows things out of all proportion.

She calls from the other room, 'Tell me which one you choose!'

'I said, SHUT UP!'

'Which one who?' comes the call from the bathroom door, where Ada, wrapped in a towel, has just come out.

'Come here and I'll tell you all the gossip about Mum and her two new boyfriends who are fighting over her!'

'Don't listen to her!' I shout from the kitchen and Ada says, 'Ooh, is it like *Bridget Jones*?!' Then I hear the pitter-pat of Ada's wet feet across the hall as she trots to the living room.

Bloody hell, I wish I'd never said anything now. For a while, Nate and Luke were all mine. My little secret chats. I hadn't told anyone, not even Brenda or Alia. They were just for me. Now, my kids know and I won't hear the end of it. Pain in the arse, kids are. They take everything from you, they inhale it like soul-eaters, all your energy, your love, your worry. And I give it willingly, because I adore them. But all I wanted was a little something for myself. I know I'm being unreasonable but it's how I feel. I just wanted that one thing, for me. Just for Heidi.

I'm putting stuff in the dishwasher in a huff, when my phone goes off and – speak of the devil – it's Luke.

Just a quick one. I'm heading out after work later to a gig at a bar round the corner from my flat here in Boston. We do a live feed. I can send you the link if you like? No worries if not. Just thought you might like it. It'll be around midnight, your time. So no worries at all if you're fast asleep by then.

That sounds bloody great! I'd love to see it! And I'm a total insomniac, so I'll be awake, most definitely. I look forward to it. Thanks!

He replies with a thumbs up. Oh, I really will look

forward to that! I'll get comfy in bed with an Ovaltine and watch that later. I finish the kitchen, see Ada off to bed, give Carly a kiss so she knows I'm not really mad at her. I mean, I am. But not her really. It's nice they're showing an interest. But they've got it all wrong. I don't want them cooking up some romcom plot in their silly little heads. Nate is just a pipe dream, a guy I used to fancy, but now lives a thousand miles away (or somewhat less). And Luke is a friend, an old housemate from a thousand years ago (or somewhat less). That's all.

Midnight comes and I'm all ready in bed with my phone, my Ovaltine and my dressing gown on. Thank God these live feeds don't work both ways. I must look a hundred and three. Luke has sent me the link and I click on it. The picture is a bit juddery at first, but then it connects and there's an empty stage – or at least, a cleared space in the corner of a busy bar with two chairs and some mic stands – and I can hear loud chattering and drinks clinking in the background, the odd person crossing in front of the screen. Crikey, this is quite exciting! Live pictures all the way from Boston, USA! I've never been to America. Always wanted to go. It's where *Cheers* was set, wasn't it? I always wanted to visit the *Cheers* place and sit at the bar with Norm and Frasier. God, I loved *Frasier* too. I always had a thing for Niles. I always like the nerdy guys.

Then, a tall, slim man probably in his thirties comes over to the stagey bit with a bass guitar and sits down. Is that Luke?! No, surely not. No, it isn't him. This guy has curly brown hair, a bit Art Garfunkel-like. He grins and then another guy comes. Ah, this is Luke! There he is! His dark shoulder-length hair is shorter now, still in a centre parting, tucked behind his ears. I can't see much grey. See what I mean about some men ageing better? It's not fair. He's not got the old wire-rimmed specs on he used to wear. Maybe he wears contacts now. He's really grown into himself. At college he was a bit of a geek and stooped a bit, jumper sleeves over his hands. Now he seems fully at ease with himself. He smiles too and then they both do a very quick tune-up of their guitars. Then the other guy says into his mic, 'Hey. We're Jones and Jones. Not related. He's British and I'm Canadian. He's Luke and I'm Bo.'

There's a few whoops from the crowd, who are still rumbling away a bit, still talking, though quieter now. That's all the introduction the Joneses give. Then they start. And – oh my word – the Garfunkel-like vibe of Bo is made incarnate, as Luke starts strumming the opening chords of 'Baby Driver'! Bo comes in with his bass and we're off. That funky little guitar solo at the beginning is note-perfect and it gives me the shivers, it's so good! God, I'd forgotten what a good guitarist Luke was. Luke watches Bo's hands as he plays, sometimes frowning, sometimes closing his eyes. Bo comes in with the vocals, high and cheery. Bo has a great voice! Clear as a bell. Then, when the chorus starts, Luke joins in with the harmonies: *'They call me Baby Driver . . .'* then *BAH BA BAH BAH*. I am sitting in my bed in my dressing gown and I am dancing! I'm dancing sitting down! It's pure fun, pure joy, just unalloyed cheery wonderfulness at the sweetness of this song, the scrunchy harmonies, the effortlessness of the excellent musicians, the way Luke's fingers move across the fingerboard. I have to stop myself from whooping when they reach the end! I don't want the girls bothering me, being nosy again.

What a song! What a rendition! The crowd love it and applaud and whistle. I watch the whole set. There's more Simon and Garfunkel, there's the Doors, Townes Van Sandt, Steely Dan, Dire Straits, Johnny Cash. It's 1am when they're done. They are BRILLIANT! Such ease and charm, such facility on their instruments. And lovely voices, both of them. I don't ever remember Luke singing back then. But he has a super voice, smooth as caramel. They're taking a break for fifteen minutes and then they'll do another set. Christ, I'm up at 6am tomorrow as usual. I really shouldn't stay up for the second set. Maybe I can watch it tomorrow. Or maybe I'll throw caution to the wind and stay up till gone 2am . . . I'm looking at the clock and considering, when my phone beeps a message.

Maybe it's Luke asking if I'm watching! I look. It isn't Luke.

Hey Hobbes

Hey Nate. You're up late?

Night owl, like you.

Well yes, I am a bit.

Thinking about you, the old you, the one I lived with all those years ago.

Ah, she's long gone, Nate!

I'd have to disagree with you there, Hobbes. She's right here.

143

I wish I still had her bum-length hair!

Your hair is cute now. Suits you.

Aw shucks.

You're beautiful, Hobbes. Always were. You still are. Even more so.

Oh stop.

Do you want me to stop?

Now then, there's an unambiguous message if ever I read one. I'm trying to play it cool but I'm thrilled with it. As John Travolta once sang, *I've got chills . . . they're multiplying . . .*

I think about how to reply.

Go on . . .

You were gorgeous back then. It's true. But you were shy. You didn't let it glow, that beauty. Now, you've grown into yourself. You have this inner confidence and it shines out of you. It's very attractive, Hobbes. It's dynamite.

Holy cow. A man hasn't said anything like this to me in years. Or perhaps . . . ever?

That's kind of you. Lovely words. Thank you.

Not just words, Hobbes. It's how I feel. Can we talk? By video chat?

What, now??

I look down at my rumpled dressing gown with an Ovaltine stain on the lapel. I can only imagine what state my bed-hair must be in, let alone not a scrap of make-up.

Not a good time?

Not really.

Another time then?

OK yeah, another time.

Good. Promise?

Promise!

Goodnight then Hobbes.

Goodnight Nate.

I sit and start panicking about what I'm going to wear for that video call. Then my phone pings again. I look down. It's Nate again.

Don't reply. But I'll be lying here, thinking of your shape.

How your hips curve like a cello. Maybe you'll think of me too. I hope so. Sweet dreams, Hobbes.

I turn my phone off for the night, switch off the bedside lamp and sink down into my bed. I sigh. I close my eyes. We're not in the same bed, we're not even in the same room, town or country. But Nate's honeyed words sweep over me with an irresistible swell of craving. I close my eyes and think of his handsome face, his blonde fringe hanging across his eyes, his pianist's hands, long, flexible fingers. It's as if I can feel his hands on me already. I'm tingling all over! That light switch of lust that was off for so many, long years is now most definitely and assuredly on.

Chapter 10

The next day, I remember when I wake up that I never listened to the second half of Luke's gig. I must see if it's saved on YouTube. I message him in the morning once I'm at work, telling him I watched the first set but couldn't stay awake for the second as it was so late (well, it's sort of true . . .) and I tell him how much I loved his music. No reply as yet. It's gone 2.30am there, so I'm assuming he's asleep.

No word yet from Nate. The memory of last night's words give me a tingle and I look them up and read them over again. Blimey! What a great night! Fantastic live music from Luke, then a bedtime lustful moment with Nate. My twenty-year-old self wouldn't have believed her luck! My fifty-two-year-old self is delighted, though I can't stop yawning. I'm not good with late nights like I used to be. And there's shitloads of work to do on my desk before my brain dies at 2pm, so I'd better get on, as dreary a prospect as that sounds. I'd much rather listen to Luke's second set, or sit here with my eyes closed and think of Nate Wheeler . . .

Better still, I could have a quick chat with him. That'll set up the day nicely. I message him:

Hey I watched a live feed of Luke Jones playing a set with another guitarist last night and it was ACE! They both had super voices too. Did a load of covers of great songs. I can send you the link if you like?

He immediately replies: *Luke was always a great guitarist. How's life today? How's work?*

It's ok. I'd love to see some videos of you performing too, Nate. I couldn't see any on your website. Can you send me some links?

I don't have any. I'm too busy performing to worry about getting someone to record me! I might have some older ones somewhere – I'll dig them out for you. How about a video of you playing, Hobbes? I want to see that famous finger work of yours again.

Ach! There's no way! I mean, firstly I've lied about still gigging and secondly, I can't let him see me play when I've only just started playing again.

Same as you, no recordings!

Then you'll just have to play for me live one day, won't you . . .

Maybe! Gotta go. Work meeting! Catch you soon.

A bientot.

Got out of that one smartish. I'll need to practise my arse off if Nate's expecting to hear any playing from me anytime soon. Plus lose three stone. No problem. Plenty of hours in the day to exercise and cook healthy meals from scratch as well as relearn the violin from scratch. If I don't sleep, that is. Who needs sleep? Sleep is for losers.

A couple of weeks later – filled with ever-burgeoning work madness and home madness of the nine-year-old-best-friend-crisis variety, punctuated by chatty, musical messaging with Luke Jones and flirty, thrilling messaging with Nate Wheeler – the second outing of the menopause support group comes around again. And this week, our topic is symptoms. I'm trying out having a different theme for each meeting, to galvanise us all a bit and avoid just rambling on about how awful everything is. Also, in these early days of the group, I feel like we need to get to know each other better, so everyone feels better about sharing stuff. So, I tell them that we're going to go round the room and talk about our main menopause symptoms. I ask everyone not to interrupt and say *Me too!* every time they hear something they identify with, only because I think it'd be best for each of us to say our piece without being interrupted. Everyone nods their agreement. To show good faith, I say I'll go first, then we'll go round the circle in turn. Everyone's sitting in the exact same places as last time, like they're set in stone now we've made those random placings. I start us off.

'I get the hot flushes sometimes. Not at night really, mostly when something stressy is happening at work or home. I'd say my biggest physical problems right now are all gastro-related. Gas, diarrhoea, acid reflux. All the fun ones. I can't drink coffee or alcohol anymore. I miss them more than I miss my kids when they're away – yes, really. The hardest stuff for me though is the psychological stuff. And the not knowing at first that this was menopause related. I mean, everyone knows about the hot flushes. But I had no idea about brain fog, or rage, or anxiety. Sometimes I get the feeling I don't want to leave the house at all. I'm not very social these days, but I've never felt afraid to leave the house, until now. And my mind . . . it's like it was an old friend and now it's letting me down. Abandoning me. I thought I had Alzheimer's. Or just pure insanity, like a madwoman in the attic type deal. I keep forgetting stuff. And losing track of time. Plus the rage. I've talked about that. It's very real. I measure my day by how often I'm able to restrain myself from punching someone in the face.'

Everyone smiles or laughs at that, but there's nodding too. Especially Rhona.

Cheryl is next. The moment she starts speaking, her cheeks bloom pink. Oh, bless her. I get the feeling she really finds this hard. And that makes me respect her even more, for coming here at all.

'I want to talk about symptoms, I really do. But . . . I find it . . . difficult. I'm . . . it's . . . they're just so embarrassing. They . . .'

She falters, staring at the floor, not raising her head. Someone makes a quiet kind of aww sound. I can tell we all feel for her.

Rhona reaches over and pats her arm, saying quietly, 'It's all right, love.'

'Cheryl, you don't have to share anything you don't want to,' I say, and she nods, still looking down. 'It's not easy talking about embarrassing bodily stuff. If it helps, please know that I have farted loudly in a meeting and also nearly shat myself in a traffic jam the other day.'

Niki bursts out laughing, then checks herself when nobody else does. 'I'm sorry. It's not funny.'

'It is funny! I mean, it wasn't at the time. I was just lucky I was sitting down in a car seat, because if I'd been standing up on public transport I'd have sprayed the whole carriage!'

Crikey, I've never shared stuff like this with strangers before – or even people I know.

I can see Cheryl has looked up now and has a small smile. I say, 'How about we come back to you later?'

'Yes please,' says Cheryl.

Now it's Rhona's turn.

'Well, you all know rage is one of my main problems. At work, when I'm cleaning floors or hoovering or washing up, I hit things a lot, bashing sieves to get the water out – BANG BANG! And smacking the mop on the tiles – WHAM! If I could afford to go to the gym, I might take up boxing! I get the hot flushes too, any time, day or night. They're rotten. Then I'd say fatigue and joint pain are my worst things. Restless legs at night, so my sleep is rubbish. My legs just twitch and feel like something's on them. It's not an itch, it's like it's coming from inside, making me want to move them all the time. It's really weird. I didn't even know it had a thing to do with menopause until I started reading up about it. I've got the brain fog too, like you, Heidi. I forget words. It's like . . . it isn't even like they were there, in my brain, ever. You know, when you're trying to think of a word. And it's on the tip of your tongue. Or in the corner of your eye. And you can't get it. But with this, there's just a blank space. Like where the word used to be. Like it's been rubbed out. That's weird too. And the last thing is a breathing thing, you know, respiratory, is it? Especially at night, again. Coughing when I lie down. Wheezy. And I get this gunk in my eyes. It's like I'm all gunked up, it's grim. Some days I get it when I'm working too. I get all dizzy and snotty and like I can't take a deep breath, when I'm standing up after bending down, at work. Those are the main ones. And same, like you, Heidi. I've had these ages and didn't know. I didn't realise it had anything to do with menopause. It's all making work really hard, to be honest, you know. Everything is so bloody hard. Everything. And it just goes on and on.'

Rhona really is a force to be reckoned with. Listening to her is energising and exhausting, all at once. She's so highly strung, so angry. But underneath, it certainly seems that she's crying out for help.

'Thanks so much, Rhona. And I'm sorry to hear about all of those symptoms. As you know, the reason we're here in the first place is because I can relate to the rage! Niki, are you happy to go next?'

'Sure. I guess the first sign for me was really irregular periods for about two years when I was about thirty-three. Then, over the space of a few months, my breasts got bigger and bigger. I grew out of my bra! I thought it meant I was pregnant, but all the tests I took were negative.'

Niki pauses then and looks down at her feet. Oh, bless her, her eyes are filling with tears again.

I say, softly, 'You don't have to carry on if you'd rather not, Niki.'

'No, no,' she says, tosses her hair and smiles that great smile. 'I'm okay. So yeah, big boobs all of a sudden. Then, I just seemed to always be having urine infections, one after another. Sorry to be graphic, but weeing was really tricky, like it was coming out in little bits, sat there on the toilet for ages. It was because my bladder wasn't emptying straight away. I'd get a blast first, then a trickle. And I'd give up and end up weeing all over my hand by accident! Then, another random thing: I started to go off beer. I just couldn't drink beer like I used to. It made me feel really warm. I can drink wine. But in the pub, I'd have to go outside, feeling all hot. I needed air. Made me gun-shy with beer. I really miss it. I loved a beer with the guys from work. So yeah, all these random things. And I didn't link any of these things together. Probably because of my age, of course, I didn't suspect it was menopause. And I don't have my mum to talk to about it, as my mum died when I was nine.'

Another aww sound from the group. Oh God, same age as Ada. I can't even imagine how it would hit Ada if I died, right now. Her dad is wonderful. He'd do an amazing job. But losing your mum, at nine. Despite my mum being a pain, it would've been an even worse childhood if she'd not been there, I suspect. My dad is even more clueless about feelings than her. She's definitely got more abrasive as she's got older. She was softer, back then.

Niki pauses only momentarily, then smiles and nods, acknowledging the group's warmth which is clearly coming

153

off us in waves towards her. As our youngest, I feel like the vibe in the room is that we're all sort of mothering Niki already. She goes on, 'Then one day I was listening to the radio and Sam Baker came on, the editor of *Vogue*. She was talking about the menopause and she had all these symptoms. All of this physical stuff, head to toe. It was a lightbulb moment for me. I had some tests and bingo, early menopause.'

She pauses again and it looks like she might be about to get upset again, or maybe she's done, it's hard to tell.

'Thanks so much for sharing, Niki,' I say.

'Well, I haven't quite finished, if that's okay?'

'Oh God, sorry! Yes, of course it's okay! Forgive me.'

'No, it's fine. I just took a little break! Okay so, then other symptoms started. Sorry again to be graphic, but I started having real problems with my vulva. And my vagina. The whole area really. It was always irritated and sore, itchy. And dry inside. I couldn't find any comfy knickers. I needed seamless ones, because that bit in the middle of the – what's it called? The gusset? Is that a word?!'

Yes, we all say and laugh. It's not a word you find yourself using every day.

'Yeah, the gusset. Anyway, where it joins, that seam used to drive me nuts. And it's so bloody hard to find seamless knickers without that join in the gusset! So I used to put a bit of Canesten on, but it never got better. I had a coil in for a while, as I said before. But when it came out – for various reasons, I won't go into now – well, the whole irritation thing got worse. So dry, painful. Awful just wiping after the toilet. Then, I'd find I was weeing a bit in my knickers, just a little bit. I was terrified.

How could I be incontinent? In my thirties? I saw a really nice GP and she said it was all linked to the menopause. The vagina shrivels up and pulls at the wall of the bladder? Something like that. It's why you can get a bit incontinent. You need a moisturiser up there, like a pessary. And she gave me some cream for the outside bit, the itchiness on the vulva. It's much better. But yeah, not easy. Any of it. Not anything I expected. And people don't talk about it, do they? Anyway, I'm done now. Sorry to go on.'

'Never say sorry about talking here, all of us, please,' I say. 'Women apologise too much as it is for talking too much. I don't know why, something to do with scolds and gossips, all that misogynistic crap about women with loose tongues. But talking and sharing information is power. And that's what we're here for.'

Everyone nods and agrees. Wow, these women. So many problems to deal with, so much suffering. It's blowing my mind, how we all walk around doing our jobs and getting on, while inside and at home, it's a bloody rollercoaster. I'm fascinated by these women, too. Their confessions, their stories. I'm all in. I can't wait to hear more. Joy is next.

'For me, I'd say the whole thing is like PMT but worse. There's the crying, at the slightest thing. After any sort of the most minor altercation or even slight disagreement with others, it feels like the end of the world. I've never been anxious about anything before, not in this debilitating way. Now, someone doesn't answer a text and I'm convinced in five minutes that they hate me. It's exhausting. That's the mental stuff. But the physical stuff is pretty awful too. It's the sweats, the flushes. They are horrendous.

This time of year is the worst, as summer heat builds up. I'll admit, I now have a pathological fear of summer. I cannot cope with heat, because of the sweating. I panic about heat. I'm obsessed with closing the windows in summer, keeping the heat in the house down. I set a timer for it on my phone, when to open and close them. It's ridiculous. I've always loved the heat. I never had a problem with summers before. It makes me feel like a failure. Sweat drips off me, onto students! I have to keep apologising. I used to have much longer hair, braided. I loved it. I've had to chop it all off. Simplify. Brain fog a bit too, yes. Losing words. That's horrible in my job, where I'm paid to pontificate all day. And memory slips, like putting my purse in the fridge and finding an onion in my handbag. It's infuriating, all of it. But there is one good thing and that's the confidence to say my opinion more freely, now I'm older. And my sense of injustice is sharper. I see so clearly now how the world is built around and for men. I'm not a man hater. But the world, the news, it's a male lens. In almost every sphere, there is an under-representation of women and people of colour and the working class, basically anyone who's not white, male and upper middle class. So, I think I'm braver than I used to be. More willing to call things out. Anyway, that's about it. Nothing unusual here. Nothing to write home about. Nobody to talk to about it though . . . Anyway, I really ought to shut up and get on with it. Time for Cheryl, I think, now?'

Joy is so confident, so assured. Yet I get the distinct impression that underneath all of that, she's vulnerable. But no time to consider it fully, as Joy has deftly moved the focus off herself and onto Cheryl. I glance over at

Cheryl, worried she'll feel put upon. But she's cleared her throat and she seems happy to speak.

'All right, then,' she says, trying to sound confident, her high voice cracking a bit. She clears her throat again and begins. 'This is me. I've not got hot flashes, or whatever they are. I get the brain fog thing some days. Mine started with my hair falling out, coming out in clumps, a whole hairbrush full some days. That's a worry. I don't want to go . . . bald. It frightens me, if I'm honest. The other thing is teeth. I've got dental problems, sore gums. The dentist says my teeth are thinning. I use Sensodyne these days. I'm not sure it helps much. So, those are the main things. But . . . there is something else. The worst thing, really. It's . . . I want to just say it. It's . . .'

She's really struggling. I want to tell her again she doesn't need to tell us if she doesn't want to. But she knows that. So I keep my mouth shut. She's a grown woman. She can decide what's right for her.

She speaks again. 'It's the same thing as Niki. Just the same. Down there. Soreness and itchiness. So dry. I've tried every cream on earth. Even yoghurt. It's not thrush, it's not infected. Nothing works. I feel like . . . like my underwear is made of sandpaper.'

Niki is nodding along, a sad smile of recognition on her face.

'I sit at the reception desk at work and some days, it's unbearable. I have to wear skirts, so I can get air up there. I wish I could perch a fan between my legs! It's that bad. I do at home sometimes, if my husband's not home. I have a lukewarm bath, then sit on the bed with my legs open and a fan perched on a chair at the end of the bed. That's the only relief I get. But then my husband comes home and I have to rush to put it away, you know.'

I'm thinking, *No, I don't know*. Why does Cheryl have to stop the one thing that comforts her when her husband comes home? I want to ask, but it feels too nosy.

'And the dryness – there. It makes things impossible. Things of a sexual nature. My husband, Clive. He doesn't understand. It's hard to explain. He gets fed up with me. He has needs. It's not right, that he has to be so frustrated. But I just can't, these days. I'd be in agony. I am in agony, just sitting there. I can't have anything else near it, not even knickers, let alone . . . a cock.'

There it is again, that little hint that the demure Cheryl has some earthiness well hidden. I love that about her. I'd love to see more of it! Maybe we will, as she relaxes more. But I do not like what I'm hearing about her husband. He sounds like a cock himself.

Cheryl is done then. It's as if once she's said the word 'cock', she doesn't want to say anything more. I thank everyone for being so frank, so brave. It's not easy, this sharing business. We discuss afterwards, sharing similarities and differences, making connections over shared woes and asking questions. It has amazed me hearing these four women's stories. Yes, we have some overlap, yet also many of our symptoms are wildly different. I had no idea menopause was such a different experience for every woman. We wrap up with my recommendation for this week, which is – only if they have time, as I don't really want to set these busy women homework – they can seek out Davina McCall's documentaries. Plus they could read her book, *Menopausing*. Those helped me in my early research phase. Joy has already read it, plus the Mariella one. Nobody else has, so it might be helpful to them. Since Niki had mentioned Sam Baker, Joy recommends her book too, *The Shift*. She says it's brilliant. I might seek that one out myself.

It's gone really well, again. People are coming out of their shells even more. It continues to surprise me. And it tires me out too. I'm fit for little after a group meeting. It's intense and draining, but in the best way. That evening, I get an early night, not long after Ada is in bed. Carly is up watching TV downstairs and I can hear the *Succession* theme tune booming through the floorboards. I'd usually be down there with her, but tonight I'm shattered. I lie in bed with *The Durrells* playing out idyllically on the telly and scroll listlessly on my phone. But I can't concentrate on anything. I can't stop thinking about our group today. I've had a few emails in recent weeks from other women at MUFFY asking about coming to the group, but none have actually turned up yet. And I realise I'm really relieved about that. Not just because it's fewer people to deal with, but because I feel like something special is happening here, in our group. And a newcomer would ruin that somehow, displace its delicate balance.

But I don't want to exclude women who need help, of course I don't. So, I decide that I'll email all those who enquired but haven't followed through yet and tell them that this group is now full and that I'd be very happy to help them set up another group run by them, as well as give them resources and advice. I do think that will work best for everyone, to have their own small group, that feels safe. I think a room of ten or twenty women or more would be too overwhelming, especially when you want to talk about dry fannies or whatever. Yes, that's definitely the way forward. I think of our band of five and I feel proud that we've already bonded. It's not about being cliquey, but instead feeling safe. Not safe in a pathetic way, but in a strong way: like it's a place where we can rage and cry and talk about intimate things with no shame and it's not weird or uncomfortable. It's our place to be ourselves, with no male bullshit or judgement or even good intentions. It's just for us. We are a female fight club.

Chapter 11

Before the third support group meeting in early July, I get an email from Niki who says that she and the other members have set up a WhatsApp group and would I like to join? She explains that I shouldn't feel obliged to, but that they wanted to ask me because – even though I'm the group founder and leader, as such – I'm also going through menopause and need support as much as the rest of us. And that's what the WhatsApp group will be for: support at tricky times and a place to blow off steam. I usually find WhatsApp groups abhorrent – group video calls as well. Honestly, I'd rather die. But, in this case, I can see that it would be really helpful to the group and I'm glad they've asked me. I reply:

> *Thanks so much for asking me, Niki. I'm not a big fan of WhatsApp group chats in general – they usually stress me out! – but in this case I think it's a great idea. With one proviso, and that's as long as it's clear*

that I can't act as some kind of leader on it or solve everyone's queries, although I'd be keen to try if/when I can. I'm happy to lurk there and offer the odd contribution now and then. Plus I will probably turn my notifications off for it so I don't get a thousand pings every time someone has a conversation. Does that sound ok?

Niki replies that she understands completely and will message everyone separately to make it clear that they mustn't use it to ask me stuff specifically and that we'll all be on equal footing in there. That sounds fine to me and I send her my phone number.

And so I get the notification on my phone and, lo and behold, I've been added to a group chat titled THE M&Ms. I type:

Hey, Heidi here. Thank you for inviting me, you lovely lot. Hey, what does M&Ms stand for?!

Joy: *We are the MUFFY MENOPAUSERS aka the M&Ms!*

Oh bravo, that is brilliant! I love that!

Niki: *Every good group needs a name.* :)

Indeed! I'm glad you've set up this group. I'm sure it'll be a great support beyond our bi-monthly meetings. (Or does that mean every two months? Gah, I don't know. Oh well! You know what I mean.)

Joy: *Agreed. People are so atomised these days. I'd say groups like these are essential for connection. I'm in another one with other female lecturers around my age. We moan about menopause and work and life. We also draft emails we'll never send just to blow off steam. A friend of mine calls them Emails of Mass Destruction!*

That is hilarious! I wish I'd had a support group to send that to instead of sending it to all the damn staff by mistake!

Niki: *But then we might never have found this support group. So I'm glad you did it Heidi!*

Well, that is true. Maybe I'm glad too! I think I'm starting to see that we all need the women in our lives more than we realise.

Rhona: *Hello Rhona here just to say my gran always said it takes a village to raise a child best advice ever that but doesnt happen v much nowdays*

Joy: *Yes Rhona, that is very true. And sadly in our society grandmother figures and older women are not celebrated as they have been at other times and in other cultures. Indeed, they're denigrated and overlooked.*

They're also absent in so many academic fields, such as anthropology and palaeoanthropology, where the history of MAN is written by men, and women are just also-rans i.e. men were out hunting and driving huMAN development forward while women were breast-feeding and doing basically nothing to advance civilisation?

I think not. It's very likely women created pottery, weaving and so on.

There's even recent evidence that women were responsible for all cave art, as the men hunted the meat, it's likely the women butchered it, when the men were home resting from their exertions. So the women butchers would have the best understanding of animal anatomy in order to draw those beautiful animal figures on the cave walls.

Also there is evidence that many of the handprints are often small, suggesting females, as well as children's handprints, showing they had their kids with them in the cave. Try the book Invisible Women by Caroline Criado Perez. That's a real eye-opener.

(Funny how we all wait patiently while we see JOY *typing* . . . at the top, and she delivers her marvellous sermon in bite-sized pieces so we know to wait for the next bit! She really is the consummate lecturer, in the best way. Also, surely she must be on her laptop to type this fast! I'm about 5 per cent of this speed on my phone thumbs.)

Cheryl: *Joy that is so interesting thank you so much I never thought of it that way.*

Joy: *My pleasure, Cheryl*

Cheryl: *My mum was in hospital lately and she said every time she tried to talk to someone she just wasn't heard she was ignored and she felt like she was invisible she said to me, women just disappear after a certain age*

The truth of that! I add: **It can be freeing though. When I see blokes gawking at my daughter Carly when we're out together, I'm actually thrilled I don't have to run that gauntlet anymore. So there are pros and cons! But yes, of course, when it comes to medicine or other disciplines, the invisibility of women is bloody awful and that needs to change.**

Joy: *Perhaps we can make our own village of menopausal women by creating support groups like this. We have to fight this silence around women's issues with talk and make it loud!*

The M&Ms continue the conversation, but I've got to get on, as I'm taking Ada to trampolining in a minute. Well, that group has turned out to be a very interesting place! Good old Joy, with her fascinating knowledge. And good on the rest of them for adding their own personal experience too. I was particularly glad to see Cheryl joining in, as I wondered if her shyness might stop her from engaging in fast-moving group chats. But maybe texting is easier for her shyness, who knows?

Anyway, a great thing to see everyone bonding further. This support group thing is going from strength to strength. Speaking of which, in the previous couple of weeks, I've had more emails from women wanting to join and I've pointed out to them the idea of setting up their own groups. I've heard about at least two other groups that have started on different parts of the campus. Do we have a mini-revolution happening here?! I bloody well hope so!

So, I take Ada to trampolining. This is a new endeavour, part of a general push to keep her busy. She has been so down lately. Not even the random appearances of Pushkin from downstairs have been enough to keep Ada happy, as Pushkin usually does. That's when you know something is really wrong with Ada, if a cat can't cheer her up. She's having some big emotional stuff happening recently, including the recent revelation that her best friend Ruby who's ignoring her (who she's been thick as thieves with since Reception and has been on countless sleepovers with) is actually a girl she wants to kiss and yet she wants to kiss boys too and is that okay and what does that mean and why is Ruby ignoring her? Ada usually plays with Alia's son Zane too – very convenient as he lives next door – but he seems to have gone off her too as he's always too busy to hang out. So, Ada has declared that she hates herself and people are horrible and there is no loyalty in the world and why is school so awful and why is the sky blue and what is the meaning of life, the universe and everything etc. etc. etc.

Poor love. It's tough being a kid. And I wish I could just tell her the answer to the meaning of life, the universe and everything is forty-two and be done with it. And I can't even tell her it's going to get easier. Because Carly's teens were a soul-crushing nightmare that nearly ended me, until the relief of her entering her twenties and more emotional resilience on her part. So, Ada's dad Geoff and I have been doing extra stuff with Ada, to get her out of the house, particularly this week since Ada's usual bad-times buddy Carly has gone on holiday to Portugal for two weeks. Geoff has taken Ada out twice this week already, once to the Story Museum in Pembroke Street and the other time for a long walk round some of the colleges as Ada likes the old buildings, especially the little cobbled roads all round Merton, Christ Church, Corpus Christi and Oriel. She likes the quads and the walls and the stone. All very Harry Potter, she says. Geoff was born in Oxford and went to Merton College, so he knows a lot about their heritage and tells her historical stories as they wander round. I count my blessings that my ex Geoff is such a hands-on dad and generally a good bloke, I really do.

It's daft how surprised we are when men are good dads, isn't it? Hence my rage when I see videos of celebrity dads out pushing their baby's pram or carrying them on their chests and all the comments are AWWW HOW ADORABLE and WHAT A GREAT DAD. Surely carrying your own child about is the bare minimum??!! Don't even get me started on when people say the dads are on 'babysitting' duties when they're referring to their OWN CHILDREN. Why on earth are we lauding blokes for performing the most basic qualities of parenting, for Christ's sake?! Where are all the posts of women cleaning their baby's arses of green shit or dosing them with Calpol at 3am or spending three hours on a weeknight on the sofa listening to their daughter cry about her best friend?? WHERE ARE THOSE VIDEOS, EH??!! Not so photogenic. And the fact remains, good fathering is seen as exceptional, whereas women get endless shit for the tiniest perceived failures in their mothering. Does my head in. Anyway, perhaps that's another thing I can rant about with the M&Ms (although neither Rhona nor Niki have kids and Niki has looked visibly upset when pregnancy and miscarriage have been mentioned, so I feel like there's a story behind that, thus I don't want her to feel alienated if we all go off on one about our kids . . .).

So, our third meeting arrives and this week our topic is treatments and assistance we've received so far for the menopause, either from doctors or elsewhere. Before we get started, Cheryl comes up to me quietly and asks if she can go last again and from now on, as she finds it gives her more courage to go last, after everyone else has spoken. Of course she can, I tell her, and so we begin. I don't say anything to the others about why Cheryl isn't going first this time. I just start with Rhona.

'I like alternative therapies, you know, so I'm going to talk about them mostly. I think some of them are working. It's hard to tell. You don't want to stop taking things and it get worse, you know. So I don't. Anyway, for my joint pain and my chest and the wheeziness and my eyes streaming. I've been thinking they sound like different things. But they're not, you know. They're related. Because they're all types of inflammation. I'd say, inflammation is the cause of most things. And there's lots you can do for inflammation. So I avoid dairy. And do daily breathing exercises. And yoga every evening. And I'm thinking of seeing a chiropractor too. And I take vitamin C, fish oil and gingko, all to reduce inflammation and promote health. I'm not sure if they're working yet. But these things need time, you know. I mean, nothing good ever comes easy, does it? I'm trying to stay calm and patient. It's not very natural to me these days, you know, being patient. But I'm trying.'

Joy says, 'Rhona, I know we've disagreed before about these things and I don't want to come across as a know-it-all, as I assure you I'm a beginner at this menopause stuff along with everyone else here. But I do think if you're getting those kinds of symptoms you really ought to have a proper asthma inhaler and with streaming eyes you ought to be on antihistamines.'

I glance at Rhona and I'm about to hop in to avoid the inevitable backlash, when Rhona snaps, 'Well, you do come across as a know-it-all actually and you don't bloody know it all, you know.'

I want to intervene, but then I think, we're all grown-ups here. And me trying to avert World War Three all the time is just my mum-self trying to smooth everything out. And maybe we don't need smoothing here. Maybe we need to let these arguments play out and see where they go. So, I don't say anything. Joy leans forward and looks at Rhona with sympathy. 'But it's just not working for you though, is it?'

'Loads of medicines don't work either!' Rhona retorts.

'That's true,' says Niki. 'I don't think the health food shop kind of stuff is a waste of money for everyone. Some people swear by some of them. I've tried a few alternative remedies – white thistle, St John's wort and sage tablets, all from Holland and Barrett – but unfortunately, I tried them all religiously for a year and none of them have worked. For *me*. So I lean more towards the medical side of things. I have actually just found a really nice GP now who is helping me, after I've been swapping around between different GPs at the large surgery I go to. Some of them were just awful, saying I was imagining it. So I'm considering HRT next. I suppose my point is, medical people don't know everything. And not all alternative people are cranks and liars.'

Joy says, 'Agreed, agreed. I think I need to interrogate my own prejudice somewhat. But this alternative stuff definitely hasn't worked for me. My sister-in-law sent a menopause survival kit packed with . . . well, before I met this group, I think I said it was packed with "New Age bullshit". There were vitamin tablets, evening primrose oil, lavender spray for my pillow, face masks, herbal teas. Out of desperation, I tried them. All of them. And none of them worked. I saw my GP who said it would help if I lost weight, then showed me her lunchbox with a salad in it and said that's how I should be eating. As if that was the cure to all my woes. At least she put me on HRT patches but they haven't really worked fully. So now I've started seeing a private gynae. She's put me on oestrogen gel. You put it on your inner thighs, one or two pumps. Do it before bedtime. You'll slop around sounding like a wet fish as it takes ages to dry. Then she's also given me progesterone tablets. You need those as well. So, we'll see how that goes. I'll keep you posted. And if anyone wants her details, I'll put them on the group chat. She's £200 for the first consult, then £150 per consult after that. I know it's pricey. And it's creating a two-tier system where only women with money can access more specialist care, I know that. And it costs a fortune. But alternative practitioners charge a lot of money too. Nothing wrong with yoga though. Yoga is good for everything. It even helps me a bit when I'm feeling low. But if that doesn't change, I'll be seeking out anti-depressants next. I'll take every chemical I can, if it helps. Because that's what we are, human bodies. We're simply chemistry.'

I glance at Rhona again and wonder if she'll launch a counter-attack. But she's looking surprisingly chill. And she speaks up, calmly and reasonably, 'And what people might not know is that lots of medicines are based on plants and things from the natural world. Like aspirin. It comes from willow bark, you know. And morphine comes from poppies.'

'And cocaine from coca leaves,' says Niki. 'I could do with a bit of that some nights after a shit day at work!'

Everyone laughs. Except Cheryl. She's not said a word throughout this whole discussion.

She's actually looking really nervous.

I say quietly, 'Anything to share today, Cheryl? No worries if not.'

She nods and says nervously, 'I'm not that keen on health food stuff. But I think I might've already told everyone I use turmeric and black pepper pills for my joints and they really do work. I'm on HRT patches from my GP and I suppose they're helping some things. I don't get hot flushes. I didn't go on it at first, because my mum comes from that generation where they made a big stink about HRT and breast cancer. But I've read that isn't a thing anymore. So I'm not that worried about it.'

'That did a lot of damage culturally and psychologically,'

says Joy. 'That link between breast cancer and HRT put women off for years.'

Rhona can't help herself and jumps in, 'But HRT isn't natural. It's a toxin!'

'It really is not,' says Joy, shaking her head and looking away.

Oh God, and just when I was congratulating myself on how mature everyone was being at discussing this calmly. Rhona won't let that stand and she raises her voice this time. 'Maybe it is! We don't know! Maybe it's poison!'

Bloody hell. Whatever this group is, I'm determined we're not going to end up like a social media storm. I'm about to intervene when an interruption comes from an unlikely source.

'Can everyone just please *shut up* for a minute??'

It's Cheryl. Yes, quiet, shy Cheryl. There comes that unexpected chutzpah she lets out now and again. We all turn to her, silenced.

'Look, I have something to say.'

She's shaking now.

'Cheryl,' I say quietly and reach out my hand. I don't know why I'm doing that. I just want her to know she's not alone.

'No. I just . . . I just need to say it. Something . . . has happened. I have to tell you. I need . . . I need advice. So . . . last time. Niki said about that cream. For her . . . dryness down there. And I have the same thing. So I took a bit of courage and I made an appointment to see the nurse practitioner. And she had a look and she sat me down and told me. She said, "You're quite raggedy down there." Because I'd had an episiotomy and it was rushed.

And she said, "No, it's not that. You've got lichen sclerosus."
Has anyone ever heard of it? It's called lichen sclerosus.'

Everybody says no and shakes their head. 'Never heard
of it,' I say and others agree.

'And I'd never heard of it either. So this nurse practitioner
goes on Google and shows me these pictures. I mean . . .
they were . . . awful.'

Cheryl puts her hand over her mouth and sobs. I want
to reassure her, but like before, I know she's got this. I
don't need to intervene. She recovers herself and continues.

'There were these photos, of women's genitals that had
. . . well, disappeared. No . . . clitoris. Lips all gone. Then
she said that she'd seen it in lots of women. And we'd
have to do a biopsy to confirm but we didn't need it really
as she knew it was that. Then she said there'd be a phone
call, with the appointment for the biopsy. Then she gave
me a prescription for some steroid cream and said that'll
slow it down, but doesn't cure it. And she sent me away.
So I came home. And I got through the evening, holding
it all in. Then Clive was saying, "What's wrong with you?
You've had a face on all night." And I broke down. And
I told him, about this condition I have. And about the
pictures. And I just sobbed. And he said . . .'

She sobs again.

'He said, "Well, if that happens, you'll be out on your
ear. So you better get it sorted."'

'Fucking hell! Why didn't you tell me, love?' says Rhona.

'Oh, Cheryl,' says Niki.

'I'm so sorry to hear that,' says Joy and reaches across
to put an arm about her, but Cheryl holds her hand up.
She doesn't want anyone near her right now, it seems.

'So,' Cheryl says, visibly trying to control herself. 'I don't know what to do. I just . . . don't know what to do. I need help. Heidi. I . . . Tell me what to do.'

And she looks at me. Nobody is saying anything. I feel like this is my first real test. I told everyone I wasn't an expert. But this is what happens when you offer support. They look up to you. They need an anchor in rough seas. And I have to help this woman and help her now.

'Cheryl, first things first,' I say, calmly. 'We can look into whatever this condition is and we can find out more about it. I bet some if not all of us are expert researchers. We'll find out more. And whatever this nurse says, we don't know for sure yet. She said you need a biopsy, so let's wait for that. I have the utmost respect for nurses, but in this case, for a condition this serious, I'd say you should wait for a doctor to confirm it, maybe even a referral to a specialist. So that's that. But there's something else I feel needs saying. And that's what your husband said. How he responded. What he said, Cheryl. It's not . . . it's not normal behaviour.'

'It really does sound like abuse, Cheryl,' Joy says, sympathetically.

Rhona snaps, clearly desperately wanting to intervene. I can see her rage is building. 'He's a bastard!'

'No, he isn't!' cries Cheryl. 'Don't say that.'

'I've wanted to say it for years, pet. He is a bastard. He's a bully and I'm scared of him.' She turns to all of us. 'I never go round her house these days because I'm scared of him.'

Cheryl looks at me and says emphatically, 'He'd never lay a finger on me!'

Joy says, 'Cheryl, I think it's important to remember that it doesn't have to be physical violence to be threatening. Has he isolated you from your family and friends? Does he text you twenty-four-seven to quiz you about where you are, what you're doing, who you're talking to, are you talking about him? Does he decide whether or not you leave the house? Does he have control of your money? That's coercive control. It's a type of abuse. And people have been prosecuted for it.'

'That's what I told her!' says Rhona. 'She should call the police on him some days! He's a bully, no more, no less. A bloody bully, he is! You don't deserve it, Cheryl – I just want you to be all right.'

Cheryl's eyes are wide open. And she grabs up her handbag and stands abruptly.

'I didn't come here for my husband to be insulted. I won't listen to this.'

Niki says, 'Oh Cheryl, please. We all mean well.'

'I'm not sure you do,' says Cheryl, her bottom lip trembling. 'I think you're all trying to tell me my husband is doing something illegal and that's just ridiculous. I'm not staying to listen to this.'

I stand up and Cheryl flinches and shuffles backwards. I just wanted to go with her to the door, so she knows everything is all right. But I stand stock-still.

'I'm so sorry about this, Cheryl. I promise you, we all want to help.'

Cheryl turns and marches to the door, saying, 'Don't anyone follow me, please!' and is out of it so quickly, the door bangs against the wall behind her.

Chapter 12

Everyone erupts. They're all talking over each other about how rotten Cheryl's husband is and why can't she see it and Rhona is saying she's known her for three years and she's been to her house a few times in the early days and this man is a shit and Joy is talking about narcissistic personality disorder and Niki is saying it sounds a bit like her dad and then laughs nervously and I'm listening, but all I'm thinking about is that poor woman careering down the corridor alone, so alone. We fucked that up, right and proper. Or rather, I fucked it up. I let it become a free-for-all. I should've had more control and kept people in check and made Cheryl feel safe. Suddenly, the awful weight of the responsibility lands on my shoulders, of setting this group up, with no training and no experience. Typical MUFFY, landing me in it, to save their own skins, to make their menopause policy seem shiny, all at my expense. And Cheryl's expense. She should've had a proper counsellor at this group, who knew what to say and what to do. I fucked it up when shit got real. I feel terrible.

'I think it's best if we finish for today,' I say, rather dejectedly. Everyone is saying nice things, that they'll message later on the group chat, see if she's okay. Rhona says she'll go to see her at reception later. Nobody is pointing the finger at me. But that doesn't make me feel any better.

I go back to work and get through the afternoon in my usual manner, scraping through with an exhausted brain. Rhona messages me privately to say that she's looked for Cheryl at reception but she's not there. Cheryl must've gone home. Now I'm really worried. I call Cheryl's number. No answer. I find a spare few minutes and I ask Brenda to accompany me to the loos where hopefully we'll have a bit of privacy and I can ask her what she thinks about it.

'It's all my fault,' I say.

'Don't be daft! You're helping these women no end. You're a bloody hero!'

'But I mishandled it. She felt attacked. She felt cornered. And she defended him.'

'Well yeah, of course she did. We all do. We all feel like it reflects on us when our partner behaves badly. Don't forget my ex was a drunk. Every time she embarrassed herself, I took it personally. That people would think I'd made this awful choice in life and what an idiot I was. It cuts deep, that stuff. It feels like they're criticising you and your choices, when people slag off your other half that way.'

'But we weren't!'

'I know that. We all know that. But you've only had nice partners in your life, really, love. Geoff is salt of the earth. You've not been with abusers. Or addicts. You don't know the guilt that goes with it.'

'Well, you're right, I don't know about that, thank God. But I must do something.'

'Let her stew. She'll reach out when she needs you.'

'What if she doesn't? What if she never comes back to the group?'

'Again, that's her choice. At the very least, she'll have heard some things today that might give her pause for thought. And with any luck, she'll leave the bastard.'

Then, someone comes into the loos and our conflab is over. I thank Brenda, work a few hours more, finish up at my desk and go home. Geoff is there sitting at the kitchen table with Ada, helping her with her maths homework.

'All right, Mrs?' he says, looking up from the sums.

'Hey, Mum,' says Ada. 'Can we have chips for tea? You said chips tonight.'

'She hasn't had her tea yet,' says Geoff. 'She wanted to wait for you at home.'

Ada stays at after-school club and he brings her home usually, after he's finished at his school, then he either keeps her with him in his flat or sometimes they come up here and do homework. I don't mind him being here. He's comfortable. It's just tonight, I could do without any extras. I'm so exhausted. And I'm so worried about Cheryl.

'Yes to chips,' I say and plonk down my work stuff and sigh. 'Yes to anything.' I walk out of the room and sink onto the sofa.

Geoff pops his head round the door.

'I'll get off now?' he says, as a question not a statement.

'Sure,' I say and close my eyes, assuming he's already gone.

'What's happened?' he says, and he's in the room now, looking worried.

'You know me too well.'

'Course I do.'

'Oh, I just fucked up.'

'Again?' he says, with a wry smile on this face. I'd already told him about the ranty email and all that fallout. He thought the menopause support group was a great idea. He even suggested it to his headteacher, that she should set one up at their school.

I smile. 'Well, not on that magnitude. But somehow worse. It feels worse.'

He sits down on the armchair opposite the couch. 'What happened then? Can't be all that bad.'

I tell him what happened with Cheryl, keeping the details vague to protect her privacy.

'That's rough,' he says. 'But how on earth can it be your fault? The only reason this Cheryl was able to say any of this at all was because she had a group of women she trusted to say it to. And the only reason she had that group of women was because you had set it up in the first place. Annnnd . . . the only reason you set it up was because you wrote a marvellous email that called out the truth of centuries-old misogyny in the workplace. So, it's not your fault. It's the patriarchy. Or God. Or just all men. It's probably my fault.'

I laugh. I don't believe in God, but God bless Geoff. He always gets to the heart of things, with that dry humour. He's a good'un, our Geoff.

'Okay, I feel better.'

'Good. Now, put your feet up and I'll ring for two pizza platters from that kebab place. That's got chips in it. And coleslaw. And salad. So it's healthy.'

'Thank you,' I say and close my eyes. We are like an old married couple, me and Geoff. Apart from the fact that we're not married anymore. Or a couple. 'And I'm sorry, Geoff.'

'What are you saying sorry to me for?'

'I don't know . . .' Thoughts are coalescing in my tired brain. 'I just feel . . . I don't know. Maybe it was a mistake, that after we split, you only moved as far as next door.'

'Why on earth would you say that? Look how useful it is, for maths homework and emergency pizza.'

'I know. I just mean . . . you should've started a new life, away from here, met someone new. I mean, close enough to see the kids, obviously. And be with them, all the time. They need us both. Of course. But . . . you know, maybe we've both been in a kind of a time warp. Not moving on. Because it's all so . . . we're so . . . comfortable.'

'You're shattered and you're talking drivel.'

I can't disagree about the first part. But I think he might well be wrong about the second, but I've never actually realised it before, or articulated it. 'Am I though?'

'Probably not. You're pretty wise, Mrs. You don't give yourself enough credit for your wisdom.'

'Thanks,' I say. I'm suddenly so incredibly tired. I know I should be doing things, but my battery is well and truly dead. I close my eyes again. I hear Geoff tapping on his phone, probably going on Just Eat to order the food.

Then my phone starts buzzing insistently in my pocket. I open my eyes and grab it, thinking it might be Cheryl. It is Cheryl.

'Hey, are you okay?'

Geoff looks up from his phone, concerned.

It's Cheryl, I mouth and he nods and goes out to the kitchen.

'Heidi?'

'Yeah, it's me. Are you all right?'

'Yes, I am.'

'I'm so sorry about what happened today, Cheryl.'

'I'm sorry. I'm the one who's sorry. What are you saying sorry for?'

'I don't know. I just felt we upset you.'

'No. It wasn't that. I think I just had a realisation. And I had to get out of there. To think.'

That makes me a feel a smidgeon better. But I'm still very worried about her.

'Where are you now?' I say, instantly feeling that's too intrusive and I shouldn't have said it.

'Well, you'll never guess.'

Oh God, what does that mean? Images from gritty cop shows like *Happy Valley* streak across my addled brain and I'm thinking she's on a bridge or the top of a high rise, looking over the edge into oblivion. And I'm not a trained negotiator and I don't know how to talk someone down from ending it all, for fuck's sake.

'Tell me.'

'I'm sitting in my car in the MUFFY car park.'

Oh, thank Christ for that! Not on a precipice then.

'How long have you been there?' I look at my watch.

It's gone seven. I worked late tonight. Reception closes at five though.

'Well, I went down to Christchurch Meadow, sat there for a couple of hours, watching the longhorn cattle graze. It was peaceful. But then there was a summer shower, so I ran back to the car and drove back here,' says Cheryl. She doesn't sound upset. Actually, she sounds extremely calm.

'Why did you go back to MUFFY?'

'I don't know really. Because it's familiar, I suppose . . . I just can't go home.'

'Why? What's happened?'

'Nothing. And everything. I mean, nothing's actually happened. But in my head, everything has. If that makes sense. I may . . . I think I might never go home again.'

I think our Cheryl might've had an epiphany.

'What do you want to do?'

'I just wondered if you knew about any women's refuges. My mum is in sheltered accommodation. And I don't have any money, you see. He took my card away.'

That almighty arsehole! I always had a bad feeling about this man, from the first time she mentioned him.

I say, 'Do you want to come here?'

'Where are you?'

'At my house. At home. Come over.'

'That'd be a big imposition on you, Heidi.'

'Not at all. Come here, if you want to. I'll text my address.'

'That's too kind.'

'No, it's fine. I've been so worried about you, it'll be a relief to have you here!'

'Only if you're sure.'

'One hundred per cent. You're not going to a bloody refuge. Not on my watch.'

'I don't . . . Clive took my friends away from me, you see. He . . . encouraged me not to have them, I mean. I don't have anyone, not anymore. It's pathetic.'

'No, it's not. Come over and you can tell me about it. If you want to.'

'All right. Thank you. I'll see you soon.'

I text her the address and where to access the front door to our flat. Wow, that's not the evening I expected. But it feels right, somehow. I didn't even stop to think for a moment when I offered. I just knew it was the right thing to do. I message the M&Ms and tell them that Cheryl's all right and she's coming over to mine and not to worry anymore.

I go through to the kitchen and Ada shouts, 'Pizza platters! We're having pizza platters!'

'I know,' I say to Ada and to Geoff, 'Have you ordered them yet?'

'Not yet. We were just haggling over extra mozzarella or stuffed crust.'

'Well, order two more, one for you and one for Cheryl.'

'Ah!' says Geoff. 'Will do!'

Ada asks, 'Who's Cheryl?'

'A very nice lady who needs my help.'

'Can she stay over?' says Ada, accepting and sweet as ever. Such a good kid. 'I can show her The Game.'

'Maybe,' I say. I really don't know the answer to that. But I don't mind either way. I don't want Cheryl going back to that wanker's house.

'Margherita for Cheryl?' says Geoff. 'It's the least controversial pizza.'

'Good plan,' I say and smile gratefully at Geoff.

He adds, 'And I've got another plan. I'll take the little monkey here and we'll have our pizzas chez moi. Then you two can talk freely. Fancy a night at Dad's, you crazy kid?'

'Yay!' cheers Ada and off they go, meeting Pushkin at the front door, begging to come in. Ada picks him up, plonks him on her shoulders and carts him off to her dad's flat next door. Toby and Danyal won't mind. They know Pushkin prefers Ada to any other living being. And I'm glad Ada so often has Pushkin's company. And that I don't have to put up with the hassle of having our own pet, another thing on my interminable list of things to look after.

It doesn't take long for Cheryl to arrive. I've been manically clearing up as the house is a bit of a tip, as per. She rings the bell and I let her in.

We do a bit of small talk in the kitchen about work, and traffic, and the group. Then the doorbell rings and it's Geoff, with the pizzas.

'Is she okay?' he whispers loudly.

'Come in and say hi,' I say. 'You're not the pizza delivery boy.'

He comes in and Cheryl stands up nervously, pulling her jacket lapels together.

'This is Geoff. He's got Ada next door, so we can have a bit of peace.'

'Nice to meet you,' he says, still holding the pizzas. He puts them down on the table, looks at his hand and wipes it on his shirt and stares at his shirt a moment, looking for pizza box grease, then holds his hand out to Cheryl. What a charmer.

'And you,' says Cheryl, shaking his hand gingerly. She's probably experiencing the pizza box grease now too.

'Listen,' says Geoff, talking to me but looking at Cheryl. 'I mean, erm . . . Heidi, I'll have Ada for the night. She can stay over at mine.'

'That's a good idea,' I say.

'I don't want to be any trouble?' says Cheryl, glancing at Geoff.

'Not at all,' says Geoff. 'It really is the epitome of no trouble. Oh damn, Heidi, forgot to say – I can't take little'un to school tomorrow as my exhaust fell off the bloody Honda.'

'Okay, no worries. What a pain though.'

'Honda Jazz?' says Cheryl.

'Yes!' says Geoff. 'Good guess.'

'Oh, their exhausts always fall off. It's a design fault. Hondas are usually so reliable, except in this regard.'

'I heard that too,' replies Geoff. 'That's why I bought one. But I'd much rather have an Audi TT.'

'Or an Aston Martin DB12,' says Cheryl.

'Bloody hell, yes! Not on a teacher's wage though.'

'Or a receptionist's!'

Everyone stands there, as the moments tick by.

'Ada doesn't like cold pizza much,' I say.

'Ah yes, indeed. I'll be off. Nice to meet you, Cheryl,' says Geoff again and off he goes. So, Cheryl is into cars. Another mildly surprising fact about her.

We eat the pizzas at the kitchen table. I feel rather self-conscious about smothering my fries in ketchup, because my family always tease me about it and Geoff calls me a philistine, and I wonder if it looks weird to Cheryl, but I think she has other things on her mind.

We're eating in silence, me mostly because I'm embarrassed and also too tired to make small talk, and Cheryl because she seems to be in another world, chewing away slowly, her eyes distracted by thought.

Suddenly she says, 'That was very clever of you, choosing margherita pizza. Because everyone likes margherita.'

'Ah, that was Geoff.'

'Your neighbour?'

'Oh God, no. I mean, yes, he is. But he's also my husband. I mean, he was. He's my ex.'

'I'm confused,' says Cheryl and we laugh.

I explain it all.

'What a nice set-up.'

'Only if you have a good ex. And he was. I mean, he is. A good man.'

'I can't imagine that,' says Cheryl, chewing thoughtfully again.

'What, living next door to your ex?'

'No, having a good man.'

I don't know what to say. Maybe I'll just wait. So I do. And when she's ready, Cheryl starts talking. And she talks. And talks. We're at that kitchen table until gone 11pm.

I couldn't possibly explain every word she said. It was nearly three hours of detail. She told me about the last twenty years of her life. About Clive, and how he systematically removed the person she used to be. Whittled her down to the slave she is now. That's the word she used, *slave*. Classic coercive control. Subtly undermining her family, her friends, her colleagues, over years. Until she had none anymore. Instigated competition between her and her daughter, until her daughter left home, unable to stand it anymore. And Cheryl doesn't see her much, because she doesn't want to come home. So she sees her secretly and doesn't tell Clive. Sees her own daughter secretly. And she tells me how she hasn't had her own bank account for about fifteen years. How all the money is managed by him, through a joint account. How he gives her her card sometimes and takes it away to punish her, if she hasn't cooked his steak right or if she's more than ten minutes late home from work. And so it goes on, the myriad tiny ways he undermines her every day, every day for decades, until there's hardly any Cheryl left, whittled down as she is, to a splinter. That's her word for it, a splinter. This wonderful woman, with this interesting mind, and overwhelming love for her daughter, and so much to say and do in the world. And he's nearly ended her.

'Well, not any longer,' I say.

'Yes,' she says without conviction.

'Having doubts?'

'No,' she says, also without conviction. I think the truth is she's just bloody tired.

'Maybe it's time for bed.'

'I'm not going back,' she says suddenly, focusing her eyes intently on mine. 'I'm never going back.'

'Good,' I say and take her hand and squeeze it. She lets me, though she's stiff. I feel like she doesn't get a soft touch from anyone these days and she doesn't know what to do with it. 'But we won't let him keep your home. It's your home too. And we'll work it out, legally. And you can stay here until we do.'

'All right,' she says, utterly acquiescent. 'But, what about my . . . vagina?'

I'd forgotten about that.

'Look, I don't think your fanny is going to disappear. Or if there's any chance it might, there must be treatment. There will be. We'll find out. One thing I've learnt over the years is not to trust every medical professional you speak to. Sometimes they're wrong. Sometimes they lie. An A & E doctor told me once that morphine tablets took a day or more to start working – and no, not the slow-release ones, the other ones, that should kick in after about an hour. Bloody liar. He just wanted to kick us out of A & E. And this nurse, she might not be qualified to make that diagnosis. And she clearly has the bedside manner of Sweeney Todd. So don't listen to her. Get a second opinion. We'll sort it, get you another doctor. Maybe Joy's private one. Together, the M&Ms will sort it.'

Cheryl looks exhausted. I am too. I suddenly remember when I was looking at that list of menopause symptoms and they scared me, that vaginal atrophy was on the list. Maybe that means this. I still think we need to do proper research on this and get Cheryl a proper specialist. I'll get on to Joy about that in the morning.

Cheryl just nods, then says, 'Can I bunk down on your sofa?'

'I can do better than that. My eldest Carly's away on the Algarve with her boyfriend. You can have her room. I'll change the sheets.'

'Please don't. I don't care. I'm sure they're clean enough. I just need to sleep, very badly.'

'All right then. Follow me.'

'Lead on, Macduff,' she says. The more I hear from her, the more I like her. Geoff would like her too. She has his turn of phrase; now she's more herself, I can hear it. She has dry wit. And his peacefulness.

I take Cheryl upstairs, showing her where the bathroom is on the way.

'I'll put a new toothbrush in there for you and a towel.'

'Thank you,' she says in a small voice. She looks like she might curl up on the stairs; she looks all in.

I take her up to Carly's floor and she sits down on Carly's bed, pushing her shoes off while I'm still in there, so I wish her goodnight and pull the door to. I go downstairs and put the pizza detritus in a bin bag and take it outside to the wheelie bins. Toby's out there too and we pull our bins down to the kerbside together for collection tomorrow morning. We start chatting about work, Toby telling me Danyal is on nights this week and he's on days, so they've barely seen each other.

'But at least it means I can catch up with my rewatch of *The West Wing*. He says it's old as fuck. I say just because something comes from twenty years ago, doesn't mean it's shit. Thus I can wallow in it to my heart's content when he's on nights. So hospital shift work has something to recommend itself.'

And that reminds me that, of course, he's a nurse and maybe, just maybe, he might be able to help me with something.

'Can I ask you a quick medical question? I know it's a pain when people say that, asking for free advice when you're not at work. But it's not for me.'

'Course, honey. Anytime. It can be for you, if you want.'

'Thanks. It's a friend. She's staying with me tonight – I won't go into it all, but suffice to say she's crashing at ours for a bit. Well, it's . . . a bit embarrassing.'

'Hey, I'm a nurse. I am bulletproof when it comes to embarrassment. Fire away.'

I explain to him all about Cheryl's run-in with the nurse practitioner and the diagnosis of lichen sclerosus.

'Have you heard of it?' I ask him.

'I have. But it's not something I have any expertise in at all.'

'Well, yes, this is what I was wondering. Surely she'd need to see a doctor about it as well. Or even a specialist.'

'Absolutely. Some of these nurse practitioners get a bit uppity in the face of doctor snobbery and start thinking they can diagnose conditions, which they can't necessarily. Don't get me wrong, we do see a lot and we have our roles which are utterly essential. But we aren't doctors and should never be afraid to be clear when we need a doctor's advice. I'd say a condition like that would need diagnosing by a gynae consultant. She should ask her GP to refer her. And please do tell her not to be embarrassed – it sounds like she's going through a really tough time and any medical professional worth their salt will empathise.'

'Brilliant. That's what I think. Thanks so much.'

Toby says, 'No worries,' and pushes his fingers through his grey quiff. He looks pretty tired. I feel bad for bothering him off-duty.

'Sorry to ask you late at night. You must be shattered.'

'No, it's not that. Just . . . we had another adoption fall through, just this morning.'

'Oh Tobe, I'm so sorry. Not another one.'

'Yeah, the mum is back on the scene, so it's all been postponed, probably indefinitely. This is our third non-starter and we're starting to feel it'll never happen, you know?'

'Keep the faith,' I say. 'If anyone in the world was meant to be parents, it's you and Danyal. You two have so much love to give. Don't give up.'

'Thanks, honey,' he says and smiles, ruefully.

'And thank you, for the advice.'

'Any time.'

Bless him. I don't know what I did in a former life to have such nice neighbours. Neighbours who've become friends. I feel very lucky.

Back inside, I pause at the bottom of the stairs to hear if Cheryl is stirring and needs anything, but there's not a peep from her. She doesn't come down at all while I'm pottering about, clearing up the kitchen, fetching a towel and toothbrush for Cheryl and sorting my work stuff for tomorrow. I think she fell straight to sleep. She needed that. She needed us. She needed me. And I feel so grateful I could be there for her. I mean, I'm fucking tired. I really am, absolutely drained of everything. I feel like I could sleep for a month. But helping Cheryl has changed something in me. I feel, for the first time in a long time, maybe in years, that I'm a good person. It sounds daft, because I'm a good mum and I always try to help my friends and family when I can, but I've felt so disgruntled with my life for so long, that I've come to see myself as an ungrateful, awful cow. Who should be thankful. Who shouldn't be so selfish. And I've beaten myself up for being so selfish. But tonight, I helped another human being. And it felt bloody good to be able to do that. To get out of my own damn head for a while. So, thanks, Cheryl, for trusting me. And thanks, M&Ms, for making it happen.

I crawl into bed. I look on the group chat and find all the messages from earlier, about Cheryl coming to mine, and how lovely everyone is, saying how happy they are to hear that and sending love. What a lovely bunch of women they are. We are. I'm about to turn my phone off, when a message pops up from Nate. And I'm about to click on it when I think, you know what, I really can't be arsed with a rock god tonight. I switch off my phone. And instantly fall into a deep, dreamless sleep.

Chapter 13

It's mid-July and nearly time for our fourth group session. Today's topic is support networks. I can't believe two weeks has flown by that fast. And what we've accomplished in two weeks is fantastic, I think. Cheryl is now living with Joy! She stayed at mine a few days, helped out around the house a lot, especially with Ada who she got on really well with. Geoff came round and he and Cheryl continued their long chats about cars, which bore me to tears, but it was nice to see someone put up with his endless interest in engines. Cheryl really has been the ideal house guest, but Carly was coming back from Portugal soon, and though she could've stayed with Matt for a while, she doesn't exactly get on great with his parents – they're not as laid back as we are and it's all take your shoes off and sit up at the table for dinner and no phones in company, which makes her feel about twelve. So yes, Carly would've stayed there under duress, but I didn't want her to have to do that. I didn't tell Cheryl this, but she already felt bad about overstaying her welcome, despite my protestations. However, the truth is, once Cheryl had gone to Joy's, I did breathe a sigh of relief. Nothing against Cheryl, but I'm so used to my own space. It's been six years of just me and my girls and it was weird having someone else in the house. We couldn't just wander around in our bra and pants anymore. Plus, the truth is, these two weeks have been harder than usual because my menopause symptoms are getting worse. I thought at first it was just because we had a house guest, but once Cheryl had gone I realised it wasn't just that. My anxiety is through the roof some days. I get this inner voice commenting horribly on everything I do, asking what if this happens and what if that happens and what are you gonna do?? Going on and on in my head, like a constant crazy narrative. Plus I'm getting migraines, which I haven't had since my teenage years. I'm really struggling. I've been chatting with Nate and Luke as usual, but not half as much. I've left them both on read far too many times. I just don't have the energy for flirting or reminiscing. It's all too much. Ada is still very needy, though she and Ruby have made up. I feel like I'm on a damn carousel again and I have to step off or I'll lose my mind . . . But it's nothing compared to what Cheryl is going through, so I park it. I have to just get on with life and make sure everyone else is okay. That's my job as a mum, and it's also quite literally my job as the leader of the M&Ms, too.

The day after Cheryl arrived at mine, Niki lent Cheryl some clothes for the first few days, as they have similar sizing (though Cheryl did tell me she was still wearing the same bra she left home in as Niki's bras were about four sizes too big for her, now Niki's boobs have expanded exponentially!). Rhona went with Cheryl at lunchtime one day to go to her house and pick up some clothes and toiletries and anything else she could get out of the house quickly. They were both terrified Clive would show up. Anyway, they managed it and a good job too, as he told her the very next day he was getting the locks changed, the bastard. Joy has been amazing. She's given Cheryl a spare bedroom in her house and said she can stay as long as she likes. She has also made an appointment for Cheryl with not only her divorce lawyer, but also an urgent appointment with her private gynaecologist, who Cheryl saw this morning, so we're all agog to hear what happened.

We're sitting in our usual room and Cheryl's brought flapjacks today, which we're all munching on (also sparking Rhona's idea that we ought to start taking turns bringing snacks, an issue on which there is 100 per cent group agreement, for once). We're all listening intently to every word from Cheryl. She looks transformed. She looks confident. Still quietly spoken, but centred, somehow. For the first time in our group, Cheryl actually asks to go first.

'Joy's doctor was lovely. Very kind and down-to-earth. She examined me and she just said simply, "You haven't got it."'

'What, haven't got the lichen sclerosus??' I ask.

'Yes, she says I don't have it.'

Everybody cheers! Oh crikey, what a relief. I'd done some research on the condition over the past two weeks. It looked pretty awful, though it can be managed with steroids and other treatments for some, it seems. I don't know enough about it to comment really, but it certainly didn't look like an easy condition to cope with for anyone. My heart goes out to anyone dealing with this right now, woman or man, and hope they get the right treatment.

'She said the nurse who diagnosed it should be ashamed of herself.'

'Absolutely!' says Rhona. 'Bloody stupid woman!'

'She certainly should not be making serious diagnoses like these so flippantly without the proper evidence,' I say.

Rhona adds, 'And now you see why I don't trust doctors? Why I'd rather treat myself most of the time?'

Nobody replies to that immediately, not even Joy. In fact, Joy's usual remonstration is conspicuous by its absence.

'Do you know what, Rhona?' I say. 'I am starting to understand that now. I think I was brought up to trust anyone in a medical uniform. Now I'm not so sure.'

Joy says, 'Agreed, agreed.' That's her version of a kind of apology, I think, for always questioning Rhona's remedies. 'There are good and bad medics, just like in every walk of life. But the bad ones can be damaging.'

'Absolutely,' I agree. Then realise Cheryl was mid-way through her account and we've gone off on one, as usual. 'Anyway, sorry, Cheryl! We've hijacked your story! Please tell us everything that happened.'

'No, it's fine. That's the headline anyway. She was very helpful and prescribed me a special cream with oestrogen in it that will hopefully solve the dryness. It's a private prescription so it's expensive, but I have some savings, so I'll use those for the moment. She's also changed my HRT to two weeks of oestrogen, followed by two weeks of progesterone, so I'm going to try that for a while.'

Niki asks, 'Can you get the cream via your GP after this?' I realise Niki has been very quiet today. I hope she's okay.

'No, unfortunately not. You can't get this particular cream on the NHS.'

'But you can get Viagra over the counter!' says Joy, with disgust.

'True!' I say. I glance at Niki while we're talking. She looks really . . . I'm not sure, but the word that springs to mind is, sad. She just looks so sad. I'll keep an eye on her. I remind everyone that today's topic is support networks.

Cheryl says, 'Just to finish off my bit, I'd have to say my greatest support network right now is you lot. I can't believe how much you've helped me, after knowing you all such a short time. I just want to say thank you. Thank you so much.'

Everyone says nice things and nods and smiles. It's an extraordinary thing that's happening here. Of course, Cheryl has a long way to go with her treatments and her marriage situation. But she's made massive strides already, with the M&Ms' help. Then it's Rhona's turn. She talks about her husband.

'My husband Joe does his own research for me and leaves these print-outs on my bedside table. And tries to do the housework when I'm too tired, you know. But he doesn't do it the way I like, so I stop him. So he said why don't we splash out and get a cleaner of our own? But I wouldn't do that. Never. I don't trust anyone else. To do my house the way I like it, you know. Anyway, he meant well. He does lots of stuff round the house. He gives me back rubs and feet massages. Neither of us are lookers, but we like each other best. Joe is so good to me. I don't deserve him.'

'Of course you deserve him,' says Joy. 'We all deserve to be treated with kindness.'

'That's very true,' says Rhona and nods at Joy. Do we have agreement between these two, twice in one session?! That's progress indeed.

'Niki, would you like to go next?' As I'm saying it, I'm already worried I shouldn't have, as she's looking so down still. And I can see by her eyes looking up that I was right. She's in no fit state.

'Maybe Joy next,' she says quietly. It's not like her. Everyone is alerted. After only a few weeks, we've got so used to each other's vibes, we all know when they're off.

'Okay,' says Joy, smoothing it over, so Niki doesn't feel embarrassed. 'Well, my support network. Truth is, I honestly don't have much of one. My parents are long since passed and my boys live all over the world with their babies, so I don't see them much. I live alone. I'd say my friends and colleagues are my main one. But I wouldn't dream of imposing on them much. They all have their own drama going on, as we all do. We have group chats, like the M&Ms one, and that helps me. We sit in Teams meetings online sometimes and message each other about the other people on the call, making droll comments. One day we'll get caught out and message the wrong group for sure! It's fun though. It keeps me smiling. But anyway. That's enough about me. I'm all right. I lump along and get on with it. To be honest, I'm far more concerned with Niki today. Something's not right. Sorry to put you on the spot, but I am worried about you, Niki.'

Niki looks up, surprised, and her eyes are unmistakably shining with tears.

'Oh, honestly, I'm fine. I'm just having a bad day. Really. Sorry.'

'If you're not feeling great, why not just go home, eh?' I say. 'I can call your line manager, let them know.'

'Oh no, it's nothing like that. Nothing physical. I don't know why. I just . . . I'm just very sad recently. It's such a small word "sad", isn't it? But it feels like a big thing. When you're feeling it.'

'Of course, love,' says Joy. 'Maybe it'd help to talk about it.'

'I can do . . . I can do. Well, it all seems silly compared to what Cheryl's going through, what you're all going through. Sounds like life gets harder as you get older, not easier, like I thought it would. I feel like the rookie complaining about stuff here. You all have kids and . . . other stuff . . . and I don't have all that.'

'Niki, everyone has their own shit to deal with,' I say. 'And your problems are no less a problem than anyone else's in this room. We're here to listen to everyone's, right?'

Everyone agrees.

'Well, all right then. But it isn't so much to do with menopause, sorry. I mean, it is. But also other stuff. So, yeah, well. My dad. So I think I said we lost Mum when I was little. I was nine. Cancer. It's just been me and my older brother and Dad since then. And the rest of the family. I have a big extended Greek family. My dad runs a Greek restaurant in Oxford.'

I'd really like to know which one, because I went to a fabulous one once with Brenda and Kim, on one of my few outings. But of course, I don't want to interrupt Niki's story.

'So my family is very keen on . . . well, on family. Everyone's got kids. My brother and his wife have five now. Five kids! And we have these big get-togethers and we cook and the kids all play. So I got married in my twenties. And we started trying for a baby straight away, more or less. We both wanted kids. And nothing happened for a year or so. And we were starting to get worried. And then I got pregnant. And we were so happy! To be normal. And then I had an early miscarriage, eight weeks. And we got pregnant again. And another miscarriage, again at eight weeks. And so it went on. I had five miscarriages, all before twelve weeks. One got to eleven and we thought we'd cracked it. But no, it didn't take. And Kel said – that was my husband, Kelvin – he said to give it a break for a while. So we did, for a year. And then I couldn't wait anymore. I wanted to try again. And then I didn't get my period. And I was excited, but scared, like before. So I did a test and it was negative. And this went on with my periods. All over the place for about two years. So many negative pregnancy tests. Just . . . soul-destroying. And, well, you know after that. I saw my doctor and they did some tests. And they confirmed, it was early menopause. I couldn't believe it. I mean, after everything we'd gone through. It felt like . . . like my body was cursed. Like it didn't want me to be a mother. Like it knew something I didn't know, that I was destined to be a terrible mother or something. That's how it felt. Well, I felt even more desperate then. We carried on, me and Kel, for a while, trying to get pregnant before perimenopause finished, because I found out you can get pregnant in perimenopause. I mean, the chances are really, really low. But it's not impossible. And I knew this was my absolute last chance. And Kel went along with it, for a bit. But his heart wasn't in it. And eventually, he just said, *I'm done*. And we realised that there wasn't really anything else keeping us together, like the baby thing had been this glue that stuck us together for years and then it was like all that . . . just dissolved away. And we were left with nothing. I suppose we were broken really. Broken by it all. And we were too tired . . . and sad . . . to fix it. So, we split up three years ago. And we sold the house, both bought flats. And I've been alone since then. And well, my dad. He never really understood. He was impatient, for grandchildren from his only daughter. And I couldn't give him any. I found out only last year that my mum had had quite a few miscarriages too, though they never told me. My mum's cousin told me. So yeah, we still have these big family gatherings. And all my cousins and aunties are there and my brother and his wife, and they all have children and grandchildren. And I'm the only one. The only one in the whole family who's single and who's . . . you know, childless. And I always will be now. I haven't had a period for a long while. I'm in full menopause. So my chance has gone. And some days I'm okay with that. And it's like my identity and that's okay, because there's work and travel and other things. I went to New Zealand last year. Canada the year before. I can do this stuff, because I don't have a husband or kids to worry about. But you know, I'd rather have all the worries in the world about my husband and kids than travel the whole world, you know? Then yesterday, I saw on

Facebook that Kel – he married again, last year – and I saw . . . his wife. She's pregnant. Already. Big beaming picture of her and him and her big belly. I don't even know why we're still friends on Facebook really. I wish I'd never seen it. I wish . . . I don't know. I don't know what I wish. Because wishes are pointless, aren't they? Wishes never, ever work. Anyway, sorry for going on.'

Oh God, it's heartbreaking. She looks too tired to cry. She just looks drained of everything. This beautiful, young woman, with her life ahead of her – what I'd give to be thirty-six again – and she just looks hollow.

'Oh Niki,' I say and so do Rhona and Cheryl, simultaneously.

'Please don't be nice to me because it'll set me off!' says Niki, sort of laughing, but there's a little sob in it too. But she draws herself in and won't let it come. I get that. I hate crying in front of people. Detest it. 'And there's nothing anyone can say, I know that. And I've kind of come to terms with the baby thing, a while ago really. It is what it is. But the thing with my family, and my dad. That's there all the time. Like, I just feel this weight of disappointment in his eyes when he looks at me. He was never that warm with me. Something died in him when my mum went. He did his best, I suppose. But he was always a bit cold, a bit hold-you-at-arm's-length. Like, he's snappy with me all the time, especially at these family get-togethers. Like he's embarrassed of me. And there's my brother, who's not only got five kids but is a solicitor as well . . . and I feel like the loser of the family. Because I'm . . . barren. God, I hate that word. But it's true. I'm barren. I'm the odd one out, wherever I go. Even here. And the

M&Ms is the best thing to happen to me in ages. But even here, I feel like the odd one out because I'm younger. I'm always . . . different. Like I feel nobody gets it. Nobody knows what it's like to be me. And that makes me feel, you know, so alone. So lonely. I'm just so very, very lonely. And that's the worst feeling in the world. Or one of them, maybe. I just don't feel like anyone understands. I wish I could meet someone who felt the same way as me.'

'Oh darling,' I say and honestly, I could sob with her. She's right about loneliness. It's a killer, it really is. 'Of course, we can't know what it's like to be you. Nobody can. But I know I can identify with the brother thing. And cold parents. Mine are both that way, no empathy really. And my brother is the golden child who can do no wrong. And he has five kids too! It does get lonely sometimes, feeling like everything you are and everything you do disappoints your family. I totally get that.'

'Thanks. It does help, actually, knowing you're not the only one.' We all smile at Niki but don't pry further, rather we all just give her the space in case she wants to keep talking.

'I want to say too that Joy has really helped me with this. We've been messaging about loneliness and she's been there for me, even really late at night. She really understands loneliness, like nobody I've ever talked to. I just wanted to say thanks to Joy.'

'It's nothing,' says Joy, quietly, with a small smile.

'It's not nothing,' replies Niki. 'I just hope I've helped you too, Joy. In a small way.'

Joy looks up, usually so self-assured, so content with herself. And there's a look in her eyes, of utter vulnerability. It takes my breath away.

'You have, love. You have no idea. I . . . don't talk about these things much. Seems . . . mawkish. And self-indulgent.'

Rhona says, 'That's what we're here for though, isn't it? To share that stuff. To listen.' She smiles at Joy and Joy smiles back.

'Well, Niki's right. I do know loneliness very well,' says Joy. 'I lost my mum too, when I was five. And my dad two years before that even, when I was three. My dad was cancer too. And my mum, well, they said it was a car accident. I've never known if she meant to do it. I don't know. I have no memories of him and fleeting memories of her, of home in Nigeria. And I came to the UK aged five and was raised here by my aunt. She had three kids already and I knew I wasn't wanted. I left everything I knew and became a British kid. I lost my accent, lost my identity. I had to fit in to survive, so I did. The family went through the motions of making me a part of their lives. But there were these micro-aggressions always, every day, little comments or movements that made it clear to me constantly, that I was a cuckoo in the nest. I married young and had three boys in quick succession. I needed to make my own family. And I raised them to be strong and dynamic. But they're so much that way, they all buggered off across the world! Sometimes I wish I had a daughter, as they tend to come home more, don't they? My sons rarely visit. Once a year, if I'm lucky. And I have two grandchildren too, in Nigeria. And I go to see them when I can. And they have the life there I wish I'd had, but was stolen from me. It's just me at home, rattling about in that big house. I divorced my ex when the boys were young. He was a hopeless father, just not interested. Not cruel, just indifferent. And I wasn't going to have that around my sons, not that coldness. Never that. So it was just me and them. And now it's just me. It's actually really nice to have you staying, Cheryl. I'm a proud woman, you can probably tell. But I'm not too proud to admit I've been lonely for years. I put on a good show, but I know how it feels to be alone, Niki. Not the same situation as you, of course. But loneliness eats you up inside. It's deadly.'

'Joy, I'm so sorry about your parents,' says Niki and reaches across and squeezes Joy's hand. Then she turns to me. 'And about your parents too, in a different way. That coldness is horrible, isn't it? I just can't understand how people can be cold towards people they're supposed to love.'

'Niki, aren't you lovely?' I say, marvelling at this young woman. 'Look at the way you reach out to others. And Joy, the same. All of us. In our own ways, putting others first and leaving ourselves till last. All of us have been through our own versions of hell. Absolute hell. And those who should've been there for you, Niki, and held you, and helped you through it, have let you down badly. But for what it's worth, you do have us. You do have the M&Ms. And we do get you. We can't know how it is to be you. But we care. And we want you to know that you are not alone. Never.'

'Absolutely, love,' says Rhona and she gets up and goes to Niki, who looks up at her, alarmed. 'Stand up, love,' adds Rhona, standing there solidly. Niki gets up slowly and Rhona puts her arms out and folds Niki into her.

And Niki is awkward at first – we all are, watching this. It's so out of character from what we've seen of Rhona. But I wonder if Rhona's rage may well have only come along with menopause and perhaps this is a glimpse of the softer side of Rhona, the real her. Then Niki just starts to sob. And Rhona holds her tight and Niki is really crying now, letting it all out on Rhona's shoulder. The rest of us just wait silently, patiently. We can wait all day, if it's necessary. Fuck the toad work.

Eventually, Rhona lets go and pulls a hankie out of her pocket and gives it to Niki. Who carries a clean hankie around, these days?! Well, Rhona does. And while Niki is cleaning up her face, Rhona says, 'We're not all mums in here. And I'm fine with that, always have been. But for you, Niki, that hurts, I know. But, you know, that means you've also got four surrogate mums in here, to look out for you.'

Cheryl adds, 'Exactly. We all want you to be okay, just like we would our own kids, whether we've got them or not. So you're not alone, Niki. Not anymore.'

'Thank you,' says Niki, sniffling. Good old Rhona and Cheryl, saying just the right thing at the right time. These women constantly surprise me. 'Thank you so much, to everyone. And sorry I hijacked the group a bit.'

I think Rhona is going to sit down, but she doesn't. She steps over to where Joy is sitting with her arms folded over her chest.

Joy looks up at Rhona and says, 'What?'

'You need a hug too, love.'

Joy laughs, looking horrified. 'I assure you I don't!'

'I know when someone needs a hug,' insists Rhona, not budging. 'And that's you.'

Joy crosses her arms even tighter, if that's possible, and glances at me as if to say, *Get me out of this!*

I'm about to say to Rhona something along the lines of that's very kind but we can't force hugs on people blah blah, when Niki says, 'Oh, go on, Joy. Rhona gives good hug!'

'I can testify to that!' chimes in Cheryl. Oh blimey, there's social pressure heaping on Joy now to take the hug. I feel like I should intervene, but again, I remember that these are grown women and they can look out for themselves, especially the indomitable Joy!

She raises her eyes to the ceiling and says, 'Oh, for heaven's sake, all right then. But I'm about a foot taller than you and we'll look ridiculous!'

Rhona says, 'I don't care!' and puts her arms out. It's an awkward hug. They fit about as well as a stork and a puffin, but the hug is achieved and though it seemed highly unlikely seconds ago, it actually lasts longer than any of us think it will. Joy seems to sink into it somewhat as it goes on. Maybe it's been a long while since she's had a hug.

Thankfully, Rhona doesn't offer me a hug. Nothing against Rhona. But I suspect Joy is like me and is not made for hugs. Not with anyone outside the close family anyway. But Rhona has put herself out there today by showing that softer side to herself and I admire her for that. I thank her when we're putting the chairs away. She beams, seeming genuinely delighted. 'I don't have much to give, but I give what I can,' she says. 'You know.'

'I know, Rhona.'

* * *

That night, I get another migraine and I spend an hour in my bedroom in the dark, waiting for the bastard thing to pass. And once I'm feeling less sick and the pain subsides, I lie there and look back on my day. I'm considering yet another incredible M&Ms session, where again we saw into the depths of somebody's soul, perhaps two, with Joy's confessions as well. And I realise that I shared very little about myself. I mean, it wasn't the right time, with Niki's crisis today. But the truth is I'm really bloody struggling. And I'm doing nothing about it. I'm doing all this stuff for other people – and that's my comfort zone, doing that stuff. It keeps my mind busy and stops me overthinking about my life. I feel responsible for so many things – at work, at home – and now all these extra people in my life too. Four new souls for me to shepherd. And I have to be all in with them, because they're suffering. I reached out to them. I didn't even want to. I never wanted to be a group leader in a million years. And now I'm stuck with them, bless their hearts. I'm happy to do it, because I care about them already, deeply. I feel utterly obliged to look after them all. But what about me? Who is there to look after me and just me?

Chapter 14

The truth is, nobody is there to look after little old me, really. I know I sound like a Moaning Minnie (that's what my mum would call it anyway) but I actually mean it, literally. Brenda and Kim are going through their own problems, as Kim's mum died the other week and they're over in Vietnam right now sorting out her estate and so forth. I still can't find it within me to impose on my kids with my problems, even Carly, though she offers often. It's just not in me to reach out to them. It feels all topsy-turvy and I just can't do it. I won't trouble Geoff with it. He's my ex and though we share a lot with the kids, I've drawn the demarcation line very clearly between us when it comes to personal stuff. I have the M&Ms, of course, and I've made a big show about how we're all there for each other. I do mean that, absolutely – but I've not yet applied it to myself. I haven't reached out to the group for anything. I haven't even shared much about myself these past couple of sessions. I've been so caught up with the others. And, rightly or wrongly, nobody's noticed that I haven't either. And I'm okay with that as, whether I like it or not, I am the group's leader and that means that I have to be the strong one, corralling the others and making sure they're all right first. And they are not all right, any of them. They all need so much. Why should I heap my problems onto theirs as well? My other confidante I've spoken to in the past is my neighbour Alia. She's a wonderful woman, really kind and generous. But she's got three kids and runs her own publishing business, so she's got more than enough on her sizeable plate. She doesn't have time to deal with all my crap. I just need to get on with it.

But this week is tough. Firstly, Geoff takes me aside one evening and tells me that he'd like to ask Cheryl out on a date and am I okay with that? I tell him, *Absolutely. I think it's a great idea.* And it is. I worry that Cheryl might not want to date again so soon after getting out of a miserable relationship, but to be honest, if anyone can help restore her faith in men again, it's Geoff. Shortly after, I get a message from Cheryl, just to me. She says Geoff has asked her out on a date. And she would like to go but she wanted to check with me first, that I'm okay with it. I absolutely assure her I am. I think it's sweet that they've both sort of asked my permission first. But also, there's a small part of me that feels lonesome. That feels . . . yes, a tiny bit jealous. Look, I know I don't want Geoff anymore, not in that way. And I've told him he should've found someone else by now and he tells me the same thing. But now it's happening, it feels . . . weird. I've got my own intrigues going on, of course . . . but it still feels weird.

I tell myself, *Get over it. You're happy for them.* And I am. It just adds a little grain of envy in the pit of my stomach somewhere and I don't like that feeling. It's as if another jigsaw piece in my support network has moved, ever so slightly, out of place. I know Geoff will always be there for me, as the mother of his kids. But now there's a possibility he might find love elsewhere . . . I truly want that for him. But at the same time, I feel the loss in that small shift away from me. I'll get used to it though.

Then I have another migraine mid-week, plus a bout of diarrhoea the next day, and by Friday I am dead on my feet. I'm coming home from work and I bump into Alia when we've parked right next to each other on the street. She's with seventeen-year-old Sienna, whose eyes are glued to her phone, as per.

'Where's the rest of the brood?' I say, as we walk down the pavement towards the house.

'At their Nanoo's, thank fucking God! I'm sick of 'em, the little creeps!'

'I'm not a creep!' objects Sienna, eyes off her phone now and searingly indignant.

'I didn't say you were. You're my good girl. It's the boys who are creeps.' Then, as Sienna goes off up the path to their front door, Alia turns to me and, lowering her voice, she adds, 'Course, when the lads are around, I tell 'em they're my dear uncomplicated boys and not a total fucking hormonal nightmare like their sis!'

Oh God, Alia makes me laugh. And I do laugh. I'm laughing and then in a split second it turns into sobbing and I'm standing on the pavement with both hands weighed down by work bags and Co-op bags and I'm sobbing my heart out. And then my handbag falls off my shoulder and thwacks onto the ground and that's the last bloody straw and I sob even harder.

I glance up at Sienna by their front door, staring at me. Oh God, how humiliating.

'Fucking hell, babe!' says Alia. 'Let's get you inside. Come to mine.'

'Won't Sienna mind?'

'It'll be good for her, to see that adults don't have their shit together any more than teens. Come on.'

I acquiesce, snivelling as I follow her to her flat.

'Is Rich in?' I say, whimpering. I really don't want him to see my meltdown. For a start, I'm embarrassed, but also he'll tell Geoff because they're mates and I don't want Geoff to know. I don't want him to reach out to help me because I know I'll take it and I can't. I just can't rely on my ex again, not after all these years. I don't want to reach out to him when he's just started seeing someone new for the first time in six years. He might think I'm jealous or trying to get in the way. Which I absolutely am not. So I don't want Rich to be there.

'Nah, he's at the golf club. Or the fucking Freemasons, I dunno what weird bloke shit he gets up to.'

'Alia, you crack me up! Thank God for you!'

'Come on, lovely. Follow me into the breach.'

The flat is littered with kids' toys and discarded hoodies and hair scrunchies and piles of papers everywhere. It's utter chaos. But it's happy chaos. We go into the kitchen and Sienna makes me a mint tea with a big glug of honey in it, while Alia pours herself a huge glass of red wine. Crikey, I envy her that. I'm almost prepared to put up with the ensuing squits that red would give me, but not quite.

Sienna says, 'I'm sorry you're all sad and that.'

'Thanks, love,' I say and Sienna slopes off upstairs. 'She's a good kid.'

I sip on my mint tea on her bar stool and Alia sits down beside me.

'What's going on then, lovely? Tell me everything.'

So, I do. I tell her all the symptoms, all the work stuff and the home stuff, all the M&Ms stuff, even the Nate and Luke stuff. Everything.

'Wish I'd never bloody asked now!' she says and I nearly spit out my mint tea. God, it's good to laugh. 'Ha ha, I'm only kidding, darlin'. Now then, seriously. You need help.'

'You know I hate asking for help. I feel bad enough taking up your time now when you could be having a nice quiet time with Sienna.'

'Quiet? With that nutter? I'm just relieved I don't have to deal with another evening of teen drama. Bless her, I love her to death, you know that. But seventeen-year-old girls are fucking exhausting. So I'm dead glad you turned up on my doorstep, you little waif and stray. But look, you really do need help. And I mean from all quarters. You need to make an appointment with your GP, like ASAP. You need HRT. Or you need something. There must be some IBS meds you can try. And migraine stuff.'

'I already take over-the-counter stuff.'

'Well, there must be IBS stuff that's prescription only. Ask for some of that. But all this anxiety you're getting. And bursting into tears. Your emotions are all over the fucking shop. You need something to stabilise that. I dunno if HRT does that job. I dunno enough about it. But ask the doctor. Tell them all your symptoms – write it down, take a list – and tell them you want some prescription meds to help with each one. Don't go away without a prescription. Make sure they bloody listen to you too. Don't let them fob you off.

'Right, next. This M&Ms business. They're bloody lucky to have you. And it sounds like it's a fab group and you can all help each other. But look, you said it to them yourself, you're no expert. And nobody's expecting you to be. And you're not their mum. Or their doctor. You're just another woman going through hell. And you mustn't take on all the woes of the world, for fuck's sake. You've got enough shit going on!'

'You're right, you're right.'

'I am. I always am. Okay, last but not least, these two fit guys you're chatting up.'

'Oh, it's not like that.'

'Yes, it fucking is! They sound like a right couple of eligible bachelors, darlin'. And they'd be lucky to have you, either of them. Or both, if you're really bored, eh? Heh heh heh.' Cue evil laugh from Alia.

'Oh stop.'

'Well, why not?!'

'Nate maybe, but Luke is just a friend.'

'Chatting with you at all hours of day and night? Keeps asking whether you're going to the reunion, even though he's thousands of miles away? He's thinking about coming, mark my words. But only if you show up. I bet you a shitload of money he'd travel across oceans for you, babe. Do you fancy him or what, the geeky one?'

Do I fancy Luke? I think about it. I watched his hands when he did that gig and I felt something, I really did. I was waylaid by sexy Nate straight after and got sidetracked . . .

'I don't know. I mean, he's lovely looking really. He has . . . such a nice face. And wonderful hands.'

'Ooh, you do fancy him! The geek and the rock god. They both have their appeal. I'd say, keep the rock god for fun and frolics, keep the geek for serious talks in the moonlight at midnight.'

And Alia saying that brings a sudden flash of memory: over thirty years ago, standing at the edge of a stretch of lawn in a little town park across the road from our Exeter house, Luke and I walking home gone midnight from a gig. *Shh!* he said suddenly and stopped. He pointed across the road at the park and there, beneath a bright moon, trotted a badger. It stopped in the pale light and sniffed the air. I'd never seen a badger up close like that before. Luke and I stood still, hoping the badger wouldn't catch a whiff of us and scarper. Then, to our amazement, a trio of badger babies came trotting out from behind a tree to join their mum, who was by now snuffling in the flower bed for slugs and worms, I suppose, or whatever badgers eat. I glanced at Luke and we grinned at each other, but didn't say a word. We held our breath and watched as the badger babies frolicked around on the lush grass, Mum keeping a close eye on them, still rootling through the undergrowth for food. We stood and watched them for an age, it felt, barely able to breathe. The moonlight was bright that night and they stood out in sharp relief as they rough and tumbled around beneath their mum's feet. Then, as swiftly as she'd appeared, she ran off, closely followed by the three little ones. Luke gasped and so did I, simultaneously. *I've never seen anything like that in my life,* I said. *Me neither. Just magical,* Luke said. And we beamed at each other again, his eyes dark and full in the moonlight.

'Are you bloody listening to me, woman?'

I'm back in Alia's kitchen again, aged fifty-two. It felt like a dream, that moonlit night. But it wasn't. It truly happened and it was wonderful. How could I have forgotten it? Was I so blinded by my lust for Nate Wheeler that I never noticed what a lovely bloke Luke was?

'Yeah,' I say. 'I mean, no. Sorry. Menopause brain. Away with the fairies.'

'Away with the geek, you mean. You were on another planet! Did you two ever get it on, back in the day?' says Alia, winking at me and taking a slug of red.

'God no. I was in love with the rock god.'

'Maybe it's time to consider the competition then, lovely. Rock gods are all very well for a fantasy, but geeks are real.'

'Nate is real! He has a website and everything.'

'Whatever you say. I still think you should have both! Now listen, first things first, make this GP appointment ASAP please. I'll come with you, if you like.'

'Oh no, don't worry. You've got far too much to deal with.'

'Well, if I can, I will. God knows when you'll get an appointment, but soon as you do, let me know and I'll see what I can do.'

216

I nod, knowing full well I won't be bothering her with that. I'm a grown-up. I should be able to go to the doctor's alone, for crying out loud.

But Alia is scrutinising me and says, 'I can tell you've decided already you won't ask me!'

'God, am I that easy to read?'

'Yeah, pretty much. Open book, lovely. But listen. It might feel like a weakness, accepting help. But you know what, it's a strength. You know my story, I've told you enough times, about running away from home. But I don't think I ever told you about what happened straight after.'

'No, you never did really. I mean, I know you knew Rich by then and you got together.' What I knew already was that, at the age of nineteen, Alia had been all set up in an arranged marriage with a man from Pakistan who was fifteen years older than her. And when he turned up at the party at her parents' house for Alia to meet him, she took one look, packed a bag and crept out the back door, never to return. It's an incredible story, so brave, so young. She's only just starting to see her parents again last year, now her youngest is nine. But for over twenty years, she managed alone, apart from Rich, as her whole family disowned her.

'Ah well, I'd snogged Rich by then, at a pub at closing time. That was about it. But when I left the house that day, I went to that pub, as my mate was a barmaid there. But she wasn't on that night and I felt lost. I was gonna go to her house, you see. And Rich was there again. And he was really pleased to see me. And he asked me about the bag and I just burst into tears. And he asked what it was all about and I told him everything. And he said,

217

"Well, I rent a room in a place down the road and there's five other blokes there, it's massive. And there's a sofa bed in the front room. No funny business. But you can stay there tonight if you want. There's actually a lock on the living room door, cos it used to be a bedroom, so you can lock yourself in if you're worried. But they're all good blokes. They won't mess about with you. Offer's there if you want it." And I thought, it's a risk. I don't really know this bloke. But I'd seen him down the pub on and off for years really, seen him around. He didn't have a bad reputation or nothing. And he looked legit. It was a risk but I took it. I went to that house and all the blokes were out and then they started coming home in dribs and drabs, most of 'em pissed cos it was Friday night. Five massive white blokes, all of them, looking pretty rough. Three scaffolders, a taxi driver and a plumber's assistant, all in their twenties and thirties. And there I was, this tiny little Asian girl, nineteen and wide-eyed, sitting on their sofa eating toast and crisps (cos that's all Rich had in). And they were so bloody respectful to me, so careful around me. And they took me in. They helped me get benefits, then get a job. They didn't expect me to do a thing around the house, even though I was the only girl. They talked to me and listened to me, but they never even asked why I was there, what'd happened. They just accepted me. I owe those guys – and Rich – my life, I think. Fuck knows what would've happened to me on the streets. I was bloody naïve. Didn't know my arse from my elbow. They taught me stuff too, how to wire a plug, how to drive even! I taught 'em how to cook South Asian cuisine, didn't I! They'll be making great curries for years cos of me!'

'Alia, that's a fantastic story. I didn't know all that.'

'Yeah, it is fantastic. If you saw it on telly, you'd think it was made up, all those rough blokes, treating me like one of their own. But it's all true. And this is what I mean, babe. You must always – ALWAYS – take help that's offered sincerely. Sincerely, mind! There's some twats out there who'll pretend to offer help but they're wolves in sheep's clothing, you know that. You're old enough to follow your gut. But when help is offered sincerely, take it. It comes from the heart. You're used to saving people, that's your problem. But it doesn't always have to be you doing the saving, darlin'.'

What a gem Alia is. I reach over and hug her and she lets me. I realise now I needed a hug off Rhona as much as anyone in that room. A hug from another grown-up. I get hugs off my kids any day of the week and they're the best. But I'm their mum and our hugs are coloured by that relationship. I haven't had a hug from a peer for ages. And I really needed it. Alia doesn't let go, she just lets me wallow in it. Then, when I'm ready – like a battery recharged – I let go. And go home renewed.

Chapter 15

On Monday I ring the doctor's. If it's not an emergency, you don't get in for weeks. But I pretend it is. I say I have severe gastro problems and I've tried everything and nothing is working. I get an appointment that morning. I email work and tell them I'll be in late. I'm not going to bother Alia with this. I'll be fine on my own. I've no idea which doctor I'll see, it's a lottery at my practice. When I get in there, it's a young female doctor called Dr Shaw. Okay, at least it's not the male one I saw before who just shrugged at me and dismissed me after three minutes. Let's see what this one's like.

She says, 'Gastro problems?'

I tell her it's bigger than that. It's all been brought on by menopause. And I want to go on HRT. She asks me for more detail. I've written down all my symptoms, as Alia advised. I read them out and which over-the-counter meds I've used. The physical stuff – gastro, migraines, hot flushes. And the mental symptoms – anxiety, negative self-talk, not wanting to leave the house, even most recently a fear of travelling, even a nervousness about driving the past week or so. None of this is normal, I tell her. None of this is me. She seems most interested in the mental stuff, asking me questions about that. Have I ever wanted to harm myself or others? No! Have I ever been unable to get out of bed? No! I wish! I'd love a decent coma about now. I ask her about new meds for gastro and the migraines. She prescribes a higher dose of a bunch of over-the-counter stuff, even though I've told her I've taken both over the counter for years and it's never worked – she says *you have to take them for at least three months to see any effect*. Then she gives me a prescription-only medication for acid reflux and another for the migraines. She says to stagger them, leaving a few days in between starting each new one, to check for side effects. Okay. But what about HRT?

'You don't need that, not with all this other stuff going on. What you need is an anti-depressant.'

'But isn't all this stuff being caused by menopause? I never had these problems before perimenopause. I've never had stomach issues. I could drink like a fish, now I can't manage a sip of wine or even coffee. I've never had migraines in my life. Plus I get hot flushes.'

'Anti-depressants are good for hot flushes. Clinically proven.'

And that's that. She starts typing, then says without looking at me that the prescriptions will go to the pharmacy next door and I can go there right now.

'Okay,' I say. I've been dismissed again. I stand up. It feels greedy, asking for more when she's given me all these other meds. But maybe I wouldn't need all these other meds, if I were on HRT? All these side effects and rattling around rotten with chemicals, when all I might need is more oestrogen, maybe? I don't know. I'm not a doctor. But my gut is telling me that this doesn't feel right.

'Off you go!' says Dr Shaw, brightly.

Off you go? This bloody child doctor, barely out of med school, at least twenty years younger than me, and she tells me *Off you go*?!

'There's no need to be so fucking PATRONISING,' I spit.

Oh Christ, where did that come from? It's Blondie, my rage! She's on the loose!

Dr Shaw stops typing and stares at me. She looks floored by that. She can't quite believe what she heard. 'Erm . . . well, we don't accept that kind of language at this practice. Everyone here is working hard to supply care for your medical needs and we don't use that kind of language here. So you'll need to leave immediately.'

'I'm sorry!' I say, terrified I won't get my prescriptions. 'Honestly, I'm so, so sorry. I've no idea where that came from. I mean, I do. It's menopausal rage. You don't understand because you're far too young, but this is what it's like. And this is why I need HRT. I really think I do! Look, I apologise. I really do. Please, forgive me.'

She looks steely-eyed at me, pursed lips ahoy. But she softens slightly and lifts her wrinkle-free chin in such a way that seems to suggest she's had her nose put out of joint but she can be the bigger person.

'Of course. Understood. But you need these meds I'm prescribing. And don't forget to stagger the gastro ones.

Migraine ones only when a headache is coming on, remember. See how you get on with those for three months, then come back if there's no change.'

Three months?! Well, it's better than nothing. And I've got away lightly after my outburst. It never does well to fall out with medical professionals. Firstly, they shouldn't have to deal with verbal abuse, whatever they've done. But mostly, it's counter-productive, because you need them onside to get where you want to be (though it's bloody hard to get there most of the time). I tug my forelock and leave the room so penitently, I may as well be exiting backwards bowing and scraping. Oh God, Blondie is out of control sometimes. Though I still think *Off you go!* was the fucking pits.

How I wish I'd accepted Alia's offer and had her there to support me. I'm an idiot. Anyway, what's done is done. So, I go to the chemist and there's a queue of nine people, yes, nine. So I'm in there for about four years and then I go home. I take pantoprazole first, as the acid has been so bad lately, not even swigging Gaviscon like a pirate swigs rum has helped. I put the others away, with Post-it notes on each as to when to start them. And then I look at the anti-depressants. Christ, I don't want to be on anti-depressants. I don't feel depressed or sad, I feel anxious and fed up because I feel like shit all the time. I look at the possible side effects and it looks like a list of stage directions from a horror film. I can't cope with all that on top of everything else. I put the anti-depressants in the cupboard, stuffed away in the corner. I won't be taking them. No fucking way. I am not depressed. I am menopausal. Anyway, let's see how these other meds go first.

I do tea for Ada and Carly and crawl into bed early. Maybe the pantoprazole is working already, but I don't have my customary heartburn after eating, and that is a relief. I sit up in bed and watch a couple of episodes of *Mad Men*. I know it's old and quite depressing, but my God, I have a thing for Jon Hamm. I could watch that man reading out the phone book and I'd be happy. Which reminds me, now I'm feeling not so acidy and rubbish, I haven't had a decent flirt with Nate for a few days. What with all the shit going on at home and work, I've not been messaging much with Nate or Luke. They're busy too, of course, so it's not been a problem really. But I've missed them both, to be honest. And they've both asked me about the reunion, which is looming in a couple of months, at the beginning of October. *Are you coming?* Nate keeps asking. Luke is still in the States, so I'm assuming he won't be. But he's asked if I am. I haven't decided. I mean, I'm barely scraping through ordinary days, let alone a trip down south. But maybe it'd be good for me. Carly thinks I should go. She and Ada are the only ones who know. And Geoff, because Ada told him about it, but not about Nate and Luke. They all think I should go. I haven't told anyone else yet. I don't want the pressure. People would say, *Oh you should definitely go! It'll be a scream!* And the old me would've agreed. The old me would've jumped in her car like a shot and bombed down there, no problem. But I'm getting to the point where driving makes me nervous, where getting dressed and looking out of the window makes me nervous. Maybe I should take that Prozac . . . No, NO. I don't want it. I'll get through the next three months, then see a doctor who's not a patronising twelve-year-old and beg on my knees for HRT.

I go on my phone and message Nate, then Luke. Nate answers first. We chat for a while. I tell him I'm sorry I've not been about much. He says, no sweat, but he's missed me.

Don't be daft.

Why shouldn't I miss you? I do. I love our chats.

Well, I do too. But you don't even know me, not really.

Yes, I do. I knew the early you anyway. And I was hooked.

Really?! I don't recall it that way!

Really? Why not?

Well, you were hardly ever home, for a start. Most of the time I was working and hanging out with Luke.

That's because I stayed away.

Why?

Isn't it obvious?

Nope!

Hobbes, can I call you? I'm tired of all this messaging. I wanna hear your voice again.

Blimey, I feel a bit sick at the thought of this. I've liked the fact we've kept it low key on our phones and no talking as yet. I know it's been weeks but I've enjoyed that. I'm nervous. Hearing Nate Wheeler's voice again. I'm trying to hear it in my mind, what it was like. It was damned sexy, I remember that.

OK, I type, then feel even more sick, as a video call comes through! Oh CHRIST, no way! I tap on the red blob that says no.

I message, *Not a bloody video call! I look like shit!*

OK sorry Hobbes. Audio it is.

It's ringing now and I tap the green blob this time.

'Hey, Hobbes,' he says. And my God, his voice is as sexy as ever it was. Not too deep, but smooth, like Galaxy chocolate.

'Hey, Nate.'

'Nervous?'

'Yes.'

I really am. I'm as giddy as a schoolgirl.

'Me too. It's so good to hear your voice again though.'

'You too.'

'Can I tell you some stuff then? About back then?'

'Sure. Fire away.'

'Okay, well, I stayed away from that house a lot, for a reason. Because I couldn't bear to be with you and not WITH you. I was going out with this other girl and I didn't want to be unfaithful. I'm not that guy.'

Bloody Nora! Now I was not expecting that. I always

assumed he was not into me in the slightest. How could I have misjudged it so badly?!

'I never saw you with a girlfriend?'

'Well . . . I'm not proud of this, Hobbes. But she was married.'

'Ah . . .' I say.

'It was all a big mess. I felt crap about it afterwards. But at the time, it was one of those heady, whirlwind things. And then she started to rely on me. And I felt guilty. And I tried to keep it going. But I couldn't stop thinking of you. So I didn't know how to handle it. She was quite a bit older than us, in her early thirties. And I was just a kid. We all were, really.'

'Well, yes, true.'

I can only imagine how attractive a stunningly gorgeous blond bombshell twenty-one-year-old Nate Wheeler would've been to an unhappily married woman in her early thirties. I don't blame her at all, to be honest!

Nate continues, 'I was ashamed of it and didn't tell anyone. It carried on far longer than it should have. It was finally over a year or so after we left uni and by then I'd lost your contact details so I never knew how to get hold of you. No social media then to hunt you down.'

Crikey. All these years and I could've been with Nate Wheeler. How different my life would have been. I can't quite believe it.

'I never felt you were into me, Nate.'

'But didn't you get the message all those times I hugged you, or thanked you for doing stuff for me, or stayed in to hang out with you when I was supposed to be somewhere else? Don't you remember me making breakfast for you all those times?'

'No, I really don't! I remember making breakfast for *you*!'

'Ah well, memories get muddled.'

Well yeah, he's got me there. My memory is utter shite.

He goes on, 'I definitely did make you breakfast, my famous pancakes. I was trying to show you how I felt, all the while knowing that I shouldn't be because I was involved with someone else. And the truth is, I didn't want you getting mixed up in all that. Because you were pure, somehow. I didn't want you sullied by it.'

'Well, that's nice. But I wish I'd known. Things could've turned out very differently. I wish you'd told me.'

'So do I. But I didn't, through a misplaced sense of loyalty. But I'm telling you now, how much I feel for you, how much I always did.'

Hearing all this is blowing me away. Nate Wheeler, pining after little old me, Heidi Hobbes, for all these years. It's incredible!

'Thank you,' I say, though that seems a daft thing to say. I don't really know what I'm saying. 'I just . . . don't know what to think about it. I'm a bit bowled over, to be honest. This changes everything, in my head, anyway.'

What am I saying?! These are the words I've wanted to hear for so long. And I'm prevaricating? Maybe I'm just tired.

'Listen, I'm crazy about you, Hobbes. Always have been. Once Facebook became a thing, I looked you up every now and again. I could see you had a bloke and then married with kids and I'd think, *That could've been me*. So I gave up looking after a while. It was too painful. I can't believe you're single now. I can't believe you haven't been snapped up.'

'Oh, I can! I'm no catch, believe me!' I'm thinking about the rolls of fat around my tummy.

'Stop joking with me, you always do that. I really feel for you, Hobbes. I want to see what develops between us. If you don't feel that way, that's cool. Of course it is. I just feel I need to know now, so I don't get my hopes up.'

If he only knew how much I wanted to hear this, thirty years ago! But better late than never, I guess.

'I definitely feel the same way, Nate. I've always carried a torch for you. I can't believe you felt the same. It's mind-blowing, to be honest.'

'Then we're on the same page, Hobbes.'

'It seems we are, Wheeler. Maybe a first step could be that you actually call me by my first name.'

'Nah, you love it that I call you Hobbes. Nobody else does, am I right?'

'That is actually true. And yes, actually, I do love it.'

'Thought so, Hobbes.'

We hang up soon after that.

Then he messages, *You OK? With what I told you?*

More than OK. I'm just tired, Nate. Sorry if I didn't sound too bright on the phone. It's been the longest day since The Longest Day.

Slight exaggeration?

Maybe . . .

Sleep well, Hobbes xx

You too xx

I can't believe it! Nate, crazy for me! That's what he
said. *I'm crazy about you, Hobbes.* Hobbes. I love it how
he calls me Hobbes. He's right, nobody else calls me that.
Nobody ever has, but him. My God, all those times I used
to sit with him on the sofa and felt weak at the thought
I could just reach over and touch his perfectly sculpted
arm and he would've responded, taken me in those perfectly
sculpted arms and kissed me! *At last,* he would've said. *I
can't fight it any longer. I must have you, right here, on
this sofa.* (Christ, that sounds like Dr Drake Ramoray from
Friends.) I'm so mad that Nate never said anything to me
at the time. But it was noble, I suppose, what he did. That
he didn't date two women at once. That he ended it with
the married one, then came looking for me but couldn't
find me. Gah! Why didn't Facebook exist then? Bloody
Zuckerburg, you took too damn long to set that shit up!
How dare you mess up my love life!

So, Nate Wheeler has been in love with me for thirty
years. Me, ordinary old Heidi Hobbes. Christ, I have –
what is it? – I count on my fingers – *ten weeks* until the
reunion. I really need to transform myself, to be the woman
he remembers. Can a person lose three stone in ten weeks?
I'm thinking, starvation. Or fasting, not intermittent like
Rishi Sunak but whatever the opposite of intermittent is.
Mittent? Mittent fasting. Yeah, that's the answer. In the
meantime, when we have a video call, which we surely
will have, I will keep the camera on my face alone. And

if he wants to see more, I'll make sure I put something baggy on. Or Spanx. And then my anxiety starts skipping ahead – *Well*, it says, hands on hips, eyeing me critically – *Well, what about the reunion then? Or the first time you meet him in real life, if not then. You can't hide your fat then, can you? Because you're going to want to get naked with him, aren't you?* And I realise that my sleeping desire has been well and truly awoken by love's true Nate. I've been off sex for years. To be quite honest, I'd lost all interest in it. But now, at the thought of this man – those arms, those hands, those thighs . . . I know I want him all over me like a rash. But my body . . . urgh. Could I do it? Get naked in front of this rock god?? My anxiety is laughing at me. I've named my rage Blondie, so now I need to name this bitch. Mommy Dearest, I call her. My anxiety is everything my mum makes me feel about how much I'm failing her and life in general. Fuck you, Mommy Dearest. If this man wants me, he'll have to take me, warts and all. (Well, not warts. Not yet. Unless that's next on the menopause Wheel of Fortune. Please, God, no.)

I want to tell the world: Nate Wheeler is crazy about me! Or do I? Only my kids and Alia know. And I made sure they knew not to spread it around, especially the girls to their dad. I don't want him knowing about it. And I've played it down since then, because I feel weird about it. I knew Nate before I knew their dad. And it seems wrong somehow. If I went on about how much I fancied him and he was the one who got away, and then I met their dad . . . maybe they'll feel they were the mistake. So I don't say any more about Nate to Carly or Ada. And I don't tell anyone else. I just want Nate and

Luke to be my thing again. Crikey, Luke. I wonder what he'll make of it? Of me and Nate? I want to tell him. I want to ask him more about that time back then, and that married woman. I want to get Luke's take on it all. After all, Luke knew Nate best back then, didn't he? I certainly thought that at the time. I wonder why they didn't keep in touch, when they were so close. I'll ask Luke . . . but if what Alia suspects is true, will Luke Jones really want to talk to me about Nate? Or does he have other ideas?

Chapter 16

I get my answer a few days later. At first, after hearing Alia's take and then Nate's declaration, I just feel too awkward raising talk of Nate with Luke. He's never mentioned him once, since our initial chats. It does feel odd that neither has mentioned the other since we all started talking again. Meanwhile, things have been escalating with Nate. After that night, he asks me for a video call. I hedge and procrastinate, but what would Miriam do? Miriam would bloody well do it and not give a damn what anyone thought of her. We all need to be more Miriam. So, I say yes. I schedule it when Carly and Ada are out. I'm not having those two mood vampires sucking all the will out of me while I try and act sexy. I'm not at Miriam's level of zero fucks given as yet, so I end up fretting about it for hours beforehand: trying on every outfit I presently own and leaving it all in an unholy pile on my bed; washing my hair and styling it and restyling it fourteen ways; touching up my make-up so many times

233

it ends up about four layers deep and I have to scrub the whole lot off and start again, which makes my face all red – FUCKING HELL. If I'm this bad with a video call, I can't even imagine going on an actual date with a real-life man. Finally, the hour of doom arrives. Christ, I hate video calls. Why did I agree to this?! I position myself on the sofa, using my phone camera to try and get the right angle so it's most flattering but in every which way I look like crap. Urgh. Oh well, the hour has come, so there's no going back. I told him I'd call at 9pm, because I didn't want to be sitting there like a chump waiting for a call that'll never come. There's still a chance he won't answer, of course . . . I hadn't thought of that. Oh bugger bugger buggeration, it's time to do the deed.

I press call. It rings. And rings. That's it, he's not going to answer. I've been a fool. I've got all dressed up for nothing and look like a prize turkey trussed up to speak to Mr Nobody and . . .

He answers. It takes a second to connect and then, there he is.

Oh my fucking CHRIST. There he is, Nate Wheeler. He's . . . utterly beautiful. His hair, his skin, the bulge in his upper arms, his blue eyes. Bloody Nora, I could drown in those eyes.

'Hey, Hobbes,' he says and I want to swoon, like those old-fashioned swoons on black-and-white movies, like a proper draping myself across a chaise longue. The wave of desire I've had every time he messages, and the peak of excitement when I spoke to him on the phone . . . NOTHING compares to this. I'm speechless. And I mean literally.

'Are you gonna say a damn word or what?' he says, lazily. Completely at ease with himself. He doesn't look nervous in the slightest. I bet he hasn't spent hours deciding which T-shirt to wear. It's a ratty old black one, with frayed sleeves. He's just one of those people that's effortlessly cool. And gorgeous.

'Hey, Wheeler,' I manage, as sultry as I can, but I haven't cleared my throat and it comes out all croaky. Is that sexy? Maybe it's sexy. I don't bloody know.

Then I don't say anything else. And then he doesn't say anything else. But it's okay. It's not even embarrassing. We just . . . stare at each other. Drink each other in. It's delicious. We're looking at every feature of each other, like we're hungry for it and not eaten in years. He's the same, I can tell. I just know he is. He laughs nervously and passes his beautiful hand across his mouth, down across his stubbly chin and flashes those eyes at me. I laugh too. We just smile at each other. I've not felt like this in . . . thirty years. That's the truth. I never looked at Geoff like this. He never looked at me like that. What is this? Lust? Love? *Stop overthinking, Heidi Hobbes. Just lap it up, this glorious moment of being.* It is electric.

We do talk after that, eventually. We talk for two hours. We talk about the times we could remember at uni. Gigs we went to – bands like Travis and Felt and The The. Nate tells me stories about musicians he's played with, like the Stereophonics and The Verve. He even had a drink with Thom Yorke of Radiohead once, which he said was the highlight of his life, as he worships the guy. I don't want to talk about me, as it's all so boring compared to Nate's life. But he wants to know. I make out my job is not as bad as I know it is, because I don't want to sound like a loser. I pretend I've been playing with fiddle folk groups for years. I lie that my hand has tendonitis and that's why I can't play for him right now. Untruths pile up on exaggerations on downplays on economy with the truth. I lie so much I realise I won't be able to remember what I've lied about. But I don't care. I can't admit to this god – and he really is a god, in every way a man could be – that I have such an utterly dreary life compared to his. I mean, I'm not much to look at and I've not much to offer, so how could I tell him the tedious truth?

But the way he looks at me, for every second of those two hours, is exhilarating. This. THIS is what I've been missing from my life for all these years. Electricity. This connection, his eyes and my eyes. Unable to stop ourselves smiling. Having to look away sometimes, it's just too intense. It's buzzing, it's captivating. It's like no other feeling on earth. It must mean something, mustn't it?

I actually end the call myself, because I literally can't take it anymore. The intensity. He wants to talk longer but I invent a childcare issue and I say goodnight.

'Night night, Hobbes.'

Holy COW.

I'm floating on air for the rest of the night. I cannot sleep. I can barely lie still, and it's not due to menopausal restless legs. Yes, I am restless, but it's for a whole other reason. I'm restless with desire. I've not felt like this for . . . I don't think I ever have. Well, I did. In 1993 to 1994. But he never looked at me that way back then. It's what I dreamed of, but it never happened, not once. But now, thirty years later, I've been handed my wish on a platter. My desire – dormant for so long – has been reawakened. And she's raring to go.

What would Miriam do? I look at the Facebook post about the reunion and change Interested to Going. Oh boy, am I going! I tell Nate and he's delighted. He's coming too. In eight long weeks, I will finally see Nate Wheeler again, in the flesh.

I've not chatted much with Luke this week. I've not wanted to. It feels weird, feels wrong. And he's held back, like he knows something. Then when I change the status on the invite, he must've noticed, because a couple of days later, he messages.

I see you're definitely going to the party then!

Yeah, I certainly intend to.

Me too.

Oh yeah?! All the way from the U S of A??

Yeah absolutely.

I think about what Alia said, about crossing oceans.

Is that a recent decision?

I always wanted to go, but it's a long way, you know. But now I know you're going, it'd be a shame to miss it. Old housemates get-together and all that.

Yes! Nate is coming too!

Yeah?

Indeed. We've been talking loads. I'm pretty blown away by his musical career, I must say. Daryl Hall and Suede and all that. It's quite something that he's played with greats like them.

Has he though?

Yeah it's on his website.

Yeah I saw that. Well, I saw pictures of Suede and Coldplay and Snow Patrol and Daryl Hall. I didn't see Nate performing with them.

Yeah, there are close-ups.

Yeah but not with them.

But there's a pic of him with Brett Anderson!

Yeah but not performing together. He could've gone backstage at a gig. Ask him.

Is Luke joking? I thought he was ribbing me at first. Now I'm not so sure.

I have. He said he doesn't have any recordings of him performing with them as he's too busy playing.

That's convenient.

And he said he'd dig some out for me sometime.

And has he?

Well no, not yet. He's dead busy.

That's convenient too.

Stop it!

He's actually bugging me now. I can feel my irritation rising. It's not at Blondie level rage yet, but if Luke's not careful, he might set her free.

I've just had this incredibly positive thing happen which is an old flame and an old friend coming back into my life.

I don't want to tell him that Nate and I might be rekindling our flame right now, because I'm still not quite believing it myself. I can't believe my luck, I mean. If I tell anyone, it might burst the bubble. So I've not told a soul about my video call with Nate and all the sexy texts he's sent me since. And I'm certainly not telling Luke. I'll conveniently keep it in the past, for now.

Well, I felt the same back then as I do now. That he's a total waste of your affection.

What?! But you two were such good friends. How can you be so negative about him??

We weren't good friends. I couldn't stand the guy.

Well, that is news to me. You moved in together!

That was just convenience. He'd seen your flyer on the music department noticeboard about two rooms to rent and I was looking too. So we came together.

Wow. I thought you two were best mates.

You thought wrong. He really is a bit of a wanker, Heidi.

Well, that's your opinion. Not mine.

Based on what though? Memories of thirty years ago? Time changes things, erases some, inflates others. It's not a reliable test of character, how you felt when you were twenty.

God, I bloody HATE that, having my own feelings mansplained to me. My rage is starting to build now.

I know that, you don't have to lecture me about memory. I know because I've spent the last few weeks talking till all hours with him. I'm getting to know the man he is now. And he is not a wanker.

OK

He really isn't, Luke. He's such an interesting person. You should give him another chance.

Whatever you say.

Oh stop it.

Stop what?

I don't know, just stop being difficult. Be happy for me instead. After all these years, I've found something again, something I thought I'd lost.

You haven't lost a thing. You're more vibrant than ever.

Oh crikey. Alia was right. Luke really likes me, I mean, doesn't he? You don't call someone you're not rather mad about 'vibrant,' do you? I'm so out of practice, reading men. But this, and his annoyance about Nate, it all sounds like pretty bloody obvious he has feelings for me. And I do for him, lovely Luke. I love talking to him. I always did. I loved watching that family of badgers with him that time. But . . . he's not Nate. He doesn't electrify me.

Honestly, Luke. I don't want to fight with you. I've been so happy getting back in touch with you both. It's absolutely made my year.

Good for you.

241

Hey, I'm trying to be nice. And you're being a prick, quite frankly.

Thanks.

You're welcome. We could've rekindled such a nice friendship here. And now your stupid jealousy is ruining it all.

Jealousy?

Yeah jealousy. Well, that's what it sounds like anyway. Get over yourself, for fuck's sake, man.

That says it all then. I think it's best if I withdraw. I hate the person this is making me become. I don't want to interfere in your life. I wish you all the best, Heidi. I really do. Take care of yourself.

What?! Don't over-react! What is going on with you?

No reply . . .

Luke, don't be like this. We used to be such good friends.

No reply . . .

OK then, be like that. I don't have time for moody men these days. If you ever feel like growing up, get back to me. Until then, enjoy your sulk.

242

No reply . . .

I throw down my phone in a fit of pique. Then it pings again. I almost leave it. But curiosity gets the better of me. It's from Luke again.

Why do you think Nate and I fell out after uni and haven't spoken to each other in thirty years?

I don't know. Because you thought he was a wanker.

No. Because of you.

Chapter 17

I demand to know what Luke means. But he doesn't reply, either that day or the next, or the next. What did he mean? I mean, it sounds obvious. It sounds like he and Nate fought over me! But it doesn't make any sense. Nate never made a move on me, despite much encouragement. Yes, he told me he couldn't, because of this married woman. But if that's the case, then why didn't Luke make a move if Nate was otherwise engaged? Maybe he didn't want to try. That does make sense actually, what with the way I used to mope about like a lovestruck teenager over Nate, telling Luke all about every shade of my feelings for the guy. Oh God, if Luke was in love with me, that must've been horrible for him. And the truth is, looking back now, interrogating my memories, I did like Luke a hell of a lot. I loved hanging out with him. I loved our trips out to country pubs, the gigs we talked all night about afterwards, his small acts of kindness every day. But I was just too wrapped up in

244

Nate to understand the meaning behind it all. And now I feel the same way, utterly enveloped in this heat of desire for Nate. It's getting even more intense, as the days go on. I don't know if I'll be able to hold out till October. I might be jumping on a train or a plane to Scotland at this rate, in defiance of my increasing anxiety about leaving the house, let alone flying up to the Orkney Isles. But at the same time, I'm missing my chats with Luke. I meant what I said to him: it was the two of them together that have given me fleeting moments of happiness these past few months. It's like Nate gives me the thrills and chills, but Luke gives me the fuzzy, warm stuff. It's like I need both, somehow.

So I decide to ask Nate.

You know I've been talking to Luke again recently?

Yeah

Well, he said something odd. He said that you fell out after uni. Is that right?

Not really. Just drifted apart. Like people do. Without the glue of uni days and Exeter gigs to hold us together. I went off gigging round Europe and he did his MSc in Engineering somewhere up north, Manchester? Newcastle? Can't remember. Somewhere like that.

So you didn't fall out?

No, not at all. Why?

Well, Luke said there was a reason you fell out. He said it was about me.

What? Nope.

What's he talking about then?

No idea. He was always a bit of a drama queen.

Was he? I don't remember him that way.

Luke was always so chill, the epitome of chill.

Yeah he was. And that's one reason why I didn't keep in touch with him for long after uni. Always exaggerating stuff or getting the wrong end of the stick. Or just making shit up.

Nate changes the subject. But I'm still thinking about this Luke business. I did not know that about Luke, about being dramatic, making things up. He didn't seem that way at all to me. But I guess it does chime with the way he was the other day in those texts. Just goes to show, you think you know a person. But you only know a sliver of a slice of who they really are.

I don't message Luke. I leave it. Truth is, I've got too much other stuff to deal with. It's August and I'm due to take Ada away on our annual holiday. We always have a week together somewhere, just me and the little'un, since Carly went to uni. She lost interest in family holidays then, but of course, Ada didn't. We've been to sunny places and cold places, cities and countryside. This year, I have so little energy, and I'm so worried about hot flushes and stress, I can't face foreign travel. So I've booked us a week in a cottage in the Lake District, in Bowness-on-Windermere. I'm dreading it and looking forward to it simultaneously. I like the idea of the beauty and the peace of lakes. But I know it'll be crawling with tourists. (Yes, I'm one of those crawling tourists, I know. But I don't count, obviously. I am a legitimate visitor who will behave impeccably, not like all these other interlopers.) But I'm dreading the travel. I was going to drive, as you would. But I'm too scared. I hate to admit it to myself, but that's the truth. Lately, the thought of driving on long, fast roads fills me with dread. So, I've booked trains to get there. I've even booked a taxi from Windermere train station to get to the cottage and a Tesco delivery to arrive at the cottage on our first evening, so it's all sorted. The only thing that assuages Mommy Dearest – my delightful anxiety – is having everything planned out within an inch of its life. It's two changes – Oxford to Birmingham, then another train to Oxenholme, and lastly a third train to Windermere. We've managed to stuff all our stuff into one case. We take backpacks with sandwiches, snacks and drinks. We have our phones, chargers, power packs. Ada has her Switch. I have enough medication in my backpack to last till doomsday. We'll manage. We'll be fine. It'll go smoothly. And if it doesn't there's no need to panic, we'll adapt. And we'll get there eventually. It'll be FINE.

Well, it's not fucking fine, is it. All goes well till Coventry, then we sit in the station for a half-hour. There's talk of points failure somewhere, then we're told to get off the train.

I lug the heavy bag off and wheel it along the platform to the next train to Birmingham. We'll have missed our connection to Oxenholme, but it's not the end of the world. We can get another one. We take the next train and we stop at Birmingham International and the conductor says the train won't be going on to New Street due to staff shortages. So we get on another train to New Street. Then we have to wait an hour for the next train to Oxenholme. By this time, I'm pretty frazzled. It is, of course, a heatwave on the day we travel. I'm sweating and feeling faint. I buy water from the fridge in the café but it's warm. I can feel sweat trickling from my head down my neck and collecting in my cleavage. My knickers are sopping wet, from sweat, not wee. We finally get the Oxenholme train and it's supposed to be direct. But it stops in the middle of fucking nowhere and sits there. FOR TWO HOURS. AND THE AIRCON ISN'T WORKING. Ada is fine. Ada is playing on her Switch. I feel like I'm going to die. I'm not exaggerating. I'm shaking. I think I might vomit all over this table. I'm drinking water like a fish and it's never enough. I'm trying to hide it from Ada. Then, the diarrhoea comes. I know it's coming. I've taken enough Imodium that morning to stun a horse. But it hasn't worked. I rush to the loo and somebody's in there. There's about six people loitering in the corridor, no seats left in the carriages. And they're all staring at me. I must look a fright, as their eyes show fear. Fear of infection. Am I really going to shit myself on a train, in front of all these people, like I joked about to the M&Ms?? Why on earth did I get the train? Why did I think I could cope with it? Finally, FINALLY, the person exits the loo and I fall into it, yank my sodden knickers down (from sweat not shit, not yet) and plonk myself down on the loo. It comes out like split pea puree. Litres of it. Christ, I think I might actually shit myself to death.

I stay in the loo for a good half-hour. You're not supposed to flush the loo when the train has stopped, I suppose. Well, maybe it doesn't matter if it's not in a station. We are lost in the wilds of Cumbria, after all. I must flush it about ten times. Two people knock on the door at intervals. I just keep saying 'OCCUPIED' very loudly. Ada comes and knocks too. She's worried. I tell her I'm okay, just go back to her seat. Finally, there's nothing left to shit out and I clean myself up and come out. It absolutely fucking stinks. I know it does. I shut the door as quickly as I can, but I know the loiterers have smelt it and they're all making faces. Oh God, I just want to die. I stagger back towards my seat and suddenly the train starts up again and I nearly fall flat on my face. Back in my seat, I put my head on the table and I feel Ada stroking my hair. Bless her, the little darling. I feel so bad she's having to put up with me flaking out, on top of this nightmare journey from hell. We arrive at Oxenholme a while after – I've lost all sense of time – and I cannot lift the suitcase. Neither can Ada. A kind man helps us. I get to Oxenholme and it's an hour's wait for the train to Windermere. I can't take any more. I find a taxi rank, feeling so faint I might actually pass out, and I tell the first taxi I see to take us to our cottage. Hang the expense. I'm not waiting for that last train. We'll get chauffeured on the last stretch.

We get there four hours late. It's a stunning cottage, part of four converted barns on farmland. We've missed the Tesco van. It won't come back till tomorrow. The key is in a locked box with a code pad. I drag my phone from my handbag and find the code they messaged to me. I put it in. It doesn't work. I try it again. It still doesn't work. Ada tries it.

'Doors should have face ID!' she cries in frustration, which is probably the most Gen Z thing I've ever heard. I try again. It works. I don't care why, I'm just incredibly relieved. I get into the house and I collapse on the bed. I have a migraine coming on and I quickly take the pills. Ada is crying. Not because of the journey. She wasn't bothered about any of that. She's crying because I look like death. She rings Carly.

I can hear them talking, Ada crying, Carly calming her down. I'm looking at my phone and I'm trying with all my might to order pizza for Ada, because we've got no food. But I can't focus on my phone. I tell Ada to put me on with Carly. I want her to order pizza for Ada.

'Mum?' she says. 'Do you need the hospital?'

'No, no,' I mumble. 'I'm just exhausted. And dehydrated. I'm okay.'

I try to get up off the bed but feel too weak to stand. My legs give way and I fall back onto the sheets.

'You're not okay,' says Ada, tearfully.

Carly's voice comes through the phone 'I'm driving up there. I'll see you in a few hours.'

'Oh, no, darling. Don't. I'll be all right in the morning.' I'm too weak to argue.

'Order pizza for Ada first.'

'All right, Mum. Ada is going to get you some water. Drink it, then sleep. She'll be okay. I'll keep talking to her.'

'I love you so much.'

'Love you too. Get some rest. See you soon.'

I wake up about midnight. The house is quiet. I look out of the cottage window – can't see a damn thing beyond the car park behind it. All that beautiful scenery that must be there is shrouded in darkness. But there is Carly's little Fiat Punto parked under the streetlamp. Oh, thank God. Thank God for Carly. Now I know why it was a pretty smart move to have two daughters years apart. The eldest can take up the slack when her mum is at the end of her tether. And I feel like I've never been this far along my tether in my whole life. I drink almost a pint of water straight down, which has been left by my bed by one of my lovely daughters. I go for a wee. No more shits, thankfully. There's nothing left to expel. I tiptoe along the hallway and glance in at Ada's room. She has a bunkbed in there – she's on the top bunk and her sister is below, both fast asleep. Good, good. I shuffle back to my room, so tired. I find my phone and turn it off. I sink back into the lovely, clean, crisp white sheets of the bed and I sleep the sleep of the dead.

Carly stays all week. She takes Ada out on trips. I stay in bed for four days, more or less. I don't look at my phone at all. I don't even switch it on. I need total peace. I go out in the garden and sit on a bench and read a bit. Other than that, I'm too tired to move. Carly sorts everything. She's amazing. She tells me that Geoff said he'd come, but he's on a weekend city break with Cheryl. I'm glad he didn't come and I'm glad he's away with Cheryl. Things are progressing nicely there. I feel proud to have been their

251

accidental matchmaker. Who knew you could find love over a margherita pizza?

By our last day, I'm well enough to go out. The heatwave has passed and the cooler air is like balm. We drive into Bowness and we take a trip on a big boat on Lake Windermere. It is still and calm, the blueness of the lake and the blueness of the sky fill my vision with tranquillity. The breeze is refreshing, lifting my hair and tickling my neck. The houses along the lakeside are serene, shimmering in the hazy sun. We see Beatrix Potter's lake house. We see the house they used in *The French Lieutenant's Woman*. Oh, to be a millionaire and live on Lake Windermere. I'm in the wrong job, I think again. When the boat stops, everybody gets off but I tell the girls I'll stay on board. I just want to sit and stare at the lake. I am so purely happy at this moment, on this virtually empty boat, moored and bobbing on Lake Windermere. I never want this peace to end.

But it will, and I will have to go back to my life, my job, my menopause. Tears roll down my face. I'm so ashamed that my daughter had to come and rescue me. I've taken my kids on holidays dozens of times. What the hell is wrong with me? I make a decision then. Never again will I let a medical professional patronise me, tell me I'm imagining things, tell me I don't need what I know I need. Never again will I force myself to undertake things I know will be bad for me, like a long train journey when I'm terrified of travel. Never again will I turn down help when I need it. I will accept help gladly, wherever it is offered sincerely, as Alia said. And never again will I wear nylon knickers in a heatwave . . .

Chapter 18

On the last day of the holiday, I turn my phone on to find several messages from Nate asking how the holiday is going and if I'm okay. Nothing from Luke. A gazillion emails from work. I ignore the latter. I message Nate and tell him I've been ill while we were away. I can't admit it's all menopause-related. I still haven't told him about that, it's just too embarrassing. So I say I must've caught some sort of virus or food poisoning. It's humiliating enough saying I've had the shits without having to admit I'm also sweating like a pig and fainting because I'm menopausal and overweight. I can't bear to share that with the rock god. Romance needs some mystery, surely, doesn't it? He sends some nice messages back about feeling better, plus a series of gifs of people vomiting to make me laugh (but actually they make me feel more sick – I can't abide seeing people vomming! And every TV drama I watch seems to have at least one scene of someone vomming! Why?!). But he means well. He asks for my postal address.

What for?? I demand. I can't have him turning up on my doorstep with me looking this ropey.

Just need to pop something in the post to you, Hobbes. Don't panic.

Carly drives us home and when we arrive, there is a huge bunch of flowers waiting outside our flat. Someone in the house must've taken them in from the delivery, knowing we'd arrive home soon. We take them inside and find there's a box of chocolates in there too. It's all from Nate. The card reads:

Be well, Hobbes

Aww, that's nice. I eat the chocolates in bed. I'm feeling a lot better.

The next day, I'm back to normal and I tackle the pile-up of emails in my inbox. On Monday, I'm back at work and coping okay. But I know now that the gastro meds the doctor gave me are not working. Maybe the pantoprazole, yes, because I don't have the acidy business I used to have. But the other gastro stuff has had no effect whatsoever. She said I have to give it three months. But is that right? Do these meds really take twelve whole weeks to start working? It doesn't make sense to me. The Prozac, yes, I get that. I've heard that anti-depressants take a while to work. But gastro meds should kick in straight away, shouldn't they? Because gastro issues come on suddenly. Plus some of these things you can get over the counter. So why would they take three months to work? I don't know. I still have at least another six weeks, till mid-October, till I'm allowed to go back and say they're not working. Urgh, six whole weeks. We put such hopes in medications, that this little pill is going to change our lives forever. And we take new ones with optimism and trepidation. Then when they don't work, we fall out of love with them and grow to hate them, useless bloody things. It's depressing shoving a pill in your mouth that you're 90 per cent sure doesn't work.

At our fifth M&Ms meeting, I realise I haven't told a single one of our group about the horrible experience I had on holiday. I didn't put it in the group chat. In fact, I've been off WhatsApp altogether for a while. I just can't deal with extra communication. I've got enough chatter going on in my head with Mommy Dearest and Blondie and the endless work emails, without adding to it. The topic I chose for this week is low days. We all have them. We hear everybody else's and we sympathise.

Then Joy says, 'What about you, Heidi?'

And I realise, that's the first time someone has actually asked me to share in the group. I'm always so busy shepherding everyone else that I usually forget to talk about my own experiences. But maybe I've been a bit quiet today, a bit subdued. And Joy has noticed.

'Well, I had one of the worst days of my life recently, actually,' I say and smile grimly.

Everyone immediately responds, with *Oh no!* and *What happened?!*

And then I burst into tears.

I did not expect that. Rhona is out of her seat like a shot, putting an arm round me. Cheryl reaches over and rubs my knee. Niki is looking for tissues in her handbag then passing me one. Joy is watching with deep concern.

I recover myself a bit and tell them I'm okay, I'll be okay. Then, once everyone's sitting down again, I tell them the whole sorry story of my holiday. I try to keep it light, but I don't succeed. Turns out nearly shitting yourself on public transport isn't so funny when it actually happens to you.

Joy says, 'What medication are you on for these stomach problems?'

Then I explain all about Dr Shaw. And *Off you go!*

'Okay, I think it's time for an intervention, love,' says Joy. And she says it so calmly, so soothingly yet firm, that I can't help but go along with it. 'We're making an appointment for you with a different doctor and I'm coming with you. We're going to get you on HRT and I won't be leaving that room until it happens.'

Everybody agrees that's much the best thing. After the group meeting, Joy gets my GP surgery number and she says to leave it with her. The next morning she rings me and tells me to meet her there at ten-thirty. We go in, we see an older male doctor, Dr Anand. Joy lets me speak, then she joins in and insists on HRT. Dr Anand immediately agrees.

'It's a mystery to me why you haven't been on it for months,' he says and Joy sighs very audibly.

'Well, maybe it might be an idea to tell Dr Shaw that, as she prescribed anti-depressants rather than allowing this menopausal woman to deal with the root cause of hormone deficiency.'

He suggests HRT pills and Joy corrects him. 'If she has

gastro issues, patches would be better, wouldn't they? I've heard of women getting nauseous from HRT pills.'

He agrees that makes sense. He says to try patches for a few weeks and keep in touch, let him know how it's going.

'We can always modify the dosage or try something different if it doesn't help.'

He's nice. He listens and he isn't snappy or dismissive, but also he isn't soppy or over-the-top, which annoys me. I like him.

So we get the prescription, for HRT patches. Joy shows me in the loos how to put one on, at the top part of my bottom, if that makes sense. Not quite the hip, the back or the arse, but somewhere in between. I have to put them on a twice a week, sticking them to alternate sides of the body each time.

'It's very likely it won't start working straight away,' Joy says. 'Give it time. A few weeks. Or it might start sooner. Everyone's different.'

'I can't even feel it,' I say. 'That's a relief. I thought it'd feel sticky as I move around, but it doesn't.'

'Yes, they're pretty good. They can leave a gluey residue on your bum and fluff sticks to it. Micellar water works well at getting it off.'

I go for a wee before we leave. Then we're standing in the loos and I'm washing my hands and I look in the mirror and say, 'Joy, thank you.'

'Oh, it's nothing.'

'I know you don't like hugs, but if you did, I'd give you a hug right now to show you how much this has meant to me. And helped me.'

Joy looks at me in the mirror and says, 'It's about time you let someone help you, isn't it? Universal mother, that's what you are. Time to accept some mothering of your own.'

The first couple of weeks I don't feel any differently on HRT, I have to admit. Well, it can take a while, Joy said. I just need to be patient. But there's a part of me that is filled with dread, that it won't work, that I'll be one of the unlucky ones for whom HRT makes no difference whatsoever. And because of that, I decide that putting the pressure on myself of attending the reunion in a couple of weeks' time is not a great idea. I'm too worried about the travelling. I don't want to go on the train, for obvious reasons after last time. But I'm too scared to drive that far either. Around town is all right, but my anxiety explodes when it comes to the idea of driving on long, fast roads. I don't know why. Just another bizarre side effect of confidence-busting menopause. I've been thinking about asking Nate if he could take me . . . Oxford could be on the way from Scotland to Exeter, if he maybe took a detour? I look on the map and it is quite a significant detour actually. And the truth is, I'm too nervous to ask Nate. It feels like an imposition, this early on in our relationship. I don't feel ready to ask him for such a favour, since we haven't actually met again yet. It feels too much. Plus there's a part of me that wants to seem like the freewheeling Heidi of my youth and not have to ask him for middle-aged help. Since I've been poorly, he's backed off the sexy stuff for a little while and we chat about more ordinary things and it's nice. One of the things he talks about quite a bit is his motorbike, which he's obsessed with. He hates cars, he says, and reveals he's going to take a road trip of a few days and come down from Scotland to Devon on his bike. So there goes that idea then. The only thing worse than being sick on a train or in a car, is being perched on the back of a motorbike for a hundred and fifty-odd miles.

So I go on the Facebook invitation and I post a comment.

I'm not able to attend now unfortunately, but I wish everyone all the best. Have fun!

That sounds chirpy enough. But I'm gutted about it actually. Nate doesn't say anything, as I don't think he checks Facebook much. I'll have to tell him soon. That can wait. I've got enough on my plate. I wonder if Luke will see it . . .

The next M&Ms meeting comes around and after the misery of the last session, I decide that successes should be our next topic. Niki's brought some Greek treats – an orangey sponge cake called revani, which is utterly divine. I've moved a kettle up here too and brought milk and sugar, and we all provide our own teabags to suit our unique needs (such as, decaffeinated for me and something to do with roots for Rhona). Everyone talks about their good days, the meds that are working and so forth. Niki in particular is doing well with her nice GP, who's really helping her. That's always good to hear. When it comes to me, I don't have much to say (and neither does Rhona, I notice). So all I can think of is Nate. Maybe, after all these months, it's time to say something about him, in the safe space of this group anyway (I haven't even told Brenda about Nate yet).

'Well, it's not a success as such, but I am chatting with an old flame of mine at the moment.'

'Ooh!' says Niki. 'Now there's some exciting news!'

'Do tell!' says Joy.

Now I feel all coy and dumb, because it's not really anything yet, is it? I feel like a bit of a fool for mentioning it.

'So, we used to share a house at uni in our final year. Me and Nate and this other lad called Luke. And I was madly in love with Nate at the time, but it turns out he was having a fling with a married woman, and he liked me too – apparently – but couldn't make his move because he was already committed elsewhere. And he never told me. And then this invitation to a class of ninety-four reunion pops up on Facebook and Nate sees me on there and messages me.'

'This is a perfect meet-cute!' says Niki.

'What's one of those?' says Cheryl.

'A way for two romantic leads to meet in a cute way. You see it in romcoms, always some interesting way. Bumping into each other with packages, sitting next to someone randomly on a plane, reaching for the same book in a bookshop.'

'Eyes meeting over a margherita pizza,' I say and glance at Cheryl and we both smirk. Geoff tells me it's going really well and they get on like a house on fire. Cheryl's divorce is well under way and she's still living with Joy and that's going fine too. The progress this woman has made in a few months is awesome!

'So, when's the reunion?' says Joy.

'And what are you going to wear?' asks Niki, excitably.

I can't bear to admit that I'm not going. Fear of travelling seems like such a pathetic thing to admit to. I mean, you don't see it on menopause symptoms lists. So maybe it's nothing to do with that. Maybe it's just me, being weak. I know they'll think I'm daft, they'll all tell me I must go. I can't deal with their admonishments right now, not while the HRT is still not working.

'Beginning of October,' I say.

'A few weeks to get that killer outfit then!' says Niki. 'Let me know if you want any changing-room advice.'

'Will do,' I say and now I want to change the subject. I'm a terrible liar, so I can't keep this up. Plus I've noticed again that Rhona is pretty quiet and subdued today.

'I know it's a good idea to share successes where we can,' I say. 'Because it can all get a bit depressing, this menopause stuff. But it can also be hard, to hear other people's successes when you're struggling. So if anyone wants to share anything today that's not on the theme of successes, or just have a rant, or whatever, do speak up, if you want to.'

There's a pause, then Rhona clears her throat.

'I want to ask something. Say something, you know. Something I'm not sure about.'

'Of course. Fire away,' I say.

Rhona looks horribly uncomfortable. They all know by now they're never expected to share if they don't want to. So we wait, until she's ready.

'So, you all know I don't like medicines much. And I always try to look out for different ways of doing things. I've been like that all my grown-up life really. And it takes a lot of faith, you know. I have faith in those things.

261

So I was seeing a therapist. This man. Quite old, well, older than us. He does acupuncture. And he does aromatherapy and all sorts of other treatments. He's in this lovely building out near Chipping Norton. I've been going there about a year. He puts waves through you. I know, that sounds a bit crackers. But it's proven, it can help. A pod on your back for the kidneys. Something around your neck and between your toes. Sends waves, like pulses. It makes a noise. Then he does massage too, but doesn't touch you. He says it isn't Reiki, he's very clear about that. It's his own version. Moving his hands over your head. Takes your bad energy away. But none of it's helped. Not any of it.'

Rhona's usual energy seems to have drained out of her. It's unsettling, to see her fiery rage so dampened down. And I feel like something worse is coming.

'And I tell him that. So he says acupuncture is the answer. So then he puts acupuncture needles in, just certain places. Around my tummy button, in my head and in my leg, lower leg, the shin bit, every week. And then more around my tummy, more often. But then . . . I had to push my trousers down a bit. For him to put the needles lower. And the next time, they'd go lower again. And then I had to push my . . . knickers down just a tiny bit. And I could see . . . well, he could see, my . . . you know. My hair, down there. The top bit of it, just half an inch of it. And he put some needles there. He didn't go into my knickers or further down or anything. But he did leave . . . his fingers there at the top . . . too long. Too often. And I didn't like it. I didn't like it at all. So I've left. I haven't gone back. And it's cost me a fortune. All my savings gone on it, on him, that man. And I don't think he should've been putting needles there. Or . . . you know . . . his fingers there. And none of it's worked. And . . . I feel like such a fool. Such a silly old cow.'

Everyone is shaking their heads and gazing at Rhona with such concern. It's uncustomary in this group to worry about Rhona. Her anger makes her seem so forthright. But she's shown us her vulnerability today and I can tell that, for every one of us, our hearts are going out to her.

'Rhona, this is awful. I'm so sorry to hear that,' I say. 'And you are not a fool or a silly cow. Don't talk about yourself that way. You wouldn't call any of us that, would you?'

'No, but you're all . . . you know. Sensible.'

'If only!' I say and everyone is nodding.

'Rhona, it's not your fault,' says Niki, reaching out and touching Rhona's knee. 'You paid good money and put good faith in this bloke and he's clearly not fit to help you or anyone.'

Then Cheryl says, 'Sounds a bit rapey to me.'

Cheryl strikes again!

'Agreed,' says Niki.

Cheryl adds, 'I mean, messing about in your pubic hair? Definitely rapey.'

Joy has waited a while to speak. But now she says it how she sees it, as she always does. 'Rhona, I'm sorry to say that I think this is an abuse of his position as a therapist. It could even be construed as assault. Have you thought about reporting him to the police?'

'Oh no, no,' says Rhona, shaking her head. 'I can't do that. I don't want any trouble. And it doesn't seem bad enough for that. I mean, he didn't grab at me or anything. It's probably nothing.'

'It's certainly not nothing,' Joy goes on. 'And I take your point, that it's hard to prove it's not just part of the therapy. But look, it's your choice, Rhona. Nobody should have to get involved in anything they don't want to, if they want to stay anonymous. But you could report him anonymously to some kind of association of acupuncturists or aromatherapists or alternative practitioners. Or I can do that for you, Rhona. I won't mention your name. How does that sound?'

Rhona smiles a small smile. 'That would be brilliant, Joy.'

'Then it's agreed,' says Joy.

'And we'll find you another practitioner,' says Niki. 'My cousin does aromatherapy. I bet she'll know some good people, who'll treat you well. And I'll go with you to the first appointment, if you like? Until you feel safe.'

Rhona is really smiling now. These women. They are the bloody best. I love them.

That night, I'm in bed and not feeling great. I'm more tired than anything, but the warm memories of the M&Ms today make me feel better. Then I realise that it's quite a few days since I've had any diarrhoea. Or hot flushes. The meds I was given for acid and also the migraines are helping, so maybe Dr Shaw wasn't all bad, to be fair. In fact, other than feeling tired, I haven't really had any health issues for about five days now. Does this mean . . . the HRT might be . . . working? It's tempting to think that, because Dr Anand was so nice, so surely his prescription will help. But life doesn't work that neatly, unfortunately. Truth is, it's too early to tell. I've had this before, brief respites. Then it comes back full force, especially when I'm stressed. And there's a lot of stress at work right now, one of our busiest times of year with so much shit to deal with. My stomach lurches at the thought of it. There it is, the old familiar gastro lurch. See, it hasn't gone away.

My phone pings. It's the Messenger sound. I'm too tired to flirt with Nate tonight. I still haven't told him I'm not coming. He's been asking which hotel I'm going to be at and I'm claiming I haven't booked it yet and he keeps telling me to. I really have to 'fess up soon. This is getting ridiculous. I open up my phone.

But it's not Nate. It's Luke.

Chapter 19

Hi there. It's Luke Jones again, sheepishly edging into your inbox. I've been a bit of a twat and I want to say sorry. So I'm saying it. Sorry. Plus I see you've said on the reunion post you're not going. I'm really sorry to hear that. And sorry it took me a while to notice. I sometimes don't go on Facebook for weeks at a time. I just wanted to see if you're okay. If it's health-related, I was wondering if I could help. If not, just tell me to mind my own business. Or tell me to mind my own business either way. Anyway, that's my sheepish and overly wordy attempt at reconciliation. Please feel free to tell me to fuck off.

That's actually really cheered me up.

I don't want you to fuck off, Luke Jones.

Hey! Are you sure?

Sure I'm sure

Good. How are you? How's your health?

I really can't be bothered to type it all, it's such a long tale of woe. Suffice to say, I'm really struggling massively with menopause symptoms and my GP just doesn't seem to be able to help me at all. It's just getting worse and worse. I don't really know what to do about it.

That sounds bloody awful. I wish I could help.

I appreciate that. I'm so exhausted with it all tbh, Luke. Sorry to be such a downer.

Not at all. I think you should get some rest, yeah? Maybe we can message again when you're feeling better.

Yeah sure. Thanks Luke.

I've not done anything. But anyway, till next time x

Till next time x

I'm glad we've made up again. It felt rotten not being friends with Luke. And it isn't long before he's messaged again. The very next night, I'm exhausted again and in bed and he pops up on my phone. It's been a long, shitty day at work and it actually cheers me up immeasurably to see it.

Hey, you ok?

**Well, not really. Another awful day at my awful job.
And I feel like shit, as usual. Oh Christ, sorry Luke. I
feel like all I ever do is complain at you!**

Not at all. But actually, I have an idea that might help.

Oh yeah?

*Yeah. It takes a bit of explaining. How about a call? Just
a quick audio call. If you fancy that. No worries if you're
too tired.*

Well, fuck it. Why not? It'd be nice to hear a friendly
voice.

Sure

So Luke rings me.
'Hi.'
'Hello Luke Jones née Beresford.'
'It's not my married name!'
'I know, I'm just teasing you.'
'I know. My dad was not a very nice bloke. We've been
estranged for years. I got fed up of carrying his name
around. So I changed it by deed poll, to my mum's maiden
name.'
'Good for you. It suits you.'
'Thanks! But seriously, how are you? How's your health
really?'

I tell him everything, and I mean everything. All about the rough seas of menopause: the tests and the Facebook groups and the M&Ms and the symptoms and the doctor visits and the holiday and the travel anxiety and everything. Even the farting and the diarrhoea. I have no shame left, no embarrassment (except with Nate, obviously). And I know Luke is a good person. And he won't judge me.

'Heidi, that's fucking awful.'

'Yeah, it's no fun.'

'Right, well, I've been thinking. It's one of the reasons I got in touch, to be honest. When I saw you weren't going to the reunion, I wondered if it might be menopause-related.'

'You thought right.'

'So listen, I have a good friend, known her for years. She's a private gynaecologist. She's not cheap. But I've taken the liberty of telling her about you. And she owed me a favour – I played guitar at her daughter's birthday party last year for three hours – and she says she'll waive the fee if you want to see her. She's up in Northumberland, but you can do it by video. She said you could have an appointment for an hour to discuss it and give you advice, then she'd write to your GP to have it sorted on the NHS. How does that sound?'

'That sounds bloody marvellous! Are you sure?'

'Absolutely. She said get in touch with her PA and she'll organise it.'

'I never thought I could afford to go private. But maybe there's a way this could work, if she's happy to write to my GP. And get it sorted with him. I didn't know private doctors liaised with the NHS ones. I always assumed it was either/or. That's really good to know.'

'Good.'

I pause. I'm feeling a bit tearful, I realise.

'Luke, that's so kind.'

'It's nothing. It's what anyone would do.'

I think of Nate's flowers and chocolates. And the fact that he hasn't asked me about my health since the holiday, not really.

'No, it isn't. Thank you.'

'You're welcome.'

'Luke,' I say suddenly. 'Do you remember the badgers?'

'Of course I do.'

'I didn't dream it then.'

'No. They seemed magical, but they weren't. They were real.'

We share a silence. We're both thinking of the badgers, I think.

'I really am sorry,' he says. 'For my textual outburst.'

'It's okay, really.'

'No, it's not. I was being a prick, you were right. And look, if you'll have me as a friend, that's what I'd really like to be. I'm no good at this phone romance stuff anyway and I'd much rather be your friend than lose that over a disagreement about Nate. And, for what it's worth, I really do wish you both well and hope it works out for you. But if you don't want to be friends with me or you feel uncomfortable – even after the doctor appointment – I totally understand and will take my leave. Don't ever feel you owe me for that. You don't. It's given sincerely.'

That's quite a speech. He's been practising it, I think. And he's offering help, given sincerely.

'I'm really happy to be friends with you, like the old days.'

'Like the old days,' he says, in confirmation. 'And look, if you change your mind about the reunion, I am going. I've booked my flight. Because of work and stuff, I can only stay in the UK for two days, otherwise I'd offer to drive you from Oxford. But I'm not arriving in Exeter until late Saturday afternoon, then I'm flying back on the Sunday night. It's nuts, I know. But it'll be an adventure. Especially if you and Nate are there. We can have a mini housemates' reunion of our own, but I won't bother you two, I promise. Plenty of people to catch up with. No pressure.'

'I'll certainly think about it,' I say.

'Take care,' he says.

What a lovely call. What a kind man. He sends through the website of his gynae friend. She's Dr Edelman up in Berwick-upon-Tweed. Thank heavens for video calls. One of the very few things we have the pandemic to thank for: remote medical appointments. Without that, I'd have to travel up to Northumberland to see her, which would've been impossible with my travel fear. I fill in the contact form on her website.

The next morning, her PA is in touch. She has a cancellation in two days' time – can I make it? Absolutely! It's at 3pm, so I leave work early and go home to an empty house and set up on my laptop.

Dr Edelman is bang on time. She's in her fifties, she's bright and chatty, yet she's a good listener. She wants a full history. I tell her everything I can think of. This is what she says:

'I feel you ought to have your HRT prescription changed to gel instead of patches, just to see if it's absorbed better. And I would also recommend a testosterone gel as well, for the fatigue and it should help with your sex drive too. For stomach cramps and nausea, I'm going to give you some prescription-only medications that are more targeted IBS treatments than anything you can get over the counter.'

I'm happy with all of that. Always up for new meds. She says she'll write a letter to my GP suggesting all of these.

'Follow up with your GP once they have the letter. They might say yes or no. Come back to me if they won't give you any of these and I can write a private prescription. It won't be cheap. But you can try them for a couple of months and see how you go, then use that as evidence to go back to your GP and demand that the NHS help, because you've proven that they work for you. Still no guarantees they will. But it's worth a try. Who's your GP? Who should I write to?'

'Please write to Dr Anand. He's the best one.'

'Super. Will do. And say hi to Luke for me, won't you?'

Well, that was brilliant. Just to have a doctor sit and really listen to you for a whole hour was a revelation. I know the NHS can't cope with that. I know it's under-funded and over-crowded and everyone is overworked and underpaid. But an hour . . . it's marvellous. I feel very fortunate.

I'm about to type Luke a message telling him all about it, when I realise a voice note would be a hell of a lot easier. So I send him that instead, telling him everything she said and how helpful it was.

'Thank you so much, Luke. For your kindness. You really might have changed my life, you know. Thanks again.'

There's no reply for a while. I get on with my evening, then when I'm making tea, my phone pings and I see he's sent a voice note back. The washing machine is on spin cycle and the Ninja's on whining loudly in the kitchen, and in the next room Ada and Carly are playing *Mario Kart* and shouting at the telly. It's a cacophony. I go into the downstairs loo for a bit of peace and press play.

The voice note is quiet at first and I wonder if it hasn't worked. Then, I hear a guitar, picking out five notes I know so well, they give me shivers. It's the opening bar of 'Wichita Lineman', the song I play on my fiddle that makes me sob. He's arranged it for guitar. And it's gorgeous. Then, his voice comes in and it's sweet and mellow. The guitar arrangement is simple yet sonorous. The instrumental in the middle is beautiful. He draws every ounce of feeling from that simple tune and makes it glow with resonance.

'And I need you more than want you . . . And I want you all the time . . .'

Oh God, I've got tears in my eyes. I'm standing in the downstairs loo in the summer evening light. And I am transported. I hold my phone tightly. I want to touch the screen, to thank it for the gift it just gave me. I want to thank Luke.

I'm about to send a heart back as reply, but I hesitate. It doesn't feel . . . right, though it does feel right at the same time.

Instead I message, ***Oh stop. You'll make me cry.***

273

Then I feel like that's a flippant kind of response. It warrants so much more than that. So I add:

That was beautiful. Thank you.

He sends a single heart back.

I listen to it again. And again. Every time I do, it transports me, to a place of utter tranquillity. It's precisely the same as that feeling on Lake Windermere, with the breeze playing about my neck. As I listen to Luke's song, it feels like he's whispering in my ear.

I can't stop thinking about it. The difference between Nate and Luke's reactions to my health crisis is stark. Nate's flowers and chocolates gesture seem risible compared to Luke's help. Is this merely the difference between friends and lovers? After all, Geoff would bend over backwards to help me, with real, proper help, not just gestures. And he was my husband and my friend. More friends than anything, most of the time. So maybe this is the difference, between romance and friendship. I'm starting to have all the feels for Luke, but it's as a friend, surely? Because every time I see Nate on video or even just a silly selfie, I feel weak at the knees. Can a person be in love with two men at the same time? And which is more important – electricity? Or tranquillity? And the more I ask these questions, the more I sound like Carrie Bradshaw typing one of her inane articles on *Sex and the City*. (Surely a gal can't afford a brownstone apartment in New York and endless couture writing one article a week?! That always bugged me.)

Then – as if by magic – Nate messages.

Hey Hobbes. You know I'll be taking my motorbike on the long road down south to Exeter? Happy to swerve by and pick you up if you fancy a ride down there with me?

Oh crumbs, exactly what I'd imagined and knew I could never do. But it's nice he's offered. Very nice. It really is more than a little detour to come all that way for me.

Thanks so much. But I've already booked the train, I lie. **I shall see you there!**

And this time I mean it. I'm going. By hook or by crook, I am going to the reunion. But who am I going for? Nate? Or Luke?

(Cue pensive close-up of Carrie with fabulous hair, chewing a pen.)

It's all very well making a decision to do something scary one day, when you're feeling fine and dandy. But actually following through on it another day, when you're feeling shit, is quite another matter. I was younger then and full of hope. Now the thought of getting the train to Exeter and meeting all those people from my past is akin to public torture.

I finally raise it with the M&Ms. And, as expected, they all excitedly try to persuade me to go, that I simply must go and not try to dodge it. That it'll be fine. But will it? When people say stuff like that to me, I always want to shout, *BUT HOW DO YOU KNOW?* There's a good chance it won't be fine at all. It might be the next worst day of my life, after the Lake District fiasco. I don't let on to the M&Ms though. I still feel silly bleating on about my fear of trains. So I leave them thinking they've persuaded me; people always feel good when they think they've done that. So that'll be nice for them. Underneath, my anxiety AKA Mommy Dearest is still hurling terrifying *What if* scenarios at me, until I'm exhausted by the thought of it. Should I go, or not?

So I'm sitting with Brenda and Kim in the canteen at work. I must admit my appetite is better than it was and I'm enjoying a nice jacket potato with coleslaw and salad. I missed Brenda and Kim while they were away in Vietnam for the summer. I ask Kim about it, see how she is. I feel I've been remiss lately and not kept up with their issues as much as I could have. We talk about the difficult business of sorting out all her mum's stuff, liaising with the solicitor about the will, packaging up heirlooms to be sent back to England and arranging valuations and an auction of the other stuff. I know it's exhausted Kim and been emotionally draining too.

Then Kim says, 'I'm bored of the sound of my own voice talking about it.'

Brenda reaches across and squeezes Kim's hand. A loving look passes between them which brings a tear to my eye. God, I'm so on the emotional edge all the bloody time. But these two, and their relationship, is just . . . I don't know. It's just beautiful. It's my aspiration. They're like best buddies and loving spouses and clearly fancy the pants off each other. I'm a bit envious, to be honest. They found their person. I wish I could.

Kim then says, 'Tell me about you. What's going on with your health? Are you better since the Lake District?'

'Yes, actually, I am a bit better in some ways. I think

the new meds are helping. I'm still terrified of travel though. I've got this thing coming up, a university reunion. Down in Devon. I can't decide whether to go or not.'

'Of course you must go!' says Brenda. 'Do you still know anyone there?'

I tell them about Nate. And Luke. The whole saga.

'You are bloody well going,' says Kim.

'But what if . . .' I begin. A thousand *What ifs* crowd my mind and I don't even know where to start. Saying them out loud would make each one sound pathetic. Nobody understands another person's anxiety, do they? Nobody gets it.

'*What if* questions will drive you insane,' says Kim. 'I used to have quite a bit of anxiety, when I was younger. I did a CBT course. Have you heard of that? Cognitive behavioural therapy. It's not soul-searching, like psychoanalysis. It's more like practical solutions to anxiety, in the moment.'

'That sounds like what I need. When Mommy Dearest is haranguing me in my head, I can't hear my own voice.'

'What's your bloody mum been saying now?' says Brenda. She knows my mum of old, and the dreadful effect she has on me when she's switched on her nasty voice. I explain who Mommy Dearest is, my anxiety monster.

'Listen,' says Kim. 'This negative self-talk stuff is deadly. You have to take control, but calmly. Ask yourself, *What's the worst that can happen?* Okay, so, you might get ill on the train. Someone would help you. Someone would. You could always go back. If the absolute worst came to the absolute worst, you could call us or Carly or Geoff to come and fetch you and bring you home.

You know we'd all do it for you, no questions asked. Or if you didn't want to wait, you could even pay for a taxi all the way home. It'd cost a bit of money but it'd be worth it. So that's that. What about the party? Well, it could be fun. It could well be the tonic you need. And give you the confidence to get out there a bit more. And you need to see these two guys, in the flesh. And decide how you feel. Virtual romance can't go on indefinitely. So again, with the party, say to yourself, *What's the worst that can happen?* You might get ill at the party. You can go back to your hotel room and recover. You can stay there till you feel better. And someone will help you. There are enough nice people around in the world, someone will. And there's always us and your support network. So, instead of asking endless *What ifs*, ask yourself *What's the worst?* And go from there. It works. I promise you.'

'I'd never thought of it that way. *What's the worst that could happen?* That really helps. Thanks, Kim. I didn't know you'd suffered from anxiety. You're always so . . . chilled out. Sorry to hear that.'

'Don't be. I don't anymore, not really. I got it from my mum. She was the most anxious person I ever knew in my life. Why do you think we always had to go over there to see her? She never came to England, not once, not even when I was here as a kid. Not even when I got glandular fever at fourteen and was bedridden for months. Even then, she couldn't bring herself to get on a plane.'

Kim was raised in Vietnam until she was eleven, when she was sent to boarding school in England and more or less never left, apart from the odd holiday visit home. She had Vietnamese relations in Oxford and spent most holidays with them. I didn't know her mother had literally never visited though.

'That is sad,' I say.

'It is. I mean, I was really mad with her for that at the time, especially when I was ill. But as I got older, and suffered with my own anxiety for a while, I grew to understand her more. But it's a terrible waste. She spent her whole life worrying. Totally anxiety-ridden. Too fearful to live a full life. That's one reason why I knew I had to deal with my own anxiety. I never wanted to live like she did. Look, you might be able to get CBT through your GP. But even if you can't, or can't be bothered, there are techniques you can use in your everyday life. It's not rocket science.'

'I'll google it later, but tell me some of yours, will you?'

'Okay, so, when your mind starts filling up with all that shit, you have to counteract it. You have to do positive self-talk, to quiet down that manic anxiety voice in your head. Start with the *What's the worst?* question and go through the answers calmly and quietly, finding solutions to each one. It works, it really does.'

'And a mantra never goes amiss,' adds Brenda.

'A mantra? Sounds a bit hippyish. A bit Beatles in the seventies,' I say, with a grimace. My favourite Beatles song is 'Drive My Car'. Simple, funny, sweet and a great beat. I can't stand it when they went all serious and psychedelic.

'Don't knock a mantra! Mantras are great!' says Brenda.

'Persuade me then.'

'I have one. I used to use it all the time with my alky ex. I'd go to a quiet place and close my eyes, regulate my breathing, you know, really focus on it, so it was long breaths, controlled. Then I'd say, *I am calm. I am whole. And I cannot change the things I don't control.'*

Blimey, I actually really like that idea: *I cannot change the things I don't control.* Ain't that the truth.

'That's brilliant, Bren.'

'Works for me.'

I think for a moment, taking another forkful of potato and coleslaw. It feels good to eat properly again and actually enjoy food.

'Are you gonna go to this reunion then, or what?' says Kim, grinning.

I'm finishing my mouthful and they're both looking at me expectantly now.

'Yes,' I say. 'Fuck it.'

'Yay!' says Brenda and Kim adds, 'Hell yeah.'

The decision is made (again). After all, what's the worst that could happen?

Chapter 20

It's Saturday the 5th of October and I'm on the train to Exeter. It's not too bad a journey: just over two and a half hours long with one change at Reading, that's all. Plus the same on the way back. *I CAN DO THIS*, I keep telling myself. It's autumn and so there's no chance of a heatwave, thank God. I'm in an airline-style seat, so I don't have to play footsie with a stranger opposite and luckily, nobody has sat down next to me, so if I do have to rush to the loo, I won't have the extra delay of asking them to get the hell out of my way. I've taken a shitload of Imodium and have multiple amounts of all my other meds, as well as a significant number of pairs of knickers, just in case a zombie apocalypse happens and I'm stuck at the Mercure Hotel for six weeks and no contact with the outside world. The hotel is a few minutes in a taxi from both the train station and Reed Hall, where the party is. I've got a train at midday, so that gives me plenty of time in my hotel room to compose myself before the party begins. I've tried to think of every eventuality and I'm feeling pretty calm. I've forgotten how nice train travel can be, when it goes well, that is. Plus I don't have Ada in tow to worry about. Things always feel far worse when I have to be responsible for another person. Today, it's just me. And if things go wrong, I'll deal with them. There, I sound convincing, don't I? Truth is, things always feel worse before you do them. Once you're in the thick of it, you just have to get on with it.

That's what Nate reminded me yesterday, and he is right. I did finally admit to him during a phone call that I had a fear of travel.

'Don't be silly,' he said bluntly. 'It's crazy to be afraid of trains. They can't bite you.'

He's right about that too. Of course he is. I have to get over this doom-laden feeling I've had about travel for months now. It really is all in my head. I need to be more Nate.

Luke sent a voicemail too and said, 'Hey, I'm off to catch my flight to Heathrow soon. I'll be driving a hire car to Exeter to my hotel and then on to the party. But listen, I know you've said you're definitely coming, but if you don't feel well enough at the last minute to go to the reunion, then that's fine too, of course. If you like, I could drive up to Oxford to see you on the Sunday, if you're well enough for a quick visit from a friend. Or not. Either way, don't worry. Only go if you feel well enough. Not that I'm telling you what to do. You're a grown-up and can do whatever the bloody hell you want to, obviously! Anyway, hope to see you soon. So, yeah. Bye then.'

That is lovely to hear too. And I realise that Nate and Luke are so different, and have such opposing ways of approaching things, but that somehow, I need both. I need someone to say, *You don't have to do this.* But I also need someone to say, *Pull yourself together. Of course you can do this.*

The train journey goes swimmingly, not one hitch. I get a taxi to the hotel. The room is smart and clean and I'm there in good time, so the room is ready plus it's still a few hours till the party. I have a bubble bath and truly relax. It's going to be okay. The first hurdle is done – the train journey. And it went so well! It reminds me that there are people out there in the world doing things every day and they just go smoothly and nothing bad happens. When I'm in the depths, wrapped up in bed in a dressing gown with an Ovaltine, hiding from the world, it all feels like a horror show. But doing something as simple as a train journey reminds me that the world can run well much of the time and that my fears are unfounded. Next, getting ready for the party. I've brought two outfits, so I can decide depending on my mood. One is a pretty skirt with pink and black flowers on, plus a sleeveless black top that hugs in the right places. Worn with tights and Spanx, it's a nice shape. I like it, feel comfy in it. It's not particularly interesting, but it's pretty and it makes me feel good. The other outfit is far more interesting but about a thousand miles out of my comfort zone. It's a jumpsuit, sparkly dark green, worn with heels. Carly and Ada have told me I have to wear it, that it's bloody brilliant and that I look a million dollars in it. But I know it shows my tummy much more than the skirt. I know it hugs my bottom and makes it stick out (though Ada tries to convince me that big butts are on trend). It's much more 'party' than the nice but dull skirt and top. But I'm terrified of looking like mutton dressed as lamb. I don't want everyone to look at me and think, *What on earth does she think she's wearing?* I actually messaged Brenda and Alia when I saw the jumpsuit online and thought about buying it, **Do women my age actually wear sparkly jumpsuits?** They both confirmed yes and also that I can wear whatever the fuck I like at any age.

Alia texts, *Who says you can't? The clothes police??*

So, I'm out of the bath. Hair is blow-dried and looking good. Make-up is done, a bit sparkly with a nice deep pink lippy. I'm pretty pleased with that. I don't look like mutton, not yet. Now, the outfit decision. I try on the skirt and top. It looks . . . nice. But . . . uninspiring. It's safe . . . but dull. Yet also comfy. Then, my phone pings.

It's Nate. I've not heard anything from Luke since last night, but Nate has messaged at every step of the journey, to let me know where he is.

At my hotel. On the road soon to venue. See you there, gorgeous!

My stomach lurches at the thought of seeing Nate again, in the flesh. I can't wait! But also I'm terrified. I've not had a crush on a man for a long, long time. How will it feel when I see him for real? Will we kiss? Will we . . . do other things?! Will I measure up to how he remembers me? I look back at the skirt and top. I finally know what I'm going to wear tonight.

The taxi drives me up from the hotel to the University of Exeter campus where the party is. Seeing the streets and buildings of my youth again brings an intense wave of nostalgia. The fear I had almost exactly thirty years ago on that first day I drove myself up to the halls – in the little Ford Fiesta my parents had bought for me, bless them – I can recall that fear so well. My parents didn't come with me. They said I needed to get on with it on my own. But they did give me that car. It was red and I called it Rosie. Girls often named their cars back then. Maybe they still do, I don't know. That fear was about the unknown, but today I have a different fear. Can I really carry off this sparkly jumpsuit?! Or have I made the worst decision of my life?! I'm terrified now it'll look like Gerard Depardieu in *Asterix and Obelix*. High waist, pot belly, corgi legs. Oh GOD . . . oh, you know what? It is what it is. And the clothes police can do one. I am Heidi Hobbes and I am going to wear this sparkly jumpsuit with pride.

I'm dropped off in front of Reed Hall. It's a beautiful Victorian building with stunning gardens surrounding it. Stone steps lead up to the main door. I feel like I should be wearing a Cinderella-style gown on those steps (and don't tell me that anything but the blue dress from the 1960s Ladybird book is the best one, because the pink was nice and the gold was a bit special BUT the blue was the most gorgeous shade of blue ever painted and it is by far the best Cinderella dress ever and there is no debate about that). But here I am, in my sparkly jumpsuit and heels, and there's a couple of other people before me and after me going up the steps and they're dressed in similarly dressy stuff and that woman there has a big arse and a figure-hugging dress and is displaying it in all its glory and I feel better about mine. I think I might actually be feeling good. Yeah, I do! Fuck it! Let's go!

Inside, there's a desk in the foyer and look who's standing there beaming, the harpist and infuriatingly positive Serena Lightfoot (and my God, what a name. Her destiny was secured at birth) and as I move closer I see . . . oh bollocks . . . yep, we have on the exact same outfit, the EXACT same green sparkly jumpsuit from Cider and I know because it's the exact same shade of dark green with the same strappy shoulders. We glare at each other and she looks me up and down and seems mortified. And for a split second I feel the same, but then I think, you know what? I have zero fucks to give and we both look great.

I say to her, 'Serena, we are by far the coolest bitches at this party.'

Her eyes widen and then she says, 'Aren't we just, darling!' and we laugh.

'Come here for a hug!' she cries. 'It's Heidi, isn't it! I'm so glad you changed your mind and could come. You don't look a minute older than 1994!'

I give her a hug and tell her she's a good liar (and imagine she says that to everyone). She gives me a badge with my name on and directs me down the corridor to the party room. I walk down, a little nervous on my heels as I basically never wear them, but feeling good. I'm scanning the others for Nate and Luke's faces, but haven't seen them yet. Down the corridor, there are other rooms and guests coming and going, then I clock the ladies' loos – I always look for loos wherever I go, a bit like cats always look for exits in any room they're in – and make a mental note for later to take more Imodium, if I feel stomachy. Speaking of which, I haven't felt ill yet and I'm cautiously pleased. Then, as I reach the door of the party room, the anxiety kicks in: what if I don't remember anyone? What if nobody remembers me? What if nobody talks to me? What if I'm left standing around on my own at the edge with nobody to talk to? What if Nate and Luke don't turn up? What if they *do* turn up? What will Nate think of me in this green sparkly jumpsuit which is far too young for me and Serena looked so much better in? What will happen when I see Nate? What will happen when Nate sees Luke? What will happen when Luke sees Nate? Will I get the shits and have to rush off back to the hotel, like Cinderella (the diarrhoea version)? What if EVERYONE THINKS I'M A LOSER?

Oh, shut the fuck up, Mommy Dearest, I whisper angrily under my breath.

'It's Heidi, isn't it?' says a voice behind me and I whip round to see someone I don't recognise in the slightest . . .

'Yeah, it's me!' I say, far too chirpily, because I'm madly trying to work out who this person is.

'It's Sally. Recorder player.' Oh God, I see it now. And I feel bad I didn't recognise her. But then I realise, her Facebook profile pic hasn't been updated for about fifteen years, I reckon. And she really has aged. Unlike Serena, who seems to have retained a youthful glow, Sally does indeed look thirty years older, but then, why the hell shouldn't she look thirty years older? She *is* thirty years older! What a ridiculous thing it is to expect any of us to look the same as we did thirty years ago. And the insane pressure on women to age well, in a way that doesn't seem to be angled at men in quite the same way.

'Sally, you look absolutely beautiful in that dress,' I say and her eyes light up with surprise and she smiles broadly.

'Well, bless you for saying that, but it's the only one that fits.'

'Tell me about it. Menopause has me rivalling the Michelin Man for fat rolls.'

We laugh and start chatting, much to my relief. I have found someone to talk to. We don't even move from the corridor, because we have so much to say and we're rushing to get it all out. She's such an interesting person. She still lives in Exeter and now works as a librarian at the Royal Albert Memorial Museum, where she looks after the archives and helps people out with their research. We talk about that for ages. Her knowledge of history is marvellous. Then we talk about music and she still plays all of her recorders in a medieval group that meets once a week at the village hall in Newton St Cyres, then they all go for drinks at The Beer Engine afterwards, one of my favourite pubs when I was at uni. Luke used to drive us there. When Sally talks about the music they play, her eyes go all misty and she still clearly loves it. I'm honest and tell her where I am in my life, the struggles I've been through. She's going through menopause too and we spend ages talking about that, leaning against the corridor wall and swapping battle scars. It's such a pleasure to talk to Sally.

Then she says, 'I must go to the loo. Bladder the size of a dried pea. I'll see you in there.' She nods towards the party room and we take our leave. Time to face the music – literally. The soundtrack to our conversation has been a medley of nineties hits that have enveloped us in nostalgia:

'Love is All Around', 'Baby One More Time' and 'Wannabe'. All songs and bands that would be at the bottom of my nineties wish list, to be honest. I hope they play some less mainstreamy stuff later. If I hear that bloody awful Wet Wet Wet again I'm going to murder that DJ. And that bloody Marti Pellow's cheeky chappy face always made me want to punch him (though I'm sure he's a perfectly nice person. It's just my menopausal rage talking. Pipe down, Blondie. The nineties is not your time). Okay, so I can't loiter in this corridor any longer. I must be brave and enter the party. Here I go . . .

The room has been decorated beautifully, I must say. There's green and white bunting along every wall, with green and white streamers and balloons everywhere. There's a table with an absolutely enormous cake on it, multi-layered and coloured in green and white icing, all of this green and white business to match the university's colours. I'm assuming this was created by Serena's Cutey Cakey . . . It is damn impressive though. Then I realise with my green sparkly jumpsuit, I match the university colours too! I don't think I've ever colour-coordinated with anything in my life. (And I bet that's why Serena chose this jumpsuit. She strikes me as a highly coordinated person in all aspects of her perfect life.) There's a long bar and three tables laden with a nice-looking buffet. Maybe there'll be some bread rolls and plain chicken I can try, something simple that won't give me a poorly tummy later. At least the energy bars I ate in my hotel room will keep me going till then. I head towards the bar and ask for a glass of iced tap water. I'm not being cheap, it's just that any kind of fruity or bubbly drink plays havoc with my insides.

So basically whenever I'm out and about I either drink plain water or decaf tea. It's deadly dull, I know, but needs must. As I'm waiting at the bar, I scan the crowd for Nate and Luke. No sign yet. I do recognise a few faces, but can't put any name to them. Some of them awaken a few sleepy neurones in the depths of my subconscious in the rusty filing cabinet labelled THE NINETIES at the back of my brain. They do look vaguely familiar but that's all. Why aren't either Nate or Luke here yet? The party started at six-thirty and I waited till seven-thirty to get here, hoping that everyone else would have arrived by now, so I'm not standing around with a handful of people I don't know looking awkward for hours till the place fills up. Serena and Sally are the only two I've recognised and now I face the horrible moment when I have my drink and I must go forth and speak to people I don't know and ask them who they are and if we did music together and what they're doing now and many other questions I really couldn't give a fuck what the answers are but I have to pretend I do give a fuck.

So, I walk over to a woman whose face looks like I may have seen it before, thirty years ago. And we start talking. And it's easy. She played piano and had a crazily tall boyfriend who played bassoon and they're now married with seven kids. Seven! And I do remember them, especially the crazily tall bassoonist. And they introduce me to a few other people they still keep in touch with, and I start to recall some of them too, and we're all talking away like we saw each other yesterday. And people can remember random stuff I'd totally forgotten, like the time someone wrote *JOHN CAGE IS A TOTAL FUCKING FRAUD* on the blackboard before the professor did a lecture and he blew his top and shouted, 'Base mockery of a great man!' and refused to give the lecture, storming out in high dudgeon. I'd totally forgotten that! And I remember thinking that too, when we 'listened' to John Cage's work *4'33"*, which is exactly four minutes and thirty-three seconds of silence. It's supposed to get you to be aware of sound and sit there listening to the hall full of expectant people while they're breathing and coughing and shuffling around, but instead it just felt like lazy, pretentious bullshit. It's so fun to talk to people about music again. And to discover that most of them have given up regular playing years ago. I'm not the only musical failure then! That makes me feel even better. And before long, I'm chatting away with anyone that catches my eye and having a whale of a time. My confidence – living at the bottom of a pit until today – has boosted immeasurably. I feel great, I'm having a right laugh and I've not felt ill once. Instead of peeking at life from behind my fears, I'm in the thick of it. And it feels bloody marvellous. I actually grin widely as I think it. Life is good.

Then all of a sudden, there's a hand in the small of my back and a voice in my ear says, 'Hey, Hobbes.'

Chapter 21

Nate Wheeler is standing there, in the flesh. And the waves of desire I felt when I saw him on video calls are multiplied exponentially as I see him there for real. The nearness of his elegant, lean body and the charged jolt I feel as we connect our gaze. Oh God, I want to kiss him. I want to kiss him now, right now and right here. But I must retain some decorum. This isn't a romcom; this is real life.

'Nate!' I say. 'You made it!'

'Of course I made it, Hobbes. I wouldn't miss out on the chance to see you in all your finery. And look at you . . .'

He takes my hand and our fingers intertwine. The touch of his warm, dry hand is electric. He opens out my arm and follows the line of my curves with his eyes, gazing at my body encased in the figure-hugging jumpsuit I'm now so glad I wore.

'Oh stop,' I say and grin.

'You're incredibly sexy,' he says, smiling and shaking his head. 'Still gorgeous.'

'Thank you,' I say, still grinning. And standing there, while Nate eyes me up, I am transported back thirty years to that house we lived in, to everything I ever wanted to happen there, but never did. Who would have thought that all you needed was patience and then your dreams would come true, decades later? And I don't even want to look the same as that girl I was anymore, I just want to look like me, because that's the woman that Nate Wheeler is looking at now and that's the woman he wants. And maybe that's the woman I want to be too. No maybe about it. Definitely. It's me, Heidi Hobbes, nearly fifty-three and menopausal, but still here and – according to the rock god – still gorgeous.

Then, 'Unchained Melody' sung by the dreadful Robson and Jerome comes on and we both grimace. Of all the nineties hits to be our backdrop when I first see Nate Wheeler again, this has to be the worst.

'That DJ needs to be shot,' says Nate.

'Right?!' I say. 'It's been like that all evening. Scraping the bottom of the nineties barrel every damn time.'

'Do you want to get out of here?' he says, looking down at my body again, drinking it in. I really, really want him to put his hands on me. But do I want to leave the party? Yes. But no. Luke's not here yet. And I haven't been here long. I want to meet some more folk from uni and reminisce.

'Erm . . . well . . .'

'I just meant the corridor. It's too loud in here with that godawful music.'

'Oh, sure!' I say, relieved.

He takes my hand again and leads me from the room and I wonder if anyone's looking at us but I can't take my eyes off Nate, the back of his head, his ruffled blonde hair and lithe figure striding forward. He's wearing scruffy jeans and a rumpled striped shirt and he looks like it took him five minutes to get ready and yet he still looks bloody fantastic.

We exit the room and he leads me up the corridor, past the ladies' loos. The corridor abruptly turns to the left and he leads me round the corner and the moment we're out of eyeshot of the general hubbub, he takes me and pushes me up against the wall. And his mouth is on my mouth and we're kissing deeply and for the first time in such a long time, I'm utterly in this moment. The voices in my head are silent and all is here and now. This man, who smells and tastes so damn good it's intoxicating, his lips on my lips, his hands on my hair. I can feel him hard as he presses his body against mine and my desire is overwhelming, to have him, right here, right now. I haven't felt lust like this in . . . thirty years, I realise with a shock, since I last saw Nate Wheeler in 1994. We come up for air.

'I couldn't wait,' he whispers in my ear.

'Me neither.'

He kisses me again and I'm hungry, so bloody starving for more. His mouth moves to my neck and his hands are all over me, and I'm glad I didn't wear Spanx tonight because he is feeling the real me. And he doesn't care about my fat rolls, or my tummy, or my wrinkles. All that time I wasted worrying about weight loss and what to wear. He wants me as badly as I want him. I can see over his shoulder now and luckily there's nobody here as he ravages me with his hands but then I realise that the men's loos are just up the corridor, and two blokes come out of the loos and smirk at us as they walk past and I feel weird about it. Then, Nate's hand moves down and presses between my legs and I pull back abruptly.

'Not here!' I laugh.

He moves his hand up to my waist and pulls me into him, kisses my neck again and I melt.

Then another bloke comes round the corner looking for the men's and, over Nate's shoulder, I look up at his face and – oh bloody hell – it's Luke.

He immediately clocks the situation and stops dead in his tracks. I don't know what to do. I stare at him. This moment feels like nothing less than betrayal. It's the worst feeling. Nate carries on, none the wiser. And Luke turns on his heel and goes back the other way, disappearing around the corner. Oh God, not like this. I wanted to meet Luke at the party, with music and drinks and fun all around us, and connect again and chat and laugh. Not like this. It's horrible.

'Let's go back to your hotel,' whispers Nate urgently in my ear.

I pull away, fixing my hair and smoothing myself down.

'What's wrong?' he says.

'Nothing. Erm . . . I want to . . . go back with you, of course I do. But . . . I want to stay at the party a bit longer. And you've only just got here.'

'I came to see you, gorgeous. I don't give a fuck about the party. And neither do you, do you?'

'Well, yeah, I do really. I'd like to talk to people a bit more. I've come all this way.'

He looks momentarily annoyed, then says, 'Yeah, course. I'm going for a slash. See you back in there.'

I hurry down the corridor. I'm breathing heavily and I feel hot. Oh crumbs, not a hot flush, please, not now. But I don't think it is. It's in my cheeks, not in my chest where it usually starts. It's not menopause. It's shame. I feel ashamed. And confused. And totally het up. That corridor kiss was one of the best moments of my life. I've never been kissed like that before, ever. But when I saw Luke, it was one of the worst moments of my life. I feel like something has been broken, more than that, smashed into smithereens. Something precious. Oh God, what the fuck am I doing? My instinct is to run, out of here and onto the street and walk swiftly all the way back to my hotel. But . . . I'm not going to. I have to face this. I have to find Luke and talk to him. I'm not going to run away.

I go back into the party room and scan the now sizeable crowd for Luke. I spot him by the cake table, chatting away merrily to a couple. I don't know them and it feels rude to interrupt, but I want to catch Luke before Nate comes back from his 'slash'. (Urgh, I hate that phrase, always have.) *Come on, Hobbes. Grasp the nettle.* I walk over to the magnificent cake and pretend to be admiring its enormity while I'm hovering near to the couple, trying to catch Luke's eye. He knows I'm there, I'm sure he does. Oh shit, is he going to ignore me and let me stand here like a fool? Then he looks up. And there's a small smile, a sweet smile, a rueful one. A smile so full of meanings, I can't fathom all of them yet. And I smile back, embarrassed, apologetic, though I don't know why, really. I haven't committed any crime.

'Heidi,' says Luke, lifting his hand over the couple's heads to motion me over. They turn round to look at me and I walk over.

Luke introduces me to them. One is an engineering student he knew back then and his wife did drama. We start talking amicably. No sign of Nate as yet, thankfully. I just need these people to stop being so nice and friendly and bugger off for a minute so I can talk to Luke alone. Even though Luke told me their names, my menopause brain retained them for about two and half seconds before they vanished from my memory forever. I'm distracted. I can't take in what they're saying to me, not just because of the loud music, but because all I want to do is gaze at Luke. Every so often I glance at him and every time I find him looking at me too. It's not lust I feel, not like with Nate. It's different, but it's just as powerful. I can't even begin to explain to myself what it is. It's something to do with a yearning, not for romance or sex, not like it's always been with Nate. But a terrible yearning, to whisk Luke away and talk to him all night like we used to – like that night during our finals when we stayed up till dawn talking about that book we both read, *The Inner Game of Music*, about how to get out of your conscious mind while you're performing and get into the zone and the moment you look at your fingers and realise you're playing an instrument is the moment you lose it and go wrong, then hearing the dawn chorus and reluctantly going to bed, Luke lingering on the landing as I went into my room and closed the door. Oh God, what a fool I was, to not see how in love with me Luke was. And how blinded I was by desire for the unobtainable glamour of Nate. Is this all a mistake? Have I royally fucked this up? I'm starting to dread Nate coming back into the room.

But I have to focus because the wife of this couple is talking to me about theatre. We're chatting away about the Northcott Theatre on the Exeter campus and how she saw a hilariously awful performance of *Medea* there in 1993, which I saw too – I used to go to the theatre all the time back then and don't know why I stopped – and the play was all set in the future and everyone had astronaut outfits on and the chorus were dressed as cybermen from *Dr Who*. We're laughing away and then 'Spaceman' by Babylon Zoo comes on and the wife says, 'Speaking of astronauts!' and I say to Luke, 'Oh Christ, do you remember watching that Levi's ad with the beginning of this song on and it was so cool that everyone went out and bought the single? But then it turns into such a rubbish song after that and we were all so gutted?!'

Luke says, 'I had a job part-time then when I was doing my doctorate and I worked at Our Price Records and everyone was bringing it back for a refund and I was like, *Yeah fair enough, it's shit!*'

Luke laughs loudly and it's so good to see him happy. If only this had been our meeting and not that shady fiasco in the corridor. And I want to talk to him about what he did after uni, because he said in a message recently that he'd done a PhD in Engineering and I'd had no idea. And I want to ask him what his thesis was and get him to explain it to me, just like he used to back then, those long talks in Dartmoor pubs about science where he'd try to explain the world beneath the world we can see and how mathematics relates to nature and how patient he was with me when I couldn't get my brain around it and how well he explained it to make me see the inner workings of the physical world and how beautiful they are. It's his mind I love, I suddenly realise. And looking at him now, his brown

eyes deep and kind and his hair gently tucked behind his
ears and all I want to do is take his hand and lead him
from that room, not for a grope in the corridor like I've
just had with Nate, but out into the Reed Hall gardens
and walk and chat with him till midnight, till we see
badgers playing again in the moonlight.

'Oh God, there's Nate Wheeler,' says the wife.

My attention immediately snaps back to the here and
now. I look round and Nate is on the dancefloor on his
own, dancing wildly and shouting 'Whoop!' really loudly.

'I'd forgotten about that wanker,' says her husband.

'Did you know him?' I ask, amazed. 'I did music with
him.' Did everyone know Nate Wheeler?! I catch a glimpse
of Luke and he is watching Nate, his face a subtle picture
of disdain.

'Yeah,' says the wife. 'He was Exeter royalty back then.
Everyone knew him. And he knew everyone.'

'And fucked everyone,' says the husband, with a hint
of envy. 'His notch count on his bedpost was infamous.'

Oh God, I feel a bit sick. And it's not an attack of IBS
coming on. I glance at Luke again and he's looking at me.
He looks concerned for me. There's no judgement there,
just care.

'Did you know,' says the wife conspiratorially, 'how
rich he was? And still is? His father was a billionaire,
apparently. Someone told me he goes round saying he's
a session musician with famous bands but it's all
nonsense. He inherited a fortune from his family and
doesn't need to work. He buys his way into tours and
they let him play because he's paying for all the hospitality
or something.'

'I had no idea,' I say, genuinely. I really didn't. He never acted rich. He always dressed scruffily, didn't have a flash car. But now it makes sense, how he's still in the industry and can afford a recording studio and two houses. And who knows what else? He's never had to work a day in his life. You can't dislike a person for being rich. But you can for lying. Or at least, being economical with the truth. All that guff about touring with Daryl Hall and Brett Anderson, like he was there for his talent alone. I feel like a gullible fool.

The husband adds, 'He's a fucking waster. And an arrogant twat.'

I look at Nate, spinning around, joined now by a couple of giggly women my age who he's thrusting his pelvis at. He keeps stopping and rubbing his nose furiously. Then carrying on dancing like a maniac. He didn't taste of alcohol when he kissed me. How is he so drunk and lairy so suddenly? I can't even look at Luke. I'm so horribly embarrassed. Whatever did I see in Nate?! He's ridiculous. And I realise that he's still stuck in the past, the rock god he used to be. He's never grown out of it, because his money has protected him from real life. All respect I had for him slides down the drain. And the lust I felt for him only a few minutes before evaporates. The scales have fallen from my eyes. Nate Wheeler is a manchild.

The couple say they're going to the bar and catch us later, and they drift away, while I'm still watching Nate throw himself around. I turn back and meet Luke's eye. In the shimmering colours of the tacky glitterball, he looks ethereal. He's the boy he was and the man he is, wrinkles and all, dressed in a suit, smart yet relaxed, hands in pockets, utterly at ease with himself, looking down at me, his dark eyes lit up by a smile. At last, Luke Jones and I are finally alone.

Chapter 22

'Luke, I want to explain.'

'You don't have to explain anything,' he says and looks down at his shoes. 'Honestly, it's none of my business.'

'But no, listen. You don't understand. Things have changed. Everything's changed.'

Luke looks at me, puzzled.

But I don't get a chance to explain, because up rolls Nate.

'Lukey-boy!' he shouts and lurches over, throwing his arms around Luke and nearly toppling both of them into the massive cake behind us.

Luke takes it well, then shoves Nate good-naturedly back onto his feet.

'All right, mate,' Luke says gruffly.

'It's so bloody good to see you, mate!' shouts Nate, far too loudly. I mean, yes, the music is pretty loud. But not that loud. People are eyeing Nate, smirking or shaking heads, or murmuring no doubt disparaging comments.

Then Nate clocks me and says, 'Hobbes! Hey, look, it's the whole house reunited. How fucking great is that!'

'Great,' I say and 'Great,' says Luke and we are about as convincing as each other, which is, not convincing in the slightest.

At that moment, while I'm wondering what the hell we're going to talk about, the desperately awkward three of us, we are saved by the DJ turning down the music and making an announcement.

'Hey there, nineties guys and gals. It's time to stop the music for a hot minute and hand over to Serena to catch those waves of nostalgia. Hang tight for a presentation on the class of ninety-four. And while you're waiting, go grab yourselves another drink at our reasonably priced bar. Buy a round. Buy two rounds. Get yourselves happy! Get ready for a toast to the Cla-a-a-a-a-s of NINE-TY-FOUUUUUUUUR!!'

'Hang the DJ,' says Luke and I couldn't agree more.

'Smashy and Nicey vibes,' I add.

Then we're distracted by Serena in full flow, arguing with the DJ. Without the music on, everyone can hear, though she's talking behind her hand, as if that makes any difference. She's telling him he shouldn't have told people to go to the bar because she's about to start her speech and she has the PowerPoint all set up and now nobody's listening. And the DJ is saying how it's part of his job to encourage people to use the bar more. And Serena is arguing back and saying it's her event and the DJ isn't backing down and they're really going for it now, while everyone else is at the bar getting another drink.

Luke and I glance at each other and burst out laughing.

Classic Serena control-freakery. It's so entertaining when people revert to type. And I know both Luke and I are thinking about the blanketed harp on the back seat of her car. But to be honest, I wouldn't want her job tonight, marshalling a bunch of drunk fifty-somethings. And I'm grateful to her for putting in all this effort to bring us together. Without Serena, I may never have got back in touch with my past again. There'd be no Luke here. But, unfortunately, there is Nate.

'Who the fuck is that woman anyway?' shouts Nate, pointing at Serena, just as loudly, even though the music is gone. Some partygoers glance round in his direction. More shaking of heads.

'That's Serena Lightfoot,' I say, watching him stagger a bit on his feet. 'She organised the—'

'I don't fucking care!' yells Nate and hoots with laughter. 'I don't give a fuck about anyone in this fucking room. They're all cunts!'

Oh, crumbs. He's getting out of control. And then he manically rubs his nose again. And it strikes me: he's not drunk. He's high. He's off his tits on cocaine, which he undoubtedly did in the gents'. Look, I'm no prude about drugs. I've not done any, but it's others' choice if they want to partake. I say legalise the lot and let them get on with it. Cigarettes and alcohol kill so many people, it feels daft that they're legal when the others aren't. But I'm not into drugs myself. And I'm not into my partner being into them, to be honest. And Nate is behaving like such an utter dick on coke, that it's the biggest turn-off yet, and that's saying something.

'Nate, keep it down, eh?' I say, holding my hand out

in an attempt to calm him. He grabs it and pulls me roughly towards him, which nearly topples him over. He's backed up against the cake table and the table judders, the many-tiered cake jiggling in place.

'Watch out, man,' says Luke loudly, grabbing on to the table.

'Oh fuck off, Beresford,' cries Nate, his face twisted with contempt. 'Nobody wanted you here anyway.'

'Hey!' I say, appalled. 'That's not true at all!' A little crowd are gathering now to watch the show. Nate pulls me towards him again and his other hand goes round my waist.

'Come with me, Hobbes. Let's get the fuck outta here. Come on my bike with me and we'll go for a nighttime drive and feel the wind in our hair and make out under the stars.'

'I'm going to stay and watch the presentation, Nate. Maybe you should go and sleep it off.'

'Come with me then!' he cries. 'Let's go back to my hotel room and fuck like rabbits.'

I glance at Luke and he's stepped forward now. He's looking murderous. Then, Nate makes a lunge to kiss my neck and I wriggle out of his grasp.

'That's enough,' I say loudly and firmly. 'I think you need to leave.'

Nate stands still and glares at me, then shouts, 'Well, you always were such a fucking boring bitch back then.'

I want to run from the room, imagining myself skittering over in these heels and falling on my arse. I'm completely mortified. Bystanders are staring and whispering. Oh God, this is my nightmare. Everything going wrong and everyone laughing at me. But, you know what, nobody is laughing.

Nate is standing there like a chump and I've done nothing wrong. Except believed Nate's hype. But not anymore. I'm not going to run from the room. What would Miriam do?

Nate adds: 'And *that's* why I never fucked you.'

There's an audible gasp from the crowd. There's no time for embarrassment. What rises in me is pure rage, Blondie awakening from her slumber and bellowing out a war cry in my brain. I've had enough of this absolute bullshit. Of thinking that I'm not enough. Of living in a world where guys like this judge a woman's worth by how fuckable she might be. That is until you hit fifty and become totally invisible. And most of all, I've had enough of this absolute wanker who I can't believe I pined after for all of these years . . .

I step forward, actually blocking Luke's path, who looks like he's about to kill Nate. But I'm there first and I raise my hands and I shove Nate in the chest, hard. For a moment he's cartoon-like, arms windmilling and panic strewn across his face. Then, he falls backwards onto the cake table and it upends, and the cake slides in horrifying slow motion off the front of the table and smashes onto the floor, destroyed. And the table flips to squish it even further at which point Nate topples over and lands on his side, his head catching the splurged top cake tier which submerges his hair and cheek in gooey green icing. I can't quite believe my eyes. This is nothing short of spectacular.

'My cake! My cake!' comes the cry, and it's Serena rushing over from her laptop at the side of the stage where she'd been waiting impatiently to make her presentation. Oh crikey, I feel bad about that, all that work on that beautiful masterpiece. But watching Nate grovel around in icing and sponge, trying to stand up with a shred of his dignity remaining, is priceless.

He gets to his feet and shouts, 'You fucking hysterical woman!'

That does it. I take a step towards him and let rip.

'Don't you EVER use that word with me, mate!' I yell at him, jabbing a finger in his direction. 'Or any other woman for that matter. I'm sick to my stomach of women being told they're hysterical, of being defined by their reproductive system, that their biology limits them, that they talk too much, that they feel too much, that they're lesser or an appendage or an addition to male normality. We are the mothers of the world, we are Mother Nature and mitochondrial DNA and we create and drive history and culture forward and we always have. And wankers like you are the worst of your kind, the man who never grows up, the man who sees every woman as his mother, his virgin, his whore or his crone. And you're fucking lucky that women haven't exercised their righteous anger to its full extent and destroyed the lot of you! You arrogant, lying, pushy, rapey, entitled WANKER!'

For a moment the whole room is so silent you could hear a pin drop. Then there's a little ripple of applause from the onlookers, then a whoop from someone and then more people are clapping and whooping and it's a roar. I can't help but smile as I look around the room and see everyone, men and women, clapping and nodding in approval. Nate is standing with his hands on his hips, glaring at me smugly, the side of his head covered in icing. He waits for the crowd to die down. Everyone wants to know what he's going to come out with next.

'I'd never fuck you now anyway, cos you're over the bloody hill and . . . and you're FAT.'

The crowd unanimously boo, like he's a pantomime villain, and I'm formulating a witty retort to this cheapest of jibes. But there's no time to answer, because Luke steps in and punches Nate square in his cakey face.

Then someone shouts, 'FOOD FIGHT!!' and before you know it, a bunch of middle-aged partygoers have descended on the buffet table and are hurling canapés at each other with wild abandon. Nate throws himself at Luke and they're struggling to stay upright as they slip around on smeary icing and cake, trying to throw more punches at each other. Fights in real life are nothing like the movies, I observe, not having seen one in real life before. Mostly it's pushing and shoving and much grabbing of clothes. Nate's nearly got Luke's suit jacket off over his head, while Serena Lightfoot is waving her hands in the air, screaming. Literally screaming, 'STOP IT STOP IT STOP I-I-I-I-IT!'

I'm just frozen there, watching the bloodbath ensue. Spring rolls and mini Scotch eggs are sailing across the room, while people are laughing like drains and falling over, while others are hovering at the edges, hands over mouths, shaking their heads in wonder or pointing in hilarity. Then even the bystanders start joining in and chucking the odd falafel ball or mini burger. And it strikes me that this is great therapy for harried and anxiety-ridden folk of a certain age like ourselves and maybe I'd make a killing if I opened a food-fight theme party business for fifty-somethings to relive their school or uni days and let rip with a few sandwiches. Fuck axe-throwing, this is the new antidote to middle-aged rage! This is bloody glorious!

But then I see Serena again and she's weeping uncontrollably, her hands over her face, sobbing her heart out. And the Reed Hall staff are gathering at the doors and looking on in horror at the mess. I didn't mean for this to happen. I didn't mean to ruin her cake or destroy their hall. And I hear one of the barmen shout, 'Call the bloody police!' and a waitress shout back, 'Police are on their way!'

And Luke hears that too. And Nate. They stop dead, Luke holding Nate's shirt collar like the scruff of a cat's neck.

'Fucking cops on their way?' says Nate. 'I'm off, mate. Let me go, for fuck's sake. I've got a shitload of coke in my pocket.'

Luke unhands him instantly and Nate stumbles as his cake-engulfed trainers slip and slide on the shiny wooden dancefloor, but he's a man on a mission and he's out of there like a shot.

'Oh Christ,' says Luke and I go over to him. 'I hate to say this, but I've gotta go too. I can't afford to get mixed up with the police. I'll be in deep shit with my employer and my job in the States. They'll probably ban me from re-entering the country if I'm arrested.'

'Oh God, yes. You mustn't let that happen. Go now. We'll talk later.'

'Yeah, look. I . . . I want to say . . . but . . . I've gotta go.'

'Go, go!'

Luke hesitates for a moment, then strides across the room and out of the door. Word about the police must've spread, as others are streaming out now. The staff don't try to stop them. I don't run off though. I'm staying. I've not thrown any food, but I did start this whole thing by shoving Nate into that cake. That beautiful cake. I look for Serena. She's seated now, beside the upended cake table, still crying. Oh God, poor woman. All her hard work. I go over to her and put my hand on her shoulder. She looks up, her face a mess of mascara and tear tracks through her foundation.

'I'm so sorry about all this, Serena,' I say.

'Well, Heidi, I am furious about the cake. It took me days of work. It was my magnum opus.'

'It really was. I'm so, so sorry. I had no idea some insane food fight would start, or that crazy fist fight, let alone the cake getting squashed. I promise you I didn't mean for Nate to fall back on it. I was just . . . I don't know . . . filled with rage and I saw red. I couldn't let him talk to me that way. I had to fight back. I know it was childish, irresponsible. But I don't regret it.'

'Oh, he definitely had it coming. I know first-hand what an awful shit Nate Wheeler is. He told me in my second year that he was in love with me, then shagged me in a cubicle in the Ram Bar toilets and dumped me straight after.'

'Oh my God! Was I the only one in the whole of Devon he didn't fuck?!'

'I think you might be,' says Serena. And we both look at each other and burst out laughing. Serena wipes her eyes carefully and can't stop giggling. I'm so glad she can see the funny side of this madness.

'Well,' she says, standing up. 'Nobody can say I don't throw a damn good party!'

'Abso-bloody-lutely! Everyone had a great time. And look at it this way, it's certainly a night none of us will ever forget, that's for sure! But look, I really am sorry about the cake. I'm going to stay and help clear up.'

'Thanks, darling. I can't have the staff doing it. It's not fair on them. Why should they get involved, when they may well be on minimum wage and long hours? If you ask for some bin liners, I'll get some cleaning things.'

And off she goes, renewed. She's not a bad egg, Serena. She's all right. She just wants things to be nice. And why shouldn't they be? I'll think twice before I slag off a woman like her again. She's just trying to do her best and help others have a nice time while she's doing it. That's something to admire, not mock mercilessly.

I do as I'm asked and manage to secure a roll of binbags from a barman and start filling one with food from the floor. The staff start to half-heartedly join in, as well as a few partygoers who haven't left yet and want to help. We do our best to clear it all up, some of the bar staff saying thanks. The police never come. I can't imagine a food fight at some posh uni conference room is the top of their agenda on a late Saturday night. Once the place looks a bit more ship-shape, we take our leave of each other.

I've booked a taxi. The driver asks me, 'Good night out?'

I pause, then reply, 'Interesting.'

'Oh yeah? Posh do, was it?'

'You'd think so, at Reed Hall. But no. It was pure and utter carnage.'

'Sounds like a great time was had by all then! A night to remember!'

'Certainly that,' I say. And though the evening in some senses was an unmitigated disaster, in other ways, I realise, it was bloody fantastic. I braved my travel phobia and got here in one piece. I chose a daring outfit and carried it off in style. I talked to loads of people I didn't know and had a right laugh. I had the best snog of my life with Nate and the loveliest moment gazing up at Luke beneath the glitter ball. Yes, I had the horrible realisation that Nate was full of shit, but then the immense satisfaction of shoving that loser into a giant cake. Plus the delectable experience of watching two men fist-fight over my honour. Oh, what a night! Heidi Hobbes is back.

I smile, shake my head and sigh. Crikey, I suddenly realise just how exhausted I am. It's gone eleven and I've not eaten or sat down for hours. I could literally fall asleep in this car, with its warmth and the rocking motion. But it's only a five-minute journey to my hotel and it's over before it begins. I pay the driver and get out. I'm saying thank you to him, when my phone starts ringing. I shut the car door and look at my phone. There's an unknown Exeter number calling me . . .

Chapter 23

I never answer unknown numbers usually, but on this occasion, I'm too curious not to.

'Hello?'

'Good evening, is that Ms Heidi Hobbes?' says a deep male voice I don't recognise, in a rich Devon burr.

'Who's this?' (I always say that whenever anyone asks who I am. As if by asking that, I don't make it already bloody obvious that I am indeed who they say I am.)

'This is Devon and Cornwall Police and this is Police Sergeant Badcock speaking.'

Police? Oh fuck! (Also, did he really just say his name was Bad Cock??!)

'Is everything all right?' I ask, hopelessly, by now convinced that they're going to arrest me for shoving a man into a many-tiered cake. My cheeks are flaring hot and I feel dizzy. Even spotting a police car on the side of the road when I'm passing makes me feel guilty, as if I've committed some crime that I've forgotten about and will be instantly arrested. Speaking to one is a thousand times scarier.

'I'm calling on behalf of a Mr Nathan Wheeler.'

Oh CHRIST! Is he going to have me arrested for assault? Is it assault, to push someone into a cake? What if it is? What if I have to go to court? What if I lose my job? What will happen about the mortgage and everything? I feel like I might faint.

Police Sergeant Badcock goes on, 'He has been arrested and is being detained. No details of the offence will be passed on to you. You are being informed as Mr Wheeler identified you as his girlfriend and thus nominated you as the person he wished to be informed of his detention. No further information can be given at this time.'

'I am *not* his girlfriend,' I say in a forthright manner. It's honestly the first thing that pops into my head. I want to make it very clear to this representative of the authorities that I have no relationship with Mr Nathan Wheeler and his nefarious activities. 'He's just someone I went to uni with. We reconnected recently via social media and met up again at the university reunion tonight at Reed Hall, but that's all. I have no relationship with him other than that.'

'Okay, well, that's as may be. I've done as Mr Wheeler has asked and informed you of his detention.'

'No maybe about it, I assure you. I don't have to come down there, do I? I don't want to see him. I don't want to have anything to do with him.'

'Absolutely not, Ms Hobbes. We're simply following PACE Code C regarding the detention of suspects. You are not required to do anything further.'

'Am I free to . . . go? Off this phone call, I mean?'

'Absolutely. Have a good evening, Ms Hobbes.'

'Thank you.'

And with that we say our farewells and hang up. I feel an uneasy mixture of queasiness and anger.

How bloody dare he tell the police I'm his girlfriend! How bloody dare he implicate me as somehow connected to him and his coke-fuelled ways! I'm furious, but I'm also curious. What was he arrested for? How did the police know about his cocaine? Whatever the case, I'm horrified to have been named by him. Yet I'm also utterly overwhelmed with relief that the police aren't going to charge me with aggravated pushing of a man into baked goods.

I go into my hotel and I'm greeted by the receptionist who politely asks me how my evening was. I momentarily consider telling her a full account of my insane night, but she doesn't want to hear all that nonsense. She's only being polite. Or maybe she does want to hear all that nonsense. Maybe it'd cheer up a dreary October night shift. Either way, I'm too tired to function and I schlep upstairs and collapse on my bed fully dressed. I'm about to pass out when I think about Nate and grab my phone and block him on everything. I also check for any messages from Luke. But there's nothing. So I message him:

Hey. Well, where to start?!

I send him a few messages, telling him stuff about the evening. I tell him about the police call and Nate's arrest. I make jokes about the madness of the party and ask him if he had food fights in his halls of residence like I did as a fresher. I know I'm avoiding the thorny stuff. I'm just so happy to have seen him again. I just want to talk to my friend. And I want to see him in the flesh again. I want to look into his eyes again. Truth is, I'm falling for Luke Jones née Beresford and I want him to know. But tonight . . . him seeing me there snogging Nate in the corridor so uncouthly . . . it's going to be hard to get past that. Very hard. If not impossible. I don't know what to say. So, I keep it brief.

Anyway, Luke, I wanted to thank you. For stepping in to defend me. That's never happened to me before and it really was rather marvellous.

There's so much more I want to say, but I don't feel able to say it yet, if at all. If I were in his shoes, whatever feelings I might have, I know for sure I would not want to start a relationship with someone who was snogging someone else that exact same evening. I then wish I hadn't told him about the police call and Nate saying I was his girlfriend. Maybe he'll think I protest too much. And that I'm actually far more involved with Nate than I am and I'm trying to pretend I wasn't. I could delete that particular message . . . but that would look awkward too. Oh well, it's done now. And also, something I've always done with Luke is tell the truth, so I don't want to start withholding information now. I sign off with grateful thanks and *love Heidi.* Then I want to delete that, or at least the word *love.* It's too early for mention of love, isn't it? Or is it okay if it's just a sign-off? Truth is I'm too knackered to consider it rationally.

No response. I assume he's in his hotel room by now. Maybe he's asleep. Or maybe he's sitting there on his hotel bed, watching my messages pop up and resolutely not answering them. Either way, he doesn't reply. I think about messaging Carly, Brenda and Alia all the gossip of the night, but truth is I'm just too damn exhausted to deal with the replies. I'll do it in the morning. I message Carly just to let her know I had a great night, I'm back at the hotel safe and sound and I'm off to sleep. Within seconds of turning my phone off, I'm asleep, fully clothed, on top of the covers. At some time in the night, I must have found my way into the tightly tucked in hotel sheets, God knows how. But I wake up under them, bleary-eyed, in the dimness. It's around 8am and just beginning to get light outside.

I forgot to set an alarm for the morning, so I'm very lucky that I woke up in good time for breakfast, checkout and train. I stagger to the bathroom and I'm assaulted with a make-up-smeared, sleep-addled visage of a woman who looks at least twenty years older than I am. I recoil and find my make-up remover, drag my clothes off and get into the shower, where I wash away last night and emerge as a new woman. Thank God I don't drink anymore. Imagine a hangover on top of it all. I check my phone – there are messages from Carly, Brenda and Alia all asking for details of my night, as well as questions on the M&Ms group chat as well, everyone demanding that I dish the dirt. Well, have I got a story for them! I reply briefly to them all saying it was a blast and I'll message properly when I'm on the train home. No missed calls from the police, thank heavens. And nothing from Luke. Oh dear. I'm not surprised. But I am disappointed.

317

Heavily so. Well, I need to celebrate the positives of this experience and not get hung up on some guitar-picking engineer. Life goes on.

I'm blow-dried, dressed, no make-up but looking fresh. And I'm all packed up. I wheel my suitcase out of there and head down to the dining room. I bloody love a hotel breakfast and haven't had one for quite a while. I'm relishing the thought of a full English, followed by toast and jam, lashings of tea (mint if they don't have decaf) and then filling a couple of napkins with mini pastries to take on the train as a snack. I mean, everyone does that at hotels, don't they? Well, if they don't, they're idiots. It's free food! (Or, at least, it's paid-for food and you've probably paid a ridiculous amount, so fill your boots.) I'm shown to a seat in the dining room and offered tea and they actually have decaf, which is a surprise. My new gastro meds are helping my tummy better than the old ones, so I feel brave enough to eat with a bit of abandon, for a change. And if I get ill on the train, well, so be it. I will handle it. I will survive. So, I'm tucking into my sausage, bacon, fried egg, black pudding, grilled tomatoes and hash browns, when my phone pings. It's Luke!

Have you left your hotel yet?

No, I'm noshing on a full English in the dining room.

Can I pop in there for a cuppa and see you?

Of course!

318

I give him the name of the hotel and my room number, so he can pretend to the dining-room waiter on guard that he's staying there. Oh crumbs, I haven't got any make-up on. Shall I run to the loos now and slap some on? I really can't be bothered and I don't want my full English to go cold and congealed. Well, fuck it. Who cares. He'll have to take me as I am. I'm so bloody happy he messaged though! I wonder what he wants to say . . .? I'm too nervous to eat. Then, I think, I've paid for this breakfast. Sod it. So I eat the lot and stow away the pastries in my bag for later. I'm spreading Marmite on a bit of toast when Luke arrives beside my table.

'Hey!' I say and awkwardly stand up, pushing my chair back and catching a waitress who I profusely apologise to. Great start.

Luke sits down and he's not smiling. 'Thanks for meeting me,' he says.

'My pleasure,' I say, trying to remain upbeat. Why do I feel like I'm about to get dumped, even though he's not even my boyfriend? But that's how it feels. 'Are you okay?'

'Yeah, yeah. I'm fine. I just . . . I need to say some stuff.'

'Sure,' I say and gulp. It feels all too soon to process last night, for me, let alone him as well. I don't know how I feel about Luke, about Nate, about the whole business. But I'm open to possibilities. Luke's face, however, looks resolute, like he's already made his decision, whatever that might be.

He says, 'It was . . . so great seeing you again last night. It was . . . well, it was pretty wonderful.'

I beam at him. And he smiles broadly in return. It makes my heart flutter, as schmaltzy as that sounds. He has such

319

a nice smile. One of those smiles that transforms a face, like Julia Roberts in *Leave the World Behind*, where she's miserable all the way through that weird apocalypse movie, then at one point she smiles and it's like, yes, there she is, the real her. And that's how Luke's smile is.

'It really was wonderful,' I say and there's so much more I want to say, but he looks like he's got a lot to say too and I want to give him a chance to get it out. He's made the effort to come and seek me out, so he deserves that, I feel.

'Look, I wish you all the happiness in the world, I mean that. You know I care about you. Very much. But, as you're with Nate, I'm just not sure a friendship would work out between us, as – let's face it – I hate Nate and Nate hates me, and we did from the end of that last year of uni and still do to this day.'

'Listen, firstly, I want to reiterate that I am not with Nate. I am not Nate's girlfriend. And last night showed me, once and for all, that Nate Wheeler is not the man I thought he was and he is the last person on earth I'd want to be involved with. I've blocked him on everything on my phone. I have no intention of ever speaking to him again. So, I'd just like to make that clear from the off, whatever else we want to talk about. He's a wanker, as you so rightly told me once. And that's a fact.'

'Okay,' he says, hesitantly. But it doesn't seem to have cheered him though. A long pause ensues, which is bearable for a few seconds, but then I have to fill it. I can't help myself.

'Can you tell me though, why you and Nate fell out? You seemed to be good mates when we lived together. I don't understand what happened. I know now what an arsehole he is, but was it just that? I mean, he has no reason to hate you. You're . . . lovely.'

Luke smiles and looks away. He definitely seems conflicted, but willing to talk. 'Well, it was about you, like I mentioned before. I just didn't feel I had the right to tell you all this recently, when you were clearly already involved. But I can tell you what happened back then, now things have changed somewhat.'

'Yes, please do! I want to know everything.'

'Okay, here goes. So the truth is, that final year of uni, Nate knew you were in love with him and kept saying he was going to do something about it, then when he didn't I asked him if he still felt the same way or if I could ask you out and he said no, hands off, that he was going to any day. But he didn't, and he was seeing all these other women and I couldn't bear that you'd just be another in a long line, while . . . well, the truth was, I was in love with you.'

He looks down at his hands in his lap and I want to reach out and touch his face.

'I wanted to tell you,' he goes on, still not looking at me. 'But Nate kept insisting you were his girl. He said you'd fucked a few times but that you didn't mind him seeing other girls.'

'That's rubbish!' I cry and nearby hotel residents whip heads round to see where the kerfuffle is coming from. A waitress stops and asks me, 'Is your food okay, madam?'

She's older than me, sixties maybe, and speaks with a gorgeous Devon burr, the accent I remember so well from the uni refectory where the dinner ladies would say, 'D'you want chips with that, my lover?'

321

'Oh yes, thank you. I'm sorry.'

'No need to be sorry, madam,' she says with a smile and takes my empty plate away.

'Sorry,' I say quietly to Luke. 'Didn't mean to cause a scene. But that is horse shit. We never had sex. We never did a thing, not even a kiss. And certainly if we had, I'd never have been okay with him gallivanting around with other women. I wasn't that kind of girl. I'm still not.'

'I was pretty sure it wasn't true. But I didn't have the nerve to ask you. Anyway, Nate and I argued badly, during finals. He said he was going to stop seeing other girls and commit to you, right after finals. And we were all under so much stress and desperate to finish our exams and do well. I just couldn't let it distract me from exams, so I parked it. Nate and I continued tolerating each other, then the minute finals were over, I left.'

'I remember that now. I remember you going the day after your final exam. I wondered why you didn't want to stay for the parties. I felt it was such a shame.'

'Yeah, well, I just couldn't stay. I couldn't watch him and you . . .'

'Well, if it's any consolation, he never did anything of the sort! I barely saw him after finals. He was out till all hours and I was going to my little parties with music friends and I never did move in the same circles as the rock god, as we all called him. I didn't even say goodbye when I left the house. He wasn't there. It was really lonely actually, packing up alone and nobody to say farewell to. It felt like my life was over.'

'Same here,' says Luke and looks at me. We look at each other. I can see the young man he was all those years ago in his eyes. Perhaps he sees the same in me, past the wrinkles of age and experience. Certainly not of wisdom. I don't feel wise at all, about anything. I feel like that girl again, twenty-one and alone, not knowing what comes next.

'I wish we'd spoken back then,' I say wistfully. 'If only we had . . .'

'Yeah, if only . . . but then, I do regret not speaking to you, but I don't regret my life. I can't live with regrets. They're such a pointless emotion.'

'Agreed. I've spent a lot of time in regret recently. I'm ashamed to admit, at one point, I even regretted having children. That somehow I sacrificed my life for them, that I still am doing that. But it's not true. They've brought me a deep joy and love I'd never have known. And how can I regret bringing these two wonderful people into existence? I don't regret anything. And it's not too late. There's still so much of our lives to enjoy. We might only be halfway through, you know? Half-time. Plenty more to play for.'

I smile at him expectantly. I hope he gets the hint. I want to look ahead to the future. A future that might have him in it.

'Listen,' he says. 'I know you're telling me it's all done and dusted with Nate. And I believe you. At least, I think I do. But that's not what it looked like last night in the hotel corridor.'

'Oh God, look. That was just a moment of madness. You know, after all these years, finally snogging the guy I had a crush on. Like, a kind of victory for that shy girl back then, come to fruition, after thirty years. That's all it was! It meant nothing!'

'But . . . it didn't mean nothing. It meant something. To you. Maybe not to him, he's such a man whore. But it did mean something to you. It meant a lot. Yeah, he revealed his true colours afterwards and you saw him for who he really was, who he always was. But that doesn't cancel out the feelings you had for him.'

'It does!' I insist. 'It does cancel them out, because I was in love with a phantom!'

'In love? You were . . . in love with Nate?'

Oh fuck. That came out wrong.

'No, I mean . . . well . . . I thought I was, maybe. But I wasn't because he wasn't real. And then you and me – we started talking. And I felt differently. I felt confused. I was all set on one direction and then . . . I realised . . . I liked you.'

'*Liked*,' Luke mouths and grimaces.

'No! I mean, yes, I did like you. Very much. I always did. And when we reconnected, and I saw you play. And you were so kind to me, so caring. And we had great chats and got on like a house on fire. And that beautiful song you sent me. It changed. From liking to something else. Something . . . extraordinary.'

'But . . . you still chose Nate.'

'It wasn't like that!' I can hear my arguments, I can see that rationally they make sense. But if I were Luke listening to this, I'd feel as shitty as he seems to feel right now. The runner-up. That's how it sounds. It's not like that. But how can I make him see that? 'I wasn't in love with Nate, I know that now. I was in lust.'

'So, you don't lust after me?'

Oh God, I can't say anything right. 'Yes! I mean, I do now. It's been a gradual process, as I've got to know you again. My feelings for you have grown into something good, so good and true, over time. I don't know what they mean, I don't know where they're going. It's very early days for us. But I want to find out.'

He wipes his hand over his face. I don't know what he's thinking, but it doesn't look good.

'I . . . I was so in love with you at Exeter. I ached for you. Didn't you know? Couldn't you see it?'

His eyes are intense and deep, deep brown. His hair has fallen across his cheek. I want to kiss him, right here, right now. He is a beautiful man.

'I didn't. I was twenty, I was an idiot. I was blind. But don't punish me for mistakes I made when I was young and foolish.'

He looks away. 'I knew it was hopeless then. I knew I couldn't compete with the rock god. I pined for you, for years after. I had a relationship here and there, but always compared them to you, to the conversations we had for those long moonlit hours. Nothing compared to that. Nobody had a hope, compared to you. I married and I was happy for a while. We couldn't have children and we dealt with that. But it faded and we got lazy with each other and eventually we got sad. And we split. There were recriminations, it turned sour. It was bloody hard. I escaped the misery of it by working all over the world. And it was easy to use that as an excuse to be single. Truth was I couldn't face another relationship. More disappointment. And I couldn't believe it when I found you again on Facebook. And then seeing that Nate was on there too, and had commented to you, I felt sick. It felt like history was repeating itself.'

'It's not, though,' I say and I reach out and touch his hand. 'I promise you that.'

He's staring at his lap again. He finds eye contact tricky, I think. I want him to take my hand and hold it. But his hand is firm, not softening to my touch. So I withdraw. Then he looks up at me.

'You're back in my life and I wanted that for years. But now you're here, and after last night, I don't think I can take it. I can't take the heartbreak, if you change your mind, if he resurfaces full of excuses and you want him again. It's not something I can take. Not after the difficult divorce, the lonely years. It's just . . . too much. You were always my first choice. I don't think I can live with being your consolation prize.'

It's a gut punch. He's wrong – I won't ever go back to wanting Nate again. But he's right – Luke *was* my second choice. If I were in his shoes, I think I'd feel the exact same way. But obscurely, I know underneath all of that logic that he's wrong. I was fooled into falling for Nate. But what I feel for Luke is natural, organic and real. I want to say all that. I think I've already said it. But I realise that words are just words and I could tell him all that a thousand times and it wouldn't make any difference. He'd still feel like a second choice. And nobody wants to feel like that. It feels like shit.

'I don't know what to say . . .' I begin and he looks down at his lap again. 'I don't think words are going to help. I could try to make you see, till I'm blue in the face. But I can't change the way you feel. I can't promise you I can change that. I can't promise you anything. My life these days feels like survival. I'm barely getting through the week without collapsing. I can't offer you much. But I would like to know you better, to have you in my life, if you want that. And see where things go for us. See if we can get past this false start. But if that isn't right for you, I understand, absolutely. And if that's the case, then so be it. But whatever you decide, I shall wish you well in the world, Luke Jones.'

I smile at him, ruefully. He smiles back, mirroring my emotion.

'I wish you well too, always. Take care of yourself, Heidi.'

He stands up, gives me another brief smile and he leaves.

I sit and stare at the cold toast with a smear of Marmite on it. It looks inordinately depressing.

'Is your toast all right, madam?'

It's that same waitress, the one I backed into, the one who asked me if my food is okay. She has a kind face, softly framed by white curls.

'The toast is good, thanks.'

'And the man?' she says, nodding towards the exit. 'Is he any good?' She grins expectantly.

'Yeah, he's one of the good ones.'

'Ah, there's not many good ones in life,' she says, nodding sagely. 'You'd better hold onto him.'

'I tried,' I say. 'I think I blew it though. I think I royally screwed it up.'

'Now then, you're a good person, I can tell, because you're polite. You talk to waitresses like they're people. You're a good woman. He'll see that. He just needs to go off into the wilderness for a while. Then he'll come right back to you.'

'The wilderness?'

'Oh, yes. It's the same for all of us, when we come to a crossroads in life. Two roads split. And we make wrong decisions. We go the wrong way. And we spend a bit of time off out there in the wilderness. We wander and think about our lives. We're all alone. But then we work it all out, you see. And if it's right and good, you'll find your way back to each other. It's like that old story. Your tears of joy will cure his blindness.'

What an extraordinary woman. Who would have thought you'd find such beautiful philosophising in the Mercure Hotel Exeter dining room at breakfast? Just goes to show, people are so often fathoms deeper than you might imagine at first glance.

'Oh! Yes, the story. The prince wanders blind in the desert, then she sings and he follows her voice. He finds her and she weeps into his eyes and . . . she had really long hair. And was shut up in a tower. What's it called? Something about lettuce.'

'I don't recall it being about salad, madam?'

My menopausal brain doesn't have a hope with this one. All I can see is a picture in my Ladybird book of a woman eating lettuce and a witch stealing their baby.

'Rapunzel!' I cry. Good old brain! It was in there somewhere.

'That's the one. You know it. Time in the wilderness. That's what you both need. You'll see, my lover.'

Before I can tell her how incredible she is, some bloke in a suit comes up to her and says, 'Tell the kitchen I want scrambled egg, freshly made. Table seven.'

Rude, I think. *She's not your servant.*

328

'Ah, there are plenty of scrambled eggs, sir. Over there at the hot buffet. Here, I'll show you, sir.'

'No,' he says and sighs loudly. 'I don't want that stuff that's been sitting there under a lamp since the crack of dawn. I want *freshly made*, I said. Are you going deaf in your old age? FRESH-LY-MADE.'

'Don't talk to her like that.'

I hear it come out of my mouth, but I didn't mean it to. I was thinking it, but my mouth said it.

'And who the hell are *you*?' he spits at me.

'I'm a mouthy middle-aged hag who's got zero fucks to give and this waitress-in-disguise you just treated like shit is as wise as the Queen of fucking Sheba, mate. And you're an absolute waste of oxygen. Now pipe the fuck down and shift your uncouth arse back to table seven and eat your bloody toast.'

And he fucking does! He just turns round, goes back to his table and sits down. Like his mummy told him off. I'm actually a tad disappointed. I was all psyched up for verbal warfare. I can't stand bullies, never could. Just shows standing up to them can work. They can't take it if you fight back.

The waitress stares at me with her mouth open.

'Thank you!' she whispers. 'You're a bit amazing, aren't you, eh?!'

'It was nothing. You're the amazing one. You're magnificent. Thank you for your wisdom and truth. Have a wonderful day, my queen. And may your door never be darkened by wankers like him again.'

I grab my suitcase and roll it out of there, straight past the wanker's table. I see a manager-looking chap standing at the edge of the dining room, looking on. I stop and say to him, 'See that guy at table seven? If he complains about that waitress there, the one with the beautiful curls, he's talking rubbish. He was incredibly rude to her and she was nothing but courteous. And she's a genius, by the way. Wasted in here. You should give her management training. And an immediate pay rise.'

I don't give him time to reply. I've got a train to catch. My adventure is done and I'm on the path home. And what a time away it's been! I faced my fears. And I came out fighting. Fuck Nate Wheeler, fuck that guy at table seven and fuck fear. Fuck yeah!

Chapter 24

It's the middle of October, it's our first M&Ms meeting since my trip and it's lovely to see Cheryl, Rhona, Niki and Joy again. I spend the first twenty minutes being interrogated by everyone about my Exeter shenanigans. They all love the mad stories but mostly they want to know about Luke. Oh God, what *is* happening with Luke?

'Nothing,' I say and shrug. 'I've not heard a word from him since. But I'm okay with that. Maybe we're in the wilderness period, like the Waitress of Sheba said. Or maybe we're destined to never connect again. So be it. It'll be sad but I'm not going to fight against the universe. I've got enough shit on my plate. Mostly, I'm just grateful I had a great time. And a lucky escape from Nate.'

Niki asks, 'Did you ever find out what happened with Nate and the cops?'

'Oh God, yeah, I forgot to say. One of the Exeter crowd – Sally, the recorder player – she messaged me on Facebook a few days after. She said she'd seen on a local Exeter group some gossip about Nate. Apparently he's still somewhat of a minor celebrity amongst the Exeter alumni, since he's toured with famous bands and all that. Apparently, he was stopped for dangerous driving on his motorbike. Swerving all over the road, by all accounts. They did a roadside saliva test and he was positive for cocaine, of course. He must've snorted a bucketful, the state he was in. Then at the station he was searched and they found the rest of the coke in his boot. He's been charged with driving under the influence of drugs and possession of a Class A substance and released, awaiting trial. That's what Sally heard anyway.'

'He could've killed someone, the bastard,' says Rhona.

'Absolutely. Lucky escape all round,' I say and feel relief all over again that I have nothing to do with that lying twat any longer.

'Anyway,' I continue, 'enough about me. We must get back to us. Today I'd like to suggest we do a Look How Far We've Come kind of thing. It's good to look back and chart your progress. Let's think back to June, five months ago, when we all first met. What's happened since then? What's improved? What still needs help and support? What goals do we have going forward, things we want to progress and aim for? If that's okay with everyone.'

Cheryl starts us off. And what a few months she's had!

'Well, healthwise, I'm on a different dose of HRT now and it's definitely helping. I'm not losing hair nearly as much as I was. I'm trying to make sure I get enough calcium and vitamin D in my diet and I do a lot more dental hygiene stuff, like flossing, which I'd never done before. I don't know if it'll make much difference to my teeth wearing away, but at least I'm trying. And the cream from the specialist for my *downstairs area* is working pretty well, most of the time, though it's not always easy to get hold of, as it's not on the NHS. So that's the physical stuff. I've filed for divorce, so I'm going through all the paperwork and all that. Clive and I are selling the house. He's not making it easy but I'm standing up to him and that seems to make him back down a bit. He's not used to me answering back. Once the house is sold, I'll be looking to put a deposit down on a new little place, with room for my daughter when she comes to see me. I'm still staying at Joy's, as you all know. And I just want to say how grateful I am to her and all of you. I don't know where I'd be without this group. I can't believe how much my life has changed and all for the better. So thanks to everyone. And thanks to Heidi for setting this group up.'

There's a little ripple of applause for that. God, it's good to hear about Cheryl's progress. It's extraordinary.

'You're more than welcome,' I say and we move on to Rhona.

'I want to say thanks as well. To all of you, you know. And specially to Niki, for putting me in touch with a new homeopathic doctor. He's really helped me. I feel like he's legit. He seems it. He knows a lot, you know. He talks about things in a detailed way and talks about research. It doesn't seem like he's talking a load of nonsense. So I'm on black cohosh for brain fog, St John's wort for hot flushes and phytoestrogens for anxiety. And I've been to the GP about my chest and eyes to get some medical treatment for that and I've started antihistamines and they're definitely helping with my eyes and I've got an inhaler for the asthma. So I want to say thanks to Joy for that. And I'm sorry it took me so long to get round to it, to get round to doctors and putting a bit of trust in them.'

'No apology needed, you know that,' says Joy and smiles. It's so nice to see these two have come together now, an unlikely team after their rocky start. They'll probably never see eye to eye about everything, but they've both been willing to move closer to each other's perspectives and that's so bloody heartwarming, isn't it?

Rhona adds, 'And feeling better all round has really done the trick with all this rage I've been feeling. I still get bad days when I want to smash things up, but mostly, I can keep it under wraps when I need to. And take it out on dirty floors instead of my family and friends, you know? Oh and yeah, I reported that dodgy therapist to this organisation called the Federation of Holistic Therapists. I did it without, you know, saying who I was. Joy showed me how. So I feel better about that now. I feel better, you know, that he won't get away with doing this to other women.'

Another round of applause.

'That is brilliant, Rhona. And brave,' I say.

Joy speaks next.

'The new HRT formulation I'm on is making things a bit better, I must admit. I also went on to anti-depressants and I'd say that made the difference with my hot flushes. I don't sweat anything like as badly as I used to. I know anti-depressants aren't for everyone, but they've really improved things for me. I still get the hot flushes, but mostly at night, when I can control it more. And they're not as intense and don't last as long. I just found that when I was taking a higher dose of anti-depressants, I couldn't feel the good stuff so much. What I mean by that, is that on good days, I still felt somewhat dulled by it. So I've gone on to a lower dose and actually that is a reasonable balance. It helps with the flushes, yet also allows me to feel fully on the good days too. Managing the dose is key. So, that's given me a bit more confidence to travel actually. You're not the only one with travel anxiety, Heidi, being perfectly honest now. I've not admitted it yet because I thought it seemed like such a daft thing to admit to and I couldn't imagine it being linked to menopause.'

'Same here!' I say. 'I beat myself up about it for ages. But then, you just need to forgive yourself and accept these things, sometimes, you know? Yes, you can fight it and win at times, but at other times, you just need to accept there are things that are way outside your comfort zone. And some days, you can tackle that, and other days, you can't. And that's okay.'

'Exactly. It's okay to say no. But that's not very me. I've always been adventurous and nothing has ever held me back. So I've managed to organise a sabbatical next spring to go and visit all of my sons. And when I'm in Nigeria, I plan to meet some of my mother's relations I've not been in touch with since I was a little girl. So I feel like I'm going to be able to reconnect with my mother's memory and find out more about the child I once was. Plus I'm going to do some work with local universities while I'm there. So it's good all round, seeing family and getting valuable professional development. I'm researching a paper on women of colour and menopause treatment too. It's fascinating. And awful. Black women tend to start the menopause earlier, it lasts longer and some symptoms can be far more severe and intense, like hot flushes, for example. And women of colour are more likely to have their concerns dismissed by the medical establishment, which means more suffering and potentially, later complications for their long-term health. I'll share it with the group when it's done. And yes, same here for being grateful to this bloody wonderful bunch of women. I'm just so happy to know you all.'

How fascinating Joy is. What an incredible experience her travels will be. I know we can't wait to hear all about it upon her return. And we'll miss her while she's gone.

Lastly, we hear from Niki.

'Physically, I'd say things are improving a bit, yeah. I'm managing the vaginal dryness okay with the cream and the pessaries. Some days are worse than others, but I'm actually managing to wear jeans again sometimes, which I went off for ages. Other days I'm in a lukewarm bath for hours, but those days are less than they used to be. Small victories, right? And my lovely GP has referred me to a consultant to look into all these UTI problems, as it may be more complicated. So that'll be a long wait probably but at least it's in progress.'

'Definitely progress,' I say.

'But also,' Niki adds, 'I do actually have some big news . . .' She pauses for effect, grinning.

'Oh my God, what is it?' I cry. We're all avidly waiting.

'I've just applied to be a foster parent.'

That gets the biggest applause of the hour!

'I've got the application pack and had a really nice phone call with a fostering adviser. I was worried they wouldn't let me as I'm single, but they said that was fine. I've got a home visit booked next month. I just really feel like I can give the time – and the love – to a kid who really needs it. And now I'm feeling a bit better physically, I feel ready for it. I know it won't be easy, and maybe it won't happen, but I've managed to overcome my fears and go for it. So, yeah. I'm feeling pretty good!'

Everyone asks her questions about the fostering process, but she doesn't know much yet, so we'll circle back to that soon.

'What amazing news, Niki! I'm just so delighted for you. It feels like the best idea that ever there was! And whoever comes to stay with you will be the luckiest kids on earth. You'll be bloody marvellous.'

We spend the rest of the session talking about symptoms we're still struggling with and making suggestions. All in all, it's a hugely positive session. To think how little we understood menopause when we started – and even how little we knew our own bodies – and now we're armed with knowledge and bolstered by support. I'm pretty darn proud of this group of ours. Vive the M&Ms!

Life goes on, work and family goes on for the rest of October. Halloween comes and goes, where Carly, Geoff, Cheryl and I take Ada out for trick-or-treating, along with Alia, Rich and their two youngest, Zane and Ricky (while seventeen-year-old Sienna is out partying with mates). Zane and Ricky are both werewolves with full wolf masks and hairy hands, courtesy of Alia's expert make-upping skill. Ada wanted to go as Elvis. Cheryl said she couldn't really as it wasn't very Halloweeny and we all looked at her like, so what? We've always let Ada exercise her weirdness and I guess maybe it can seem a bit odd sometimes. Cheryl will get used to it, when she knows Ada better. But I felt bad that we all looked at Cheryl that way and was about to smooth it over – I mean, it must be bloody hard coming in to an established family unit like us, especially where the exes live next door to each other and are still pretty thick as thieves. Then Ada, sweet as she is, said to Cheryl she'd be a Dead Elvis, with scars and blood on her face, to make it 'more seasonal'. What a clever, nice kid she is, bless her heart.

As we start down the street, Alia says, 'I wish I were out at a fucking party like Sienna. I hate wandering around the neighbourhood and begging strangers for sweets. Who the hell thought this crap up anyway?' Zane and Ada, besties again, tell her off for swearing. Alia replies that she doesn't give a shit. I love a bit of Halloween, personally. I'm dressed as some kind of psychotic, mouldy pumpkin-head zombie thing, the cheapest thing I could find on Amazon. Whatever it is, the pumpkin mask terrifies all and sundry, plus I have the added bonus of hiding behind it, like Luke and his umbrella.

Ah . . . Luke. Still no word. It's been weeks now. At first, I tried to stop thinking of him. It didn't work. Then, I decided to wallow in it. I keep listening to his voice note of 'Wichita Lineman'. I can't stop listening to it. Sometimes I have my earphones in and just tap it ten or fifteen times in a row, while I'm doing emails or whatever. I just need it as the soundtrack to my life some days. I even log in to watch his live feeds from Boston on YouTube, which he now does at a new venue on Friday evenings, a long bar with a little stage at the end. Can whoever runs a YouTube channel see who's watched their stuff? I don't know, but I decide I don't care. Maybe he'll see my name on there and . . . and what? I don't know. I'm not pining for him. I'm just keeping in touch. Actually, I'm a bloody liar. I am completely and totally and utterly pining for him. I feel like I opened an attic door onto a cornucopia of treasures, that had been locked away for years, and only now I was able to enter and explore their riches. And now the door is shut. Locked. I was distracted by something shiny and I missed my chance. I blew it. When I realise that I'm not getting over this easily, that in fact I don't want to get over it at all, I decide to reach out. Maybe the Waitress of Sheba was even more right than I first thought. She said we needed our time in the wilderness. Well, that's definitely what this is. But what else did she say? Rapunzel sings and the prince hears her. He follows her voice. And she heals him with her tears of joy. Now, I don't have hair down to my bum anymore, not like the magnificent mane I had at twenty. And I don't live in a tower with a witch in charge. But maybe, just maybe, I could sing to Luke. And I'm not talking about a voice note. I'm talking about something far more brave than that. I'm talking about a grand gesture. Luke's pride was hurt but I know he still cares about me, deeply. It won't have worn off that quickly. And I need to prove it to him somehow, that I feel the exact same way. Life is too short, especially in its second half, after fifty. No time to waste. Seize the fucking day. I have this crazy idea, that might be scary, that could well be foolish and will definitely be expensive. But you know what, I'm gonna do it. I decide alone. I don't discuss it with anyone. I finally know my own mind without seeking out a hundred other viewpoints. Luke Jones sang 'Wichita Lineman' to me when I really needed to hear it. And now, it's my turn.

Chapter 25

'Mum, I am telling you, you HAVE to do this,' says Ada. 'It'll be a totally amazing adventure!'

She's hopping up and down on the rug, while Carly sits beside me on the sofa, legs crossed, nodding sagely.

'The kid's not wrong,' she adds.

'I'm not wrong!' cries Ada.

'That's what I said, cloth ears!'

Can I do this? Can I fly to Boston and coax Luke Jones back in from the wilderness?

'But what if I get ill?' I say to Carly. Ada doesn't see the problem with all that, despite our Lake District disaster. Carly understands it more, the anxiety, the risk.

'You'll manage. Like you told me yourself, someone will help,' says Carly. 'Just think what you would do if you saw a woman alone who really needed your help. You're not the only one out there. There are nice people everywhere. The world isn't as scary as it feels sometimes, sitting here, on your safe old sofa.' How did she get so wise, so young?

'I just don't want to get there and end up ill in a hotel room for the whole trip, then slink back home with my tail between my legs, too poorly to see Luke. Just think of the money, the waste. It just feels . . . too risky.'

Ada jumps on the sofa and snuggles up to me. 'Is he nice?'

'Who, Luke?'

'Yeah. He looks nice. But is he nice to you? Like properly nice?'

'Yeah, he is. He's very nice to me. He's a really good man. One of the best men I think I've ever known.'

Ada says, 'Good. Cos you deserve a nice man, Mum. The nicest.'

Carly, adds, 'Then he's worth it. Isn't he?'

I think of Luke's eyes, his hands, his voice. I feel a tingling all over. It's not like the pure lust I felt before. It's something new. Something that comes from deeper inside me than I knew it could. It's taken its time to arrive, this knowledge, this love. But yeah, I love Luke Jones. And I need to tell him, face to face. He's worth it, all right.

Ada and Carly are staring at me, waiting. I'm thinking, what would Miriam do? I grin. They grin.

'Fuck yeah, Mum!'

'Carly!' I scold her, for cursing in front of the little'un.

'Fuck yeah!' cries Ada.

And we all laugh like drains.

So, here I am. I'm driving to Heathrow through the darkness of an early morning. It takes me back to pre-dawn drives to Torquay on holiday when we were kids, my dad insisting we left in the middle of the night and arrived at the hotel for breakfast to avoid the mad summer traffic. I was always fascinated by the yellow headlights on the country roads, capturing the fleeting views of rabbits skittering away into hedgerows as we ploughed onwards. Later this morning, if all goes well, at 11am-ish I will be boarding a plane to Boston, USA. It all seemed such a thoroughly romantic idea last week. And now, on Friday 15th November, I'm about to travel across the Atlantic Ocean. Alone. I've left home ridiculously early, just in case there's an unforeseen historically atrocious pile-up on the M40. I have to navigate my way round the chaos of the airport roads to find out where to park at Heathrow. I have to find how to get to the right terminal from my car. I have to find the right check-in gate. I have to go through security and suffer the scrutiny of the guards as I fumble about with my handbag and cabin bag. I have to find the right gate for my plane. I have to get through a trans-Atlantic flight in one piece, without being sick or developing crippling diarrhoea. I have to get through all the customs and control kerfuffle at the other end, after having researched that there are certain materials my violin may be made of that I can't bring into the US, including Brazilian rosewood, tortoiseshell and elephant ivory. Luckily none of these apply to mine, but I'm still worried it might be refused. It has to be stowed inside my hand luggage, which leaves little room for anything else. I have two pairs of trousers, a dress, one pair of boots and another of shoes, one nightie and four tops for my two days and two nights in America, arriving 2.05pm on the Friday and going home on the 6.55pm flight from Boston Logan Airport, arriving Heathrow at 6.30am Monday morning. I've taken the

Friday and Monday off work. I've told Brenda and my boss I've taken a long weekend for myself, no particular plans. I only tell the kids the truth because I have to. I need this trip to be largely my secret, my business. I just want to do it. I don't want expectations or advice. I have enough anxiety without people getting excited or nervous for me (much appreciated, of course, but I can't deal with that right now). I have stowed every pill known to humankind in my luggage, just in case. Once I get through customs at Boston, I have to get a taxi to my hotel. I have to settle in and probably sleep the rest of the day till 6pm-ish. Friday evening at just before 8pm I have to walk down the street to the bar where Luke plays. What if they randomly decide to cancel it that week? Even if they don't, I have to get into the toilets without him seeing me. I have to tune up my violin in there. I have to wait in there until he finishes his set. Then, once he's done, I need to sneak into the audience and when his musical partner Bo throws the floor open to other performers, I have to put my hand up and then . . . he'll see me. What will he do? Will he look embarrassed? What if he's gone off me? Will he have a new girlfriend in the audience who'll say, *Who the fuck is this?* That's assuming that all of the other steps go swimmingly. Any fuck-ups and I might not be there on time. I might not have my violin. I might be too ill to leave the hotel. But the HRT has kicked in better in recent weeks. The new IBS meds are helping, not always and not completely, but I'm definitely having fewer attacks than before. And they're not lasting as long. Not as debilitating. So, I'm gambling I'll be okay. The whole thing is a gamble. I think I may well be completely insane.

I can see the signs for Heathrow now. The driving has been fine, no problems at all, no anxiety. Can it really carry on this well? Could I really be that lucky?

You'll be glad to know I'm not going to bore you with every single moment of that massive journey across the sea. Suffice to say, it goes okay. I don't fuck up anything too badly. I don't get the shits or vomit. I feel a bit sick in the airport, but I've taken an anti-nausea medication before I board and it helps. I'm actually feeling okay. Customs at Boston Logan is long and a bit nerve-wracking, especially when they search through my violin case and shoot questions at me. But it's fine and they let it through. And I find a taxi okay. It's bitterly cold outside. The sky has a bright, yellowish tinge to it. Looks like snow. (What if I get snowed in and they cancel all the flights home? Okay, enough with the catastrophising, Mommy Dearest. I'm in actual Boston, USA. Focus on the now.) The ride from the airport to my hotel is the first time I've truly relaxed in nearly twenty-four hours. We drive across the river, and I can spot the New England Aquarium across the water. I hope to go there tomorrow on my tourist day. (If everything else goes tits up tonight, at least I'll get a day of sightseeing in Boston. The Cheers Bar and the Aquarium are my two must-sees, along with about seventeen other must-sees I won't have time for. Wish I could've come for a week.) We drive on through the North End, the West End and into Back Bay.

I'm staying at the Newbury Guest House. It's a gorgeous-looking place, three townhouses joined together on a tree-lined street. Check-in is easy, the receptionist is charming and I get to my room. I collapse on my bed.

I've been awake since 5am and in the UK (and my brain) it's now about 8.30pm (five hours earlier in Boston time). I sleep the rest of the day, about two and a half hours. My alarm goes off in good time and I feel like death. But there's no rest for me and my stupid damn idiotic romantic gesture I thought was a good idea until right now. But it is what it is and I'm here in the US of A and I need to move my arse. I get up and get ready.

I walk to the bar down Newbury Street and I'm so glad I brought my warm winter coat. It's black and fluffy and has buttons all the way down. I need it and it's bloody freezing and . . . is it? Yes, it is! It's snowing! Watching the first few flakes drift down from the night sky is so charming, I momentarily forget my anxiety about return flights. The bar has a blue frontage and is buzzing with Bostonians coming and going. I go in and scan the place. No Luke. Not yet. And I see they've changed the times. Usually at this bar, he plays at 8pm. The chalkboard on the wall says Jones and Jones will start at 10pm. Before that there's some comedy on. It's bloody awful. People are laughing but I just think it's dumb, like the worst kind of *Hey it's just the worst when you trip over in public, huh?!* I keep monitoring the crowd for Luke, worried he'll see me before the open mic bit and I'll spoil the surprise. But I can't wait in the toilet for two hours plus his whole set, that's nuts. The women in there will think I'm a lunatic. It's a pretty bar with low-hanging lamps with blue shades and strings of lights adorning the walls. It's packed with people mostly in their thirties, with a few oldies like me here and there. I find a place in the back corner and wait, watching the show, watching the crowd. In between sets, I hear the voices of Bostonians all around me and I feel like I've fallen into a Ben Affleck movie. That famous Boston accent is loud and clear, the one no actor who isn't from Boston can ever get away with in a movie and, as hard as they try, always end up being absolutely rinsed on social media. I've always had a thing for Boston movies: *Good Will Hunting*, *The Departed*, *Patriots Day*, *Spotlight*, *Fever Pitch* – not the British footie one, the American baseball one. (I'm also randomly obsessed with baseball movies. Don't get me started on *Field of Dreams* and *The Natural*. I bloody love them, plus the books of Ring Lardner. I've no idea why. I've never even watched a baseball game. There's just something about the romance of the game. There's nothing quite like it, the bats, the gloves, the caps, the pants, the weird stance of the pitcher. I can't imagine a romance movie about cricket, can you? Gap in the market there.) If I were staying longer, I wish I could've seen a Red Sox game. I'm loving the atmosphere here. I want Matt Damon and Minnie Driver to swish past, talking about caramels. I see some other instrumentalists – a guy with a mandolin, a girl with a bodhran, the Irish hand-held drum. Love those things. Suddenly, it dawns on me, what I'm about to do. I've been so caught up with the grand gesture of turning up to Luke's open mic and playing for him, that I'd forgotten that I'm going to be playing for a room full of strangers as well. I haven't played in front of a soul for over twenty years. I haven't even played for my kids yet. I made this decision so rashly, I never stopped to think about performing. What if I go up there and he sees me and he's all dewy-eyed about this great romantic act of love and then I play with the grace and musicality of a panda and fuck it all up completely? What the fuck have I done?!

Oh God, there he is. THERE HE IS! In the flesh, in Boston, USA! The last comedian has finished, finally, and Luke is setting up on stage with Bo Jones, his Garfunkel-esque partner. Oh Christ, Luke looks great. He looks so bloody good. He's wearing a plaid shirt, faded red T-shirt and blue jeans. He's so utterly at ease with himself. Meanwhile, I feel like I'm about to give birth to seventeen kittens, or something more wriggly, perhaps porpoises. Yeah, I've got baby porpoises thrashing around in my innards right now. *Calm down, Hobbes. You can do this. It's insane, but it's happening. And you look good. Relax.* I'm dressed in black – I found a cute little black dress which I'm wearing with thick black tights and Dr Martens. My hair behaved tonight and is holding a rather lovely wave. My dark clothes and my seated position in the back corner hopefully ensure he won't see me. I keep my eyes down and only glance up occasionally. He's not looking at the crowd. When he turns his back I scan the crowd madly to see if there are any likely females gazing at him proprietorially. Does he have a girlfriend here? Even if he doesn't, maybe he has one somewhere else? But then, he did say, he's been avoiding relationships the past few years. So what are the chances that he's suddenly met someone important in the last six weeks? Just my luck if he has. But let's stay positive. We have to honour the wisdom of the Waitress of Sheba. She knows best. She told me to do this . . . well, more or less. My interpretation of it anyway. And while I'm hiding in the

corner of a Boston bar, clutching my violin case and
glugging on my pint of tap water, since my mouth is as
dry as a cuttlefish in a budgie cage.

Luke and Bo are ready. He still hasn't spotted me. They
start their set. It's as good as last time, better even. Such
an eclectic mix: 'Little Girl in Bloom' by Thin Lizzy; 'And
It Stoned Me' by Van Morrison; 'Thank You' by Bonnie
Raitt; 'Save Me' by Aimee Mann. Exquisite taste! Classics
all! And they sing their harmonies so precisely yet easily,
as if the chords are as old as the hills. And Luke plays like
a dream, picking out the beauty of each song with his
long, elegant fingers. I cannot take my eyes off him. When
he closes his eyes, taken away by the music, my whole
body responds. Oh bloody Nora, I've really got it bad for
this man. I'm gone, I'm lost, I'm all his. If it all goes to
shit tonight, I don't know if I'll ever get over it. But at
least I tried. At least I fought my greatest fears of all –
travel, potential humiliation and love. My God, the journey
I've been on this year blows me away. I'm suddenly struck
by where I am and what I'm doing. I couldn't be happier.
Whatever happens, I'm so glad I did this. I'm so glad I'm
on the earth at this moment in a bar in Boston listening
to beautiful music. And it's about to finish and then comes
. . . the open mic. I down my remaining tap water and
feel sick. It's time.

'Thanks for the appreciation,' says Bo, who does most
of the talking for these two, Luke being the shy one. 'We
appreciate you too, coming out into this snowy east-coast
November night. And now please show your appreciation
for some other talented folk here tonight. Any offers for
the open mic, raise your hand now.'

I see the guy with the mandolin and the woman with the drum raise their hands. They're together. It's now or never. I've got to do it. I raise my hand. Luke's not looking. He's moving away from the stage to the bar. He's not seen me. Bo says, 'You guys here. And the lady at the back? Not seen you here before, honey. What're you gonna play?'

It feels like every damn person in the bar turns and stares at me. Oh crikey, this is like a weird dream. But it's bloody happening. I hold up my violin case and grin nervously.

'Oh wow, a fiddle player,' says Bo. 'You're first then, lady. Come on up. Love me some fiddle on a Friday night.'

I put my case on the table and open it up. There she is, my darling fiddle, in all her curving glory. I've not tuned her since the hotel. I hope she's still all right. I take her out, hold the bow over the strings and give each one a quick bounce. Sounds fine. Still in good order. It's then that I look over and see Luke is staring at me, eyes like dinner plates. Is he happy to see me? His mouth makes a perfect O. But then, as I shuffle and swivel around the crowd and make my way up to the little stage, I can see that O turn to a huge shit-eating grin, as they say. That gives me a boost. He doesn't say a word and I don't look back at him as I'm settling myself, placing the rest on my shoulder, the base beneath my chin, my hand gripping the bow ever so lightly, the bow resting a half-inch above the taut strings. People are low-level chattering away, filling the silence, thank God.

To calm my rising anxiety, I'm thinking about the song I'm about to play. It's a song about loneliness and longing, about needing someone and wanting someone endlessly, like the endless roads and the endless telephone lines that span them, about being so in tune with a person, you can even hear their voice singing through the lines as you go about your everyday business, a strange and beautiful image. It's like a moment in time, a glance at a figure in space, there and gone, lingering in the mind. To me, it's a simple, short and sweet love song. And I'm going to play it for Luke.

I'm tuned up, I'm miked up, I'm ready. The talking fades and all eyes turn to the stage. I thought it'd be more casual than this, but no. Everybody is looking at me. I glance to my left, to the bar. Luke is still there. He hasn't moved a muscle. His eyes are not so wide now, but they are intense. I close mine. I have to focus now. I play this song in G major, my favourite key on the fiddle. It just sits so nicely under your fingers. The melody is simple – go listen to it. It's not the first choice a violinist would usually make. It's mostly covered on guitar or piano. But from when I was about fifteen, I started playing my own version. I started by picking out the tune alone. As I grew to know it more, I added in grace notes, little turns, mordents, trills and hemiolas, to folkify it, expand on it, play with it. Depending on my mood, I might add in some double stopping to provide a bit of harmony. I might riff on the dit-dit-dit rhythms of the Morse code-like figure between verses. I played it differently every time. Tonight, I have no idea where my bow will take me. I just know I have to close my eyes and let my muscle memory kick in, then after that, give myself up to the place where the inner music takes over and you're out of your body, out of your conscious mind and you're out there, way beyond anything you know.

I play the first D and I'm nervous, it judders and I press down, bending the bow and strings to my will, gently yet firmly. I'm onto the G now and I'm off. The song is unspooling and it's clear as a hand bell, even in this crowded, warm bar. As I play on, as the song rises to its top E, I feel as if the roof has lifted off, the Boston night sky swirling with snow, the longing in that lingering E, rising on the warm air from the bar into the cold and dissipating into the dark, wintry beyond. I'm there, I'm lost in the song. I have no idea where my hands will take me, my bow has a will of its own. The music unfolds in grace and beauty, filling the room with flowing filaments of sound. It's the performance of a lifetime. I've never played better. I know I'm coming towards the final notes and I don't want it to ever end, this moment in this Boston bar, the man I'm in love with watching, listening, with me in this place and in this moment. When it finishes, I'll have to face him, face reality and face the possibility that he feels just the same as he did that morning in Exeter: melancholy, disenchanted. But as I play the final notes and draw this mellifluous melody to its final long, high, E note stretching out along the telephone lines into the infinite distance, I glance up from my violin and I look directly at Luke Jones. And I know, whatever happens tonight, tomorrow and beyond, I will remember for the rest of my life the way Luke looks at me in that perfect moment in time, the light shining in his eyes, streaming from him across the room and holding me motionless as we connect. And we smile.

EPILOGUE

It's 29th December, you know that time between Christmas and New Year where nobody knows what day it is or how much cheese they have really eaten. It's time for my annual post-festivities lunch I do for my neighbours. Now that I'm feeling better in myself, I've been looking forward to getting back into the kitchen and cooking for everyone again. It's pretty marvellous how much things have changed since the lamb shoulder à la dishwasher on Easter Sunday. I'm cooking two large lasagnes. But it's not just any old lasagne. It's the Best Lasagne in the World Ever (that's official, according to Ada). It's a recipe developed over the last forty-odd years of making the thing, from my mum's bog-standard but still very nice method she taught me when I was a teenager, using minced beef, bacon and Worcestershire sauce. Over the decades, I've incorporated new additions from various friends and acquaintances, until it's become its very best self. I start with onion and garlic, add finest quality beef mince, spicy Italian sausage meat called nduja, oregano, basil, roasted tomatoes blitzed down and sieved, passata and red wine. I let it cook slowly for a couple of hours, with a big carrot thrown in whole while it's simmering, to give it a hit of natural sugar, then remove the carrot at the end. For the cheese sauce I make a béchamel with nutmeg, then add parmesan and mature cheddar, plus a teaspoon of English mustard. I chose to make lasagne for everyone today as it's my favourite, it's my comfort food and also we're all sick to death of Christmas turkey leftovers (though my turkey pilaf – using mum's old recipe written in her sloping hand on yellow notepaper from around 1974 – is legendary).

It's been a really nice Christmas, quiet and relaxed, just how I like it. We virtually didn't leave the house for days, apart from – at Ada's request – going to Midnight Mass at Mary Mags, that is, the Mary Magdalen Church in central Oxford. Geoff and I are both total atheists, but Ada is toying with religion at the moment, so we wanted to be supportive. And Christmas is the time of year when atheist me can feel somewhat sentimental towards the church, because it certainly gets you in the spirit of the season, watching the Blessing of the Crib and singing Christmas carols at 11.30pm on Christmas Eve. However, Ada had a similar response to what Rhona once told us put her off church: too much standing up and sitting down and standing up again. Religion lost its allure for Ada after that, I suspect. Ada's favourite thing about it was being out on the hallowed streets of Oxford past midnight, a true adventure for a nine-year-old. She says she wants to try Buddhism next. That's the flavour of the week this week, anyway.

I'm just finishing off the prep for the meat sauce, cooked slowly in a huge cauldron inherited from Geoff's mum, which will bubble gently away on the stove all morning, while guests drift in and out and chat with me. It's my happy place, again. Serving food and sharing stories with friends and family, old and new. This time, there's no hot sweats, no lost lamb, no stress. Everyone from 28 and 30 Walton Crescent is here, the cheery chit-chat filling my four walls. The kids are on the iPad at the kitchen table and Alia is telling me about her trip to the Frankfurt Book Fair in October, she and her small publishing company's staff – i.e. her mate Sylvie (they set it up from their kitchen table, where so many great endeavours of women begin) – the first time they've ever been to an international book fair, and she's full of it. I'm so proud of her. They're signing new writers all the time and getting some Amazon bestsellers. What a legend. Our youngest, Ada and Zane, are fascinated by something Zane's thirteen-year-old brother Ricky is showing them on the screen, talking in their ears conspiratorially.

'They're not watching porn, are they?' I whisper to Alia and grit my teeth.

'SIENNA!' shouts Alia.

'Ah, leave her be. She'll be very busy TikTok-ing or whatever other apps the youths use these days.'

'Then she needs something useful to do,' says Alia and shouts for her again. Sienna slouches in and looks disgusted to have been roused from whatever it was she was doing of great import. 'Get over there and supervise those monsters. They're up to something shifty.'

'Why can't you do it? You're in here. You're on site,' says Sienna, arms folded. Alia gives her daughter the mother of all hard stares. With immediate effect, Sienna tuts and slouches over there.

'What are you doing, you total and utter wastes of space?'

Ada pipes up, 'Ohmigod Sienna, you're not gonna believe it but there's this thing on *Minecraft* called Herobrine and he's a really really scary character like Minecraft Steve but with white eyes and if you see him, you DIE and it's real. One hundred per cent real footage and also cursed telephone numbers you must NEVER call at 3am and I mean NEVER cos you'll be possessed and it's true and you'll DIE. One hundred per cent true and—'

Sienna pushes Ricky hard on the shoulder and says, 'What're you showing them that scary crap for? Give them nightmares, you little tosser.'

Zane adds, 'But it's real cos we saw it and this guy rang that number at 3am and it was Momo that horrible bug-eyed woman thing and she was—'

'Oh, shut it,' snaps Sienna. 'Here, give me this. I'll show you something really scary. Ever seen a Damascus goat? They look like bloody aliens and it's all because of selective breeding and it's dead cruel. Hang on . . .'

Alia says to me, proudly, 'She's going to be a vet, that one. All science A levels. Wants to save the world, bless her.'

Then all the kids go URRRGGGGHHHH when they see the Damascus goat. Alia wants to see it too, so off she goes over there and into the kitchen come Carly and her boyfriend Matt. Oops, I mean fiancé Matt! Yes, they just got engaged – Matt popped the question on Christmas Eve – and what's more, they've got hold of the last chunk of a deposit for a flat from a well-off uncle of Matt's, so they're looking for the iPad to check out the latest local flats to buy. I'm so thrilled for them that they're finally able to start setting up home together. Matt is a kind, easy-going lad. Kindness is so damn important, isn't it? When it comes to my daughters, it's kindness that's my number one priority. Anyway, they're chatting away about a flat they're thinking of putting in an offer on, weighing up its pros and cons.

'It's above a kebab shop,' says Matt to Carly. 'Which is of course excellent news because kebabs are food of the gods.'

Carly argues with the kids about taking the iPad and she loses, wandering back out with Matt looking at the flat particulars on her phone instead, jostling in the doorway with Geoff and Cheryl, coming in with Alia's husband Rich. They're all talking animatedly about something to do with cars, while Geoff is grabbing the corkscrew and another bottle of white.

'My dad had a TVR Griffith,' says Cheryl. 'Did it up in his garage. I loved that car.'

'TVRs are class, proper class,' says Rich.

'Cheryl knows everything there is to know about classic cars!' beams Geoff, proudly.

And as they leave the kitchen with fresh glasses of wine, they're all off on one about *The Grand Tour: Sand Job*, which Cheryl also loves apparently, which is so nice for Geoff as I can't stand cars. They're just metal boxes to transport us from A to B and I have no interest in any of them until my car breaks down this time and I can't get Ada to her Taiko drumming class (her latest craze – and musical! I'm delighted!). It was Joy who told us about Taiko drumming, as one of her boys used to do it back in the day and it turned out the same community group was still going. Ada gets to bang about on huge drums one evening a week. And speaking of Joy, I'm delighted to report that she and Rhona teamed up and went to see Stevie Queef together. Joy persuaded him to give an over-priced solar-powered desk fan for FREE to every office-based menopausal woman on campus. And Rhona argued that all staff should be valued equally, that not all women who work at MUFFY have desks. Some of them are on their feet all day, doing the more physical jobs that are just as crucial to the smooth running of the college. So Rhona persuaded Stevie Q to confirm he'll look into changing the contracts of these kinds of jobs, providing more regular breaks and the right to go home if needed when their symptoms become severe. Good for Rhona! Bless her bolshie heart. I say persuaded, but knowing Rhona, it's much more likely she marched in there and gave him an order. Thank fuck for women like Joy and Rhona in the world, getting shit done. Speaking of getting shit done, we M&Ms held a workshop recently where we taught one another some more coping mechanisms for when things get tough, as we all know they still will. Rhona still sometimes struggles with her rage, so she taught us all how to give ourselves an essential oils hand massage, which was wonderfully calming. Joy showed us some yoga poses too, which set us all off in fits of giggles like schoolgirls. I suggested that the M&Ms might need a works trip out to Ada's Taiko group to bash the living shit out of those massive drums and Rhona thought that was a grand idea. I added that I'd quite like to set fire to the thing and burn the whole fucking place down afterwards too, just for kicks – so yeah, both Rhona and I need to work on our rage just a little bit more. But we're getting there. Plus I told Rhona about Brenda's mantra. If anyone needs a mantra to calm the fuck down, it's Rhona and it's me. But I also hope we don't lose all of that fury. We need furious women in the world too.

And Ada's not the only one who's joined a musical group. I've started playing with a monthly folk fiddle group at the Iffley church hall, a gorgeous listed building of that luscious clotted-cream-coloured Cotswold stone. We play Irish, Scottish, Appalachian fiddle and others, jigs and reels and hornpipes and all sorts. It's the most fun you can have with your clothes on, believe me. I feel incredibly alive when I'm there. I can't wait for the next one after Christmas. Music is back in my life and it is here to stay.

Speaking of which, in come Danyal and Toby, and Danyal is carrying my violin.

'When are you going to play this thing for us, like you promised?' says Danyal. 'So we can hear it properly instead of just through the ceiling.'

'Later, you'll see. All will be revealed . . .' I say mysteriously and they look intrigued.

'Are you up to something, madam?' says Danyal with a wink.

'I might be. You'll see . . .'

'Actually,' says Toby, clearing his throat as if about to make a significant pronouncement. 'We've been up to something too, something very close to our hearts.'

I stop chopping up yet another Romaine lettuce head for the accompanying green salad and put down my knife.

'Is it . . . could it be . . .?' I don't want to say it, in case it's not and then it'll be a downer.

'We're nearly there!' cries Danyal.

'We're going to meet Ben and Hannah again tomorrow!' says Toby, his eyes bright with tears.

'Fucking brilliant!' I cry and the kids shout at me for swearing. A couple of weeks back Toby showed me pictures of two heartbreakingly beautiful kids they'd met with twice, a two-year-old boy Ben and his little sister, one-year-old Hannah. It was so obvious that both Toby and Danyal were in love with them already. I hoped they wouldn't be disappointed again. Gosh, I really bloody hope this one works out for them.

'It's not finalised yet, of course,' says Toby, prudently. 'We have to meet and spend a bit more time with them and then we'll get the final call. We've gone with a different adoption agency this time and they've been much more helpful and transparent about everything.'

'Oh, that's brilliant. Actually, I have a friend who's looking into fostering, Niki, in my menopause group. She's mentioned adoption too the other week. Message me the contacts for this agency and I'll send them on to her.'

'Sure, definitely. It's a really good one,' says Toby. 'We are . . . cautiously optimistic.'

'It's going to happen this time,' insists Danyal. 'I can feel it.'

Toby smiles at me, his eyes still shining. I know he's more wary than Danyal and fearful of letting Danyal down, somehow, even though of course it wouldn't ever be his fault. Just the luck of life. I give Toby a big hug and whisper in his ear, 'You'll be fine. It'll all be fine, whatever happens.'

'And we have news for Ada!' says Danyal loudly, grinning in her direction.

'What? What?!' she cries and skips over to us.

'Well,' says Toby. 'We were going to ask your mum first, but since Danyal has let the cat out of the bag . . . literally . . .'

I think I know what's coming. 'Ohhhh, okay, are we talking . . . Pushkin?'

'What about Pushkin?' Ada is electrified by curiosity and hope now.

Danyal says, 'Well, since we're hardly ever around and always at work and since . . . well, things just might be changing around our place soon . . . maybe . . . we want you to have Pushkin, darling!'

Ada literally screams and everyone is saying *What? What?* and it's chaos, every single person who's come for lunch has crowded into my kitchen to see what's going on, but instead of it being a disaster – like Easter Sunday – it's a joyous moment, even though Ada is crying buckets – emotional little monkey, bless her – and hugging Toby and Danyal and saying *thank you thank you* and everyone is relieved it's good news and not a crisis, for once. Ada runs from the room and finds Pushkin in her bedroom where he's been sleeping peacefully since his (ex) owners turned up. She drapes him across her shoulders and comes back into the kitchen, proud mother to a black and white cat with sleepy eyes who doesn't know what the hell's going on right now, as he's surrounded by humans wishing him hearty congratulations. And in all the hubbub, we must have missed the doorbell going, because someone is banging loudly on the front door.

'Who the hell's that?' says Rich. 'We're all here, aren't we?'

Carly and I shoot a glance at each other and she grins. We're the only two who know who that is. We didn't tell anyone else, as Ada would never be able to keep her mouth shut and also I didn't want her to be disappointed if it didn't happen, because of flights and delays or whatever. Nobody else knows.

'That'll be for me,' I say and I'm met with a barrage of questions as I manhandle my way through loafing guests sipping wine to get the hell out of my own kitchen and down the passageway to the front door.

And there he is, guitar case in one hand and travel bag in the other.

'Room for a knackered-out, jet-lagged, middle-aged musician?' says Luke.

'Put those bloody bags down,' I say and he does and then we're kissing and kissing and kissing.

The next couple of hours is pure, unadulterated but lovely chaos. Everyone wants to hear the story of Luke and Exeter and Boston and all of that, throwing questions at the poor guy who does his very best impression of an extrovert and is charming company. I keep getting winks and excited thumbs up from all and sundry, while the meat sauce sticks to the bottom of the pan and Alia says she'll do the cheese sauce and we finally get the damn things – two massive lasagne trays – in the oven. Eating it is chaotic too but, blimey, it's a bloody good one. I'm very proud of my lasagne and Geoff calls it a triumph and gives me a hug. I know he's talking about Luke more than the food and I appreciate that.

After eating, the assorted-aged kids all clear up the kitchen, directed by Alia and Rich, and I'm sent to sit down in the living room with Luke and relax a bit. Cheryl and Geoff are still going on about TVRs in the hallway, while Luke and I chat with Toby and Danyal on the sofas. Toby gives me a special look – I know he approves. I'm watching Luke talking to Danyal and I feel like I'm going to well up. I can't believe my beautiful man is here, with me, with us all, at Christmas (ish). We wanted it to happen but weren't sure what Luke's work would say, as he was in the midst of a project, but it's all come good and he managed to get a flight. He was going to try to get here for Christmas itself but didn't quite manage that, so lucky him, he managed to miss our video call on Christmas Day with the grandparents, which the kids and I call the Christmas Curse. (Curse or not, I'm just relieved that my parents stayed in Norfolk with my brother Lance and co for the whole of Christmas and we stayed well out of it, thank God.) Actually, when I told the olds about Luke, Dad in particular was delighted, Luke being a systems engineer. (Though I'm not sure Luke's non-army-regulation-length hair will please either him or Mum. Well, good. He can join Ada in the so-called weird hair brigade.)

As I'm watching Luke talk, I realise tonight we'll be alone in bed again, the first time since our two nights of debauchery spent almost exclusively in his tiny apartment in Boston. And yes indeed, they were wild and wicked, from beginning to end. I'm thinking about later tonight and I have a tiny spike of anxiety when I consider him seeing me without make-up or Spanx or whatever, even though he saw me like that in Boston, but it felt unreal there somehow and the light from the snow-lined streets that filtered through his apartment windows was magical and very flattering to a woman in her fifties. But here at home, the light isn't so kind and he'll see me in my scruffs and with all my wrinkles and my muddle of a messy life: the real Heidi Hobbes. But do you know what, I realise that I don't actually give a fuck about that. And also, I'm sure as eggs is eggs that he doesn't give a shit about any of that either and would find me sexy in my scruffiest of scruffs. I don't have to be fake-sexy to make him like me; we just fancy each other rotten anyway and all that bogus stuff is nonsense and really fucks up your sense of self-worth. I don't need to be dolled up like I was in Exeter or Boston, perfect nights under the glow of coloured lights, the way we stood together in that Boston bar and drank each other in, the moment after the appreciative applause died down and I walked over to him. We talked about the 'Wichita Lineman', our favourite lines – mine's the bit about the snow down south on the line that'll *never take the strain*. (I understand that feeling, Wichita Lineman, I do. But sometimes, you know, things turn out okay and, despite your worst fears, it turns out, you really can take the strain.) We danced to the next musicians, the mandolin guy and bodhran girl, whipping up Irish jigs and bringing the crowd to life, everyone on their feet. We laughed and laughed and danced and stopped and kissed. And kissed. And kissed. And went back to his apartment nearby, eagerly hurrying through the cold, arms linked tightly, feet slippery on the freshly fallen snow, squeaky underfoot. All day Saturday we never left his bed, except to fetch my things from the nice hotel I never got to stay in. I never got to see the Aquarium either, but he took me to the Cheers Bar before the airport, so at least I could say

I'd seen something iconic in Boston. Saying goodbye at departures was the sweetest agony, our last kiss the perfect end to the perfect weekend.

But life isn't like that most of the time; life is the harsh light of day and the darkness of the witching hour, watching your child throwing up for eight straight hours, suffering at work while your arse aches from piles, opening another damn bill with price rises, lying awake wondering how you'll ever afford your kid's three years at uni, driving away from the house where all you feel is sad because your marriage is over and you both know it. Life is struggle. But, oh my, there is beauty and there is magic. I need both and I need a man who understands both, deeply. And I know Luke gets it. He gets me too, he always did.

Suddenly, small arms are about me and Ada is giving me a full-on hug. I think back to when Carly tried to hug me all those months ago and how uncomfortable it made me feel. How unlovable. I'm so glad I don't feel that way these days.

'Can you believe it about Pushkin?! He's mine, he's really mine!'

'Nothing less than you deserve,' I tell my crazy, adorable, fascinating and gorgeous girl. My other gorgeous girl is standing nearby and looks at me. We grin at each other.

'Proud of you,' Carly mouths. And I don't need to hear the words. We can read each other like a book, my first-born and I.

'Love you,' I mouth back.

Toby taps me on the knee and says, 'When are we going to hear you two play then?'

I look at Luke, he nods and smiles. We've been practising

a few songs together by video call all through December, ready for this moment, we'd hoped. And here it is. And the good news is, that we won't have to rely on video calls for much longer either, because Luke's tenure in Boston ends in three months and then in the spring he'll be transferred to Aberdeen. A bit of a schlep up north, but a darn site easier than Massachusetts. We will be on the same land mass at least! And therein lies acres of possibilities for the future, for our future, me and Luke, whatever that might be.

I go to the kitchen where Toby's left my violin case and I meet up with Luke in the hallway, where he's fetching his guitar. For a few precious seconds we're alone and sneak in a lovely, long, slow kiss there, before anyone finds us, before we head back into the fray with my dear friends and they'll see the true Luke and the true me, playing our music together. And I think how misanthropic I was so recently in my life, how much I wanted to stay home forever, preferably in bed alone, and never venture out again, that this was somehow inevitable at my age and would just get worse as I got older. But I know now, that's absolute bollocks. What would Miriam do? She wouldn't stay in bed for the rest of her life. She's out there right now, having adventures all over the world. And I'm so glad I tapped Interested on that Facebook reunion invite; I'm so glad I sent that ranty email at work; I'm so glad I had to set up the M&Ms and I met those incredible women; I'm so glad I made the trips that scared the hell out of me, to Exeter for the party of a lifetime and then all the way across the sea to Boston, to play my long-lost fiddle for strangers and for one old friend. It's been nine months since I washed a shoulder of lamb in the dishwasher until it was squeaky clean. Nine months of change, of growth, of restoration and newness, or fear and failure and bravery and success. Nine months? That's a handy metaphor for gestation if ever there was one. I'm finally looking forward to the second half of my life and fear has been replaced with excitement at whatever comes next. Menopause is not the beginning of the end, as I once called it; in fact, it's the end of the beginning. And it ushers in a new phase that can be gruelling and scary, but at the very same time can be liberating and truly magnificent.

Luke says, 'Ready?'

And I say, 'Fuck yeah.'

AUTHOR'S NOTE

This book is a work of fiction. As such, it should not be used as any kind of source of information on menopause, a complex subject into which research continues to evolve. Readers looking for information and advice into treatments for menopause symptoms should approach qualified medical practitioners and seek out appropriate non-fiction sources of information.

ACKNOWLEDGEMENTS

Rachel Hart, my superlative editor at Avon, the dream team, my Maxwell Perkins. However random my tangents are, at least I don't deliver 5000-page first drafts like Thomas Wolfe! Huge thanks to the Avon team as well, for the whole Harper Ford package.

Laura Macdougall and Olivia Davies of United Agents, for savvy and superb support always for this author, whatever she's writing this week.

Menopause interviewees: Kyllie Booker, Jennie Grieve, Pip Jones, Georgia Lewis, Lynn Richardson, Debbie Taylor and Sue White, for your candour and bravery. This book would not be the same without you wonderful women.

Sumaira Wilson, for all things Alia.

Kathy Kendall, for information on sociology lectures to medical students and issues of gender, class and race in menopause studies.

Early readers – Lucy Adams, Kyllie Booker, Lynn Downing, Jennie Grieve, Pip Jones, Pauline Lancaster,

Georgia Lewis, Lynn Richardson, Sue White and Sumaira Wilson – for your quick reading, your support and your super comments.

Mark Brownless, for his shoulder of lamb recipe, side dish suggestions and the Heston Blumenthal dishwasher fact! Plus support for this author's books and physio queries.

Lasagne ideas from Sue Baker, Talya Baker, Sally Berneathy, Vicki Bowles, Darren Cooper-Holt, Chloe Hammond, Ben Illis, Susie Lynes, Orla Mcalinden and Katie Rawlins.

Laurah Gower and DC Kristene Lawrence, and Kyllie Booker, for information on police calls.

Erica Harris, Customer Service Support Officer, Office of the Police and Crime Commissioner, Devon, Cornwall and the Isles of Scilly, for excellent help on procedures regarding arrest and detention.

Sarah Waights and Eleanor Small, the GPs and other medical practitioners, who've listened patiently, taken me seriously and helped so much with recent health investigations. Thanks to my family and friends too, for their patience and support.

Poppy, for all things Gen Z, from face ID to *Minecraft* and everything in-between, as well as hungry otters, butterfly rescues and mega birbs.

Clem, who is the best work buddy this author ever had, who sat beside me on the sofa while I finished the final chapter I'd been putting off for days. For all your support, always. (And sourdough of the gods . . .)

And lastly, all those wonderful readers, reviewers and bloggers who bought *Divorced Not Dead*, kept it in supermarkets for months, pushed it high up in the charts and shared their reviews, taking Frankie to their hearts.

This author could not have wished for a better bunch of reading pals. You guys are the best. So glad you're here again for book number two. And if you've not read the first Harper Ford book yet, WTF are you doing with your life?? Get buying!

Love Harper x

We're going to need a bigger drink . . .

Fans of Alexandra Potter, Marian Keyes and
Caroline James will love *Divorced Not Dead*,
a no-holds-barred, heartfelt and laugh-out-loud
hilarious romcom about being fifty,
but absolutely not yet dead yet!

OUT NOW